Dear Reader,

For those of you who have never read a Mallory Rush or Olivia Rupprecht novel, I'm so glad you've picked up *Off Limits*. I hope you enjoy reading *Love Game* and *Love Play* as much as I enjoyed penning them.

As for my devoted fans who have written to me over the years asking for more books and wondering just where I've been…well, girlfriends, if life's an adventure, then I've had one incredible Wizard of Oz ride. And no, it wasn't to Kansas, Toto. But I have been traveling this amazing world, raising five great kids with my dreamboat of a husband, sitting on the other side of the desk as an editor for an international association of novelists, and despite all evidence to the contrary…writing! Really fun stuff, like ghostwriting for a Hollywood celebrity and other cool nonfiction projects. A part of me really misses fiction, though, and I'm awfully tempted to be a professional daydreamer again. Especially since I miss my readers most of all….

So until we meet again, may you have an extra pair of ruby slippers in your closet and an abundance of love in all its rainbow hues.

Mallory Rush

MALLORY RUSH

is an award-winning, bestselling author whose favorite claim to fame is having *Love Game* appear in a *Ziggy* cartoon. While her sizzling, innovative story lines have made her a reader favorite, she believes the reason for much of her success is that she can relate to the women for whom she writes. A romance fan for years, this busy mother of five began her writing career after buying an old manual typewriter for fifteen dollars at a garage sale. Six years and four unpublished novels later, she sold her first book. What she remembers most about book number five was nursing baby number five while pecking at the keys with an index finger. Mallory lives in Florida with her husband and their children.

OFF
LIMITS
MALLORY RUSH

HARLEQUIN®

TORONTO • NEW YORK • LONDON
AMSTERDAM • PARIS • SYDNEY • HAMBURG
STOCKHOLM • ATHENS • TOKYO • MILAN • MADRID
PRAGUE • WARSAW • BUDAPEST • AUCKLAND

ISBN 0-373-83635-X

OFF LIMITS

Copyright © 2004 by Harlequin Enterprises Ltd.

The publisher acknowledges the copyright holder
of the individual works as follows:

LOVE GAME
Copyright © 1995 by Olivia Rupprecht

LOVE PLAY
Copyright © 1999 by Olivia Rupprecht

CONTENTS

LOVE GAME

Of all the books I've written, only those indelibly marked by others bear the distinction of a dedication. And so…

To Chris Pacheco,
writer par excellence and dear friend,
who kicked me in the butt when I wanted to roll over and play dead. You believed in this book when my own faith was shaken, and for that I am truly grateful.

To Malle Vallik and Birgit Davis-Todd,
editors both of amazing courage and vision.
My deepest thanks for taking the risk, for loving, respecting this genre enough to let it grow.

Take a bow, ladies. Without you, what miraculously is, simply would not be.

PROLOGUE

"STOP THAT! Did you hear—Mark! Stop it, Mark, that—that tickles!" Her knees hitched over his shoulders, Chris used her heels to pound his back in time with her squeals of laughter. A playful shove at his head dislodged a fluffy red-and-white cap that skittered beneath the Christmas tree. With a firm clamp on the legs she'd squeezed shut, he spread them and nipped an interior thigh.

"Ho, ho, ho," her equally naked lover replied. "Quit squirming, Chris, and let me give you a hickey."

"No hickey! No hickey, please…" Amid wiggles and giggles and pleas for mercy, Chris tumbled them off their secondhand couch. Rolling over the creaky wood floor, she reached for a long candy cane and smacked him with it.

"Ouch!" Sitting atop her hips, Mark rubbed his jaw.

"Did I hurt you?" Suddenly still beneath him, she touched his mouth—which curled into a suggestive half smile.

"I'm in agony." He bit softly into the heel of her palm, then leaned over her, all playfulness gone. Sifting through the tangle of her hair, he took a dark strand and teased it over her lips. "You love me."

"I love you too much," she answered truthfully. "Mark, I don't think I could live if I ever lost you."

"Then don't think it. You're stuck with me for life."

She drew his mouth to hers. They kissed with tender emotion until their lovemaking escalated and he impulsively pushed into her. Then quickly, he began to pull out.

"No, please no," she whispered, gripping him. "Please, Mark. I want a baby. Your baby, my baby. *Ours.*"

"Chris." His gaze was steady, wise, patient. That was Mark, CPA, MBA, wing tips shiny and conservative suits Martinized clean. He was her rock. "We've only been married two years. We just signed our lives away on a mortgage and we'll be needing a new car before we can—"

"Start a college fund," she finished by rote. Mark was right, she knew. They were young, their future bright. That was logical, and the almost-frantic instinct to conceive that had been in her for the past year wasn't. But there it was. "We can get by. So what if we can't afford formula, I want to nurse our babies anyway. As for clothes, I'd rather sew with remnants than have ready-made."

"Anyone ever tell you that you sound like a home-ec teacher?" He squeezed her hand, gentling the brewing storm. "A sexy home-ec teacher who's married to a guy with a cash register for a brain. At least, that's what you said the last time we got into this."

Turning her head to the side, Chris stared at the slim pile of presents under the scraggly pine they'd cut from her parents' yard in Dallas and hauled all the way to Lubbock. The tree hadn't cost a penny but had more meaning than a hundred-dollar flocked fir.

A baby would be like Christmas. A present to be unwrapped each day of the year, an ever-changing surprise of life and wonder.

"Money is fine and good," she said quietly. "But a baby doesn't care about anything but being wanted and cherished." She implored him with her eyes while seducing his agreement with the upward tilt of her hips. His gaze locked with hers and they shared a taut silence in this, their battlefield, a place where their allegiance was increasingly torn.

"All right, then. If we have to make a few sacrifices, it won't be at the expense of our marriage. A rift between us just isn't worth it." He took a deep breath and committed himself with a thrust. "You're my life, Chris. No man should ever love a woman as much as I do you."

Good and sure was the rock of his hips. She held tight to the arms anchoring her against the floor, desperate to never let him go. What they had together was too wonderful.

The feel of his body emptying inside her own was a bond they sealed with soul-deep kisses. "No regrets?" she asked, just to be sure.

"No regrets, hon, we'll do fine." They hugged each other with fierce affection. "Maybe next Christmas we'll have more than cookies in the oven."

"You'll still want me, even if I'm tipping the scales?"

"You betcha. At least then you can't outrun me if I want to give you a hickey." His grin got him a pinch on the butt.

"For a numbers kind of guy, you sure know how to make a woman feel like she's in the chips."

"Mmm. What do you say that we open our presents, then take another crack at investing in futures? Once my personal stock's on the rise, I'll put up the liquid assets."

"The bank's open and ready for your deposit, sir."

"Deposits. Much more to my liking than withdrawals are, any day." His hands stretched over hers. Their wedding bands fit snugly between the grooves of interlocked fingers. "Jingle bells, jingle bells. Kiss me and let's make them ring."

The scent of drying pine needles and woodsmoke mingled with their hushed, intimate laughter.

CHAPTER ONE

THE SCENT OF DRYING pine needles and woodsmoke mingled with the sound of family laughter.

Chris opened her eyes and smiled as six-year-old Audrey tore open another package from the mountainous pile of gifts. Most had Audrey's name on them. Chris thought it an awful lot for one little girl when so many other children went without. But Audrey went without in ways, too, and she wasn't overly spoiled. Besides, judging from the beaming faces of her own parents, Anna and Don, they were having as much fun as their only grandchild. And if Rick and Tammy, her brother and his wife, had gone overboard on the gifts, Chris knew their hearts were in the right places.

"Wow, neat! Look, Mama, look at what Uncle Rick and Aunt Tammy gafed me." Bounding from the floor, Audrey rushed to the couch and thrust her newest prized possession at her mother. "Isn't she pretty? She looks just like Aunt Tammy. 'Cept Barbie doesn't have a baby in her tummy."

"That's because Ken's not a stud like me, right, Tammy?"

"Whoa, big boy, that's some real competition. A rubber doll who's not even anatomically correct."

Chris watched her brother pat Tammy's stomach as they shared a grin. They were an inspiration and one Chris needed, a reminder of how rich life could be. It seemed that her own heart's good fortune was spent, and she couldn't deny that poverty had taken its toll. Not bad on the outside for thirty-three, but where it counted, inside, she felt like a woman past her prime. Washed-up, hollowed out, hanging on to the fringes of other people's lives to fill up the gaps in her own. And smiling, always smiling until she thought her jaw would break from the effort. But for now, it was easy enough.

"What do you say to Uncle Rick and Aunt Tammy, Audrey?"

Dutifully, the little girl thanked them, then threw in two big hugs before she tore into the next foil-wrapped box.

An hour later Audrey was tucked into the old double bed that Chris had slept in as a child. Audrey was a good little snuggler, but she couldn't take the place of a large, comforting body to warm cold toes on. And she wasn't a listening ear that shared secrets on a pillow deep into the night. Not for the first time, Chris wished she'd never had that comfort. Never to have it was never to miss it.

"Did you have a good Christmas Eve, sugar?"

"It was great, Mama. Super good. Almost, anyway."

"Almost? You mean there was something you wanted that you didn't get?"

"Uh-huh. But Santa comes tonight so maybe he'll bring me what I really, really want." Audrey looked confident.

"And what's that, your two front teeth?"

"Uh-uh. But can't tell or maybe I'll jinx it. Only God knows since I told Him—but He's good at keeping secrets." Audrey's quiet smile was poignantly familiar. The hair belonged to her father too, pale colored, fine textured. Chris stroked it back, and touched him through their child. The soulful, deep brown eyes that blinked away the sandman were the only trait she'd passed on to her daughter. In all else, Audrey was Mark's; even his wisdom was reflected in her maturing baby face.

Please don't grow up, don't ever leave me. I need you

too much. Swallowing the words, Chris kissed her—a tender kiss that imparted her desperation to hang on to yesterday while her child was slipping too fast into tomorrow.

Leaving on the night-light, Chris left the room. She paused behind the cracked door and, curious, listened.

"Now I lay me— Aw, shoot, You've probably heard that a jillion times. Besides, You know I'm just sayin' it to get to what I want. Please, God, make Santa bring me a daddy. I want one really bad. All my friends have one and they think they're awful neat. And besides, Mama— Well, she doesn't say so, but I think she's lonesome and she'd like it lots if you sent my real daddy back. But if he's too busy with the other angels the way Mama says he is, I bet she'd be happy with someone nice and funny and—"

Chris moved quickly away. The hall, suddenly too narrow and dark, lent its support as she skated her flattened palm against the wall. Once alone in the bathroom, she turned the lock and slumped against the door. No light. No sound, except for a heart that beat dully in her chest, her ears.

"Were you listening, God?" she whispered sharply. "Is there a goddam chance in hell that You listen to little children? Do they possibly get through when a deaf ear's all You gave me when I was on hands and knees and—" Pressing a tight fist against her mouth, Chris bit into her knuckles.

Stop it, she silently railed. *He's gone.* Gone. And no amount of anger, regret or sorrow would change what was. She had to go on. She had to make everyone believe that she was fine. Then maybe she could convince herself. She had worth; she had purpose. Audrey needed her. The family needed her. Even some of her students needed her.

She needed them to need her. Without them, where would she be? *Who* would she be? Chris knew too well they were her only defense against this bitter woman cursing God in a dark bathroom on Christmas Eve.

"Well, Lord," she muttered, trying to summon a bit more respect. A caustic laugh and she went on, "If I couldn't fool Audrey, I might as well quit trying to fool myself. I *am* lonely. But I've had my slice of the pie, so I don't expect a motherlode of generosity. My little girl is something else. She deserves more than presents to make up for what money can't buy. Audrey wants a daddy. Got an extra, by chance?"

Silence. What had she expected? Jingle bells? A kiss to make them ring? With a snort, Chris flipped on the light and fished a cigarette from her pocket. Despite the cold weather, she opened a window to puff the evidence into the frosty night air. Smoking. Just one of the things she hid from those who loved her and thought they knew her best.

They didn't know her, she just let them think they did. Hell, half the time she wasn't sure if she knew herself. Heel hitched onto the toilet lid, she stared into the starry sky and absently finger-drummed her knee.

Make You a deal. Find Audrey a decent daddy and I'll quit bitching. I'm not asking for love, just so he can love her and support PTA. You know, a good guy who likes kids. He doesn't have to be rich or handsome, but a sense of humor would be nice. A few common interests, not too tough to live with—as in, demanding, macho types need not apply—and, say…mutual respect. That'll do it for me, and I'll try hard not to slip and call him the wrong name at the wrong time.

Chris glanced down to where she'd instinctively tensed. Her fingers inched up and brushed the place she'd ignored so long that she'd begun to wonder if her sexuality had decided to go away and never come back.

While we're on the subject... If You can dig up a daddy for Audrey, even if he's not good in the sack, I'd appreciate it if he could spark a tingle. I'd like to like his kisses. But I'm not greedy, he doesn't even have to give hickeys.

Window closed and cigarette butt flushed, Chris gargled, then made a spot check in the mirror. No smoker's breath and no tears. Except for the stray gray hairs she plucked and a few well-concealed lines, she decided she didn't seem much changed from when she'd left for college in Lubbock: pretty and polite, cheerleader vivacious and an honor-roll listee, just the kind of girl a boy's parents liked to meet. *Groan.*

A convincing smile firmly in place, Chris marched out. Before she reached the den, a knock sounded at the front door.

"I'll get it," she called, wondering which relative it would be. Thank goodness she had met her husband at Texas Tech and he hadn't wanted to move away from his Lubbock roots. Even if it did smell like cow shit when the downwind brought the stockyards home, the outskirts of Dallas were far more cloying. In the Adams clan, smother love went way past doting parents.

Pulling open the door, she pitched her voice low to imitate Santa. "Mer-ry Christ-mas...?"

"Chris? Chris Adams?"

"Yes. Well, no. Chris Nicholson."

The man she stared at stirred a wisp of memory. High school. Her, a freshman, with a major-league crush on a senior. Wanting more than anything to wear his letter jacket. Even better, his high school ring; each wrap of surgical tape to take up the slack would be a band of honor.

Three dates that ended with kisses. On the fourth, ending

up in the back seat of his parents' Buick. Half an hour past her curfew, Dad meeting them at the door. The fast boy had proved he was an even faster talker. Apologies made, he'd promised it wouldn't happen again.

It hadn't. He'd moved on. While she spent a month with tears on her pillow after listening to the phone not ring, he'd chosen a girl who put out over one with standards. That's where she'd lost him, both of them knowing he'd have a long wait to get more than kisses, a quick feel and...

A hickey.

She touched her neck. A smile spread from her lips and lit up her eyes.

"Greg Reynolds! I haven't seen you since— Come in, get yourself out of that rain."

"No argument here. And just for the record, I haven't forgotten 'since,' either." He grasped her extended hands and stepped into the warm foyer. His gloves were wet and she felt his shiver beneath.

He let go but the shiver remained in her fingertips. It was from the cold, mostly. But a flash of steamy windows in the back seat of his parents' car caused the shiver to linger.

"You're the last person I expected to see at my old doorstep on Christmas Eve. What *are* you doing here?"

"I was on my way to surprise Mom and Dad when the car I'd rented at the airport had a radiator blow just down your street and wouldn't you know, my cell phone ran out of juice. Much as I hate to barge in, I was counting on your parents' goodwill toward men. Thought they might let me use their phone."

He doffed a military dress cap. Marine, she thought. A slight recession of his hairline reminded her more than she liked of just how many years had passed since they'd parted. What she did like, however, was that he brushed his hair straight back, not trying to hide time's progress with an overlong front strand draped over a prominent forehead. Several lines were creased there, from laughter and maybe some worry and sorrow.

Altogether, the years had treated him well. His jaw was a little large, but firm, and his chin had a small indentation in the middle, as if a fingertip had been pressed into it. His eyes were flecked with several colors, none taking the lead. His nose had been broken in the interim and, if set, it was not a good job. The thick, sandy hair was clipped close to ears into which she suddenly, vividly remembered whispering, ''Greg, no, I can't.'' He hadn't pushed her to pet him again, but a part of her had wished he'd been more persistent.

A slight clutch in her belly took her by surprise. Glad as she was that her body was miraculously showing some signs of life, Chris was sorry it stemmed from an adolescent crush on a boy who was now a man—a man who was sure to be married or divorced and carrying around a lot of emotional baggage.

And you're not? came a small, nagging voice. Shutting it out, she said brightly, ''If your car had to break down I'm glad it was here. Where did you fly in from?''

''D.C. Got assigned to the Pentagon after traipsing the globe to wherever Uncle Sam needed me. Man, is it good to be back stateside. Never knew how much I took for granted until it was gone. Sure does make a body appreciate what they've got the next time around.''

''You can say that again.'' Chris, amazed at how easy it was to talk to him after so many years, decided she wanted to talk some more. ''You're welcome to stay for eggnog,'' she said hopefully. ''And I'm sure Rick would love to hear about your pro-football days.''

''That should take all of two minutes since I didn't make

the final cut.'' Greg's smile was craggy, a little weary, but just as infectious as she remembered. He had a nice smile, with a touch of something else that wasn't so nice. ''I'd like to stay and visit, but it's getting late and I'm eager to surprise the folks. If I could use your phone, I'll give them a call to come get me.''

''And spoil your banner entrance at their front door? Hang on while I get my coat. I'll drive you.''

''You're sure? I hate to take you away from—''

''Sure I'm sure, and Santa can simply eat her cookies and milk when she gets back. Besides, I'd rather hear more about you than pig out on some sweets I don't need.''

She squeezed a waist that looked thinner to him now than it had when she was fifteen. He thought her face slightly drawn, too. But it didn't detract from the wholesome prettiness that had matured into a frank beauty—a beauty he found all the more interesting for the character lines life had crafted.

Watching her as she strode away for her coat, Greg was caught by the way she carried herself. There was a stiffness to her spine he recognized as almost regimental, a bearing that was proud, as if trained not to show any hint of weakness. It could have been the same walk as the men he had once commanded, except for the fluid swish of her hips showcased in black leggings that seemed to have no end.

Chris the Dish was still a dish. Straight toothsome smile, high rosy cheeks, Ivory-soap complexion and a mouth to dream about. The dark hair was shorter—just to her shoulders and she wore it in soft waves.

Too bad she was married. One look at that ring on her finger and he knew there would be no making amends for past mistakes. It ate at him some. Chris had a distinct manner that told him she'd realized her potential admirably well.

"Ready?" Keys in hand, she paused in the entryway, beneath a sprig of mistletoe.

"Not quite." Leaning down, he kissed her. Why the hell he did it, Greg didn't know. But he did it just the same.

CHAPTER TWO

IT WAS ONLY HER CHEEK he kissed. But still, her husband might not appreciate the way he lingered. The hint of cinnamon on her breath and the scent of apples lifting from the hair he impulsively fingered, prompted a quick bite of envy inside him.

Judging from Chris's high color she was either embarrassed or transported with him to another place and time: necking like crazy to make-out music on the car radio until he was ready to say he loved her, anything, if she'd give in. His "Please, let me. I won't hurt you, I promise." And then her grip on his wrist, leading his hand away from her panties.

He was there again and feeling the yank in his groin. It was crazy, insane. A man his age didn't get a hard-on with the turn of a dime. *Married.* Shit, wouldn't you know it.

"Let's go," she said suddenly. Once in the car, he started to give her directions. "No need," she interrupted. "I still know the way by heart."

"But I only took you home to meet my parents that once."

"But I only drove by with my girlfriends to check up on you at least a dozen times. I quit after you dumped me for Tiffany Goodbody. Remember? The bad girl with a good body."

"I remember." Groaning, Greg shook his head. "I'm not proud of the way I treated you, Chris. I was immature and a little too full of myself, putting more stock in scoring with a bimbo than waiting for an extra-special girl. There's more than one thing I'd change if I could turn back the clock.''

"Same here." That said, she let it drop.

As they tooled down the rain-slick road, neither spoke. The swish of wipers and the patter of a heavy drizzle seemed louder than it should. Didn't they have anything left to say? Strange, but he felt a loss that they had crossed paths again only to part with a "Thanks for the ride and take care." Then again, maybe they'd run into each other at a checkout stand and wave, or fumble for conversation now that they'd hit another dead-end street. Second verse, same as the first.

Their arms and thighs were separated by a stick shift between bucket seats. He took up a lot of room but the car felt crowded with more than the space their bodies consumed. When she turned on the radio he sensed it was more from a need to fill the silence than to listen to "Carol of the Bells."

"Are you sure it won't be an imposition to leave my car in your parents' driveway until the—"

"Of course not." She slid him a brief smile.

"I hope you don't mind what I did," he offered, turning down the radio. "You know, kissing you in the foyer."

"Mind? Hardly. It was the best Christmas present I've had all night."

"No kidding?" At her nod, he touched her hand, which gripped and ungripped the four on the floor. "You look great, Chris. Even better than I remember. Who's the lucky guy?"

"His name was Mark, but I wouldn't exactly call him lucky. Thirty years old and he had a heart attack. It happened when he was jogging, trying to work off the love handles he'd picked up behind a desk." She laughed—a brittle sound. "Staying-in-shape heart attack, get it? Life's a real joke. It sure had the last laugh on me."

"I'm sorry, I had no idea."

"Yeah, well, it was a surprise to me, too."

"Recent?"

"Almost four years ago."

Reaching over, he tapped her gold band against the steering wheel. "Four years and you're still wearing a wedding ring?"

Her shrug he took to mean indifference, but the passing streetlights illuminated the strain in her profile.

"I've had trouble letting go." She glanced at him sharply, then returned her attention to the road.

Another two miles and they'd be at his drop-off. Another mile and a half...then, maybe a mile to go. Why did her wedding ring bother him? Why did her loss of weight, the tension in her smile? He'd seen friends die. He'd made plenty of personal sacrifices and they'd aged him, too. But none of that seemed to compare with the emptiness he read in the shuttered gaze of a woman who seemed too old too soon.

"We're here," she said, pointing a red fingernail at the solid-as-they-come ranch house.

Who had she done her nails for? he wondered. That ring declared her still bound to a dead man, so she'd likely painted them for herself. Yeah, women were funny that way, making themselves look pretty on the outside when they didn't feel so pretty in places the eye couldn't see. He saw...a terrible waste. Chris probably wouldn't like what he had to say. Tough, Greg decided. He was saying it anyway.

"I've never gone through your situation, so if I sound insensitive, I don't mean to be. But look, you're plenty young to make a new life for yourself. Seems to me you've hung on to your grief, Chris, that you're still tied to the past. Not to say you need a man to make your life complete, but surely it would be fuller with some company. A wedding ring does *not* spell opportunity for any man who might be interested in getting involved with you.''

She said nothing but stared straight ahead. Before his parents peered out the window, he killed the engine and turned off the headlights.

Chris slowly turned to him. Even more slowly she slid a finger down his gloved hand.

''And would you be...interested?'' A smile crept to the corners of her lips, then wavered. ''I can't believe I said that, Greg. Flirting, I was actually flirting with you!'' She laughed self-consciously. ''Trying, anyway. It's been so long, I don't even remember how. I'm sure your wife wouldn't like me brushing up my skills on her husband.'' She paused, waiting for confirmation. He gave her none, wanting a confirmation of his own. ''You are married?''

''In a manner of speaking.''

''Oh.'' She summoned a jaunty smile that didn't quite make it. Giving it up, she admitted, ''Wouldn't you know, I finally hook up with someone whose company I like and—bummer, he's taken.''

''Yes, ma'am, he is. Worse than married, he's sworn to a jealous mistress—the Marines.'' Greg tipped his hat. ''Sorry I set you up but a week's leave doesn't give me much slack for subtlety. I want to see you again.''

''For old times' sake?'' Even in the dim light he could see the hint of a blush. Oh yeah, she remembered the magic they'd made. Question was, just how open was she to making some more?

''Old times are just that. I'd rather enjoy the present than dwell on the past.'' He caught the lapels of her coat and pulled her closer. Her willingness to let him kiss her, as he fully intended to do, didn't mesh with the apprehension etched in her face. "I'm sorry you lost your husband but I am glad that you're not spoken for."

"But I am! I mean…I have a little girl, Greg. Audrey, she's six."

Hiding behind her child, was she? Chris, he decided, was actually afraid of a simple kiss. Hard to imagine that, but the last thing he wanted to do was scare her off. Besides, it wouldn't be much of a kiss if she didn't loosen up.

"I'll bet Audrey's a cute kid," he said, easing his grip.

"Darling. She looks just like her dad."

"And every time you look at her, you see him, right?"

"How did you know?"

"Doesn't take an Einstein to read between the lines." He pried free the fingers she'd frozen over the stick shift. A soft kiss to their tips, then he urged her arm around his neck. Even through the layers of her coat, he could feel her shaking. His sympathy mingled with frustration as he watched her left thumb work that damn ring like crazy. "Are you cold?" he asked when her teeth began to chatter.

"Freezing," she confirmed.

"I can't imagine why. After all, there does seem to be four of us in here—a ghost, a daughter, you and me." When she blanched, he paused. The most decent thing he could do would be to send her running. "Hey, what say we have a party, add in a few more guests. Think we can make room for my two ex-wives? And how about my hellion teenager? That should heat things up considerably. Warm yet?"

He was glad her shaking stopped, but regretful he'd surely eat her dust without so much as a goodbye kiss.

"So, you have a teenager. What's her name?"

Hot damn, surprise, surprise. Maybe she was staying to chat, but even hanging out with bad news wasn't smart for a woman as vulnerable as Chris obviously was. Greg studied her, eyes narrowed on her too-soft features.

"Arlene. She's fourteen."

"From your first marriage?"

"If that's what you want to call it. A paper with an unwilling signature does not a real marriage make."

"I see," Chris said with an understanding he hadn't expected. "Even if you weren't happy about it, you did do 'the right thing,' which is more than a lot of boys are willing to do these days."

"At twenty-two, I wasn't exactly a boy. I was old enough to live up to my responsibilities. Unfortunately, Arlene's mom didn't take hers seriously enough. To be exact, she wanted to get married but I wasn't ready to settle down so she conveniently forgot a few pills." When Chris nodded sympathetically, he went on. "Once it was a done deal, I tried—but I didn't try hard enough. I cheated on my first wife, Chris." He touched his nose. "Frying pan, right between the eyes."

"She caught you?"

"No, I confessed. I didn't love her but I did have a bad case of the guilts—until that cast-iron skillet cleared my conscience. I told myself she deserved it, that it was her fault I was trapped with a wife and baby I didn't want. Her fault that I didn't make the pro-ball cut because my head wasn't in the game. Because it was her fault that I was already worried about finding a job with a history degree that was fairly useless in the job market."

"Oh, Greg," she said softly, "you must have been terribly unhappy."

"Miserable. And misery liking company, I made sure she was just as miserable as me."

"You mean, you kept cheating to get back at her?"

"That look on your face tells me you're almost as disgusted as you are curious." He laughed at her, and then, at himself. "The hell I ever cheated again. I didn't feel man enough to satisfy one woman, let alone two. The truth is, if I'd really been man enough, I never would have stepped out on her. It was inevitable that we'd split, but after we did I came to terms with where a good part of the blame belonged."

"And where was that?"

"Right here." He tapped a finger to his chest. "Of course, that didn't keep me from making bigger and better mistakes. After divorce number two, it dawned on me that I make a lousy husband."

"Maybe the third time will be the charm." Greg stared at her red nails as she patted his gloved hand. He wasn't one for playing on a woman's sympathy and the fact Chris's felt so good and welcome was enough to make him wish those nails of hers were clawing his back. That was familiar and safe; this warm-fuzzy something he felt wasn't.

"Won't happen, Chris. Three strikes, you're out. I'm not going back to bat now that I've finally reached a place where I'm satisfied with my life. Living alone suits me. So does having no demands other than my career. If I get lonely sometimes, Arlene comes to visit me every other summer and that's enough to make me appreciate loneliness for company."

"I take it you don't get along."

"It's not so much that as the fact she scares the hell out of me. Arlene is The Teenager from Hell. She's the kind of bait that can't wait to get bit, and all I can do is shake my head from the sidelines. It's where I've been all her life, so, as you might guess, I'm no better in the Daddy department than I am at marriage." *Why was he telling Chris this stuff?* Comfort and conversation were luxuries in his wasteland of a personal life and he had no intentions of developing a taste for what he couldn't have for keeps.

Quickly, he shifted the conversation her way. "You, on the other hand, strike me as a devoted parent. It's my guess you won't have the same problems when Audrey's older."

"They grow up no matter what, don't they?" Chris sifted her fingers through the hair at his nape, the motion more distracted than intentionally provocative.

"We did, didn't we? Some of us just take longer to grow up than others." The feel of her nails skirting his neck was intensely arousing. He wanted a kiss—a deep, wet kiss— and he wanted it now. Only he didn't get the feeling it would be wholeheartedly returned. Yet. Intimacy—the emotional kind that Chris demanded—was not his forte. But if that's what it took to get the kind of kiss he wanted, well, a man had to do what a man had to do.

"You know, Chris, I'm a very private person. I've told you more tonight than I've let on to friends who have known me for years."

"Then, why me?"

"Oh, I dunno. Maybe because I'm hoping you'll ditch this 'I'm okay, you're okay' attitude that I don't buy for a minute. I'm *not* okay, Chris—unless we're talking professional. I think you know where I'm coming from and that's where I'm trying to connect. Do we?"

"Enough that you're making me feel uncomfortable."

"Nothing wrong with that. Uncomfortable's up-front and personal. And personally, I could use an okay feeling with someone who doesn't have any expectations of me. You?"

Something flickered in her eyes—an eager, hesitant something. "Yes, Greg, I *could* use an okay feeling for a change. I need it so much I'll even return the doubtful favor you're asking for. I'm a mess. A god-awful mess. You're looking at a closet basket-case who can't get her act to-gether. My life—'' Her catching sob tugged at him with a force more startling than the raw pain he saw in her eyes before she turned away. ''My life is so screwed up that I wouldn't mind trading places with you. I mean, you're happy with what you've got, right? I'm not. I hate my life the way it is. I *hate* it.''

''Then why don't you change it?''

''Because... I want to. It's just that I don't know how.''

He had hoped her exposure would tumble some walls and get him the touch he was after, but this was more than he'd bargained for. He felt no pride for his selfish manip-ulation, but he did feel a keen compassion as he absorbed what he'd laid open.

Drawing her close until she buried her face in his neck, Greg asked gently, ''Want to talk about this?''

''No.'' She caught her breath and took a dry heave. Clasping his shoulders, she pulled away and gave him an overbright smile. ''I'm fine, really. I don't know what got into me. The holidays, I guess. They're always the worst. It's a shame, but I can't wait to get past New Year's Day. Less than a week and I'll be—''

''In no better shape than you are now.'' When her fragile smile crumbled he felt a triumph he didn't take much plea-sure in. ''Look, I'm not happy with the life I've got, just satisfied. Sometimes that has to be enough because it's bet-ter than nothing. But to get there, a person has to cut their losses and move on.'' Swiveling her wedding ring, he said firmly, ''That's what you have to do, Chris. You've got to get rid of this and move on. I've been lobbying for a kiss like never before, but ain't no way that's gonna happen— not with me or anyone else—until you let go.''

She was silent for a while, staring at her gold band, and then at him. Quietly she said, ''Do you actually think my kissing a man who admits to making a mess of his own life will make mine better?''

''Couldn't hurt. After all, what do you have to lose?''

Too much when I've got nothing as it is. She didn't say it, but she didn't have to. He could do one of the things he did best—find the path of least resistance and get what he wanted—but he didn't. Instead, he waited, trying not to hope too much but hoping too much all the same.

When patience became an awkward lapse of words and movement, he decided to stick with what he did better than best: cut his own personal losses and move on.

''Thanks for the lift. See ya...maybe in another eighteen years?'' As he reached for the door handle, Greg felt her grip on his arm, her nails biting softly through the heavy layers of winter clothing.

''Stay? Please, Greg. Stay.''

He paused, giving her time to reconsider. The concern she dug up inside him made *him* uncomfortable. Whatever was going on between them was...unusual. As for Chris, the safest thing she could do would be to open the damn door and push him out faster than spit could hit ground.

When he didn't move, Chris fought a wave of panic. Why didn't he say something? she wondered. And then she wondered, *Why didn't she? Say something, do something,* she ordered herself. *For once, take control.*

Adrenaline mixing with the rush of anticipation, she pressed her lips to the back of his neck. Her nuzzle was a decision of forward momentum. Flushed with excitement, she took another step with an exploratory flick of her tongue from behind his ear to the starched rim of his dress shirt.

He tasted of ache. Achingly masculine, a composite of the day's last traces of cologne, the faint salt flavor of skin diluted by the rain that had brought him here. Here, in a closed car where the sounds of their breathing mingled. His, heavy and deep; hers shallow as he turned and opened his coat, inviting her in.

"Not yet." Decisively, she raised her left hand, poised between their faces. The moon's watery light haloed her slow lift of gold. The ring, departing from her finger, felt as fragile as life's precarious balance, and then, like Mark, it was gone. Chris kissed the band she should have parted with long ago. This she well knew, just as she was aware of a worse folly: She had loved Mark too much, and not even he was worth the price she had paid. Never again would she risk such vulnerability; never would she forfeit the autonomy she now claimed. And with that silent vow, she laced tight her heart.

Her heart was where she slipped the ring, between breast and bra. Greg's eyes followed the movement and lingered as she began to rebutton her red silk blouse. Pausing there, she decided to leave it undone, exposing a wisp of white lace.

His brow lifted. So did the side of his mouth.

"I'm impressed." He kissed the satin riding over the swell of her breast. "I'm impressed by this almost as much as I am with what you did. That took some guts, Chris."

"More than guts." She tossed his hat onto the dashboard and savored the freedom she claimed in that small act. Pulling him forward by his tie, her grip ate its length until they were separated by a whisper's distance. "It took you to help me find them." And then her whisper brushed aside the final barrier. "I want to kiss you."

"Then do it."

And do it, she did.

CHAPTER THREE

"CHRIS? HELLO, anybody in there?"

"Huh?" She'd zoned out again, Chris realized. So far, she'd escaped a family inquisition as to why she'd been so late getting back the night before. Much more of this and they'd drive her nuts trying to find out what was up. "Sorry, Tammy, what were you saying?"

"Not much. Just that I'm dying my hair purple next week, Rick's been elected to Congress and Mom's having an affair with Tom Cruise. When you said, 'That's nice,' I figured I'd lost you." Topping off their coffee cups at the breakfast nook where they sat, Tammy asked nonchalantly, "So tell me, how does he kiss? After all, it does give a lot of insight into a man's character. You know, sensitive or aggressive. Both and more if he's a really special kind of guy."

Chris chewed on a doughnut, trying to form an answer—more for herself than Tammy. Greg didn't kiss like he used to, when he'd plowed ahead for a touchdown and dropped the ball where she'd drawn the line. Last night he'd kissed like a man who knew how to get what he wanted from a woman's mouth and savored every inch of ground they covered together. It had been an intensely personal kiss that went beyond the usual lip-to-lip, slip-of-the-tongue, I'm-out-of-here-unless-you-slip-yours-back sort of predictability.

Nothing had been predictable about that kiss. Not the way he spent more time on her neck and in her hair than on her mouth. Not the frank way he spoke about how she tasted—''damn good''—or wanting to know how it made her feel when he teethed her nipple between bra and blouse. Apparently ''Dear God'' hadn't been answer enough. He'd drawn away then and stroked his chin while she clenched his shirt and gasped for breath. His affectionate peck on the cheek had been the last thing she'd expected. That and his sudden ''Let's sleep on this, Chris. Sweet dreams. Merry Christmas and…good night.''

''How does he kiss? Tell me and we'll both know,'' she finally said. ''Look, Tammy, I'm a little confused and I'd like your input. But you have to swear to silence.''

''Gag order, no problem.''

''Not a word, not even to Rick.'' At Tammy's nod, Chris held up her left hand.

''Your ring! You took off your ring!''

''Mark's dead, Tammy, and he's not coming back. I've known it all along, but I wasn't willing to accept it.'' Glancing out the window, Chris thought how much clearer the sky looked, how much brighter the sun appeared than it had the morning before. The day was too beautiful to weep over a closed coffin. So much time wasted. But no more. *No more.* ''I let my life go stale and I'm disgusted with myself for wallowing in the dregs.''

''Wallowing in the dregs?'' Tammy repeated. ''How can you say that? You're strong. You've survived.''

Chris shook her head. ''Going through the motions of living isn't the same as getting on with life. Greg gave me a taste of life last night and now I'm ready to make up for lost time.''

''This Greg, he must be a special person.''

''He's special but he's not for me—or anyone else—in the long run.''

''A confirmed bachelor?''

"Worse! The man's been divorced twice and he's got a teenage daughter who scares the pants off him."

"A lot of parents don't know how to handle their kids when they start demanding their space, so he's not alone there. But the ex-wives? That doesn't sound so good."

An unexpected urge to come to Greg's defense rose up in Chris. But what could she say? That he'd cheated on one wife and after the second marriage didn't pan out he'd realized he made a lousy husband? She'd found herself wondering about those women. Relationships did take two people to make them work, and Greg's willingness to assume the blame did count for something. Didn't it? For some reason, she wanted it to.

"Wives or no wives, he's only here for a week. Then back he goes to Washington to huddle with his fellow warmongers. And back I go to Lubbock. Playing Mommy, teaching school, and keeping my eye out for a decent daddy who won't mind ironing his own shirts and eating take-out Chinese. But before I get sensible, I could use a hot date with a hottie." With a sense of personal victory, she announced, "I've decided to ask Greg out for New Year's Eve. Cool, huh?"

"Not Greg Reynolds, I hope?" Rick said as he entered the kitchen.

Tammy got up and hugged her husband while Chris busied herself by pouring more coffee, intent on ignoring the earful of advice she was sure to get.

"Reynolds was a hell of a football player, should've made it with the Cowboys. I'm glad you're getting out, but don't forget his reputation for scoring wasn't limited to the playing field. Maybe he's changed. Maybe he hasn't."

"Yes, brother dear," Chris simpered. "But may I remind you that your reputation wasn't any better before

Tammy settled you down. So there.'' She stuck out her tongue at him.

"Cute tongue you've got, sis. Just be sure to keep it in your mouth when he's around or you might not get it back." Rick meowed. "Then again, maybe that's not such a bad idea. You wouldn't have it to lash me with—*ooof!*''

Tammy's punch to his stomach coincided with Chris's fling of a doughnut. She hit her target: his nose.

"PHONE, CHRISSY,'' Anna called to her daughter. Chris felt her heart speed up and her stomach drop. Forcing herself not to run like a starry-eyed schoolgirl, especially when it was bound to be a relative or a friend or— Who was she kidding? *Please let it be Greg,* she prayed, forgetting she had no faith in prayers. "It's a man,'' her mother whispered.

Yes! *Yes!* "Hello?'' she answered, waving Anna away.

"Merry Christmas, Chris.'' His voice washed over her and made her feel too good, too young, and all-too-alive. Her palms were wet, her throat was dry. Lord, even her knees were shaking! And her breath—she couldn't catch her breath.

"Greg, hi! I didn't expect to hear from you today.''

"I called to find out if the car was picked up.''

Her high spirits immediately sank, reminding her of those days once made or broken with a phone call from Greg. It had been a long time since she'd eaten a quart of ice cream to pick herself up after he'd dropped her. "Yes, they came. We had the pickup guys in for a cup of eggnog. Must be a drag to have to work on Christmas Day.''

"Yeah, it is. I've done it a time or ten.'' He chuckled then. "Actually, Chris, the car was just an excuse to call. I've been thinking about you and I wanted to hear your voice.''

For a moment her voice was nowhere to be found.

"Chris? You still there?"

"Yes, I—" She laughed at her own foolishness, the delight she took in being foolish for a change. "Know what? I think I've got a crush on you again."

"I know I have one on you. It's a kick, isn't it? At least when it's not being horrible. I've been circling this phone for most of the day, telling myself to be cool and not pick it up because then I'd be very uncool and tell you how much I want to see you again. Guess I'm not as cool as I used to be." And then she heard it. A kiss. A soft, short kiss that sent silver bells ringing. "Anyone ever tell you that you've got a mouth that won't quit?"

She'd been told she was a good kisser but a mouth that wouldn't quit, that wasn't exactly the same. It made her feel, well, *carnal*. Carnal? *Her,* the good widow and hovering mother, *carnal?* It gave her the strangest sensation, like peeking into an open bedroom and witnessing an act of mindless sex. Knowing she should move away but too mesmerized, too aroused by the view to leave. And then, the shocking realization that the woman writhing on the bed was her. She, the intruder merely watching herself from a distance.

"Are you free tomorrow night?" Chris suddenly asked.

"As of now, I am. Can you be ready by seven?"

A vision of Audrey looking Greg up and down, then asking, "Are you going to be my new daddy?" sent Chris scrambling for an out. "Since you don't have a car I'll pick you up."

"No need. I'll borrow the keys from Dad." Laughing, he added, "Maybe he'll slip me a twenty after Mom reminds me not to show off behind the wheel and to be home by midnight."

Moments later Chris stared at the cradled receiver. Apprehension swirled in the pit of her stomach. Excitement, smacking of a delicious, dangerous risk, stole away any desire for dinner. It was an oddly nostalgic moment, reminding her of the horrible, wonderful effect hormones could have on appetite.

She wanted to be alone. Curled up in bed, painting her toenails to the tunes from a classic rock station, nirvana.

"Who was that man calling you?"

Chris managed a stiff shrug for her mother and a casual "Oh, it was just Greg. We're going out tomorrow night. You won't mind watching Audrey, will you? Maybe you could even take her to McDonald's while I'm getting ready." *And please, take the rest of the troop with you. Big Macs all around, my treat. Just don't show your faces until I'm gone.*

"Why, Chrissy, a date with your old boyfriend! Where are you going, honey? Are you nervous, excited—"

"Really, Mom, it's no big deal. Pass the word?" Chris pecked her cheek and headed for the bedroom that still had cheerleading pom-poms tacked next to a high school pennant.

Door closed, she went straight for the closet.

What did she have to wear? Nothing too great. She'd hit a mall first thing in the morning. Her hair needed trimming, but a fresh wash and blow-dry would have to do. Fingernails? She could use a manicure....

GREG CHECKED HIS WATCH. Ten minutes early. Should've driven around, checked out the old stompin' ground. Alone. *Jeez, what was he doing here?* Sitting in her driveway—better check his watch again. CD, which CD?

Let's see. *The Best of Heart...Journey's Greatest Hits...100 Groovin' Oldies*—better shove that one back in the glove compartment, too nerdy to shell out $18.88 for a late night TV pitch aimed at those of a certain age.

Ah, Norah Jones *Come Away With Me.* Slip it in…check the watch— *What the hell was he doing here?* Feeling like some green kid worried about getting a good-night kiss while he worked up the nerve to knock on a door, sling back his front hair and say, coolly of course, "Hi, ready to roll?"

Like he still had the hair to sling back. Checking his image in the rearview mirror, Greg suddenly laughed. *Aw, man, you oughta be sweatin' bullets. What'd you think this was, a date for dinner? Uh-huh, sure. That's why you flipped a coin when you couldn't decide between white briefs and black boxers. Why you just happen to have a rubber stashed under the front seat.*

Poor Chris. He never should have called her, never should have kissed her. That kiss, it wasn't just a kiss, and he had no business messing with a woman who put so much gut emotion into a kiss.

Leaning back, he considered that kiss, the reason he was really here. Simple. She'd been needy and he'd eaten it up.

Long time since he'd felt needed for more than balls on a battlefield—be it for country or in a bed. Well, he slept alone mostly. What with being a little needy himself, recreational sex just didn't cut it anymore. Pity he'd lost his appetite for it—about the time his hair began its slow but noticeable retreat. Funny, he thought, how a man's priorities could rearrange themselves when his body started doing the same.

Sex. He loved it. The sounds, the smell of it, the way a woman tasted, how she looked when she came. The sweat, the fit, even the awkwardness of trying to find the right fit with an unfamiliar body. But screwing, it wasn't enough anymore. He wanted a woman with character, class, lots of nooks and crannies upstairs. Someone who knew how to laugh and live for the moment because tomorrow was tomorrow and demands weren't part of the bargain.

Poor Chris. She deserved better than the best he had to offer. Damn, but he wished that he didn't like her; even worse, he respected her. She was the kind of woman who would win a whistle and keep walking without so much as a turn of her head. Bad luck—she'd turned his.

Getting out of the sedan, Greg leaned against the door and waited for the cold air to work against nature. Amazing that Chris could still do it to him at his age. Then again, maybe not. From what he'd seen so far, she was like a vintage wine: the blush, a deeper shade of pale; the crisp flavor, more mellow and rich; a bouquet that was meant to be savored.

Yeah, she'd go down easy.

"STAY PUT, I'LL GET IT!" Purse in hand, Chris rushed to the door on ready. And then she wasn't ready at all.

She'd always felt creepy about men who looked a woman up and down—but judging from Greg's lazy smile, he didn't mind a bit when she surveyed him. Two nights ago he'd looked good, even plane-rumpled and tired. But freshly shaven and dressed in a soft white sweater with pressed jeans, Greg was *mur*-der. The bushy poinsettia with a fat red bow and the easy confidence of his stance as he held it out proved the real killer.

Dying had never been so sweet.

"Why, Greg, how thoughtful of you."

"Think your mother will like it?" She hadn't planned on inviting him in, but in he came anyway. "It's a little thank-you to your folks for lending me their driveway and a big suck-up in advance—just in case I get you home past curfew."

Chris set the plant on the hall table and was trying to figure out how to make them scarce without seeming rude when Rick made his entrance.

"Hey, Greg Reynolds, good to see you." The two men shook hands and she noticed it lasted longer and they gripped harder than a friendly greeting would dictate. "Chris says you're one of a few good men these days. What's your rank?"

Chris gritted her teeth. Credentials, intentions, warnings with a handshake. Less than a minute and Greg was getting grilled before they could take off for a simple date.

"Major, as of last month. You're Rick, right?"

"That's me. You've come a long way since skirmishes on the twenty-yard line. Chris says you've been assigned to the Pentagon. That's quite a coup, isn't it?"

"I guess you could say so. But like anything else, it's a matter of what you want and how much you're willing to sacrifice to get it. I've paid my dues, proved myself in active duty. Once I did that they caught on where I really belonged was behind a desk. Go figure."

"Must be boring to shuffle paper after seeing that kind of action."

"Top secret, Rick, so my agenda's not exactly boring. I still get around."

"I'm sure you do."

Chris grimaced. *Oh, this was embarrassing, ridiculous. The only thing worse would be—*

"Hi! I'm Audrey. Who are you?"

"So, you're Audrey." Greg bent down and formally shook the small hand that disappeared in his. "I'm very pleased to meet you, young lady. Call me Greg. I'm an old friend of your mom's. Maybe we can be friends, too."

"Neat. Want to come with me and Grandma to McDonald's?"

"I'd like that, but maybe another time. Your mother and I are eating out at a competitor's—"

"A what?"

"A com—somewhere besides McDonald's." As if realizing he wasn't speaking her language and wasn't sure if he could, Greg rose. He towered over the child Chris suddenly wanted to whisk away. A suitable father he wasn't, and she felt a nudge from her conscience for wanting to be with him instead of with a daughter who was counting on Mama's good judgment.

"Tell you what, Audrey. Since you're loaning me your mother for the evening, I'll bring her back with a surprise to put under your pillow. What's it to be? Candy?"

"I'm tired of candy."

"Then, maybe a present?"

"Nope. Do you believe in Santa Claus?"

"Uh, sure."

"Do you like kids?"

Scooping Audrey into her arms, Chris gave her a fierce hug. "Mind your grandmother or the only surprise you'll get is a piece of coal."

"You're squishing me, Mama!"

Chris put her down and tossed a withering glare at Rick. She grabbed the coat she'd conveniently hooked by the door. Greg took it and spread the lining. One arm was in when she heard her parents' voices close by.

"Let's go, Greg," she said abruptly.

Chris bolted for the exit. She didn't say goodbye.

CHAPTER FOUR

"GREAT RIBS," GREG of Memphis pronounced. "Only place to compete is Kansas City. But I'll take Dallas any day, just so you're here."

"I'm glad I'm here. You're good company, Greg. Sorry about Rick."

"Don't be. He was looking out for his sister and I give him credit for that." Leaning closer, Greg said in a private tone, "If it was anyone but you, I would've ordered a steak instead of the ribs I wanted. They're a little too messy to impress someone you don't know too well on a date. By the way, you've got sauce on your upper lip." When she reached for her napkin, he caught her hand. "Funny, I never realized barbecue sauce could look sexy on a woman."

The air fairly hummed with an illicit vibrato that shut out the voices surrounding them, and she thought he was going to kiss her at last. Eyes half-closed and lips parted, Chris felt the glide of his wet fingertip wiping away the last traces of sauce. Then his finger was no longer there but at his own mouth where he discreetly sucked the remains.

Somehow, that seemed a lot more intimate than a kiss.

"Dessert?" he asked politely.

Two bites of pecan pie was all she could get down and he finished what she couldn't. Rather than seeming rude or overfamiliar, his use of her fork, his sharing the same plate, rivaled his finger kiss of the sauce. Those liberties were subtle but telling, as was his prudently generous tip, his slide of her chair and "Ladies first" as he held open the restaurant door. Altogether, they heightened her desire for the kiss so much that Chris considered stopping him and *taking* what she wanted.

She couldn't bring herself to do it. Old habits died hard.

"You're hobbling. New shoes?" he asked, slowing his pace.

"Half a size too small but they looked so good, I couldn't resist. This is absolutely *the* last time I buy for appearance instead of the right fit."

"Sounds like me and marriage." He laughed, making himself the butt of the joke. Chris thought it a rare ability and an immensely appealing trait.

"I could learn from you, Greg."

"How's that?"

"You don't let life beat you down by taking it too seriously."

"Don't be so sure." He stopped her with a firm clamp on her waist, a narrowing of his eyes that spelled *t-r-o-u-b-l-e*. Suddenly, her feet left the ground and she was in his arms laughing with abandon as he growled ferociously against her neck. She yelped when he threw her in the air, catching her just when she was certain she'd been dropped.

"Put me down!" she shrieked, not caring about onlookers or reputation, simply cutting loose, not giving a damn, for once— Oh, when had she had this much fun?

"Wanna race me to the car?"

"I'll be a cripple before I get there!"

"In that case, enjoy the ride." His easy shift of her weight over his shoulder amazed her a little. A young athlete's firm muscle could go to flab by the time he was eyeing forty. It seemed that Greg had avoided the pitfalls of comfort the same way she sidestepped even the hint of a conflict. But watching the way his legs moved, two trunks of equal sureness and strength, attached to the tempting view of tight buttocks, Chris decided a conflict might not be so bad after all. She swatted his backside.

He swatted hers back. "You've got a great ass," he said conversationally, and then he bit it. "Betcha taste even better without your clothes. Ah, here we are."

He tumbled her into the car. On his side.

Her first instinct was to scoot to the opposite door—a generous length in a luxury sedan—and think about the last half-minute. Compromising on her sudden cowardice, Chris opted for the middle and put her purse between them.

Greg cranked the engine, slid in a CD and pitched her purse into the back seat. He patted the spot beside him.

She inched closer until their hips met. The feel of his arm around her, the slow rub of palm to shoulder, raised gooseflesh beneath her coat.

"Where to?" asked the man who bit butts in parking lots and thought she'd taste better without her clothes.

"Do you like to dance?" she ventured.

"Slow's no problem, but a fast number and I'll trample what's left of your feet."

Did she really suggest *dancing?* A lesson in humility she didn't need. "We could hit a club and have a nightcap."

"Tell you what, if you don't like my idea of a good time once we get there, say so and we'll catch whatever's playing on the big screen, then top off the night with a drink."

With a calmness she wasn't feeling, Chris agreed to his small intrigue. There was an edge of purpose she sensed in him and it felt more darkly suggestive than a kiss. By the time he drove into a deserted shopping center, her palms were pumping sweat. When she began to wipe them on her new suede skirt, he quickly placed her hand high on his thigh.

"Your skirt's too nice, wipe your palms on me." The firmness of thick muscle flexed beneath her touch and she was caught between a tingling quiver and chagrin that Greg was aware of her slipping composure.

He circled the parking lot—ensuring they were alone, she suspected—then, once in the back, pulled into a reserved spot.

Off went the car lights but the engine still idled.

"Know where we are?"

"It's familiar but—no, I can't place it."

The brush of his lips was a restrained hunger. Her own hunger mingled with taut nerves and she hoped he'd keep kissing her until the first consumed the other.

"Do you remember now?"

"This is where we used to go parking."

"The concrete walls weren't here, but you had some walls of your own I did my best to crack."

"You made more than a dent." Her smile was a little wobbly; so was her voice. "After all, you gave me my first hickey."

"The most persuasive thing I knew to do with my mouth. *Then*." The engine continued to idle against the innuendo that he wanted more than a repetition of old memories. She'd heard the dating game had changed since she'd been an active player, but it distressed her to think Greg would hold her in such shallow regard.

When Norah Jones began crooning a new song, Greg switched on the lights. "So what movie do you want to see?"

"Wait." Chris gripped his hand on the shift. "I have to know, did you expect casual sex as payment for dinner?"

"Casual sex?" he repeated, a hint of amusement in the lift of his brow. "Why, Chris, surely you realize any sex

we might have would *never* be of the casual variety. And
there's certainly not much variety to be had in a car.''

''Then what are we doing here?''

''I had hoped,'' he said slowly, ''we might make some
good memories to keep us warm when life turns cold.''
Shifting into reverse, he added, ''I'm somewhat offended
that you thought I would pressure you for sex because I
sprang for the meal. That's not my style and I've yet to
take anything from a woman she wasn't more than willing
to give.''

Truth or dare; Chris twisted the key. The engine ceased
to purr and she imagined he could hear her dry swallow.

''Forget the movie. Unless it's at a drive-in.'' It was she
who turned off the lights, and it was she who said in a
trembling whisper, ''Wanna make out?''

Determined to forge past her qualms, she closed her eyes
and waited. And waited. Until finally, she blurted, ''What
are you waiting for?''

''You.'' His lids were lazily drooped over his eyes.
''You're tense. Like this is something you're bent on doing
because it's good for you, not because it's easy and natural.''

''Of course, it's not easy,'' she retorted, flustered. ''And
you're certainly not making it any easier for me, staring at
me like that, like…like— Ah, hell. Maybe *you* want to take
in the last show.'' Why was he making this so difficult?
Scrutinizing her until she couldn't stand it a second longer.
She turned away. ''I'm not too good at this, Greg.''

''On the contrary, I think you're doing great.'' He
pushed off her coat and got rid of his. Their blended wool
heaped on the floorboard, he smoothed the fleecy angora
spilling around her shoulders. ''Tell me what you're thinking.''

''I'm thinking that I'm making a total fool of myself and

I should be embarrassed, but I'm not. That I'm scared of what I'm feeling because I'm not even sure what it is—if that makes any sense.''

"Makes sense to me.''

"It does?'' His nod, the stroke of his thumb over her cheek, had a wonderful, soothing effect. She relaxed, feeling...okay. Okay with him, with herself. How he'd done it, she didn't know, but somehow Greg had shifted the moment into one of natural ease. "Do me a favor?'' she asked.

"For you, anything.''

She believed that, just as she believed he could guide them more smoothly than could her rusty confidence. "Would you take it from here?''

"Love to. But Chris, how far we take it, that's up to you. I won't stop until you tell me. It's not in me to be noble when you make me hard with just a smile.''

"You're very good for my self-esteem.'' *Whoa!* She was flying on the wings of his earthy praise, giddy with the thrill of a woman empowered by her sexual allure. Testing it, she murmured, "I'm smiling, Greg. Are you...hard?''

He kissed her palm, then settled it over the straining of his fly. The air trapped in her throat rushed out as he slid a hand up her skirt. A single finger licked her crotch.

"Are you wet?''

"Heaven help me.''

"Let's hope so, because any intervention won't be coming from me.'' He pressed her down on the soft leather and shifted them until her knees were spread and his were bent against the door. Greg tossed off her shoes. His thumb worked the arch of a stockinged foot as he said quietly, "I dreamed about you last night. It was a very erotic dream.''

"Then maybe we were having the same dream.'' He

rubbed against her, reminding her of how empty she'd felt upon waking. More, how empty and aching she was now.

"I always did wonder if women could have wet dreams. Should I take it there's at least one woman who does?"

Chris began to wonder if a woman could orgasm in the front seat of a car without so much as a kiss.

"Kiss me," she demanded, desperate for the taste of his mouth, for more than the slow lift and press of his hips.

The sound he made was somewhere between a profanity and a blessing. Then his mouth was everywhere but on hers, laving her neck and bathing her ears between whispers of hot, urgent words. She ravaged his mouth, frantic to shut him up before she begged him to make good on his wicked suggestions. He returned her kiss with a stunning fury while his hands traveled under her sweater and slowly inched it up until he was fingering the front clasp of her bra. "Let me," he said in a low, persuasive voice. "Let me." And she did.

It was the touch of a man who knew exactly how to touch. And it was the tentative touch of memory, discovering the wonder of a female body. She was coming undone and Chris didn't have the want or the will to stop him, not even when he released the button of his jeans. She knew what was next, and then, there it was, his hand moving hers to the zipper.

"Do it," he urged her. "You want to, Chris. Do it."

She hesitated. He wedged a thigh between her legs, then pressed with a steady rhythm. "While you make up your mind, let's see if I can sway your decision."

He was good at this—too good. But she couldn't fault him. Greg was honest in his seduction. And Chris was honest with herself. She very much wanted to be seduced.

She drew down his zipper.

"Don't stop there. Take me out. Touch me."

Being seduced was one thing; seducing him, another. As if he sensed her desperation to let go, he kissed her with a tender patience. Sometime in the midst of that kiss, he took hold of her hand and guided it to do what he wanted. *What she wanted.* She wanted to feel him; she *did* feel him, warm and sleek, virility pumping within her fist until she pressed him against the barrier of hose and panties.

"Pull them down," she said urgently. "Do it before I change my mind."

CHAPTER FIVE

HE WAS QUICK TO accommodate her, taking them down as far as he could. The small space of a front seat made it awkward, but no less exciting or agonizing as he played her so right that she gripped his wrist and led him to finger her inside. His rough groan was infinitely arousing, calling up the whimpers, mewling little gasps, that broke from her throat.

But then he was no longer stroking and neither was she. Together they held him poised, dangerously close to the point of no return.

"I won't hurt you, I promise. It'll be good. I'll make it so good for you."

"No—no. Anything but. I'm not ready for this, Greg."

He nudged her with a tempting glide between the slit of her folds. "Your body says that you're plenty ready, baby."

"My body, yes. But..." She wanted to cry. She wanted to say the hell with it and just do it. She'd thought that she could, but now that she was here— No, she *wasn't* ready.

His breathing was ragged, his face etched in pained, severe lines. And his voice, it hurt a little to hear because it was terse with the effort to sound calm.

"You're telling me 'No' and I'll honor that. Your body, your choice. But to come this far and leave me hanging— Chris, I feel like I deserve an explanation."

Chris couldn't bear for him to think she had less respect

for his body than he'd shown for hers. And so, painful as it was, she forced the words.

"There was a man I got involved with about a year ago. An old friend, actually, who did a lot of hand-holding before he admitted to wanting me for a lot more than a friend. I knew he cared more in that way than I did, but I was lonely and the hurt wasn't going away. I told myself that I could heal faster, come alive again, by going to bed with him. I did...but it didn't work out. I—I..." A tear slid down her cheek. Greg's eyes glittered with an incisive hunger, but the fingertip he swept over the tear was amazingly tender.

"What happened?" he asked gently.

"I did something wrong. Our clothes were off and—and I did something wrong. It was just that I loved Mark so much, I missed him so much. Time was supposed to make it better, but—I couldn't get rid of his clothes, couldn't stop waking up every morning and my first thought was 'Where's Mark, why isn't he in bed? Oh, that's right, he's dead. Dead, dead...*dead.*' How could he have done that to me? Leaving me before I could tell him that I loved him, one last time. Make love to him once, just once more. I never got to tell him goodbye. He was there and then he wasn't and if I just could have told him—but I couldn't and so I did something wrong."

"Shh, shh. It's okay, you don't have to say any more."

"But I want to, I—I need to. I've had this bottled up so long, it's been like a cancer eating me alive. That night, while another man touched me, I closed my eyes and pretended Mark was there, that it was him instead. I wanted him to be inside me and...and..."

"You said his name."

"Mark," she whispered brokenly. "I called for Mark and then—then I was alone. Lying naked on a bed and watching this man I thought was my friend fling off the sheet. Not a word. Then he was jerking on his clothes and I was talking, trying to explain, to apologize—but he was walking out. Out of his own bedroom where I couldn't get his name right, out of the house I couldn't drive away from fast enough. Out of my life. We'd gone to the same church and he even transferred his membership. I think maybe he loved me but he knew I could never love him back.''

''Chris.'' There was a wealth of sympathy in the thumbs that stroked the wetness coursing down her cheeks. But there was more, a certain male selfishness Greg didn't try to disguise. ''He shouldn't have left you like that. I'd like to say I would have behaved better, but I'm afraid I might have been worse. I don't think I could have managed the grace to stay silent.''

''I wish he hadn't been. The silence was ten times more horrible than anything he could have said. I felt like I'd cheated on two men, not one, and... It was a nightmare, Greg, a nightmare.''

''I'm sure it was.'' His simple acceptance was exactly the right amount of comfort and Chris took it. All cried-out, she felt cleansed, freed from sickbed sheets that had been mummy cloth silencing her body, her breath.

She wanted to thank Greg but it didn't feel right. Something about him said her gratitude would take away from what he'd gladly given.

''You know, Greg, I can hardly believe it myself, but in a matter of days you've come to know me better than the people who've known me all my life.''

''I like that. I like it a lot.'' He didn't return her smile. Indeed, he got rid of hers with a sudden and hard, tongue-thrusting kiss that left her speechless when he was done. ''Know me better, Chris. Know me well enough to realize I won't be any man's stand-in, ever. Let's find out who you're really with tonight. It's something you need for yourself, and I want to be the one who sees to that need.''

"Greg, I—''

"Don't say my name again. Don't say anything until you don't know where you are or what you're doing, you only know you're calling for someone to be inside you. Me, Chris. It's going to be me who takes you there. And it's going to be me you ask for when you're ready to take it all the way. I'll make sure you get the name right, trust me.''

A man in his element, he made all the right moves. Kisses and more kisses, hot and deep. Hands wooing her with a perfect balance between gentle persuasion and rough demand. There, on the breasts he bared to the chill air and heated in his mouth until steamy windows shut out the pale sliver of a moon. And there—"Yes, please, there"—where he drew fluid circles and her body grasped for more than a mock coupling.

Greg…Greg…

That's it, yes…yes, that's it. Good, so good, baby. But it's been too long. Again, you need it again…. That's right, take it. Take it and say my name.

How many times she said it, she didn't know, only that it was his name she cried out, pleading for him to be inside her and why, *why,* wouldn't he be there? His hands, his mouth, his teasing thrusts, they were everywhere but inside her.

He didn't stop until she sobbed for him to quit, she couldn't take any more. Her body listless, her head slumped to the side, she couldn't bring herself to look at him.

Perhaps he intuited her need to regain some sense of self, or maybe he was struggling for his own control. Chris was too fragmented to care about the reason, just grateful he gave her time to collect the scattered pieces of herself before he firmly turned her face to him.

What she saw was a starkly honest man. One who was pleased with himself and with the woman he had so well pleasured.

"Just a little incentive, something for you to think about." He folded her palm around his erection. "You're a sexy woman and I'm a needy man who doesn't have time to waste. Cards on the table. I want to keep things square."

"I have no false illusions, Greg. We have no future."

"Maybe not, but that doesn't mean we can't take something with us when we go our separate ways."

"I'm not sure what you're after."

He was quiet, pensive, as he stroked her hair, and then he said, "Tell me, Chris, did a man ever talk dirty to you in bed, or explain, graphically, exactly what he wanted you to do to him?"

What? Startled beyond speech, she was glad the word hadn't slipped out and given her away for what she was: a woman who'd lost her virginity to the man she'd eventually married. A wonderful man who most certainly had *not* talked dirty and still made her feel plenty satisfied in the sack. She hadn't needed any comparisons to know what they had was good.

"Why do you want to know?" she finally asked.

"The same reason I want to know if you ever told a man exactly what you wanted."

"Well, I…I never had to. I mean, he always—"

"Knew what to do?"

"Yes."

"But how could he know exactly what you wanted if you didn't tell him? Was he a mind reader, by chance?"

"No, an accountant."

"Well, that certainly explains it."

Chris wasn't sure, but she thought Mark had just been insulted. Or maybe Greg was making a joke about her evasion. Whatever his intent, he'd definitely gotten her attention.

"I wonder," he said casually, "do you like oral sex?"

"Oral—" Good Lord, where was he going with this?

"A nod or a shake will do."

Finding her voice, she blurted, "It's fine!"

"Fine. Hmm...I see." He tapped his chin and stared at her quite thoughtfully. "Do you swallow?"

"Sw-swa— Are you trying to shock me?"

"If I wanted to shock you I'd tell you exactly what I'd like to do to you. But if you want to know, you'll have to ask."

Did she swallow? At the moment she was swallowing what felt like cotton. Greg obviously had a purpose, a goal she was suddenly curious to have defined. Licking dry lips, she made herself say, "And what exactly is it that you'd like to do with me?"

His smile was thin but definitely pleased. She felt as if she'd passed some sort of test from a tough teacher who very much liked her answers.

"To be exact, I want to make love to you like you've never experienced it before. Very nice, very slow and easy—for starters."

"For starters?" she repeated.

"Surely you don't think that's where it would end."

Not sure if she wanted to know, but too curious not to ask, she did. "Where would it end, Greg?"

"I have no idea, but I'd like to find out. I'm very open to suggestions and I'm not shy about making my own requests. If you want me to be more explicit, I'd be more than happy to give you a taste of talking dirty in bed."

"*No!* I mean, no, that's not necessary. I get the picture." When he grinned, she added, "I think."

He kissed her then—a generously sweet, disturbingly demanding kiss that confused her even more.

"You're killing me, Chris, killin' me. Don't keep me hanging, I need your answer."

"You'd get it a lot sooner if I knew the question."

Something between a groan and a frustrated sigh passed his lips. "Look, I realize what kind of woman you are, and I respect you for not being cut out for an affair with no promises attached. What I want with you isn't so simple or cheap. See, I have an appetite that hasn't been fed in some time because I've become rather particular. You suit my tastes and they're…unique."

Hesitantly, she whispered, "Perverted?"

He considered that. "I don't think so, but I suppose it's a subjective opinion. I'd never want you to do something you didn't enjoy. Like I said, that's not my style, and besides, it would defeat my purpose."

"Which is?"

"To explore each other. No expectations, nothing to lose, the field wide open—between our legs and, where it gets really interesting…in the mind."

Chris tried to absorb what he was saying. An affair, unique tastes, exploration. It began to fall into place and she realized he'd left something out. *Discovery.* But discovery meant change, and change was often threatening.

"Does this mean if I want to see you again, you have some expectations, after all? That if I simply want to take in a movie and enjoy your company, it's a no-go?"

"We can go wherever you want and talk until the conversation runs dry. But it'll always come back to this." This, where he pressed himself against her and remained with a still pressure. "I want this with you too much. You deserve to know I won't play fair, that I'll press every button you've got to get what I want."

"You're warning me, that seems pretty fair."

"Not hardly. It's strategy." He shook his head with a laugh that wasn't really. "What I wouldn't give to be the kind of man you could love as much as you did your husband."

"No man, Greg, *no man* is worth loving that much again. I'll never let it happen," she vowed. "It's taken me too long to find my way out. I won't be setting myself up for another fall."

"But you'll remarry, won't you?"

"I hope so. You might like living alone, but I don't. I'm a nester and I'd like another child before my time clock runs out. The problem is finding a man who doesn't expect too much emotionally and can settle for what I can give."

"Lets me out. I could never be that man any more than the one who spoiled you for the likes of me. You'll meet someone, though. Someone willing to just 'settle.' I doubt you'll be happy, but maybe you'll be satisfied with the lucky bastard who wins the girl I let get away twice."

"Thank God I'm not in love with you." Tracing the line of his thinned lips, she was honest about the threat he posed: "You're everything I'm not looking for and I think you could still break my heart."

"Mine's already broken. You're everything a man could want and fall in love with way too easy. You're poison, baby. Pretty poison for someone like me."

It was, without doubt, the sexiest compliment she'd ever received. But from whom? The more she learned about him, it seemed, the less she knew.

"And what are you like, Greg?"

"I'm not so sure if I want you to know." His gaze locked with hers while she waited him out. "All right, then.

There's a good dose of anger, even some hurt, but I bury all that in my work. I've dished out my share of heartache and moved on while doing what it takes to climb up the ladder. I like being top dog, power's my fix. I try not to abuse it, but I have. Sometimes regretting it, but never when the means are worth the end. I know what and who I am, and make no excuses either way. I'm not a bad person but I do have some critical flaws. Now that you have more goods on me than most, will you see me tomorrow night? We both know the score.''

He'd told her more than she wanted to hear. The score was: There was a lot more at stake than what she was ready to risk. Maybe Greg wouldn't break her heart, but he'd make sure she never forgot him. Once she hooked up with an altogether–decent man who made a model father, she'd have more than one ghost to deal with in and out of bed. One was dead, but as long as the other was alive, one chance meeting could pull the rug from under her firmly planted feet. No matter how much she had, that's all it would take for her to know she didn't have it all.

"I have to think about this," she finally said.

"Fair enough. You've got a phone book. Use it when you decide you're ready to move on."

CHAPTER SIX

"CALL ME." Greg kissed her cheek beneath the front-porch light. He waited until she'd passed through the unlocked door before returning to the car. There, he gave a short wave.

Chris watched until the taillights disappeared, still unsure if she would see him again.

Passing through the hallway she heard her father's snore from an open door, then low murmurs from the bedroom Rick and Tammy shared. Chris's smile held a bit of a smirk. For once, they weren't the only ones with a private agenda.

Her knees were still shaking. Wanting a man who thrilled her with a whisper of "You're poison, baby" was dangerous for a woman who'd always believed in commitment before sex. This time there would be no commitment, and she still wanted the sex. Passing her finger through a candle flame was one thing; walking into a bonfire was a good way to get burned.

Changed into her flannel pajamas, Chris sat on the edge of her old bed and stroked Audrey's hair. This was her ultimate responsibility. This child who had kept her going when she'd wanted to give up. A little girl who prayed for a daddy she didn't have.

"Maybe in a couple of years. I'll hold out for the best, when it comes to you," Chris whispered to the tight ball hugging a Barbie doll. Though Greg wasn't in the running for future dad, he'd proved a real ace when it came to a child's whimsy. Slipping the note he'd suggested under Audrey's pillow, Chris was certain a mother-daughter date for the skating rink and a bunch of quarters for video games was a super-good surprise.

The possibility of a movie and popcorn she'd left out. After all, she might still be foolish enough to dial the number she didn't need a phone book to recall.

"YOU'RE DOING IT AGAIN," Tammy observed.

"What?" Chris drummed her fingers on the breakfast-nook table while she eyed the kitchen wall phone she'd monopolized as a teen. And now, here she was, an adult visiting her parents, afraid to go near the thing lest she use it.

"*That*. Are you expecting a call?"

"Yes—no." She'd hoped for one to nudge her decision. Clearly, Greg had meant it when he'd put the ball in her court. More than in her court, the damn thing was pinging around her brain like a pinball machine stuck on automatic return. Even in her sleep she'd been betwixt erogenous re-plays and half-awake glimpses of Audrey's trusting face on the next pillow.

Chris looked at her watch: Six-thirty and counting. If she counted much longer they'd lose one night out of five that couldn't be recaptured. If she could just keep counting, he'd be gone and so would she. She'd pack Audrey up and head for Lubbock with morals and pride firmly intact, an untainted woman, suitable for a man looking for more than a hot fling.

No expectations, nothing to lose, the field wide open— between our legs and...

"Chris, are you feeling all right?"

"Huh? Oh, sure, I'm fine. Why?"

"Nothing, just that noise you made. Kind of a...groan?"

Between our legs and in the mind... Six thirty-three. *I'd never want you to do something you didn't enjoy.... I want to make love to you, very nice, very slow and easy....*

"You're sure the leftover ham didn't upset your stomach?"

I have an appetite that hasn't been fed in some time....

"Or maybe it's the flu. You look so flushed and— Why don't you go to bed and get some rest?"

A vision of Greg in bed didn't provoke thoughts of rest. One call and... And what if she couldn't face the mirror in the morning? She could bail out, some the wiser for her bad judgment, couldn't she? And at least she wouldn't spend the rest of her life wondering what discoveries she might have missed. *You need it. You want it.*

She was taking the risk.

"Think you could help Mom watch Audrey tonight?"

"No problem. Are you going to lie down?"

"Not here." Rising, Chris put a finger to the secretive smile framing her lips.

"Are you sure about this?" Tammy stroked her stomach like a worry stone, but the smile she returned was intrigued.

"I need some memories, Tammy." The previous night's images continued to barrel through her brain and shoot down to her belly, pulling it tighter than a piano wire. The chord it struck rippled into a crescendo, giving a quiet passion to her voice. "I need new memories to compete with the old ones that I've let hold me back."

"Then what are you waiting for? Go for it." Tammy gave her a thumbs-up as Chris headed for the phone.

Not giving herself time to hesitate, she dialed. On the fifth ring Chris silently damned herself for assuming Greg was sitting by the phone, waiting for her call.

"Hello?" he answered, out of breath.

"It's me. I was afraid you weren't at home."

"And I was afraid I'd miss your call while I jogged off almost a day's worth of pacing the floor."

Taking heart that there was at least one man who baby-sat the phone, she said clearly, "I'm ready, Greg. Ready to move on."

An hour later she turned from his side at the car to wave. From the front door, Audrey waved back, looking curious, confused. And hopeful.

The next one's for you, daughter. But this one's for me.

CHAPTER SEVEN

"YOU DON'T WASTE ANY time, do you?"

"No time to waste." Greg's grin was cagey as he watched Chris's foot tap against the thick carpeting—high dollar, in keeping with the posh lobby, which she apparently found preferable to look at than him while they waited for the elevator.

The doors slid open but she didn't move. When her hand shot out to catch the closing metal, Greg breathed a sigh of relief. Though they were alone, Chris stared at the escalating numbers until they reached the top floor. He noticed she seemed to flounce her way beside him as they strode down the gold-sconced corridor.

"Why do I get the feeling you're a little irked?"

"Maybe because I am. I thought we'd slide into this instead of me feeling like a call girl who phoned up her john."

Greg subdued a chuckle. Enjoying himself at Chris's expense wasn't really fair, but he wasn't above making her sweat after she'd kept him sweating all day.

Wanting her to verify her decision in no uncertain terms, he tapped the electronic entry card against the door where they stood. "Sure you're ready? You can still back out."

Chris grabbed the plastic and shoved it into the slot. At the sound of a buzzer, she thrust the door open.

"Wait." He tossed a light bag through the doorway, then scooped her up. Carrying her over the threshold, he realized how fragile she felt in his arms. The dress she wore was designed for a leggy, thin frame that could use the illusion of an extra ten pounds. Maybe he should have fed her first. Better yet, room service; they could feed each other.

The door closed and he heard the catch of her breath in the dark. The effect it had on him wasn't to his liking, making him want to ease the apprehension he suddenly felt badly for creating.

"You think we're here so I can get a piece—no champagne, no flowers, lie on your back and spread 'em, let's do it so we can do it again before the clock strikes twelve—right?"

"Aren't we?"

Greg slid her down his length. He could feel her trembling and it touched a soft chord inside him, damn her. And damn her some more for shaking even harder as he turned her in his arms and pressed his hardness against her belly.

"If you're so nervous about being here with me, why aren't you making tracks to one of those taxis outside? It's not too late. In fact, I'll even pay your fare."

Her arms were slow to come around his waist but once there, she clung tighter than a miser to his last dime.

"It's not you, Greg—it's me. I *do* want to be here. Just give me a minute to get my bearings."

"A minute? Take an hour, take the whole night. I'm in no rush unless you are."

Her shivering stilled. "Then why are we here?"

"A piece of action, Chris, isn't simply permission and submission. That won't cut it with me. Nothing's going to happen unless you're in heat."

"What's that supposed to mean?" There was an edge of indignation in her tone and he was glad to hear the spark.

"It means you have to want me enough to light *my* fire. You're not an easy lay. These days, neither am I." Her off-the-shoulder dress gave him access to her collarbone. Lips pressed into the indentation of soft flesh, he murmured, "When you can't get my clothes off fast enough, when you can throw out every inhibition and feel good about it, *then* we can move on. The first move has to come from you."

"You're asking for a lot."

"Yeah, I am. No shutters, no limits, adults only and regrets not allowed. Those are my terms and you might as well know that I'm not one for compromise." When she stiffened slightly, he asked, "Remember what we agreed we missed most during the holidays?"

"The privacy of our own homes. Some room to breathe."

"I didn't give you a Christmas present. Consider this a belated one for us both." He flicked on the lights. Her gasp of delight made the trouble he'd gone to well worth the effort. Greg watched her lean over the entry table where two dozen roses bloomed in rainbow hues. "I never send flowers if I think they're expected. So I'll know next time you least expect them, what's your favorite color?"

"Yellow. Purple. Red. Any of them! All of them! *Flowers.*" She sighed. "It's been so long—thank you, Greg."

The hint of moistness she blinked away squeezed something inside him. *Not the heart, can't be the heart.*

"Glad you like them," he replied gruffly. "Go on, kick off your shoes, make yourself at home. No need to be polite or watch what you say. Wanna strut around naked? Be my guest."

Her lilting laughter as she flung both shoes away accompanied a soft thudding sensation in the region of his solar plexus. It grew louder, harder to ignore, as he helped her out of her coat, then louder still as he hung his herringbone jacket next to her gray wool in the entry closet. Staring at the hard wooden hangers, companionably nestled side by side, he jerked them to opposite ends. Jaw clenched, he hooked an arm around her shoulder and led them to the kitchen.

"High on style, low on function. But it comes with a microwave and I happened to bring along the popcorn. Not theater fresh, but it'll do. As for the movie, if you don't like what's showing on pay-per-view, the management told me they have a load of DVDs to choose from." His kiss was short but not too sweet. Sweet was dangerous, a lowering of defenses he couldn't afford. Chris was too sweet, that was the problem; but once she cut loose and quit being such a good girl, he'd be fine. "Still irked?"

"Are you kidding? This is great!"

"Let's check out the rest." In the bedroom, a big mahogany poster bed with a lace coverlet was the centerpiece of the inviting antique decor. The bottle he'd ordered was snuggled in a silver ice bucket and positioned where he'd requested it: in the middle of the bed.

"Champagne! And look, pink flowers painted on the glass! This is marvelous, Greg, just marvelous."

Did she have to sound so ecstatic about the very things he'd hoped would impress her even half this much? Ah, hell, he'd milk it while he could and impress her some more.

"Perrier-Jouet, 1995. France. Not their best year, but it'll do." He grabbed the bottle and offered it to her flung-out, I-don't-believe-this arms. "A tiny region in France thought up champagne and after spending some time there, I don't think much of impostors." Rolling up his sleeves, he turned his attention to a cheval mirror angled in the corner.

Covertly he watched her as she traced the hand-painted glass, green against a ruby nail—sliding it against the trickling moisture and making his testes ache for her palming, the light flick of her nails searching, moving, pressing.... Tearing his gaze from the mirror, Greg silently counted to ten, then turned to face her, still unsure if he was capable of vocalizing more than a succession of groans.

"Want me to order up some caviar and chocolate-dipped strawberries?"

"And spoil dinner? Popcorn and champagne, sounds like a feast to me." He coveted the fine arch of her neck as she threw back her head and laughed joyously. "Greg Reynolds, where have you been all my life?"

"The Middle East. Russia. Thailand. Europe. You name it, I've been there. But if I could choose any place in the world, this is where I'd want to be." Fishing a coin out of his pocket, he brushed his erection and winced. "Let's try out the bed." He made a hard toss on the mattress. "Didn't bounce. But I'll forego demerits if the sheets are extra crisp and clean."

"Should we turn down the covers and find out?"

"If we did that, they wouldn't be too crisp and clean by the time we crawled away." When she bit her bottom lip, he lifted two crystal flutes from the nightstand and pinged rims. "It's your call. Flop on the bed while I spring the cork or get your butt out of here before I start talking dirty."

"Don't forget your quarter," Chris said over her shoulder as she made for the door. "You might need it later for a tip on the pillow."

The coin he left behind for good luck but he brought the glasses along. He settled them by the champagne she had placed on the mantel, above the gas logs that he turned on in the hearth. Amply realistic, the fireplace was a nice touch, set a cozy mood.

Chris stood at the picture window, surveying the vista of headlights far below.

"They look like stars on a clear, black night."

"Damn pretty sight." And he didn't mean the skyline.

"It's beautiful," she breathed. The touch of his broad palm tightening on her waist made her feel utterly feminine and deliciously warm. Pivoting, she laid her hands on his chest and leaned her forehead against his silk tie. Was she really here? Wooed with champagne and flowers by this mysterious man.

Finger to chin, he tipped up her face and kissed her softly, deeply—a kiss he spiked with a taste of demand. It left her feeling a little woozy.

"This doesn't seem real."

"Believe me," he assured her with a gentle bump, "this is as real as it gets."

His smile, that trademark naughty-nice flash of his teeth, should be illegal, she thought. It simply wasn't fair for any man to be able to turn a woman on with an easy half-twist of his lips. Staring at them, she wondered how many women had fallen victim to their lure. It bothered her to think of herself as the latest number in a long line of predecessors. And so, she tried not to think it.

"What I mean is, for our lives to go in such different directions and wind up here. It's too crazy. I keep expecting to wake up and realize I dreamed the whole thing."

"Does that mean you'd look on the next pillow and wonder why *I* wasn't in bed?"

His reference to her painful confession caused her to step back. He bridged the slight distance with a firm grip on the hand she'd laid over her heart. Pulling her to him, he stroked her arms, warming their sudden chill.

"Supposing you did," he went on. "I can only hope you'd wish I had been more than a dream."

No dream, this. Greg was a wild card and his squeeze of her buttocks was more than a reshuffling of the deck.

With his soft bite to her earlobe, his murmur that the next move was hers, Chris felt she was playing fifty-two-card pickup.

"What are you in the mood for? I mean, what kind of movies do you like?" Breaking away, she hoped her lunge for the movie guide didn't look as frantic as it was. "Let's see, what shows do they have that won't hit the video stores for another month?" Flipping past the Adults Only section, she tapped an action-adventure flick. "How's this?"

"I got enough of that on the job to last me a lifetime. No thanks." His gaze distant, he was staring out the window gathering wool. Chris had the feeling she was the wool. A quick embarrassment for her skittish reaction caused her to toss aside the movie guide.

She touched his fist, pressed against the glass.

"Tell you what, Greg. Why don't we forget about the movie? I can channel surf while you make the popcorn—or vice versa."

The gaze he turned on her was incisive, challenging her precarious composure. He studied her awhile—long enough that Chris was torn between telling him to bring the popcorn into the bedroom and making a mad rush out the door, grabbing the flowers on her way.

"Two televisions," he finally said. "You know where they are. Decide which one you'd rather watch and I'll meet you there."

CHAPTER EIGHT

CHRIS FELT MORE in control by the time Greg met her on the couch with a bowl of Orville Redenbacher's best. When he gave her a "That's what I figured" chuckle before landing the popcorn on the cocktail table, she decided the night might be salvageable after all.

Extending the remote, she said, "Want a turn?"

"First things first." Greg's reassuring pat on her knee relieved the last traces of tension.

His discarding of foil and wire shield seemed an omen of sorts, as did his adroit lift of thumbs to the cork. As it flew, effervescent bubbles spewed upward. Before she could grab a flute, the best champagne she'd never drunk in her life went everywhere except between their lips.

Chris put her mouth to the frothing glass. With a gurgling yelp of dismay over the waste, she pointed for him to do the same, certain she had the equivalent of ten bucks in her mouth and another twenty was headed for the floor.

"A lady shucking her manners. If that's not rich, I don't know what is." Rather than slurp up the expensive brew, he slapped his palm against the rim and shook hard. The bottle ejaculated with an enthusiasm to match their grapple as he aimed for her mouth. "Open up and let me watch you swallow."

"You open up and swallow!"

"I knew you could talk dirty if you put your mind to it." He grinned and lifted the bottle to his mouth. With a swish and a wink, he gulped. Both their faces bathed, the champagne almost gone and precious little consumed, Greg licked her cheeks, then sucked her drenched chin. Doing her part in the game of cleanup, she ran her tongue against the slope of his jaw. Each shaved whisker was a reminder of their opposite genders and just how much opposites apparently did attract.

"A glass, *monsieur?*" she offered, twirling the stem.

"Throw it." He lifted its twin and tapped their rims.

"But this is good crystal," she protested.

"So? They can bill me." Pointing to the fireplace, he tossed up his glass and caught it neatly. "Ready if you are."

Chris looked from the fine crystal to the hearth to Greg.

"Okay, bud, it's your dollar." Rearing back, she hurled with gusto. He was two seconds behind her but his flute took the lead. Her own fell apart in three sections, a puny ping to his resounding shatter.

"You throw like a girl."

"I *am* a girl."

"So I noticed." Surveying the bottle, he said, "Low tide. A swig apiece and it's empty. Want to take another shot? Put some arm into it and keep the wrist stiff."

"Give me that!" Snatching the painted glass from his grip, she decided to save the remains of her encounter with a small region of France that had invented champagne. Maybe she was too American, her tastes too unrefined, but André hadn't lost its appeal. Still, what she now held was more than the prettiest bottle she'd ever seen; it was a memory they shared, and that much was for keeps.

"I'd like to have this if you don't mind."

"Want me to order another so you can take home a pair?"

Eyeing the service-bar cabinet, Chris felt a tug she hadn't acknowledged in several years.

"I'd rather have a real drink." Deciding she felt closer to being a lady of the night than the unmerry widow, she asked for and got a double brandy, straight up. Greg poured himself a stiff Scotch and settled beside her on the couch.

Chris felt him watching her as she downed a manly portion in one draw, stopping to cough, then wince before she took another gulp.

"Just curious, but did you order that because you wanted it—or needed it?"

"Both," she confessed. "It's been a while, but there was a time when I drank a lot more than I do now."

"With friends?"

"No, alone. After Audrey was asleep and the lights were out. It kept me company in bed until I decided if I didn't clean up my act, I'd have more problems to deal with than I already did. I made myself buy a new bed and once I did that, out went the bottle."

"That must've been a bad time for you."

"Bad?" She swam her tongue through the taste of memory. "Bad was good, back then, comparatively speaking."

"Wish I'd been there."

"I'm glad you weren't."

"But you are now? Glad to be with me?"

"I am. You're good for me, Greg—in a bad sort of way."

"You make me feel like a vice."

"You are!" Chris teasingly bit his earlobe and whispered, "Want to hear about my other vices?"

"Only if they're awful."

Loose was fun; another two sips and she'd be sloppy. She swirled what was left of the brandy.

"I smoke on the sly. At first I figured it might eventually kill me, then it became a nasty habit I liked too much to give up."

"I can only hope for as much for myself."

She hooted and began to wonder if she was closer to sloppy than not. Strangely, she didn't care either way. Greg had a subtle humor, and a special knack for bringing out her own. It was, she decided, one of the sexiest things about him—next to his smile. No judgment calls from him; why the hell should she judge herself?

"If the First Methodist Church could see me now, I'll bet I could get out of playing piano for Sunday school."

"From what I know about Lubbock, you might even have a good chance of getting out of your job."

"You're right," she agreed, sobering. "Sometimes I get really tired of it—the school politics, neighbors knowing each other's business, watching what I say and do so my Snow White reputation stays intact. Trying to be the perfect mom, the perfect daughter. Well, I'm *not* perfect."

"The things we have in common, don't they beat all. Seems you're a vice for me too, Snow White." There was a darkness in his gaze that had the feel of a deep, wet kiss in a public place, an urgency too strong to wait for the closing of doors.

Chris tried to look away, but couldn't. When she took a quick sip of her drink, his eyes followed the movement and remained fixed on her mouth.

"So, what other vices do you have?"

Vices...vices. She was sure she had some besides her recently acquired taste for Greg. Did reading for an hour in the tub qualify? She didn't think so. What about hating housework and having a home that showed it? Not down and dirty enough, either.

"I always pick the longest line at checkout stands. That way I can flip through the tabloids without having to hide the trashy things at home."

His low laughter eased into an indulgent smile. "Is there

a chance that you ordered a collection of Groovin' Oldies for $18.88 from the tube when everyone with a life was already asleep?''

"I was tempted, but I didn't. They lost a sale when 'Yummy, Yummy, Yummy, I've Got Love in My Tummy' rolled up the screen. Not that I didn't like the song as a kid, but hey, I've got some pride.''

"Since we're baring our souls, I have a confession of my own to make: I was weak and totally without pride.''

"No. Get outta here!''

"It's in Dad's glove compartment, along with some other CDs I didn't want to move. Again. I should pay rent for the stuff they hang on to for me.''

"*You* bought 'Yummy, Yummy, Yummy, I've Got Love in My Tummy'?'' She cracked up and he joined her. "Boy oh boy, have I got something on you now.''

"Mutual blackmail, Chris. Never can tell when a *National Enquirer* might show up in your mailbox.''

"Don't you dare! I wouldn't be able to show my face to the mailman for a week.''

"Want to know what's your worst vice? Worrying too much about what other people think.''

"And well I know it. That *is* my worst vice and ten times harder to kick than stealing smokes in the bathroom.''

"No need to steal them here.'' He shoved an ashtray her way on the coffee table. "Light up whenever you get the urge. Maybe I'll even join you with the cigar my brother-in-law stuck in my pocket. I'm an uncle again, as of to-day.''

The fact he hadn't said anything until now told her where babies fit into Greg's scheme of importance. Had Tammy just given birth, Chris knew she'd have camped out at the hospital to beg, borrow or steal any cuddles she could.

"Did you see the baby yet?''

"This morning. Cute little sucker—until it wet on me. Reminded me why I'm a lot more comfortable holding a football or a front line than babies." He studied his drink, then downed it. "Sometimes I wonder if I'd given fatherhood a second shot, if I would have done better.... Hell, couldn't do worse. But I don't ever think about it too long. I've got enough guilt to deal with as it is. A double dose of shame, I don't need." He shoved his empty glass next to hers and reached for the remote control. "Oh, by the way, I'm clean."

"Better than clean, you smell great."

"Not what I meant." He shook his head and laughed as if she'd just played straight man to a one-liner. "After ending up a daddy because Arlene's mom skipped her pills, I haven't had sex without a condom since. What with the current climate, I thought that might be a concern you weren't sure how to bring up."

"Actually, I hadn't thought about that."

"Do me a favor? Think about it the next time. I'd hate to see anything happen to you. The world, Chris, it's a better place with you around."

The warm hug he gave her played havoc with her head and had an unexpected pull on her libido. His bluntness, his comfortable familiarity with the nitty-gritty of sex, seemed healthy and yet another something she could learn from Greg. Odd, though, that he was more relaxed about sex than holding a baby.

"I'll turn off the lights," she offered, needing some distance from their close encounter of the comforting kind. But his hurt spot, his sense of failure as a father, stuck with her. Trying to escape it, she hastened her pace and snapped out a silent order. *Sleep with him, laugh with him, anything. Just don't let yourself start to care.* To care was to risk that black, terrible tunnel she would never again go near.

Greg had helped her to escape, and for that she was grateful, but an emotional entanglement she had to avoid at any cost. *Especially* with Greg. Audrey aside, he was too tempting and too lethal, like cheese baiting a steel trap.

Chris stopped in her tracks as he kicked off his shoes. They landed on top of the heels she'd shucked off with a laugh. No longer laughing, she watched him prop his feet on the coffee table and stretch out. His arms on the sofa's back was a natural posture for a... "Family man," she whispered, while an image of a cheese wedge sliced through her mind.

"Did you say something?" he asked, looking away from the tube.

"I said that I'm glad you thought this up. A relaxed evening has a certain charm for a woman who's got a sore rear end and ate leftover french fries at the rink so they wouldn't go to waste." *Good, very good,* she told herself. *Hook it to the kid and make him bring it back to the bed where he's comfortable and this whole crazy thing belongs.*

"Then it's okay by you if we don't hit the bar where we could take on the 20-somethings? Maybe show them how to swing to Springsteen—move over, alternative rock."

Time out! Okay, here's the plan—no self-respecting player could possibly find a woman in support hose and up to her elbows in arthritis worth the chase.

"The older I get, Greg, the slower I go."

"That's good to hear. Otherwise, I couldn't keep up."

Chris frowned. He was too easy to be with, too easy to talk to. She couldn't seem to quit telling him things—little things that were somehow more revealing than big secrets. Her affection for him was genuine and that was fine. But what she couldn't—repeat, *could not*—do was let herself think of him as more than a good time on the fly.

His fly was where she angled her gaze since she deemed it safer than his couch-potato slouch.

"Sit with me?" He patted the sofa and looked even more dangerously domestic. "I won't bite."

"I'm disappointed." Her retaliatory defense got the reaction she needed to put Greg in his proper perspective. A dark brow rose over a darker glitter in his eyes. His slouch straightened and his crossed ankles came off the table. "Wouldn't you be more comfortable with your shirt off?" she prompted, ignoring the prickling sensation on her neck.

He tapped his fingertips together, as if contemplating his answer. Suddenly, he reached for the remote control. The television silenced, only the light of the screen illuminated him as he pushed the coffee table away.

And then, he worked loose the knot of his tie. Slipping it off, he slowly, suggestively, ran its length over his palm.

"Come here." His voice was smooth but rough around the edges.

Her feet were slow to acknowledge the command. Once she stood where he had indicated, between his spread legs, her lungs shut down, her stomach rolled over, and the sound of her thrumming heart filled her ears. The only thing that seemed to be in working order was her vision, locked in on the thin silk he continued to feed through a loose fist.

What was he planning to do with it? Why did he keep staring at her that way, saying nothing, and making her imagination leap in these crazy directions? She had no idea where she was, only that it was someplace promising, erotic, frightening.

His slide of the tie around the small of her back caused her to breathe out in a rush. Using it as a pulley, he drew her forward until her knees met the couch. Thank goodness for the couch, something solid to keep her knees from hitting the floor.

He gave a quick yank and she felt herself falling, guided by his hands on her waist until she was spilled over him. Her head against the crook of his neck, she felt his fingers twisting into her hair, then pulling until he stared at her, hard. Their faces so close, her halting gasps fanned his lips. The taste of danger, thick as the scent of Scotch on his breath, his voice gritty, challenging and...amused?

"What did you think I was going to do with it?"

"I—I didn't know."

"Were you scared...even a little?"

"Yes."

"Curious?" When she jerked out a nod, he said, "Curious, that's good. What about...excited? Were you?"

She was shaking, even her lips were shaking. Forcing them to move, she answered, "I was."

"Excellent." He led her hands from his shoulders to the first button of his shirt. "Anything and everything you can possibly imagine...*I want.*"

CHAPTER NINE

IF PATIENCE WAS TRULY a virtue, she decided that Greg was either remarkably virtuous or had a keen appreciation for suspense. As for herself, Chris felt like a sixteen-year-old about to lose her virginity to a much older man. Her fingers, slow and unsteady, had an uncommon amount of difficulty in releasing the first button on his shirt.

"Good," he murmured, drawing out the word like a line he slowly reeled in while she, the slippery catch, tugged against the hook she never should have nibbled. Too late to undo her decision, she tentatively pressed her lips against his throat. He tasted no less than delicious, and the sound she heard was like a low rumble of seductive thunder spurring her on. When she reached the button above his belt, he slid her fingertip over the buckle and said, "There's more."

Willing herself to shut out all thought, she allowed the flow to take her and pulled free the strip of black. The sight of mingling leather and silk did something strange to her senses. *Anything and everything you can possibly imagine.* Chris imagined the contrasting textures sliding snakelike around her waist, her wrists. Closing her eyes, she imagined his large hands, sure and sinuous in their seesaw movement, plying the binding between her legs. She felt an immediate twinge there, tightening, lingering, as did the forbidden fantasy.

It shook her, the startling image called up from some dark place she had never roamed; it did shake her. *How could she think such a thing, worse, feel so unbearably aroused by it?* The heat in her womb gathered momentum and spread up to her breasts, to her cheeks. Even the roots of her hair seemed to pulse with a peculiar warmth. They, and the rest of her, grew even hotter as his palms embraced either side of her head where he exerted a gentle but firm pressure.

"Look at me." Reluctantly, she met the scrutiny of his gaze. "You're very flushed and I'm seeing smoke in your eyes. Leaves me to wonder if you're fantasizing about something other than getting rid of my shirt, or if you're imagining being with *someone* other than me."

"No! No, Greg, I swear I wasn't pretending to be with—"

"I believe you," he said, cutting her off as if even Mark's mention would intrude on their intimate space. "Care to tell me what I caught you at?" When her eyes darted guiltily to the floor, he made an *ahhh* sound of approval. "Have you ever—"

"Certainly not," she said quickly.

"There's always a first time and I'd very much like to be the first to introduce you to that kind of pleasure."

"That kind of pleasure?" she scoffed. "Don't you mean that sort of deviant behavior?" His low chuckle made her feel like a prude just caught ogling a naughty magazine on the pretext of shaming him for his prurient interests.

"Pick them up. Both, the belt and the tie. Go on, just do it." When she began to protest, he smiled with such open encouragement that she hesitantly lifted them from the floor. "Tell me, how do they feel?"

"The silk, it's smooth and cool. The leather, warm and sturdy. The buckle's a little heavy."

"Do you feel threatened by them?"

"No." Quick to qualify that, she added, "But I'm holding them, not you."

"So you are." He took the belt from her, folded it in half and snapped the middle. The hands she'd imagined sliding the belt between her legs returned the leather to her with a casual grace. "Should I feel threatened? After all, that's a thick belt and you could hurt me with it if I let you."

"I'd never do any such thing!"

"That's good since I'm not into pain—giving or receiving it. Big difference between that sort of thing and a bedroom game of mutual trust. Believe me, Chris, bondage isn't about abuse, it's about freedom, giving each other permission to explore a very special kind of pleasure." Lifting the belt's pointed tip, he tickled her nose with the leather.

It smelled earthy, masculine, like an extension of its wearer. Impulsively, she then sniffed his tie. The subtle absorption of his cologne provoked images of clean rain and a twist of citrus on the rim of a tall, icy glass. The scent of him mingled with a vision of silk tethers gently binding wrists and ankles to the four corners of a poster bed.

Her hands began to move with a sudden impatience and she parted the starched white material. A wide expanse of blocked muscle was covered by a thick mat of dark gold sprinkled with silver.

"I want this off. Take it off," she demanded.

"You want it off? *You* take it off."

Hungrily, roughly, she swept her palms over the ridge of his shoulders and down his arms. Cotton joined leather and silk on the floor. She rubbed her cheek against soft hair and tough muscle, drinking in more than his cologne. It was Greg she inhaled; the unique scent of his skin, his person.

He was an intensely arousing man. Without even a hand on her, she felt as if he'd reached inside to stroke the tip of her womb.

"I want you," she said.

"Then take me." Arms spread over the length of the couch in submission, he shifted his hips downward in demand.

What she felt, Chris wasn't sure; several sensations all at once, separate but interlocked. Wanting, but afraid to want this much. Standing on a precipice of dizzying height, breath held while teetering on the edge. Wings spread, feeling the power, the thrill of charting a new course, she freed his erection and thus something in herself.

Taking him, teasingly then aggressively, she was filled with wonder. It was the wonder of discovery, finding an unexpected treasure. He had given her the means, his body a pliable shovel, to unearth a gift too marvelous to be hoarded.

She shared it generously, delighting in his delight as she bowed before the giver.

WHEN HIS HEART QUIT racing like a marathon runner and his breathing was no longer a groan after groan after groan, Greg looked down, a little amazed, at the head resting in his lap.

She looked up and their eyes met. There was a glow in her face, enhanced by a mischievous slant to her smile that he'd never seen before. Not in her; not in any woman.

For once in his life, maybe he'd chosen an intimate companion worth the keeping. When her gaze lowered to his crotch, leading his to follow, Greg was sure of it.

Laughter rolled from his belly as she lifted his softening erection by the loops of a bow.

"Poor man." She sighed, "All tied up with nowhere to go."

The sight of her swirling ruby nail stopped him in mid-laugh. And then, the touch of her finger to her tongue created a sliding sensation inside him, drizzling through his chest and pooling in his gut, which felt a sudden clutch.

"I don't swallow," she murmured.

The woman was lethal. With her dip into his leavings, the skate of her fingertip over her mouth as if it were lipstick she applied, she was lethal.

Greg caught her wrist. "Feeling your oats?"

"Umm. I think I am." Softly, she confessed, "If I'd known being a bad girl could feel so good, I would have sown some wild oats before now."

His soaring elation at being the wild oats in question coincided with a disturbing stab of possessiveness. He felt like a transient staking squatter's rights, fierce in his want of the virgin soil on which he could never lay legal claim.

Legal claim be damned. *He didn't want to share.* Not with a dead husband and not with any future prospects. It was an extremely upsetting and unfamiliar sensation, not part of the game plan he'd had in mind. It gave him a sense of lost control—of himself and of the situation. Instinctively, he tried to regain what he'd lost to the woman on her knees; a woman he was beginning to fear could bring him to his.

"Unless you like the floor, I strongly suggest that you head for the bedroom." Greg had the pleasure of seeing her swallow as she rose, a bit wobbly at those knees. "Oh, and take the champagne bottle with you."

"Aren't we a little old to be playing spin the bottle?" she asked, eyeing it uncertainly.

"Absolutely."

"Then why bring it? It's almost empty."

Angling his gaze to the apex of her thighs, he said quietly, insistently, "Take it."

The wariness of her gaze, the unsteady reach of her hand, stroked his dominant nature. He wouldn't hurt Chris for the world but a small taste of danger wouldn't be bad for her, either. Besides, the danger he was tasting was no little bit, and that much he was inclined to share.

Though she gripped the bottle to her as if it were a potential weapon to ward him off, Greg admired the lack of cowardice evident in her walk. *Lethal,* without a doubt.

As he untied the bow in his lap, he found himself already regretting the moment he'd have to let her go.

A grim smile touched his lips. He had no illusions about what he had to offer. Yeah, he was a poor bargain, for sure. But that didn't keep him from considering how he might manage to get a just-fallen angel to strike a deal with the devil.

CHAPTER TEN

CHRIS CHAFED HER ARMS as she stared at the bottle on the nightstand. What was he taking his sweet time doing while she ate the Godiva chocolate laid on one pillow? Deciding Greg didn't deserve his, she ate the second while she fought the urge to shove the bottle under the bed.

This was all so disorienting, so unfamiliar. Lights out, under the covers, *that* was the normal thing to do—which meant it just might upset *his* equilibrium.

Deciding the dark was an ally, she went for the switch beside the door. Her dress was halfway over her head when the lights came back on.

"What are you doing?"

"What does it look like? I'm taking off my clothes. Would you please turn the lights off?"

"No." He did, however, dim them. "Ask me what I think is the sexiest thing a man can do to a woman."

As she shoved her dress back down, her glare wavered. Shirt off, pants on but zipper not quite up and black boxers nuzzling his navel, he was discreetly overwhelming.

"I'm afraid to ask."

"Ask anyway." He started to bypass her but retraced a step and lifted her left hand. On her ring finger, he placed a kiss, then moved on to the cheval mirror. Picking it up without so much as a heave-ho, he brought it closer to the bed and angled the mirror until she was the central reflection.

"You're a voyeur, aren't you?"

"I like to watch, but I'd rather be a participant than a spectator." He came to stand behind her and she shivered at the feel of his palms riding down her sides, then clenching the material at her hips. Pleating it, raising the hem higher, she quelled the instinct to cover her knees. "Ask me," he said again.

"All right, what do you think is the sexiest thing a man can do to a woman?"

"*This,*" he answered, shifting the soft angora to her waist. "Undressing a woman is like unveiling a work of art. One of a kind, no two alike, in shape or tastes in underwear. Will she be a Picasso, a Rembrandt, a Warhol? Arms, lift."

If he'd told her he got off on threesomes in a vat of melted butter, she would have been less shocked. But feeling his slow peel of her dress, his nuzzle at her neck as she stood there in a French-cut bra and a lacy half-slip, she was between curious and worried about his artistic opinion of her.

"Well," she asked hesitantly, "what do you think?"

"Olga, 34C," he answered with certainty as he fingered the front clasp of her bra.

So, he was a connoisseur of women's lingerie. Certain that Greg would find her lacking in comparison to his Victoria's Secret Matisses, she caught his wrist.

"I'd really prefer the lights out." And then, with rising anxiety, she implored him with a "Please?"

"Why, are you ashamed of your body?"

She wanted to say no but that wasn't altogether true. Foregoing the bra, he hooked a thumb at the waistband of her slip and began to inch it down.

"I've had a baby, Greg."

"Um...yes, Audrey. I like her, she's a sweet kid."

"I gained a lot of weight when I was pregnant." Unable to watch, Chris shut her eyes. "I have stretch marks."

"Stretch marks," he repeated in a whisper, amazingly seductive. So was the glide of his teeth against her neck. "Where are these stretch marks...on your breasts?" At her stilted nod, he lifted her clenched fists to the bra's clasp. "Take it off? I'd like to see."

She hadn't expected his gentle coaxing; she hadn't expected her undressing to be such a painful exposure. But then, she'd done it, the bra was off while she tried not to think about the worst part to come—her lower body.

The feel of a blunt nail tracing the silver paths radiating from her areolae to the whole of her breasts sent ripples of sensory delight racing along her nerve ends.

"These actually bother you?"

"They do. I wish my body was perfect...the way it used to be."

"Not me. Maturity in a woman's body is something earned and a lot more to my liking than some teenage blonde in a thongback. The whole package, not the wrapping, that's what moves me." The slow roll of her nipple between his fingers, as if he were contemplating, appreciating a very fine cigar, caused her to whimper his name. "Open your eyes, Chris." She did and his own gazed back at her from the mirror. "I mean, *really* open them. Look at yourself and tell me what you see."

What she saw were two pale breasts that were firm, nipples tilted up and haloed by dark pink circles. More, she saw his open desire for them, felt it in the strain he pressed against her buttocks.

"I see...a woman who's a little thin and more than a little nervous. But she has good taste in lingerie and her breasts, they're—" Her throat was tight but as she studied herself, dark hands lifting the color of heavy cream, she whispered, "My breasts, they're pretty."

"Not pretty. Baby, they're beautiful." He slid her palms over their smooth texture, then led her to cup their weight. "Touch them. They feel even better than they look."

She couldn't believe what she was seeing, actually caressing herself in front of a mirror while he watched her and groaned. But that wasn't half as astonishing as hearing herself moan her arousal at what she felt, what she saw.

"Still want the lights out?" he asked, stroking a broad palm over her belly.

"No." Leading his hands to her slip, she told him exactly what she wanted. "I'd like you to take off the rest."

"My pleasure." His pleasure was deliciously slow and incited more visions of erotic games of trust. By the time her slip and hose were off, her spine was wet from his licking kisses and she had begun to hope he'd brought along his belt and tie. A glance at the bed assured her that he had. Their presence gave her no pause for, amazingly, she felt no threat. Just anticipation of what awaited if she dared to brave a freedom she'd only ventured in her imagination.

Panties were all she had left when he softly bit the heel of her palm and then urged it over her pubis. Curling her fingers in, she felt herself through the weightless lace.

"Feel good?" he murmured.

"Yes," she answered, almost trancelike. Yes, she must be in a trance, watching another woman who'd borrowed her body all but fondling herself in front of a mirror—for an appreciative audience of two.

"Let's make it feel even better, shall we?" Together they drew down her panties and Chris wondered at what she felt: a quiet sense of bonding that was different from any she'd experienced before. Even with Mark.

The thought slipped out before she could stop it. Strangely, she realized it wasn't Mark, but Greg who would be wronged by any sense of guilt she had for their intimate connection. Mark had no place here, and here was too special to taint with regret for the comfort she greedily took.

Fingers laced with hers, Greg roamed the slight outward arc of her belly. "What's this?" he asked, tender in his tracing of a thin silver streak.

"A stretch mark."

"And this?" He guided her nail over the flair of her left hip.

"The same."

"Do you think they're ugly?"

"Not anymore."

"Glad you realize that." His palm over her belly, he drew her to him and ground himself against her bare behind. "You've got sexy stretch marks. Don't ever forget it. I love your body, Chris. Renoir would, too—all those soft angles and classic curves. A Renoir, that's what you are. And your taste in lingerie is, well, it's you. Elegant." He dropped a kiss, a very straightforward, unembellished kiss, on her shoulder. "For the record, I've never called a woman 'elegant' before."

She was a Renoir. She was elegant.

She was in heat.

"Make love to me." Grasping his hand, she pressed it against her groin. *"Now."*

Her gaze riveted on his reflection, she saw the pleased curve of his mouth and then, something she hadn't expected—a sly expression, as if he was the host of a surprise party for her, the unsuspecting guest of honor.

Suddenly, cool air brushed her as he fanned open her lips and stared at what he exposed to the mirror. "Look at that—mmm, what a gorgeous view. Help me out and tell me what you'd like me to do with this beautiful little joy toy of yours.''

"Greg, *please.*"

"Greg, please," he echoed. "I like the sound of that. Go on, then. Please…what?''

"Touch me," she whispered. When he hesitated, she demanded, "*Touch me.* I want you to touch me.'' Then she added, "Please, Greg.''

"Ever the lady, aren't you? I'll have to see what I can do about getting rid of some of those manners.'' He touched her then, a svelte glide, a single stroke. "There. Now what?''

"Damn you, Greg," she cried, panting.

"I like that even better than 'Greg, please.' Once more now, but this time with feeling.''

"I don't believe this—damn you!'' Swinging around, in frustration she struck her fist against his chest. He gripped her wrist and jerked her against him.

"That's it, that's exactly what *I* want from you.'' She yelped in outrage when his fingers bit softly into her behind, then struggled in earnest as he lifted her until she was squirming against his open fly. "Passion, Chris, that's what I want from you. *Passion.* And unless I'm terribly wrong, the kind of passion I'm after isn't something you've ever had.''

As if he'd accused her of being frigid, she glared at him and snapped, "That's not true.''

"Are you sure? When was the last time you looked at yourself naked in the mirror and liked what you saw? When was the last time you were so hot to have a man touch you that you told him so instead of assuming he knew that's what you wanted? And when, tell me when, have you ever hit a man because he wanted an equal partner in bed and you didn't want to accept responsibility for your needs?''

No longer resistant but still flushed with the fight, she met his narrowed gaze and shivered. "Meet my need and tell me yours," he said with an ache that stunned her. Touched her. Undid her.

He began to slide her down. Chris shimmied up and locked her legs around his waist.

"Carry me to bed, just like this."

"And then?"

"Then I want you to undress for me and after that, I want you to kiss me."

He rubbed his lips over hers. "Here?"

"Yes, there."

Lifting her higher, he tongued a nipple. "And here?" Her languorous sigh proved answer enough. "Anywhere else?"

"My sexy stretch marks need you."

Her soft laughter trailed them to the bed. There, he laid her beside leather and silk, wondering if Chris would sweep them away. But no, she stroked them, allowing him to watch her shed old notions for brave new ideas. Greg considered it a priceless privilege to expand intimacy's vistas with this woman he coveted for his own. But as he slowly disrobed, he was aware of another feeling he wasn't particularly proud of: smugness born of jealousy.

Passion. Her passion belonged to him and that was something her dead husband couldn't claim. The dead husband who had taken her love with him to the grave. Greg couldn't deny that he hated the bastard a little for that. Yet his own emotions for Chris were strong enough, he believed her better off for refusing her heart to a man who'd often wondered if he was capable of that tender emotion, love.

Passion, he understood. And passion he did get.

Her body thoroughly kissed, exactly where she asked, he

didn't stop until he'd reached the soles of her feet. Glorious she was in her writhing impatience, but he had a need to make it last.

Greg eyed the game pieces surrounding them on the bed. Both players were ready, bound by rules of trust. With belt and tie in hand, he held aloft the champagne bottle.

Seemed to him they had some celebrating to do.

CHAPTER ELEVEN

"WE HAD LOTSA FUN AT Auntie Marge's last night."

"Uh-huh." Foot propped on a pillow in the middle of the bed, Chris painted another toenail and suppressed a moan. That toe, that very toe had been sucked less than twelve hours ago. Sucking toes, where in the world had Greg picked that up? The Middle East, Japan, maybe in France while he sipped real champagne—*who cared?*

"But the mostest fun was when Uncle Rick and old Uncle Harvey sorta had a fight playing cards. Uncle Rick said makin' up new rules was cheating and Uncle Harvey said..."

What should she wear tonight? The Olga was her best bra but the Vanity Fair was lavender and *très* risqué. Did black go with lavender? Or maybe the white tap pants.

"And then they threw popcorn balls at each other and then they hit Aunt Tammy's bee-hind with one and then..."

Then again, she did have the whole afternoon to shop. Only, would a Renoir wear red?

"But it was lotsa fun and— Mama, what's this?"

"Maybe ivory." Finished with the last nail, Chris capped the polish and stretched.

"But ivory, that's from elephants, right? This doesn't look like it came off a elephant."

"Audrey! What are you doing with that?" Heedless of her wet toes, Chris lurched from the bed and seized the champagne bottle. "Stay out of my suitcase, young lady."

"Why're you yelling at me? I only wanted to see the pretty bottle."

Arms crossed and hiding what she held, Chris forced herself to calm down. "I wasn't yelling."

"Were too! And that's not all, you weren't listenin' to me. Ever since your friend started comin' over, it's like you're gone all the time. Why can't I come, too?"

"Because—because children aren't allowed where we go. And besides, I save all my days just for you." Dropping to her knees, Chris laid the bottle aside and, in contrition, held out her arms. "Give Mama a hug, sugar."

Audrey stepped back. "Tonight, Mama, I want you with me tonight." With a note of hope, she added, "It's okay with me if he's with us, too. We could all go to the movies and—"

"When we get back to Lubbock, I'll take you to the movies. We'll eat all the popcorn we want and—"

"But he won't be there, and I like your friend. Let him come to a movie with us. Please? Then we can be like a family goin' to the movies instead of just you and me."

"No." Her firm denial won a pout. But better a pout now than letting Audrey get her hopes up for something that just couldn't be. "Tell you what, I'll ask Aunt Tammy and Uncle Rick to take you."

Audrey emphatically shook her head. When Chris reached for her, she shot to the door and said with a sniffle, "You don't wanna be with me tonight."

"That's not true." Chris went to her and stroked the pale blond hair. "You know that's not true, Audrey. I *always* want to be with you. Tomorrow I'll make up for being gone tonight. We'll spend the whole day together, okay?"

Audrey looked away. Following her gaze, Chris saw that it was on the bottle. Deep breath. *Stop cringing, damn it.*

"He doesn't like kids, does he? I thought he was nice and he liked me, but he's not nice."

"But he *is* nice, Audrey. Greg's just not cut out to be a daddy, that's all."

"Then I don't want him to be with you. Tell him to go away, Mama. Tell him we don't like him anymore."

"I'm sorry, but Mama likes him and I—"

"Uncle Rick doesn't like him neither. I heard him say so to Aunt Tammy and—"

"Stop it!" Chris froze as she realized she had almost gripped Audrey's shoulders—to shake her. Never had she shaken Audrey, never. Only once had she even been spanked, for running in front of a car. Chris wanted to spank her now, paddle Audrey good for her childish resentment of Greg's inability to meet her expectations.

Staring at her poised hands, then the streaks resembling pale pink bracelets on her wrists, Chris shuddered. *What was happening to her?* She didn't know the woman these wrists belonged to. She didn't know this angry mother who felt violated by her child's curiosity over a bottle.

Chris shoved down the cuffs of her blouse. Gently, she cupped Audrey's cheek. "Mama's so sorry we had a fight. A few more days and we'll go home and—"

"I wanna go home now. Please, let's go home."

Chris withdrew her apologetic touch and looked away, needing to distance herself from the sight of Audrey, the shrill pitch of her demands. Waves of confusion beat at her but receded beneath the lapping vision of a white-hot night too stunning for any sane woman to regret.

Avoiding Audrey's gaze, she patted her head. "We'll go home on New Year's Day, just the way we planned."

"No!" The stamp of a small foot emphasized her shout.

"Damn it, that is enough out of you! The world does not revolve around you, Audrey Nicholson. When Mama says it's time to go home, *then* we'll go home. Do you understand me?''

''You old meanie! I'm glad you're goin' away, *glad.* I hope you stay away with your dumb old Greg, and never, ever come back!'' The door slammed and Chris could hear Audrey sobbing as she ran down the hall. She heard Rick's, ''Slow down, half-pint, what's wrong?''

What was wrong? *Nothing's wrong,* Chris told herself as she covered her face with her hands and struggled for as many breaths as it would take to clear her head. She had to think. *Think,* damn it. Damn it, she'd actually cursed at Audrey, lashed out at her child as she never had before. They had always been so close, and at the moment she was glad, really glad, that Audrey was gone.

God, she felt guilty for that, and for so many things. For wanting her child gone, for selfishly wanting some private something just for herself, for letting Audrey think the worst of Greg because it was easier than admitting *she* was the one who didn't want the intrusion on her sex life to-night.

Chris chafed her wrists. She wasn't herself, not at all. Maybe she *should* go home.

Her mind was in chaos, a battleground where Audrey's retreating sobs gave way to a rich dreamscape of deca-dence. She didn't want to be here, she wanted to be there. *There,* on her back, feeling the mattress beneath her, taking Greg's weight, reveling in being covered by his body's pressure. There she wanted to be and it was there she es-caped, to a precious place of discovery, frightening and full of wonder. A place where she was anything but a mother....

LEATHER AND SILK CINCHED *in one fist, his other like a steel band gripping both her wrists. His knees straddling her chest, he loomed large, towering above her like some mighty warrior with the spoils of victory at his feet.*

His whisper then: "I'd never hurt you. That's why I want to know everything's all right between us here before we take this where I'm wanting to go."

"And where is that?"

"Somewhere we've never been, a place we create just for ourselves to see what we find along the way as it happens. But to get there you'll have to take the first step: I want you to give me permission to take control."

Eyes fixed on the belt and tie, she said quietly, "You'll be wanting to use those."

"Absolutely. But they're merely a means to an end. What I'm asking for, Chris, is for you to trust me to treat your body with the same care you'd treat mine were our roles reversed."

The clutch of anxiety she felt as he asked for absolute control, absolute trust, collided with a daredevil high that was more frightening than lying prone and helpless and at his mercy. How well did she know Greg, *really?* It was then she realized this was more than a game. He wanted to strip them down to the core, expose them both for who they really were beneath their civilized veneers.

Her courage faltered even as anticipation soared.

"What if I ask you to untie me? Will you?"

"Only if you say…'Roses.' *Roses,* that's the password to signal me to stop. If you say 'Stop,' I won't. You see, I want to play out a fantasy where a 'Stop' from you might be very exciting to me."

"A fantasy? You mean, pretend something that's not real?"

"A fantasy is no longer a fantasy when it becomes reality, *ma chérie.*"

"Excuse me?"

"*'Non, non, monsieur! S'il vous plaît, non!'* would be a more apt response from a prisoner I've captured and intend to use for my own pleasure. It's a neat bit of revenge I can't resist since you're a fair *mademoiselle* born and bred by my enemy. The keep you call home is soon to be mine, just as you will be. I lust for your family's land. I lust for you."

"But why?" she asked, intrigued by the story he wove. "Why are we your enemy and why do you want to steal what's ours?"

"There's bad blood between us, *ma fille*. The land is rich and many hands tend the grape arbors your father stole from my own before you were conceived. As a boy I watched my father cut down. Only I escaped, and now, with twenty years of rage for injustice, I've returned to seize back my rightful claim. It is a day of reckoning for which you will atone, as well."

"But you said I wasn't even born and—"

"Silence! I'll have silence from you who have slept in my bed while I made my own on the grounds of strangers. You've eaten at my table and feasted when I made my meals from wild game and scraps of bread. No one to turn to, our allies were overthrown as we were. But a bitter wind blows and with it comes war. The men riding with me I've chosen for their skill with a saber, their loyalty proved from our days spent as renegades—but we are outlaws no more. We *are* the law and I am the officer in command. They follow my orders now, circling us in the woods where I rode you down.

"See the wildflowers you were gathering crushed beneath my horse's hooves, feel the warm air on your breasts, barely covered. Your clothes are in tatters. How foolish but how brave you were to struggle with me. Scratches cover my face and my blood runs hot as I force you to the ground.

Look around you and see four saplings—two at your head, two at your feet. Is your heart pounding?''.

"Yes...*yes.*" The four posts took on the semblance of tree trunks and she jerked her head from side to side, staring at their ominous positions, suddenly struggling to free her wrists.

"That's it, *fight me.* You know what I mean to do and—''

"Stop!" Grappling with him, she freed one hand and thrust at his chest. His laughter was dark and mocked her lesser strength as he easily pinned her flailing arm beneath her twisting weight and she again cried, "Stop!"

"Stop? I don't think so. The more you fight me, the more I want you. Feel how hard I am bearing down on your hips, my mouth covering yours to taste the sweet sound of your cries for help." His lips were brutally sweet, stealing her breath while she felt the cinch of silk around her wrist before he led her to grip the wood. Holding it tight, holding on for dear life, she whimpered, "No, no," and made a token resistance as he knotted the tie around the sapling post.

And then her other hand was pulled from beneath her. The tingle of circulation rushed through her fingers and ripples of arousing sensation shot from the soft scrape of teeth on her palm to the fierce tug low in her belly.

His nipping bites became a giving kiss pressed to where her pulse leapt in her wrist. She was riveted by the sudden snap of his belt cracking the sense-thick air, and then came the stern feel of leather looped around her wrist and fed through a buckle. It felt snug and warm as a harness while his murmured words in French mingled with the sight of him twining the belt around and around the wood.

A satisfied smile was on his lips as he taunted, "For shame, *chérie,* you've given up to the enemy much too easily. I'd hoped for a challenge but you're simply lying there while I stand over you and start to unfasten my breeches. Listen to my men cheering me on, eager for their turn at you once I'm through.''

"You mean to rape me?" Fantasy and reality merged and she jerked against the restraints. "The hell you'll do such a thing! Let me go now. *Now!*''

"I'll let you go when and only when you're too weak to stand, much less walk. But as for rape…no. Rape would be too easy and I want a better victory.'' His thighs clamped around her legs that kicked futilely beneath him. "What spirit you have, after all. Certainly a worthy opponent to battle in bed. No, I don't believe I'll share you with my men. In fact, I've decided I don't even like them looking at you, so I order them to move on, to scout the area until I join them. And should I not appear by sunset— which is a distinct possibility—they are to make camp. You would do well to please me since it would buy your family freedom for another day.''

Rising up, he clamped a palm between her legs and she bucked against his possessive grip. "I'll have this and you'll give it to me willingly.''

"Never,'' she gasped. "Never under threat by a tyrant who wants to gloat over his conquest.''

"I can see that bringing my feisty prisoner to heel is a worthy vengeance in itself. You'll vow your fealty to me once I prove what a generous master I can be. Indeed, I should think you grateful for me staking my territory and dispatching my men. Not so bad a fate, being afforded my protection.''

"Grateful? Once you're finished with me, you plan to attack my family and I'm supposed to be *grateful?*'' She stared at him, shocked to realize this was more than make-believe. He was giving her a rare access to his soldier's mentality.

"Yes, grateful. I'm powerful but I like to think of myself as fair, even when I'm taking the life of someone I don't even know. It's power that I thirst for and it's power which allows me to show mercy to those who deserve freedom. But, unfortunately, *you* don't deserve freedom or mercy at the moment. No battle is begun without the intent to win and I intend to win the ground I covet between your legs." Suddenly, he was off the bed and holding up a Swiss knife he'd taken from the pants he'd left folded on a boudoir chair.

The pants, the chair, they seemed strangely foreign to her, a wrinkle in the fabric of another time, a civilized age that bowed to his savage yank of the white sheet at the foot of the bed. But it wasn't a bed, it was the cushion of thick grass awaiting them, and the two carved posts framing her feet were saplings.

She heard the rending of thread as he sliced down. Three long strips he cut, then left the rest for waste.

"Your petticoat, *mademoiselle,* has met a terrible fate. Prepare to meet yours. Spread your legs."

"I won't!" His hands moved so fast, with such focused purpose, he simply batted away her kicks to his chest and made short work of securing first one foot and then the other to their binding stations. Speechless at his easy mastery, she felt the rub of wood and the whip of smooth cloth that held her fast and spread her apart.

Coming to the side of where she lay, he swayed the remaining white strip between her legs, then slowly lowered the end to tease the pink tip of her exposure. Pride demanded she not give him the satisfaction of the wail trapped in her throat; but her hips felt no pride in martyrdom and thrust up, up as far as the bindings allowed.

Laughing low, he brushed the cloth over her belly, around each breast, then dangled it above her head.

"Let's see, what should I do with this?" He tapped his lips with a finger. "I suppose I could wrap it around your mouth so I won't have to listen to you scream...."

Gag her? He was actually considering gagging her? *What was the word, the password? Flowers. No, some kind of flower.* Wildly she cast about for the word that was buried somewhere and refusing to surface. And then she had it. *Roses.* "Roses" was on her tongue but in the space of a single gasp for air, his mouth was on hers. Kissing her madly, hungrily, and with a thoroughness that left her dazed, he finished with a lingering suckle of her chin.

He pinched it and shook his head.

"No, I don't believe I want this covering your mouth now that I've assured myself any screams I hear will be music to my ears. I think there's a better use for this.... Yes, perfect. But let's do this quickly because the sun is setting and I wish to see my victory in your own pleasure. Pleasure that I'm certain will be all the greater if *you* can't see." The fabric whispered over her eyes before he lifted her head with a gentle pressure. She felt the tug of a knot and then the sifting of his fingers through her hair.

No sight. She heard the rasp of his breath, the absence of hers. She smelled the scent of his lust and the escalation of her own as her breast was sucked up into a haven of wet heat. Wet, dear God, she was wet, and well he let her know it with the startling upthrust of a single finger. And then she felt two, reaching so high she moaned.

"I have a taste for virgins," he whispered. "Is there a chance that a virgin you might be?"

She felt like a virgin and there was no doubt that in this place and in this moment, a virgin she was.

"I am. Please, please, be gentle with me."

"Oh, but I will. I'll fuck you ever so gently." With that vow, he withdrew his hand and she gasped at the feel of ribbed glass easing inside her. And then, then she felt the cool trickle of effervescence mingle with the stream of hot tears her body wept.

Awash in sensation, she was suddenly drowning in it, pulled under by the suckle of his mouth, the sipping sound she heard. He drank from her as if she were a golden chalice, her ecstasy a rare and heady nectar. And when he ceased his leisurely tasting, she screamed a cry of protest.

His breath on her face was flavored with the scent of woman and wine. "Could it be that my virgin captive is now a prisoner of her desire for me?" he whispered.

"Yes, whatever you say, *yes.*"

"Whatever I say, is it? I say...I want to hear you say 'Fuck me.'"

"Fuck me," she whimpered, the sound of a plea she'd never spoken before.

"How I've longed to hear those words from you. After all, some time has passed and my virgin captive is now my virgin bride. Remember with me now...how I spared you a ravishment on the ground, how I was so taken with your beauty and courage that I wanted your passion without the same resentment I harbored for the man whose name you bore. I won back my rightful claim. And I won your willing hand by my show of mercy to your kin. So merciful I am, your wish I now gladly grant."

Suddenly, the blindfold was off. She blinked against the light and saw his face bearing down on hers with an awesome intensity of raw passion. Amazingly, his initial thrust was a slow glide that stretched and filled and didn't stop until he pressed, then remained still, sheathed against her womb.

His head descended and she tasted herself on his tongue,

tasted the hint of a sparkling vintage. It was a boozy sweet kiss, one she never wanted to end.

But had it not, she never would have heard his seductive whisper of, "Baby, I never knew champagne could taste so fine."

CHRIS CONTINUED TO STARE at the champagne bottle, then lifted it, kissed the rib of glass. Had it really been there where she now felt such a keen ache? And had their fantasy given way to a carnal gluttony that eased to a playful frolic, to naughty jokes and laughter? And had Greg then carried her to the sunken tub while she pretended the bottle was him and gave it a blow job to die for?

Had it really happened? It had.

So, what was wrong with Rick? Didn't he consider this man suitable for his widowed sister? And what was wrong with Audrey? Why couldn't she understand that daddies weren't the sort of lovers who made a woman beg for him in the lewdest of languages.

What was wrong with them? Rick, the protective brother with his head on straight. Audrey, the model child who had never before made such a scene as the one today and...hadn't it been said children could always spot a phony a mile away, that they gravitated to adults who genuinely liked them?

Chris dismissed the idea. Greg was no phony and Audrey wasn't used to being excluded. The problem wasn't theirs; it was hers. Her needs, so long buried, were demanding attention. She was starved for it and the man who filled those needs so frightfully, deliriously well, was feeding her greed with a voracious appetite she'd never dreamed of sharing.

Reluctantly, Chris tucked the bottle under her lavender bra and white tap pants in the suitcase. She then divided her attention between the door and the phone on the night-stand.

More than anything, she wanted to shun her responsibilities and wallow between the sheets with a man she couldn't let her child get attached to. But the right thing to do would be to find Audrey and spend the night with her alone instead of going where she already longed to be.

Chris made it as far as the door. Her hand hovered over the knob. *How many nights alone had she already spent with Audrey?* Too many. *How many more nights alone would they share?* Too many.

And how many nights did she have with Greg?

Too damn few.

Fingers curling in, her nails bit into her palm. Give in to guilt and give up a once-in-a-lifetime experience? Or spend some extra quality time with Audrey during the days to make up for the nights she desperately needed just for herself?

Making her choice, Chris put her guilt on hold, certain she'd have to deal with it later, and picked up the receiver. The wait for his voice was an eternity.

"Can you be here an hour early?" she asked. Two hours early was better for Greg. Before she could tell him to step on the gas even as they spoke, Chris hung up.

Going to the vanity, she flicked aside the blue-and-gold tassels of a pom-pom and faced herself in the mirror.

It didn't crack. She didn't look away.

"Black," she said aloud to her reflection. "Black bra, panties and hose. They match, even if you and Greg don't."

Turning from the mirror, Chris decided that she'd never looked better in her life.

CHAPTER TWELVE

HE COULDN'T PUSH IN. Even after an hour of foreplay, he couldn't push past whatever barriers her frantic hip jerks said weren't there.

Rolling off, Greg looked at the ceiling while Chris stroked his chest and asked, "What's wrong?"

"You tell me."

She gripped his erection and pumped several times. When he didn't respond, she let go and assumed his own back-to-the-mattress posture.

Their silence stretched out and she fumbled for her purse beside the bed. They'd gone there directly—the same bed as the night before, but not the same bed at all.

He reached over to his nightstand and found a match. Lighting her cigarette seemed the most intimate act of the evening.

"There's nothing wrong," she finally said, studying the smoke she sent into the tension-thick air.

"You're full of it, Chris." He plucked the cigarette from her lips, took a puff, then gave it back. "You were tight the first time, but ten vestal virgins combined couldn't be tougher to work past than this," he said with a terseness born of frustration.

He'd been so damn hungry to kiss her that he'd pulled off the road twice before they'd made it to the hotel. Even as he'd tumbled her to the bed, he'd tried to dismiss her emotional distance with every bedroom trick he knew and some he invented as he went along. Nothing.

She turned to him, head propped on her palm. And then she said, "Audrey."

"What about Audrey?"

"She neutered me, as you apparently noticed."

"I take it she doesn't approve of me."

"If she did, I'd be worried."

He managed not to flinch. Could a man feel like a hooker? Maybe so. *He* did.

"But it's not you," Chris hurriedly explained, while what had gone soft was now limp. "It's us."

"But after last night I thought— Ah, hell, I don't know what I thought. Just that it was great and we were good together."

"Better than good, Greg. Last night was incredible. It was all I could think about today until… Audrey, this afternoon, she picked up the champagne bottle."

"Nothing left to drink, I finished it off."

"You practically finished me off, doing it!" Relaxing, she laughed. He couldn't laugh with her, but he relaxed some, too, and traced her lips. Her nip of his fingertip was the second most intimate act of the night. "The problem is, Audrey wants a daddy and it's up to me to find her one."

"And a daddy I'm not, right?"

"Of course not!" Forget being a prostitute; he felt like he'd been emasculated. "C'mon, Greg, we both know what this is."

He'd thought he did, but somewhere along the line they'd bypassed the merely titillating and shared what felt like substance. It had nagged at him all day like a sore tooth he couldn't quit tonguing: What had happened? When had it happened? And did whatever the hell had happened cut both ways?

"Just curious, but what exactly do you think this is?"

"What we agreed on to begin with. 'No expectations, nothing to lose. No limits, adults only, and regrets not allowed.' A few more nights, that's all we've got, all we can ever have. After that, I go home and pick up where I left off."

But things have changed, he wanted to say. A few measly nights weren't enough to play this to its end and same time next year was too long to wait. Chris could meet someone else and there he'd be in D.C. without a chance to compete.

Sounding as casual as he could, he asked, "How would you feel about me coming to visit, or flying up to see me?"

She paled before crushing out her cigarette and immediately going for another. "I don't think seeing each other after we say our goodbyes would be a good idea."

"Why not?" he pressed, his guts knotting.

"I don't want to talk about this." She reached for the bedside light. He gripped her wrist and rolled her back. He leaned over until he was in her face. No longer pale, her cheeks were bright spots of pink.

"Know what, Chris? Every time you don't want to confront something, you go for the lights. I want them on while you answer me."

They were locked in a staring contest. Finally, she broke it. He wanted to grip her jaw and snap her around but instead, he caught her chin and firmly turned.

"All right," she said, sighing. "First of all, I have an example to set, a reputation to maintain. If we see each other, we'll sleep together—or make that, not sleep—and I can't risk getting caught."

"We could be discreet." Even as he said it, the suggestion turned his stomach. Sneaking around meant there was something to hide. No, he didn't think it cut both ways with them, after all. He could just see Chris making excuses, trying to explain him to her friends. And him? If he had her on his turf, he'd flash her on his arm like a Rolex. Hell, make her a movie marquee: *Now Showing...Man Goes from Rags to Riches and Ain't She a Million-Dollar Doll?*

"Even being discreet, Greg, it wouldn't work. As long as you're in my life I won't be able to, as you say, move on. How could I possibly go in search of The Great American Daddy if your shoes are under my bed?"

Suddenly, he wanted the lights off. Greg bummed a cigarette and lit up.

"Are you looking for someone like—" He couldn't bring himself to say the name and "dead husband" seemed a little cruel, though a little cruel he felt. Something told him that cruelty wasn't a qualification for The Great American Daddy. "Are you looking for a duplicate to replace the first father?"

"There could never be anyone like Mark. And even if there was, I wouldn't want him. He'd deserve to be well loved and that's something I'm not willing to give."

"But don't you think you're cheating yourself of something that could be good by keeping that kind of distance?"

"Maybe. But it's more important to me to survive. You lost two wives. Not to death, but divorce is the next closest thing. Surely you went through some grief—"

"No grief here, just regret for bad judgment."

"Then surely you've loved *someone* enough and lost them to understand what that does to a person."

"Not yet. But...I guess it could happen."

"For your sake, I hope it never does. Wanting to touch someone, to ask how their day was and really care about their answer, but knowing the closest you'll ever get is a memory—"

"So, once I'm a memory to stash away with your others—not together of course, mine in the closet, the others on their exalted altar—just what kind of a guy will you be on the prowl for?''

Direct hit, he noted with satisfaction. There was a shocked quality to her quick intake of breath, the rapid blink of her eyes as if she couldn't believe he would be so mean, that he would deliberately hurt her with his words.

"If you must know, there's a man at church who happens to be the assistant principal where I teach. We're chaperons for a school dance coming up and he's let me know that he'd like to make it a date. I think I should pursue it."

"I'm impressed. Go on."

"He's a widower with two teenage daughters. They sing in the choir and make straight A's."

"They sound even more interesting than him." A heartbeat passed and she didn't fling his own less-than-successful attempts at fatherhood at him. *Why* was he doing this? Unless he backed off, he could forget about the few nights they had left. "Sorry, guess I'm jealous. They seem like the perfect family and that gives you a lot in common."

"He's president of the PTA." As if she wanted her lover's approval of the potential husband, she rushed ahead. "And he's very good with children. The worst discipline cases at school get handed over to him."

Yeah, great, but how does he screw? Husbands, of course, didn't *screw* their wives. At least, junior-high assistant principals who chaperoned dances and shared a hymnal with straight-A daughters—shit, that's right, they sang in the choir—didn't screw. God, he hoped not. They did, however, make love—at least often enough to have kids—and Chris had said she wanted at least one more.

Not his, surely; but The Great American Daddy had the plumbing to get the job done.

Greg shut his eyes against the image of Chris going through the motions of conception. She wouldn't love the man, be it this one or another, but there would be affection, mutual respect and the standard trimmings for a commitment. To make her loveless bed and lie in it, she'd need that much.

That much was more than he wanted her to have. Selfish, uh-huh. Went right nice with a mean streak. He was some stiff competition, yessir.

Stiff he was not at the moment. But he wanted to be. He wanted a raging hard-on to drive Mr. Goody Two-Shoes out of the running, make her so sore she'd still be hobbling at the stupid dance—chaperoning with her precious reputation intact.

"He sounds like a super guy for you, Chris. Say, if he's so good with discipline cases, maybe he wouldn't mind taking a crack at Arlene." *And while she's making him itch for a new job, what say the two of us slip into the nearest broom closet and get it on until the janitor turns us over for next in line after Arlene?* Strategy. There was an angle.

"From what you've told me about Arlene, I don't think even Jerry could handle her."

Jerry. So, the jerk had a name. Easier to like him without a name, but either way, Greg didn't like him one damn bit.

"I'm sure he'd try his best, given his track record. As for mine, it speaks for itself."

"Hey, don't be so hard on yourself." After lifting the cigarette that had burned down to the butt from his lips, she brushed the ashes off his chest and kissed him where his heart thudded dully. "If it makes you feel better, you make me wish I wasn't a mama when we're together."

"You mean if you weren't, you'd want to meet me in the locker room after the first half's over?"

"I'd want to keep you there until the clock went into overtime. Heck, even when I think about you, I feel like a teenager with more hormones than good sense."

"I'll take that as a compliment." Lord knew, he could use one from her hallowed halls of motherhood. "So what about tomorrow night? Kid or no kid, I want to see you. I'll cancel our reservations and the three of us can arm-wrestle each other for the last greasy french fry, if that's what you want."

"No," she said abruptly. What had been limp was now closer to shriveled. "Don't get me wrong. Audrey thinks you're nice—she told me so."

"Then what's the problem?"

"She's upset because I'm neglecting her to see to myself. I need you, Greg, but the way I need you doesn't have room for Audrey. Bringing you on the scene would only confuse her when the two of us are temporary. I wish things were different, believe me I do, but I'm not the only person I have to think about."

What about me? He clamped his jaw before he could ask. Surveying the surroundings, the answer was all too clear. This was it. Still, he had to push.

"Audrey seemed to like me." Weak defense but it was the best one he had.

"She did." Chris's nuzzle to his chest only made him feel worse. "And I think you're a wonderful man."

"But you don't want me to spend time with your child."

Groaning, she flopped on her back. "Damn it, Greg, I don't need this coming at me from both ends! I feel like hell after Audrey gave me what-for today and wanted to go home. Much more of you putting the screws to me and home's where I just might go."

He hadn't lost her yet and yet he was losing her already. Was it her, or was it him? Emotional introspection wasn't his strong suit but he saw far enough: Chris could love deeply, too deeply, so she refused to even give him a chance. He'd never been able to love deeply enough, a control freak who liked to get his way and usually did. She wasn't giving him his way and he was sulking. No wonder his marriages hadn't worked out. No wonder Chris wouldn't have him.

But he'd have it from her as to why not—in his face and straight from her mouth. Maybe they should end it here.

"It's clear, perfectly clear, that I don't fit into the big picture. But even in the short term, I've got some pride. You're ashamed of me and I've got a problem with that."

"Ashamed of you?" Her eyes had never looked so brown, so deep. So affronted. "Where did you ever get that idea? If I'm ashamed of anyone it's me. You're honest, I'm not. I've lied to my daughter, my family, I've lied to myself. I've lied to everyone but you—and only because you won't let me. You've been a real friend to me, Greg, and I'm already dreading goodbye. All the more reason that after we're over, we *have* to be over. Not because I'm ashamed of you—that's ridiculous—but because I could care for you too much. And that's the one thing I can't afford."

"Does this mean…" *Deep breath, just say it.* "Does it mean you could fall in love with me if you let yourself?"

She took a while to answer. "I don't know. But it really doesn't matter because I can't, I *won't,* ever let that happen. It's all or nothing with you, and falling for someone who makes those kinds of demands is the most self-destructive move I could make. Audrey aside, there might be a chance I could fall in love with you, and that's the biggest reason

I won't be seeing you again once we finish what time we've got left.''

She could love him. If only he hadn't been such a loser as a parent, a husband. If only she knew how deeply, how often he wished he could rise above past failure and prove himself as a father and a man. *Let it go. You ain't no daddy but your libido's working again.* Chris's confession had aroused him more than a fevered touch. She could love him—what a rush. Addictive stuff; he was already hooked.

The realization hit him with the impact of a brass-knuckled fist and all he could think was, *Ah shit, man, are you in trouble. Give her some room and get some for yourself.*

"Look, if you need to spend time with your daughter tomorrow night, I can make myself scarce. I don't like it but I understand. Whichever way you want to work it, we will.''

Chris did a finger-drum on his chest. "Jelly beans.''

"Say again?''

"Audrey has a weakness for jelly beans. I have a weakness for you. One pound of the suckers—bubblegum, her favorite flavor—and maybe we can reach a compromise.''

"And if you can't?''

"Don't cancel the reservations anyway. Only, don't you think we should move to another room? This suite must cost a mint and we're spending all our time in bed anyway.''

"You're watching my checkbook?'' Greg laughed around a groan. How many women would push for a Motel 6 when they had the Ritz? None that he'd ever met. Served him right, for Chris to end up screwing with his head. Had to get it on straight before he lost his heart to a woman who took no prisoners. "It's this joint or a fast flight to Lubbock. I'd like to check out this Jerry So-and-so and warn him that he'll have me to deal with if he's not good to you. Take a second and choose."

"I choose…you." She kissed him soundly. "You have smoker's breath."

"So do you. Want to share a toothbrush?"

"And give you girl germs? I wouldn't dream of it."

"I like your germs. Admit it, Chris, a champagne bottle's safer for you than getting toothbrush cozy with me."

"Like I said, you won't let me lie. As for whichever way I want to work it, tell me, *exactly,* how you'd like me to."

As she felt for him beneath the covers, Greg stared at the ceiling. Options…strategy…. He could make sure she thought of him tomorrow with every step she took. He could make her salve his bruised ego and pump hers up so much she'd realize she had too much going to settle for a wing-tipped bore. He could make her think. He could make her pay.

If he did it right, he could possibly manage all four.

"Get dressed if you want to come with me. If you don't, I'll be glad to order up a bottle of champagne to keep you company while I'm gone."

CHAPTER THIRTEEN

STUFFING HIMSELF INTO his pants, he watched Chris shimmy into her bra, then reach for the panty hose—*ug-ly,* whoever thought those up deserved to be shot. Greg slipped into his favorite pair of loafers— *Forget the socks.* She pinched her own feet into the high heels and raced him to the door.

There, he zipped her dress—damn, but he could get used to this easy—while she adjusted the shoe that fit no better than Cinderella's glass slipper had on the bitchy stepsisters.

Chris wasn't a bitch but he'd be tempted to give up his considerable nest egg if she could see her way to becoming a bitch first-class. Then they could split, no problem.

"Where are we going?" she asked, panting.

"Shopping." He punched the Down arrow, then pinched her butt. Glancing around, she made sure no one had seen.

"Go shopping for what? It's nine o'clock."

"So?" The elevator was empty. As the doors slid shut, he pressed her against the leather-cushioned wall. Palms on her hips, he shoved his own against her and rubbed.

"What do you think you're doing? Someone could—"

"Don't worry." Hitting the Stop button between floors, he pushed up her skirt and insinuated a hand beneath her ugly panty hose. Fingering her, he said roughly, "You're wet. First time tonight. Maybe I should rent out the elevator."

"I thought we were going shopping." She clutched at

his hand, but he waylaid her efforts with a persuasive entry that left her poised on tiptoe.

"What are you hungry for? I might not be The Great American Daddy, but I am one helluva cook and since you're so concerned about me wasting my hard-earned bucks, far be it from me to let the kitchen go to waste. How about leg of lamb with mint jelly—back up. No time to marinate. A tray of canapés? Perfect. They look tempting, taste delicious, and whet a person's appetite for more."

"Hamburgers," she gasped. "Hamburgers are fine. Sonic burgers are my favorite."

"Quit worrying about my financial status, would you?" Pretending to remove his hand, she gripped his wrist and squirmed down. His laugh was low and immensely satisfied. "I'm plenty solvent even if you have to be so stingy that you can't afford me. What about smoked salmon with white sauce and a few capers for garnish? Should be just your speed."

He released the Stop button.

Her hand slammed down. One on the button, the other shoved his retreating fingers back under her panties.

"Finish it," she begged with such demand that Greg decided he could be generous.

"I'm crazy about you, Chris. Every time I think of you, I want you. When we're together, I can't hold you tight enough or get in you deep enough. Crazy, you're making me crazy and I want you just as crazy for me. Only for me."

Okay, Jerry, match that. And if by some miracle you can, let's see you top this. Thumb to cleft, fingers spread against inner walls and moving, he knew how to make them weep.

Mouth open, her breath a shuddering, silent cry, she climaxed with an intensity he felt in his fingertips and elsewhere—in a place he couldn't locate but still it was there, warming him, touching him, making him feel more vulnerable and more a man than he'd ever felt before.

This part of her belonged to him and him alone and not even The Great American Daddy could take it away. Greg's smile was grim. Maybe he couldn't stop her from throwing in her lifetime lot with another man, but he could still come between them if she called for "Greg" at the best possible wrong moment. His desperation for that hold over her, his need to intimately triumph over a dead man, was a little sad, pitiful to him. That he had come to this did not make him feel proud. It was wrong, and he knew it; but he was hurting in a place she'd created, an empty spot she was refusing to fill.

The elevator phone rang.

"Should I answer?" he asked quietly as Chris put herself back together and moved to the far end. Hands gripping the shiny brass bars, she seemed to shrink into the corner. Even from his position by the doors, he could see her shaking.

"I don't care. Just hit floor number three so we don't have to face anyone who's making that call from the lobby."

At the third floor several people stepped on. When she made to get off, Greg caught her arm.

"Wrong floor," he said loudly enough for everyone to hear, then whispered, "Hang loose, okay?"

Chris worried her ringless ring finger. She reminded him of himself as a kid, stealing a candy bar at the five-and-dime, then being marched by his mother to the manager's office where he was sure a policeman with handcuffs was waiting. A confession and an apology had won his freedom, but he'd taken a good lesson home to remember.

If he could do the same with Chris, he might have a prayer for an extension of time.

A "ding" and an illuminated L marked their arrival.

"Let's go." Greg gave her a gentle shove and she reluctantly went. From the side, he could see her eyes darting around for a watchful guard, her feet slow but ready to run at the first accusing finger. "No one knows who we are." He felt her arm tense under his grip.

"I feel like it's written all over my face." She looked at the floor and he subdued the urge to give her a shake. "What we did was insane. What if we'd gotten caught?"

"But we didn't. The desk's over there if you want to turn us in and clear your conscience."

Her glance at him was sharp. "I can't believe you're so calm, like this doesn't even bother you. It doesn't, does it?"

"Bother me? Hell, no." He wanted her to admit what she'd so obviously enjoyed; her shame over it maddened him, dug and bit at that empty spot of his. "I loved every gasp out of your mouth, every wet grip of my fingers, every—"

"Stop it," she snapped.

"Last I remember, it was your hand on the Stop button."

"That's right, rub it in."

"Once we get back to our room, I'll do more than that."

"Don't be so sure, you cocky bastard."

He stopped her near the exit, palms firm on her shoulders. When she tried to break away, Greg held fast.

"Unless you want to make a scene and bring the concierge over here, settle down."

"Why? So you can feel me up while he watches?"

Hmm. Chris wasn't a bitch as far as bitches went, but there was enough bitchiness there for a yelling match to clear the air. Hell, she might even have it in her to throw a thing or two. Fine line between love and hate; one could trip into the other. If he couldn't have her love, he'd take hate over indifference any day.

Greg took heart since there was nothing indifferent about the grinding of her teeth.

"You're right, Chris, I am a cocky bastard. Cocky enough to hold out on you until you ask for it. Even then, I'll hold out until you get mad and demand I give you what you want."

"The last thing I want right now is your smug attitude."

"Talk about attitude, you're pissed. And why? Because I don't play clean but you still want me. And that scares you."

"Damn right, I'm scared. I'm scared of what I do when I'm with you." Waiting for a couple to pass them, she shivered, then whispered, "Last night it was bondage—"

"But you wanted it, babe," he reminded her.

"Greg, please, listen to me," she said urgently. "I was as much to blame for what happened in the elevator as you—"

"Blame implies guilt for some harm done. No one was there but us, so it comes down to you and me, and I'm fine. Did I hurt you somehow? Is there blame to be had that I don't know about? Tell me, because I'm confused."

"*I'm* confused. Maybe blame was the wrong word, but I do know that we're pushing the envelope a little more each time and what seemed right when it happened leaves me in a cold sweat once I step back and ask myself, 'Good God, what have I done? This isn't me.' But it *was* me, and I'm having trouble dealing with that."

"Then let me help you deal with it and tell you where the trouble really is. It's in your secret garden, the one you neatly tend after dark with me. If you hadn't noticed, I like the light. Because it's the light, Chris, that makes your garden grow.'' He softly knuckled her jaw. ''Think about it.''

He released her and walked on. Hard as it was, he left her behind to retreat to the room; a room that would be empty when he returned if she hailed a cab instead.

Needing the crisp night air to clear his head, Greg waved away a valet's offer to deliver the car.

Only willpower kept his feet from racing in reverse, and that almost made him hope she'd be gone. Chris was scared? *He* was scared, more scared than the time he'd pissed his pants when a covert operation had him in a foxhole, hearing a kid on his first mission crying for Mama while four of his other men lay mangled all over his feet.

He got out with the boy. Shell-shocked, the kid ended up playing tiddledywinks in a nut ward. As for himself, he wrote to the families of the deceased, then did his damnedest to purge it all away in two weeks of R-and-R hellraising. Eat, drink and be merry, for tomorrow ye may die.

He'd had a better chance to survive than most, sensitive situations being his specialty. But none so sensitive as this. Yeah, Chris had him scared. Even more scared than dying.

As he rounded the car, the strike of his fist on the hood coincided with the rapid click-click of high heels that went off like a machine gun in his head.

It took everything he had and then some to slide into the driver's seat without a glance in her direction. Greg gave her long enough to get in before he cranked the engine.

Breathless, she took off the shoes she never should have tried on, much less bought.

Seemed those shoes and he had a lot in common: giving Chris hell while she broke them in against the laws of nature.

The silence was taut as he drove, his pride demanding she be the one to reach out first. So far, he'd been doing all the reaching. Her turn. It was her turn, damn it, and until she took it, he was doing what he'd been trained to do so well: show no emotion while he picked up the remains of unbeating hearts and their shattered dreams of a future.

If he could do it for a few good men, he could do it for himself.

CHAPTER FOURTEEN

CHRIS STARED out the window, the passing streetlights with Christmas decorations on their posts a blur. All she could see was Greg in bed, in the elevator, in the lobby where she'd sensed his anger was really hurt.

Terrified, she was terrified to touch it. Still, she did touch him, his hand tight on the steering wheel.

"I'm sorry," she ventured.

"For what?" Voice curt, eyes straight ahead.

Actually, she wasn't sure what she was apologizing for, just that he'd seemed to expect one and she felt badly for calling him a cocky bastard. Only he'd deserved it; had even agreed and taunted her with her weakness for him in bed.

"I'm sorry that we had words. Our time together is so short, I don't want to spend it arguing."

His profile could have been carved from marble. He wanted more than an apology, she realized. Why she should be surprised, she didn't know. He *always* wanted more. For every inch she gave he wanted a dozen, and she wasn't up for the distance. Why couldn't he understand that? Him, of all people, who'd twice proved that he was no long-distance runner himself. Did he think she could break his no-win marital streak? Surely not.

Even the thought of marriage to Greg was absurd. As absurd as the Kissin' Don't Last, Cookin' Do sampler she'd embroidered for her kitchen warmed up to his spare, spotless style.

Chris wrinkled her nose with a slob's snobbish distaste for immaculate addicts. Everything in order, their obsession for just-so neatness, as if their lives would fall apart if a dish was put in the wrong cabinet—*pu-leez*. Greg was one of *those,* and what made it worse was him being a man, for Chrissakes. Last night, after he'd stripped for her, he'd folded his clothes and eyed hers on the floor. And before they'd left, he'd cleaned up the glasses they'd thrown, then checked for stray popcorn kernels. But it was his making up the bed and tightening the coverlet when the coin didn't bounce that pronounced him a neat freak of the highest order.

Funny, it hadn't bothered her last night. Then again, his demands had been of a different nature. Ever since he'd picked her up, he'd kissed with too much feeling, touched her with an emotional hunger that was all the more piercing because it was tentative, as if he was new to touching that way and wasn't quite sure how. As for his jealousy, his pressure to expand their relationship, her head was still spinning and her heart was still pounding.

Marriage to Greg? Banish the thought. He would want to possess her, consume her, and the more he pushed, the further she'd retreat. Just like tonight. And just like tonight, he'd punish her for denying him what he wanted.

Punish her; yes, that's what he'd done. He'd punished her by pleasuring her and making her admit to the dark side of her sensual nature. He was punishing her now. With his straight-ahead stare at the road, his heavy silence, he was bullying her into a confrontation.

And then, she realized. Greg wanted a fight. He was setting her up to take him on.

Chris's lips twitched with amusement as she plotted her revenge. Besting Greg at his own game was too tempting to resist. And besides, this way they could both win.

"I... Greg, I thought about what you said, about my secret garden and wanting to tend it in the dark. I decided you were right. That's why I came after you."

When he glanced at her, she removed her conciliatory touch from his ungiving hold on the wheel. He quickly recaptured her hand and brought it to his thigh.

Voice soft, with just the right hint of innocent seduction, she explained, "This garden of mine was awfully barren until you came along and gave me a taste of forbidden fruit. It scares me because...well, I do run the risk of getting snake bite. You know how snakes like gardens." She felt his thigh flex against her smooth upward brush, and then his immediate thickening beneath her cupping palm.

"I have a garden at home, Greg, a small vegetable patch, and a snake slithered out while I was hoeing one day last spring. I chopped its head off and then its tail when it kept on wiggling." The flinch in his groin did not go unnoticed.

"Anyway, after you left me, I thought about how much gardens need both night and day to grow. And how it's the same but appears so different in the dark when I can't tell what's what without a light. I'm a little night blind, so I eat a lot of carrots. I decided you're like a carrot for me."

"A carrot, huh?" His slight chuckle told her she had gained the advantage. "A fat one, I hope."

"Long and fat, definitely a major-league carrot," she assured him. "It's a real joy to me, Greg, seeing all those colors and shapes leave my garden in a big wicker basket that's headed for my kitchen. So, there you have it, the reason I ran to you, instead of away."

"A basket of vegetables is why you're here?"

"Why, sure. I knew if I left, I'd keep seeing you as all those veggies in the basket and kick myself because—" she clicked her tongue "—oh, gee, I could have had a V8! And there I'd be rummaging in the pantry for some junk food I didn't even want.'' She leaned down and kissed the straining of his fly. ''I want you, Greg. You *are* my secret garden. Let's harvest everything we can, while we can. Please.''

She looked up to beseech him and saw everything he didn't say. The frustration, the distress of a man who was not a graceful loser. Maybe he didn't want her to see, or maybe he simply decided to take what he could while he could, but his palm gently stroked her head as he pressed it down.

''We'll be there soon, but it won't take much.'' His voice had an odd sound, like sandpaper brushing velvet.

He covered her head with a portion of his coat. It took a minute perhaps, before he came. The muffled groans she heard were quickly followed by the sound of tissues pulled from a box on the dashboard and nudged toward her mouth.

Chris pushed off the coat and sat up, heedless of any oncoming traffic. Greg, backhanding sweat from his brow, appeared confused as she shook her head at his offering.

Sure he was watching, she swallowed.

''HEY, GUESS WHAT!''

''What?'' Greg called back from the kitchenette as he tossed a cherry tomato into the air and caught it in his mouth. A snap of his teeth and down his throat it went. If only Chris's defenses were so easily downed.... Had to be a way; he just hadn't figured it out yet.

''There's a Harvard prof who swears Earth women have given birth to alien babies and an intergalactic race is only a generation away. Neat, huh?''

Laughing, Greg put the finishing touches on the platter and, balancing it on fingertips raised high, strolled into the living area. There he paused, absorbing the pure pleasure of seeing her sprawled on the couch, wearing his shirt and nothing but, a heap of trashy tabloids scattered on the floor.

Grinning, Chris looked up from the one she was reading. Their gazes caught and held. Her expression sobered.

"Why are you looking at me that way?"

"I like what I see." He placed the tray on the coffee table, wondering as he did what sort of home Chris had. Probably a quaint bungalow with pine floors and vintage furniture, some worn white wicker rounding out the spaces as soft and warm and invitingly messy as herself. And a porch swing. Yeah, she'd have a porch swing. One that needed painting and creaked. But she'd like it that way— lived-in.

"So, come nice weather, do you drink lemonade and sing to Audrey while you swing on your front porch?"

"How did you know I do that?"

Greg shrugged. "I just do. The same way I know you sit out there alone in the dark and listen to the crickets while you try not to think too hard but end up doing it anyway."

With a look akin to amazement, she said, "Are you sure you haven't been spying on me?"

"Not yet. Scoot over and make room for—" *Daddy.* One of his favorite old re-runs as a kid, but Danny Thomas he wasn't. Or at least, he hadn't been. Chris made him want more than ever that second chance to be the kind of father who'd swing on a porch while he read a fairy tale to his kid.

Jeez, talk about fairy tales. The odds of that happening were on a par with spinning gold out of straw.

It felt like straw clogged his throat, a whole roomful of it, and he coughed dryly as he pulled Chris onto his lap.

"Are you okay?" she asked, putting a cool palm to his forehead. "You feel a little warm."

Toast was more like it. With her concerned little gesture, Chris was making him crash and burn, here and now. He was falling in love with her, he realized, wishing fiercely for some way to break the fall. Worse than bad, he could see the writing on the wall.

He was going down like never before.

But the hell if he'd suffer alone. Jaw clenching, Greg swore to himself that Chris was going down with him. Be it fellow survivors or casualties, they'd share the same fate.

Grip stern on her wrist, he bit into the heel of her palm— a soft, teething gnaw that won a sigh, and then a sharp gasp when he clamped hard on flesh and muscle.

Tracing the imprint of his teeth, he said quietly, "Good thing I can't eat you alive since there wouldn't be anything left. Even for me. And it sure wouldn't be fair to Audrey, much as she needs you, along with that daddy you're hoping to find for her. Problem is, Chris, she needs more than two parents who wrap their lives up in a child because they don't have much else holding them together."

Chris glanced away. "Since when were you an expert on what kids need from their parents?"

"Since I screwed up with Arlene and got the distance to realize where I went wrong. And looking back on my childhood, I can see where my own folks made some big mistakes."

"But your family seems so stable. I assumed your parents had a good marriage."

"Depends on what you call good. They have the kind of marriage you're after. Passionless, but amicable. Not that I'm looking to lay blame—they did devote their lives to making mine the best it could be. But I've wondered at times if my problems in the relationship department weren't rooted in being the center of attention growing up."

"I wonder what's on the tube." Chris reached for the remote. Beating her to it, Greg knocked it to the floor.

"Anyway, I don't think that's healthy for a kid. They can end up real selfish people who don't know how to put someone else's needs above their own. And what comes of those who build their lives around a child who'll eventually be gone is a pretty sad thing to witness. My mother treats my old bedroom like it's some kind of a shrine. Hell, Dad says he can hear her talking to me like I'm in there and—"

"Enough."

"And there's something wrong with that. Why isn't she talking to him instead of a memory who picks up the phone when guilt kicks in? They don't have anything to say to each other, that's why. The only thing they had in common is gone, and some great job he's done so far with his own life, right?"

"Damn it, Greg! *Enough.*" She lunged from his lap. He heard the soft whoosh of her breath as his chest came down on hers, his weight pinning her to the floor.

"Wanna hit me, Chris? Go ahead, take your best shot if you want to shut me up. You're not doing Audrey any favors by hooking up with some man who doesn't love you enough to demand more than a mockery of a marriage. Is that what you want to teach her—better to feel too little than too much?"

"Stop," she whimpered.

Stilling her with fingers wound tight into her hair, Greg savaged her mouth until she returned the force of his hunger.

"That's it," he whispered roughly. "That's it, babe. Caring enough to fight and then to kiss and make up, that's what kids need to see. They learn a helluva lot more from two people who have soul between them than a couple of emotional strangers who happen to sleep together could ever teach.''

Chris went limp beneath him. She felt as if she'd been pummeled with a stinging truth, her emotional cowardice shoved into her face and down her throat.

His palm was on her throat, fingers stroking her jugular. How easily he could break her neck with a single snap of his powerful hands. *Greg had killed.* The thought came from nowhere, but she suddenly realized she was staring into the same eyes that had no doubt looked much the same as he'd committed murder. Murder in the line of duty, but murder nonetheless.

His was the look of a man who sympathized with his victim but felt no remorse for the course of action he was compelled to take.

''You are merciless,'' she whispered.

''I am.'' Slowly he lifted his chest, sat astride her hips. From her vantage point on the floor he seemed larger than life, a skyscraper of a man, made of tough muscle and possessing a will of steel. From her throat to the opening of his shirt she wore, he drew down his hand. Eyes like the pinpoint sear of a laser burned into hers as he gave a fierce jerk.

The sound of buttons stripped from thread filled her ears and she felt the cool lick of air on her bared breasts. Greg reached for the tray filled with vegetables and scooped a celery stick into the brimming bowl of creamy avocado dip.

''Green, such a suitable color,'' he murmured, painting her nipples with dabbing strokes. ''Green as spring grass after a cold and lonely winter. Green with jealous envy. I'm jealous, Chris, jealous of any man having you except for me.'' As his mouth descended he warned softly, ''A lesson to remember, babe. You're about to find out just how merciless I can be.''

CHAPTER FIFTEEN

CHRIS WORRIED HER bottom lip as she fingered the envelope Greg had slipped her after "dropping by" shortly before noon.

He hadn't stayed more than thirty minutes but it had felt like hours. Agonizing hours of polite chitchat with her mother and what seemed to be an inordinate amount of attention lavished on Audrey. The little girl who had done a quick about-face once Greg had told her she was the reason for his visit.

She'd gobbled it up, as if starved for attention. Never mind that Mama had poured it on her all morning, trying to placate a conscience working overtime. Chris hated paper dolls but Audrey loved them, so play with them they did. Audrey wanted to go to the park, so to the park they went. No matter it was cold and Chris wanted to be inside instead of chafing stiff fingers and paying her penance with each push of a swing. She'd done everything except buy jelly beans.

Those, she'd planned to buy this afternoon but Greg had saved her the trip. Well, Chris thought with a huff, maybe Greg could fool Audrey into thinking he was a "super-cool dude," but she knew better. He was a super-smooth operator who was trying to convince both child and mother that he was something he wasn't: Daddy material. Good thing she knew him as well as she did, or Greg might have fooled her, as well. He'd actually gotten on his knees to say goodbye to Audrey and give her a high five.

Audrey had giggled as they slapped palms, then had thrown her arms around his neck. Standing protectively close, Chris had heard her whisper, "Do you like kids?"

Greg's resounding, "You bet I do, and I especially like you" was accompanied by a challenging smile shot at Chris.

Just remembering it had Chris grinding her teeth while her throat tightened all over again. She couldn't deny that she was almost as touched as she was furious with the man. That Greg was trying to move their relationship into deeper waters was obvious. But even if she could shore up the guts to give them a chance, it couldn't possibly work. Greg wasn't paternal; he was a strategist and she was his target for conquest.

For all his seeming sincerity with Audrey—and perhaps he even believed it himself—the bottom line was, he was using a child to manipulate the situation to his advantage.

"Oh, Greg." Chris sighed. "If only you were less of what you are and more of what Audrey and I need." Glancing around her old bedroom, Chris tried to imagine sharing such simple, domestic surroundings with him.

But when the vision came with surprising speed, she discarded it just as quickly. Too risky to let herself even think such things. She was vulnerable and he was dangerous. Greg thrilled to a challenge; winning was the name of the game for him. And should he win her, the challenge would be over.

Steeling herself for what was sure to be an assault on her defenses, Chris opened the envelope, fully expecting a love letter minus the gush. Sappy wasn't his style.

And neither were love letters, even minus the gush. His script and the message she read were as bold as the man himself.

Several packages will arrive this afternoon. I want you to wear the items I've selected just for you—nothing else beneath the wrap, please. A limo will pick you up at five and deliver you to my requested destination. Expect an evening of the unexpected. Till then, might I suggest a nap?

A nap!

Somewhere in the back of her mind she heard Greg's low laughter. He knew very well that even if she was dead on her feet she wouldn't have a prayer of sleeping after this. Which only made her flounce onto the bed and bury her head in a pillow. By golly, she'd take a nap just to spite him!

Ten minutes later, Chris gave it up. No use, her stomach was churning in anticipation. And apprehension. What game was he playing? What adventures might the night hold? And *what* had he bought for her to wear? Nothing else beneath her coat? Heavens, what if he'd sent a merry widow with fishnet stockings and spike heels? And if he had, would she be brazen enough to meet his challenge and wear them?

The sound of the doorbell had Chris racing for the door, certain that Frederick's of Hollywood boxes awaited and how in the world would she explain *that* to her mother?

With a sinking sensation she saw Rick accept the packages. Next to Anna and Don, her brother was the worst person to get a hint of the double life she was leading.

"These are for you, sis." He gave her a probing look.

Heart in throat, Chris claimed the pile of distinctively wrapped boxes with a breathless, "Thanks."

"Neiman Marcus. Hmm."

Hmm, indeed! She had to admit, whatever Greg lacked

in paternal attributes he more than made up for in the ability to surprise and impress.

"I've gotta hand it to him, Chris, his taste in stores is right up there with his taste in women. But I can't help but wonder about his intentions. You're my sister and I don't want to see you get hurt."

"That makes two of us, Rick. Don't worry about me. I'm a big girl who's simply enjoying a whirlwind romance."

"And that's all it is for him, too?"

Chris shrugged. "Don't tell anyone about these, okay? I'd like to check it out without an audience."

"Sure." Rick caught her arm as she turned. "You know, I never thought I'd play the devil's advocate, but a man does not go shopping at Neiman's for a woman unless he's after more than a whirlwind romance. Like the saying goes, the bigger they are the harder they fall. I think I hear a timber going down with a really big crash. Just something you might keep in mind."

"I do." Boxes piled to her chin, Chris took off, perturbed that Rick had spoiled her enjoyment with a guilt trip. She had enough of that to deal with already as a mother without adding her lover to the emotional heap.

Of course she didn't want to hurt Greg. And as long as they abided by the rules they'd agreed on, he'd be fine and so would she. She'd have to remind him of that tonight.

And then she'd have to put her foot down about any future visits with Audrey. No more steamrolling his way into the carefully orchestrated life she'd put on hold for a week, period. That was that and if he didn't like it, then…

Then they'd both be better off calling it quits now. Before either of them got hurt. *But could you do it, Chris? Could you walk away tonight without a backward glance?*

The question haunted her as she unwrapped the smallest box and found—

Stockings. But not just any stockings. A black seam up the backs with rhinestones circling one ankle; silky and transparent, they slid through her fingers like a French kiss wrapped in a whisper.

Eagerly opening the second package, she caught her breath.

A lacy black chemise with tiny jet pearls embroidered over the bodice joined stockings on the bed. Nestled in delicate paper beneath she found a matching garter belt.

No panties.

Lord, it was wicked! Absolutely the most wickedly gorgeous lingerie she'd ever seen.

Two boxes left and Chris allowed her imagination to romp naughtily. Perhaps a sheer black cocktail dress, split up either side to the thigh, lacy garters and hose tops peeking coyly through? Or maybe a black leather miniskirt with a next-to-nothing top?

With visions of decadence dancing in her head, Chris pulled off the lid and gasped, amazed to discover a flowing dress, the fabric velvet, the design a collage of vibrant red roses and rich purple irises on a background of black. The hem zigzagged in a scarf effect from knees to mid-calf; the neck was scooped, the see-through sleeves sheared in graceful tatters like flag strips circling a Maypole and cinched at the wrist. Even the sash was a work of art: a length of supple black velvet with a mingling of purple and red silk tassels at the ends.

Holding the dress to her, Chris waltzed to the vanity mirror. It was a magical dress, unlike anything she'd ever seen before. And the woman she saw in the mirror seemed transformed by the magic it worked. Her eyes were Mona

Lisa mysterious and her face had a rare glow, the sort of illuminated flush people had when they were in love.

In love? Chris shook her head, hard. Given that she most certainly was not in love and had absolutely no intentions of inviting such foolishness, she could only assume that the dress had a good dose of fairy dust sprinkled on it.

Moving quickly from the mirror, she shook out the dress. This was not reality, she sternly reminded herself. It was a waking dream, no more. After all, only in a dream would she open the final package and stare in awe at the contents.

A purple velvet cloak lined in black satin, with a voluminous hood. And a pair of matching ballet slippers. But it was the grace note she found, a single line on a piece of folded paper, that took her breath away.

See yourself as I do—Greg

This was how he saw her? Chris gave in to the luxury of imagining she was worthy of the compliment. An elegant, sensual woman who could inspire such enamored praise from a worldly man like Greg.

The problem was, she was playing a secret fantasy role in the fantasy world they had spun, one that had about as much real substance as cotton candy.

Chris stroked the velvet cloak. What little remained of her prudent nature advised her to return the packages to Greg and explain the gift was deeply appreciated but too expensive to keep. A lot like him.

Still, she couldn't resist at least trying on the ensemble. Gazing in the mirror, Chris could only think she did see herself as Greg did. At least for now, and now was all that mattered. She'd worry later about accepting such an outrageous gift from a man who brought jelly beans to her little girl and made a woman want more than anything to live happily ever after in a fairy-tale world where cotton candy was meat-and-potatoes real.

CHAPTER SIXTEEN

IT WAS A CALCULATED risk. Gloves off, screw the rules, he was invading her turf.

Chris wouldn't like it. At least not initially. Then again, one look at that plane ticket to Lubbock, and she might have tossed it into the trash, then hightailed it back the way she'd come.

But he didn't think so. If nothing else, she'd make the hour-long flight just to order him off her front porch before the neighbors got curious. Which they already were, judging from the blinds lifting across the street. He was in clear view, the porch-light timer having clicked on shortly before.

Greg waved. Down the blinds went.

The swing that needed a fresh coat of paint creaked in the crisp evening air as he continued to rock easy on the home front; soon to become the front line.

Spying the headlights of the stretch limo he'd assigned pickup duty to, Greg took a deep, bracing breath.

And grimaced. Cow shit. Jeez, how could Chris stand smelling the stuff? He'd lay a thousand to one that the only reason she lived in Lubbock was because she'd met her husband at Texas Tech and his job and family had kept them here.

How…predictable. And safe. A whole grand world awaited and here she was, rutting her life away. Too bad D.C. took three times longer to reach via air; he could've gone at this resident turf problem the opposite way.

He watched the back door fly open a second after the driver put the limo in Park. Yep, those neighbors of hers were getting an eyeful now. The driver getting out, Chris telling him to wait, and, as instructed, the driver taking off despite her frantic "Stop!" followed by a four-letter-word shout that pretty much described the air.

Cloak flowing, Chris looked like a queen marching up the cobblestone walk. A very pissed-off queen, to be exact.

All but stomping her slippered feet over the steps and onto the smooth pine porch, she stopped and glowered down at him, demanding, "What are you doing here?"

"Swinging. Care to join me?" he asked, patting the space beside him.

"No. No, I do *not* care to join you."

"Then why don't you ask me in? I'd like to see how the dress fits and it's a little too chilly to take off the cloak out here. By the way, it looks dynamite." Actually, so did Chris. Not only was she red-hot gorgeous, she looked about ready to explode. Hooking a thumb across the street, he slyly added, "I'm sure the neighbors agree."

Ruby lips pinched tight, she promptly rummaged through her purse, cursing softly until she dug out the elusive keys. Jamming one into the front lock, she gave a neat kick when the door stuck to the frame. The bottom needed planing. Greg wondered how many other odd jobs needed to be done around the good widow's house. He'd take a lot of pleasure in seeing to them. Maybe Jerry would, too.

Just the thought of another man leaving his mark on Chris's domestic domain had him clenching his jaw. It got tighter when she flicked off the outside light, as if hiding him and her traffic-stopping appearance from view.

"Well?" she said sharply, tapping her foot. "Are you coming in or not?"

In answer, Greg continued to swing, the metal link's *creak-creak* piercing the charged silence.

With an exasperated sigh, she huffed her way over.

"So? What is it you want now?"

"Not much, really. Just the same politeness I'm sure you'd extend to any other guest. That is, anyone but me."

"What did you expect? You came here knowing full well how I felt about—"

"Defiling your home and reputation with my presence?"

"I never said that!"

"No, but the way you're acting says plenty. You don't want anything to do with me outside a rented room. I hear ya, Chris. Loud and clear."

She was quiet for a while. When she spoke, her voice was subdued but not exactly calm. "I think you're being very unfair about this. We had an understanding, and you're the one who's pushing to change the rules that were your idea in the first place. They were smart rules, Greg."

"I thought so at the time. But I didn't count on you getting in my head and running roughshod over just about every working organ I've got pumping in my body."

"This is getting too complicated," she whispered.

Greg noticed she didn't worry her ring finger despite her obvious distress. He took some consolation from that.

"Yeah, it is getting complicated," he agreed, getting up. Palms on her shoulders, he stroked the velvet that felt as soothing as Chris did when he buried himself inside her. "Personally, I'd like to simplify things. How about you?"

"No argument here," she said, pulling away slightly.

Cinching his hold, Greg chose his words carefully. He didn't want to run her off by coming across as desperate and demanding as he was beginning to feel.

"I want you to acknowledge me. Maybe not as a permanent fixture. But couldn't you at least accept us as more than lovers? I consider you a friend, Chris. A very special friend who I care about just as much out of the sack as in. Don't shut me out just because the sex is good.''

In the moonlight, he could see her tight swallow. Was she hesitating because she knew as well as he did the sex was good—hell, incredible—because of the emotional chemistry they generated? The irony of it was, those emotions she was so afraid of were the very ones that turned her on.

''I... Let's go inside and talk, okay?''

''Should I take that to mean the welcome mat's out?''

''For now it is'' was her evasive reply.

''Good enough.'' *Like hell.* Keeping that last thought to himself, Greg followed her inside. She turned on the overhead entry light, a small stained-glass fixture that gave the foyer a warm, rosy glow.

As she went about lighting up the adjoining living room and smoothing out a vintage shawl draped over a Duncan Phyfe couch covered in aged brocade, Greg smiled. Her home was just as he'd pictured it.

Except for the wedding picture prominently displayed on an old upright piano.

An urge gripped him to smash the frame onto the wood floor and tear the picture into a thousand mangled pieces. Damn, but he'd never felt so threatened before. And jealous. God, he was eaten up with the little green monster. Better get that smile back into place before Chris saw. *Do it,* he ordered himself. *Fast.*

His lips straining with the effort, Greg said, ''Nice place. It's got your signature all over it.''

''It's home. Make yourself comfortable and I'll see if there's some wine left in the fridge.''

''I'd rather have hot chocolate if you've got some.''

''Hot chocolate? Um...no problem.'' Truth was, he

wanted Scotch, a stiff one, but cocoa set the mood he was after a lot better.

Chris turned toward the kitchen and he swiftly came up behind her. She stiffened when he caught her arms.

"Greg, please, I let you in to talk, not to—"

"I just wanted to help you out of your wrap, not get into your pants." *She didn't have any panties on.* Just a chemise and a garter belt holding up a pair of silk stockings. Sweet Jesus, he was suddenly so stiff that he hurt. The ache intensified to near agony as she slipped out of the gift he'd taken a gamble she'd accept, and pivoted.

"Thank you," she said stiffly. "I've never owned anything so beautiful. You're very thoughtful, Greg."

Thoughtful? He'd let her think so. But the gesture was more selfish than not. He had wanted to dress her with his money, cover her from head to toe as if she were his most prized possession.

"My pleasure. But Chris, you make the dress look great, not the other way around."

In Chris's gaze he saw a keen delight mingle with a kindling of arousal. Despite herself, she wanted him. Too bad for them both, he had no intentions of doing more than fanning the flame.

"I'll go make the chocolate."

"Want some help?" The quick shake of her head caused him to laugh wryly. "Don't tell me a man in your kitchen is more intimidating than sharing a toothbrush."

"In your case, only about double. If I know you, you'd wrestle me for the apron and probably organize my shelves after checking out the magnets on my refrigerator."

"Got some of Audrey's artwork displayed, do you?" Her wary expression confirmed it. "Relax. I know better than to push my luck in that direction tonight."

"Thank God for small favors," she muttered, heading toward the kitchen.

Watching the provocative sway of her hips, Greg endured a moment's masochistic pleasure before turning his attention to setting the trap.

CHRIS LET GO A SIGH of relief once she sensed his eyes were no longer devouring her retreating back. In the kitchen she tried to calm herself with the familiar surroundings, touching this and that. All was as she'd left it. And yet, she felt strangely removed, as if she'd departed the owner and returned a back-door visitor.

The milk put on to heat, Chris gripped the tiled countertop's edge and leaned her forehead against a cabinet door, seeking their inanimate strength.

Finding none there, she smacked her fist against the countertop and paced the kitchen's length. *Damn him.* Damn Greg for weaseling his way into her home. Hard as it would be to leave behind those places they'd marked as theirs, at least she wouldn't have constant reminders around her. But she had to come back here, live here, and remember that his physical presence had once filled her home.

Would she ever be able to swing on the front porch again without thinking of him? And would she ever hear the rusty creak of the chain without hearing his plea for friendship, spiked with pride and demand?

He had no right, no right whatsoever to steal the peace she would desperately need once their affair was over. If he'd really wanted to be a friend to her, he wouldn't have done that, and she didn't think for a minute that Greg didn't know exactly what he was doing.

Much as she hated confrontations, they were due one now. At least the memories she'd return home to wouldn't be sweet or happy or passionate. *Especially* not passionate.

As for the desire he'd already stirred up with no more than a look and a casual touch, she'd just have to deal with it. Anger would help. He'd defused it too easily on the porch; she couldn't let him do that again.

Chris made hot chocolate for Greg and poured a generous glass of wine for herself. Girded with as much self-righteous temper as she could muster, she strode toward the living room.

Anxiety rose when she saw he'd shut off the lights and turned on the twinkling ones wrapped around the Christmas tree beside him. Crouched in front of the fireplace, he pumped the bellows as if he had every right to make a fire in *her* house with *her* wood, and use *her* tools to change the atmosphere from quaint to intimate and make it their space instead of hers.

"Here's your hot chocolate," she said briskly to his shadowed back.

"Thanks, babe." He looked up with a gaze as warm as the fire he stoked.

"I'm not your 'babe' here, Greg. I'm your friend, remember?"

"You don't sound too friendly to me. Seems I should have elbowed my way into your kitchen, after all."

"Why not? You elbowed your way into my parents' house to see Audrey today and bulldozed your way into mine tonight."

"Taking back the welcome mat, Chris?" He made a *tsk-tsk* sound of disapproval. "That's no way to treat a friend."

"I thought about it, Greg. We're not friends."

"No?" He stood and accepted the mug she held out. At her soft gasp, he smiled innocently. Her palm tingled where he'd flicked a fingertip before claiming the cup. Taking a sip, he licked his lips and Chris caught herself about to lick hers in response to the movement. "Ah, it's even better than Mom's. But don't tell her I said so. It'd hurt her feelings and I wouldn't want to do that.''

Chris took a gulp of wine and immediately wished she'd brought the whole bottle.

''What about *my* feelings, Greg?'' she demanded.

''Tell me what they are and I'll see what I can do about them.''

''I feel violated, that's what. This is my house and Audrey is my daughter and that's what I've got to come back to in a few days.''

''Don't you mean *all* you've got to come back to? Except for your job and your search for Super Dad, of course.''

''That's right,'' she whispered fiercely. ''It's all I've got and the last thing I need is you taking that away.''

''Let me think about this.'' He left her standing in front of the fire and sat on the couch facing it, his posture a comfortable lounge. His gaze trained steadily on her, he sipped at his chocolate. ''Why don't you sit with me?'' he asked companionably. ''Let's just sit and talk.''

''I don't want to get that close.''

''Because you don't trust me or because you don't trust yourself?''

''If you must know, both.''

''That's honest and I respect honesty above all else. It's the thing I prize most about our relationship. Sure, I admit it, I've done my best to take advantage when I can, but I've been honest about that, too. As for yourself…''

He lingered over another sip and she silently damned him for looking so natural on her couch, for making her feel so ridiculously pleased he liked her hot chocolate better than his mother's.

''Go ahead and say it,'' she challenged. ''Say that I'm

a coward who'd rather lie about her feelings than admit them."

"Actually, I think you're doing a fine job of expressing yourself. Even if they're not what I want them to be, I'd rather you expose your gut feelings than hide them from me. But I wish...I wish I understood a lot of things better. Like your choices. Why, Chris, *why* would you rather go back to living a life you told me you hated and wanted to change, when I'm offering you an alternative that—"

"Stop right there." Chris held up her hand, warding off the seductive lure of his suggestion. "The only alternative is an on-again, off-again affair. When the nights get too lonely, a stolen weekend at some clandestine meeting place before we go back to our separate lives and—"

"Why do they have to be separate? Why couldn't we work something out so we could see each other once, twice a month? We could talk, exchange e-mails in between. It'd give us a chance to see if our relationship's as dead-end as you seem to think, or if what we've got is as special as I believe it to be. Time would tell, Chris. Give us some time."

"I can't do that." She drank deeply, willed the wine to give her the borrowed courage she needed to stand firm. "I'm getting very tired of telling you this, so for once would you just listen. You don't have a child to consider, I do. Last night, you brought up some good points about what children learn from their parents. But they learn moral standards from them, too. If you came here, we'd end up in bed. Audrey would discover us sooner or later."

"Probably." His pause was weighty and Chris felt the gathering momentum of a bomb about to be dropped. "But by then, she'd surely realize that her mother was sleeping with a man for reasons other than lust. And as for that man, me, she'd know I care deeply for her mother. Who knows?

In time, she might even decide, along with you, that I'm the perfect daddy for her.''

"No," Chris said emphatically. "I want you to stay away from her, Greg. And after tonight—'' Her hand shook as she tossed down the remains in her glass. Almost choking on the words, she made herself say, "After tonight, I want you to stay away from me.''

CHAPTER SEVENTEEN

CHRIS BRACED HERSELF for the hurl of his mug into the fireplace, the lover spurned to surge off the couch and oppose her with an eruption of fury.

But no, he simply put down his mug and tapped his fingers to his lips. Her own fingers wrapped so tightly around the glass it was a wonder the stem didn't snap.

"Okay," he said, shrugging slightly.

"Okay?" she repeated, certain she hadn't heard right.

"Sure. If after tonight you want me out of your life, gone I'll be. But you're stuck with me for—" he checked his watch "—a few more hours before the charter plane I booked leaves for Dallas. No commercial flights out that late, so you'll have to endure my company another hour there. You can take a cab if you don't want me to drive you to your folks'."

For a moment Chris was speechless. Nothing was as she had expected. Not the defensive words she'd heard come out of her mouth before she fully considered them. Not his easy capitulation. And not the horrible sinking sensation in the pit of her stomach.

The least he could have done was argued with her, fought for the two nights they had remaining.

Two nights she had thrown away.

Chris was suddenly as furious with herself as with him. She wanted those nights back. Desperately. But her pride was at stake, and backing down would mean she'd have to swallow it.

Even now, her pride demanded she strike back and incite the argument she wanted.

"So much for your future vision, Greg. You obviously hold as fast to potential relationships as you do to marriage."

"Hey, you're the one who insisted I drop it."

Not so much as an "ouch" his way. Unlike her, who wanted to pinch herself black-and-blue for saying what she'd programmed herself to think before weighing the consequences. And now she didn't even have a decent comeback.

"I shouldn't have accepted these clothes."

"Then give them back." He leaned forward, opened his palms; his gaze flinty, dark, it matched his challenge. "Go ahead, Chris. Take them off. Then put on whatever it is you wear in the role you play around here."

The role you play around here. Was it a role she played here? Or was it a role she was playing now, dressed up and acting out in a way she'd never imagined herself capable of?

Returning his level stare, Chris realized she wanted to hit him. She wanted to tear off their clothes and wallow all over the floor, bodies angry and hot, fighting each other for supremacy.

Who was she? What kind of woman was she to feel these primal urgings? And what kind of man was he to make her crave them? God, she didn't know. Greg made her so confused.

"I think that's the best idea you've had all night," she said unevenly. Yes, go to her room, put on her own clothes, wrap herself in the familiar and get some breathing space. It was absolutely the best thing she could do.

Chris took a halting step away from the fireplace.

"Where do you think you're going?"

"To my room. Alone." Alone, just as alone as she'd been there for years. For Greg to step a single foot inside her bedroom was unthinkable. "Feel free to read a magazine or something. I'll be back when I'm back."

"I don't think so." He pointed a finger to where she stood. "Here. You take them off here. In front of me."

"I can't do that!"

"Why not? It's not like I'm going to see something I haven't seen plenty of before."

That wasn't true, she wanted to rail at him. To bare herself here, she would be stripped of more than clothes. Here, she was so much more vulnerable than in a hotel room.

The scent of drying pine needles and woodsmoke mingled with the memory of hushed, intimate laughter. The memory slipped away before she could cling to its bittersweet hold. Greg's waiting silence was broken only by the sound of wood crackling in the hearth, the tap of her nails drumming the wineglass.

"I don't want to undress here because..." Chris took a steadying breath. "Because I don't want you to watch. And—and this is where I got pregnant with Audrey. Here, in this room, beside another Christmas tree."

"All the more reason, then."

"What do you mean?"

"Quite simply, you accepted what I gave you and now you regret it—apparently much the way you feel about ever getting involved with me. If you're shunning my gift, and us, I deserve to watch you do it. As for you, what better statement of independence could you make? Free from the past you kept yourself tied to, free from any ties to me."

Eyes narrowed, lips thinly smiling, he touched himself. A lingering stroke over his groin that made her belly draw tight and her fingers pulse with the urge to grip him.

"Don't worry," he said with a mocking chuckle, "I

won't be taking this out or putting it in. So, go ahead, off with my clothes, on with yours.''

When she hesitated, he snarled, "Take them off! Goddamn it, do it now or leave them on and keep them. Where're your guts, Chris? Where're your guts to do one or the other?''

Goaded by his insinuation that she had none, Chris hurled the wineglass into the fireplace. The sound of its brittle shatter coincided with her cry of "You wanna see guts? Then look all you like and see them.''

Grappling with the sash at her waist, her hands were shaking so hard that she wished fiercely for a pair of scissors to cut the beautiful binding in two. When it was finally undone, she flung the length of velvet at him. His gaze simmered with the same white-hot light she'd seen as he'd pretended to be a vengeful warrior tying her to four saplings.

But that was pretend and what she saw in him now, what she felt in herself, was real. They were engaged in a battle of wills and she realized that Greg had employed yet another subtle maneuver to bend her will to his.

He wanted her naked. He wanted her to beg him to make love to her and then beg some more—for the two nights back. And he wanted her to leave in the clothes she had come in.

Oh, yes, she knew *exactly* what he wanted. Chris was disturbed to realize that for now, at this moment, they wanted the same thing. Minus the begging.

Chin lifting, back straight, she held herself with pride. Her gaze challenging, she watched the shift of his eyes to her hands as they slid over the swell of her breasts.

Taunting him, she stroked down the length of her body until ever so slowly she raised the hem to just above her knees. Holding it there, she stepped out of the slippers, lightly rubbing her legs against each other. Then she parted them.

She smiled upon hearing his muted groan and inched up the velvet with a procrastination certain to bring him to the knees she wanted him on. Chris counted three groans before she drew the dress over her head. And tossed it to his feet.

His eyes did not follow the movement. They were glazed, fixed on her open thighs.

She widened her stance and felt the fire's heat lick at the moisture of her own arousal. Never had she felt so glorious in the fullness of her own sensual prowess and feminine strength. And what triumph she felt in holding them over the man who had led her, challenged her, to discover this heady power within.

"Like what you see?" she asked in a throaty murmur.

"I..." Like it? He coveted it. Greg told himself not to watch anymore. Not the way she baited him with the caress of her palms to her breasts, the intentionally seductive removal of the chemise. And he had to be a glutton for punishment to stare ravenously at her fingertip touching once, just once, the peak of her cleft.

"What are you doing?" he demanded in a voice so guttural he didn't recognize it as his own.

"Only what you want to be doing to me." Her laughter low and sultry, she fanned open her lips. "I'll let you, Greg. *If* you promise not to do anything else...unless you ask first and I agree. Certainly not your style, I realize. But that's the rule and this game's up if you break it."

Jesus, he thought, the woman had discovered she held a whip. And what a fast learner she must be, bringing him to heel with the crook of her finger and without a glimmer of mercy.

Standing, Greg grimaced. He had a raging hard-on and

it hurt like hell to walk the few feet it took to reach her. Strange that he towered over Chris, but she seemed as tall or taller than himself. Something had definitely happened to tip the balance of power between them. Maybe he could figure it out later. For now he could barely think.

"I didn't say you could touch me there," she whispered.

"I'm not touching you." And he wasn't. His palms traced her arms in a phantom caress, stroked without contacting the warmth of her skin, which gave way to the rise of gooseflesh. A current of energy so strong it was electric leapt between them as over and around he passed his palms, bathing her back and breasts with the charge of kinetic sensation.

At her belly, he stopped, hovered. Unbidden, a vision filled his mind and pulled at his heart. Chris, her belly rounded and full, their baby growing inside her—testimony to the purity of passion, the destiny of two souls bonded, the miracle of life. And a new life for him, enabling him to prove himself worthy as a father, a man who was committed and would never stray from his mate, his lover.

Greg swallowed hard. The vision was pure torment, just as Chris was standing there, enticing him with all the possibilities and refusing him access, eluding his every attempt to have and to hold.

Forcing himself not to grip her to him, he cupped her pubis and finger-stroked her with the delicate maneuver he knew she responded to best.

Several minutes passed and Chris was breathing erratically when she faintly protested, "I said you could only touch me there once."

"It's still once." Deepening his intimate massage, he pointed out, "You didn't mention any time limitations."

"All the same, I think you're cheating."

What did he have to lose? Taking the risk, Greg said

with conviction, "I would never cheat on you, Chris. If that's part of what's holding you back, let it go. I'm not the man I used to be. And you're not the woman you were a week ago. We're good for each other, so damn good."

A sad sigh mingled with her moan. "We're good together in bed, Greg, but we can't live there."

She moved against his hand while unzipping his pants. When she dipped inside to release him, he caught her wrist.

"I said I wouldn't be taking that out."

"You're not. I am."

On a breathless little catch, she added, "I want you to come." But rather than feel subjugated by her whim, he found a transcendent freedom in the searing jolt of release.

Through slitted eyes, he had watched her wield the control he had given her over his body, elation rife in her smoky gaze as she exulted in that power.

Power was addictive, as he well knew. Chris had liked it, and, strangely, he was excited by her discovery.

She released him and Greg dropped to his knees. He pressed a lingering kiss to each interior thigh, then lifted his head and whispered, "Whatever you want, it's yours."

"I...I want those two nights back."

"Done."

"And I want to keep the clothes you gave me."

"We'll forget you ever wanted to give them back." The fire cast a warm glow over the garter belt and her skin. "Anything else?" he prompted.

Her gaze veered to the Christmas tree. Voice soft and tremulous, she said, "Make love to me with your mouth."

"Here?" Knowing that she had conceived Audrey in this very place, he was somewhat amazed by her slow nod. As he took her his amazement gave way to a secret triumph.

Chris believed she was conquering the significance of this room, and he supposed she was. But what she had failed to consider was that her objective was made possible by creating a memory as indelible as the first.

Their memory. One he filled with such heart and heat, he knew she could never erase what they'd shared beside this tree. And unlike a discarded evergreen, memories were for keeps.

CHAPTER EIGHTEEN

DRIVING AWAY FROM THE hospital, Greg was still smiling. He'd been visiting his sister daily. Her delivery had been a difficult one but she was bouncing back from the emergency C-section.

Glad as he was of that, he knew the smile he couldn't wipe off his face was owed to the cute little sucker that wet on him every damn time he volunteered for diaper duty.

Despite his initial hesitation to do much baby holding, he'd found himself becoming increasingly eager to cradle the infant in his arms and coax a tiny hand to wrap around his finger. His sister had teasingly said that his off-key singing was sure to give the baby gas, and after several loud toots that left them both laughing, he'd reluctantly handed over his nephew for a feeding.

Though he'd seen her nurse his twin nieces years before, and felt awkward enough to excuse himself from the room, his current reaction was different. It was a beautiful sight, the most nurturing and pure vision a human could ever behold. It had moved him deeply. Hell, he'd even had a lump in his throat.

Maybe that's why he'd decided it was time to leave and had offered to take his nieces for the day so his brother-in-law could spend some alone time with his wife and newborn son.

But he'd no sooner gotten Laura and Stephanie buckled into the back seat and driven down the street than they started to squabble over the doll both insisted they had brought along.

"Hey, double trouble, either hand that thing here or quit your fighting and share." Arm over the seat, he snapped his fingers, then opened an "I mean business" palm.

All immediately quiet, he glanced back and saw the doll nestled between the five-year-old twins.

The hell he couldn't be a good father, Greg thought. King Solomon couldn't have handled them better himself. Deciding to try out his paternal skills, he said, "Good behavior deserves a reward. How would you girls like it if I took you to the zoo?"

That won him a duet of "Goody, goody" and a rise in his confidence. It rose amply for him to entertain a sudden idea.

Acting on it before he lost his nerve, Greg took a roundabout route that had Laura saying in dismay, "I thought we were goin' to the zoo."

"Me, too," Stephanie joined in. "This is the way to Grandma and Grandpa's."

"Not quite," he hastened to assure them. "I thought we'd swing by another grandparents' house. I know a little girl who's visiting there, just about your age. Let's go see if she's home and wants to come along." Their enthusiastic response helped steady the limb he was going out on.

Chris had been adamant that he steer clear of Audrey but she couldn't make too much of a fuss in front of three little girls over a simple invitation to join them at the zoo. Still, as he took the twins like so much arsenal to the front door, Greg knew he might very well be courting her protective wrath.

"Hi!" Audrey greeted them with a grin. The coat she had on implied she'd either just returned or was about to leave. Hoping greatly for the former, Greg stooped down and picked up a mitten she had dropped.

"I brought some new friends for you to meet, Audrey." In the midst of introductions, Rick appeared behind her and Greg stood, bracing himself for a repeat of sparring directed at his character and intentions.

"I hope you don't mind, Rick, but I was just passing by and thought Audrey might like to spend some time with my nieces since she doesn't have any playmates around."

"Hey, that's great." Rick offered his hand and his friendly man-to-man grip was as surprising as his chuckle when the small glove wedged between their palms. "Glad you caught us. It's just Audrey and me hanging out today and we were headed for the zoo."

"What a coincidence! So were we." Coincidence? More like heaven cutting him a break. "Care to make it a five-some?"

"Sounds good to me. What do you think, half-pint?"

Both men's gazes followed the three girls racing each other to the car.

"I think that's a yes," Greg said, not bothering to hide his grin. It faded as he asked, "Where's Chris?"

"She just left with Mom and Tammy. Audrey didn't want to go along and just between us, I think she's about to OD on her mother's TLC. Anyway, they talked Chris into clearing out some clearance racks. My guess is at Sears...not Neiman's."

Caught off guard by the silent question in Rick's raised brow, Greg awkwardly cleared his throat. "Only the best for the best," he slowly replied.

"That's good enough for me." Rick gave an approving nod.

It wasn't like him to ask another man for advice or reveal

his deeper feelings, but this was Chris's brother and a potential ally. Hard as it was, he told it like it was.

"I, uh, wish Chris felt the same way. I care about your sister, and not just a little. Unfortunately, she doesn't think I'm cut out to be more than a...a—"

"Fling?" Rick bluntly supplied.

"That's not what it is to me."

"If I didn't think so, I would have stepped in before now. Not that I wasn't tempted after Chris kept tiptoeing in at two in the morning and Tammy let me in on her whereabouts once I sweet-talked it out of her."

"Chris actually told her where we were?"

"Mother hens never go anywhere without leaving all the particulars in case of an emergency."

Greg felt a mixture of discomfort and satisfaction that their private sanctuary was sibling knowledge. "I don't like sneaking around as if there's something to hide. There's nothing shameful about my feelings for Chris and if I had it my way our relationship would go way past a hotel door."

"She should know better than to be there but I've gotta give you points for taking her to one with some class."

"She's a class act," he said, quick to defend Chris. Seemed to him that Rick disapproved more of his sister's behavior than he did the man who was responsible for it. Greg didn't like that. "She's also a grown woman who can make her own decisions without needing her brother's approval."

They exchanged a level stare until Rick chuckled softly. "You're looking better and better to me, Major. In fact, you're starting to look so good, I'll give you a little tip. Audrey's the one you really need in your corner. She's got a lot more clout with her mom than me."

"So I figured. Dropping over to see Audrey wasn't exactly accidental. I want you to know that I appreciate you letting me have some time with her.'' He glanced at the car and waved back at the three little hands motioning them to hurry up. ''But in case you're not aware, I've been put on notice that Audrey is off-limits for me. Chris doesn't want her to form any attachments that aren't guaranteed to stick. She's not going to like it when she finds out I spent the afternoon with her daughter.''

''Unless you tell her, I see no reason why she has to find out. A word to Audrey from me and she'll keep quiet—she likes secrets almost as much as bubblegum jelly beans.'' After a pause he added, ''By the way, you get points for those, too.''

As they walked toward the car, Rick went on to say, ''My sister's a good woman, Greg, but as a mother she's overly protective. I think losing her husband is what's made her a little obsessive about keeping Audrey safe. It's a blind spot of hers, so try not to take this back-off thing with Audrey too personally.''

''But I do. I take it very personally, Rick.''

''If I were in your shoes, I'm sure I would, too.'' The slap to Greg's back was one of commiseration. ''Tell you what, while we're at the zoo I'll keep an eye on your nieces and give you a chance for some one-on-one with Audrey.''

''I owe you for that.''

Two hours later, Greg decided he owed Rick big time. As he took a lick of the ice-cream cone Audrey had insisted on sharing, he tried to remember when he'd ever felt so completely accepted and just simply *right* with a child.

He couldn't draw any comparisons because there were none. And Lord knew, nothing could compete with those adoring brown eyes staring up at him, the wistful little voice saying, ''Gee, you're big, just as big as Superman. I bet if you wanted, you could touch the clouds.''

His heart squeezed even as his chest puffed out. She made him feel like Superman; and what a rare feeling that was, almost believing he could leap buildings and take to the sky, exalted there by the wonder in a little girl's eyes.

Greg stretched high, then shook his head. "Seems I can't quite reach it. But maybe you could." Leaning down, he opened his hands. "How about it, sweetheart? Want to try?"

Audrey was in his arms faster than Superman could change in a phone booth. Over his head she went with a giggle of delight as he said, "Up you go on the top row!"

She rode on his shoulders until it was time to leave and it was with regret he gave up her slight weight to buckle her into the seat while Rick did the same with the twins.

"That was a great ride, even better than a Ferris wheel. Thanks lots." For such a little thing, Greg decided Audrey packed a punch with her hug. Fact was, he felt like a fist had landed in his chest when she whispered in his ear, "I sure do like you. Please make Mama let us be together again. I can't ask since Uncle Rick told me this was a secret visit and Mama's not s'posed to know."

"I sure do like you, too, Audrey," he whispered back. "And I want more time together just as much as you. But I can't make any promises. The problem is, your mother… Well, she loves you an awful lot. And she seems to think it would be better for you to get close with someone besides me."

"But I don't want somebody else. I want you. I think you'd be a super-great da—"

"Shh." Greg laid a silencing finger against her lips. Pulling slightly away, he willed himself not to turn from the confusion and hurt in her soulful brown gaze. Only a child would be so open, so disarmingly honest. And only a heartless adult would abet a child's hope for a dream that reality could shatter. He couldn't do that to her; no more than he could let Audrey think he was rejecting her, as obviously she did.

"Listen, sweetheart," he said gently. "These things take time to happen, just like your teeth growing back in, and that means we have to be patient. Just remember that no matter what, I think you're very, very special, and anyone who could have you for their little girl is the luckiest person alive." Greg pushed back the pale, fine hair from her forehead and softly kissed her there. "Okay?" he asked.

"Okay." The spark of determination he saw told him that Audrey wasn't going to give up easily. *Good.*

"Then give me a high five." They slapped palms and in that brief joining he felt an uncanny sense of alliance, a connection that bound them in a shared cause.

As he drove, Greg noticed that the twins' animated chatter emphasized Audrey's silence. He glanced in the rearview mirror and their gazes met. She grinned and he wondered how long she had been watching him; if his unguarded expressions had revealed the turmoil of his thoughts.

Reaching over the seat, he patted her knee. Audrey caught his hand and squeezed it.

If Chris didn't break his heart, Audrey would.

Their destination reached, he helped her out of the car, intent on making a fast getaway before she got to him more than she already had.

"Thanks for a great day, Audrey," he said, playfully tousling her hair.

"It was the best," she pronounced. "And so are you."

God, how he wanted that to be true. But the fact simply was, he wasn't the best. He was only a man wanting to be the best he could be, a man who had fallen in love with a woman who doubted him even more than he doubted him-

self. A man who could easily love the child whose unconditional belief in him almost made him believe it wasn't
misplaced.

Almost. Greg shook his head. "I'm sorry, Audrey, but
I'm afraid there are better people out there than me."

"That's not true!" she protested.

"How do you know?"

Her little arms went around his legs and she looked up
at him as if he were some great god in the sky.

"'Cause when I was on your shoulders, I touched the
clouds."

Greg couldn't get any words out and so he lifted her up
and let Audrey imagine she touched the clouds once more
while he pretended he was Superman a little longer, just
for the space of time it took him to deposit her at the front
door.

A quick hug and he was out of there. Halfway to the
car, a clamp on his shoulder stalled him.

"Hang in there, man."

"Yeah," Greg gruffly replied. "Thanks for everything,
Rick. It was, uh…it was a really special day."

"And not just for you. Here, I've got you something to
remember it by."

Greg took the small mitten that Rick held out, clasped it
in the haven of his palm.

"Thanks, I'll consider it my good-luck charm."

Quickly, he drove away from the house he would return
to in a few short hours and pretend along with Audrey that
something wonderful hadn't transpired between them.

It had been so hard to leave her, yet he'd left with so
much more than he had come with. Greg knew he had
given something to Audrey, as well. Himself. The best of
him, buried so deep he hadn't known it was there until she

had dug it up with the ease of a child building a castle from sand.

The image of a wave hitting carefully piled white grains came at him and he could see the castle's threatened devastation.

Chris was that wave. Or rather, it was her consuming need to protect, her fear of allowing herself to love again.

Greg's jaw tightened. He couldn't make her love him. But intimacy was a doorway that could lead to emotional journeys and weaken defenses.

Tonight, he determined. Tonight he would push that door wide open. If Chris knew what was behind it, she'd surely slam it shut and run for safety with the speed of light.

And so, he'd entice her inside as he had before and once she was in too deep to escape, he would take them to a place where defenses had the substance of tin soldiers on straw ponies.

They wouldn't stand a prayer of surviving. Not when he could cut a path to her heart with the ultimate weapon: intimacy. A very unique expression of it. One that would strip away all barriers and lay their souls bare in a sexual arena where few lovers would ever dare venture.

CHAPTER NINETEEN

WHY HAD SHE AGREED to this—this crazy bedroom game? Was it because after tonight there would be only one remaining and she wanted to sow as many wild oats as she could before living out the rest of her straight-and-narrow days? Or was it because she'd developed a taste for adventure, the arousing hint of the forbidden in a dangerous liaison?

He hadn't touched her once since picking her up and already she was aroused. It was as though the absence of his touch made her want him that much more.

Perhaps that's why she had agreed to the fantasy he had requested—a fantasy that smacked of the forbidden. Yes, danger was in the air, invading her senses with the visceral thrill of a risk. Odd that she was a little scared but felt a sense of security, too. Maybe it was because of the password.

Roses. Chris's trust in him was ample to believe he would stop if she said, "Roses." *Why hadn't she cried "Roses" in her living room last night, or screamed it at the top of her lungs later, in her bedroom?* No matter that his lovemaking had been so tender it had bordered on sweet, why hadn't she called him off when reality had been ten times more dangerous than this exotic fantasy?

She squinted to better see the dark rider, all shadows and shifting movement in the unlit suite. Only they weren't in their motel room, either.

"Tell me where we are," he softly commanded, his

voice holding a note of some secret mystery. And much of it was a mystery, their given roles to unfold as they went. All that was certain was the simple muslin blouse and long, full skirt he had brought for her to wear, a complement to the fantasy setting and century they were to pretend they were in, and an oil lamp, the only prop. As for the other item—she suddenly found it difficult to talk.

"Tell me where we are," he repeated. There was a hypnotic quality to his whisper. "In what time are we living?"

"It...it's the late 1800s."

"Yes. Now I want you to describe our surroundings."

"We're in a stable, near the Mexican border." When he remained silent, she took it as her cue to draw the setting in their minds. "It's a large, fine stable filled with riding gear, sacks of oats, a long row of stalls. A few are empty but most are housing purebred horses. Arabians, I think."

"Arabians, yes. Most are quiet now, since it's dark. A few are moving about, a little disturbed by our presence, but their movements are muffled by the hay under their hooves. Fresh bales are stacked near us. Can you smell them?"

She sniffed and imagined she could, that and more. "I smell clean straw. And leather. A storm is brewing and the air, it's heavy with the earthy scents around us."

"Earthy," he murmured. A match flared and illuminated his shadowed face as he held it to a cigar. Their eyes met and what she saw in his was both compelling and ominous. He shook out the match, cloaking them once more in darkness except for the glowing red tip that caught and held her gaze. She wasn't sure if it reminded her more of a warm, glowing coal or a single, glittering serpent's eye.

"Do you mind the cheroot?"

"No, I don't mind. The smoke, it's...faintly sweet."

"And so is your cologne. Tell me what else you smell."

"You. Even from here, I can pick up traces of sweat and leather—" *and lust* "—and rain. You've just ridden in after an extended time away."

"Nearly a year. Such a long time to travel abroad and leave my ranchero in the care of an elderly father and a foreman. Your older brother, *bambina.* The two of you were orphans and my family took both of you in as children. Now, tell me why I was gone. I'll hear it from the young woman who was the reason I left."

"You left because—because you no longer thought of me as a sister, not since that night you found me at the lake, naked in the water." Lucia shivered. Yes, Lucia was her name. And she was eighteen now, nearly an old maid by current standards.

"You were angry with me," she went on. "I remember you throwing my clothes at me, saying, 'Put them on, Lucia. What were you thinking, coming here alone after dark? A stranger could have found you, done something terrible to you. Put on your things, damn it, and don't ever let me find you like this again.' I remember you turning your back but stealing several glances while I dressed. I was shaking. But it wasn't from the night air on my wet clothes."

"Then what was it?" he asked in a silky whisper.

"You seemed like a stranger. A stranger who had found me and wanted to do something unspeakable to me."

"Most unspeakable, Lucia," he assured her. His draw on the cheroot, a brightening red circle, seemed to concur with his carnal desires. "You were only sixteen and there I was, a man of twenty who had knowledge of harlots and brothels. The acts I suddenly wanted to commit with you, no proper woman would do. And you were not only proper, you were like my kin. But after that moment, I never thought of you as a sister again. You were the water nymph in my dreams and I damned you each time I woke up with my sheets soaking wet. Finally, I couldn't bear to see you and not touch you.''

She laughed softly, accusingly. "And so you did touch me. You gave me my first kiss. In the glade beside the lake, it became our meeting place. You fondled me there. And it was there that I offered you my virginity.''

A moment passed before he said, "But I refused.''

Why? she wondered. But then the answer came; she knew it because she knew him. Honorable though he was, he was equally selfish in his need for absolute possession.

"Yes,'' she agreed. "You refused. You said it was your fault things had gotten out of hand and it was for the best that you leave. I begged you not to go but you did.''

"If only you'd been a woman who knew her own heart, I would have stayed.'' The regret in his voice gave way to a startling anger. "Did you actually think I didn't notice how you flirted with the shopkeeper when I took you to town?'' he snarled. "And those boys at the church social, the barn-raising dance, God, what that did to me. You were trying out your feminine wiles and the hell if I was about to risk getting you with child when you were still such a child yourself. So, tell me, who have I come home to?''

In her uncertain silence, he snuffed out the cigar with an agitated grind. "I'm waiting, Lucia. Tell me if I've come home to a fickle girl...or a woman who had the sense to wait for a man who would gladly give his life to protect her.''

Of course she would have waited for a man as mature and fine as he, she started to say. But something held her tongue. Resentment, she realized. Resentment of the desertion that in her innocence she was responsible for. And he was a lusty man; had surely kept intimate company with other women while she cried herself to sleep at night, lit candles and said prayers for his safe and speedy return.

Oh, yes, she resented this man for awakening her desires, then leaving, forcing her to realize that the suitors who had come to call were callow boys, their kisses chaste and passionless.

"Wait for you?" she taunted him. "Why would I waste my time waiting for an arrogant old man—or should I say, stud? You do smell a bit like one, sniffing the tail of a mare who finds you not the least bit appealing. Perhaps if you took a bath I could tell the difference between you and these horses in their stalls. But you'd best be quick about it. A lover awaits and I'm already late for our rendezvous."

"Who is he?" His demand was so sharp, so harsh, she jumped. But he couldn't see the apprehension sure to be etched in her face, nor sense the delight she took in his jealous response. Toying with him, she said nothing.

"Answer me, damn it!" The sound of a match struck roughly against a boot's sole gave way to the rattle of a glass chimney. Moments later he was bathed in lantern light. His countenance could have been that of a demon risen from hell, the blue-white light flickering over him, flames from the nether world he'd sprung from to exact a frightful vengeance.

Indeed, she felt the tug of fear. Danger was near. *He* was the danger. Tearing off the white riding shirt he wore, the expanse of his chest terse and awesome, he bore down on her, raw virility personified. His paces, measured and slow, the crunch of hay, the nicker of horses filled her ears.

She told herself to run, quickly, to hide herself in the night from this familiar stranger in black breeches and high leather boots. But she couldn't move, couldn't force her gaze from him.

Or the riding crop he tapped into his open palm. She'd never seen one quite like it—thin leather strips, perhaps a foot in length, dangling from the tip, both exotic and menacing. Two halting steps back she took, and he advanced at a leisurely stride that was somehow more threatening than if he'd lunged. His was the walk of a man who was confident in his just retribution. And her inescapable fate.

Whatever it might be, she knew in her heart he would never truly hurt her, his jealous rage no match for the tender emotions he bore her. And so, she tilted her chin up, faced him with the arrogance of his most prized and spirited steed. The one only he could ride. Bareback. For not even he could break it of its unwillingness to accept a bit or a saddle.

The tips of his boots nipped her bare toes. Glowering down at her, he growled, "What man has claimed what was, and is, rightfully mine?"

"Ask me no secrets and I'll tell you no lies." Her eyes slitted catlike and she licked her lips—only for them to part in a startled O at the crack of the tassels whipping the air. The slow shake of his head, the light tap of the crop against her thigh, gave her to feel she was in the presence of a strict taskmaster who regretted his wayward charge was in dire need of a lesson to remember.

"You have been a very bad girl, Lucia. But fortunately for you, I am a fair man. I'll forgo the punishment you've earned on two conditions. First, I want to hear you say that you love me and will never betray me again. And then, I'll have your confession. Five words—'I was a bad girl.' All or nothing, you know that's my way. It's your choice, *bambina.*"

His stern whisper carried over the air. How far was she willing to go to mend the damage done before they did more? That was the real question, and one she couldn't possibly answer to his satisfaction. Or hers. Compassion for them both competed with an urge to rebuke him for putting her in such an impossible position.

No, she would not tell him what he wanted to hear. Even if it might hold some truth, putting aside the past wasn't that easy. And besides, if she obeyed, he would become the man she knew and she rather liked this dominating side of him.

"No, I won't say it."

A poignant disappointment flickered in his gaze before he swiftly disguised it with a look of stoic resignation. With a heavy sigh, a weary shake of his head, he stroked the dangling leather over her breasts.

Her nipples beaded and her pulse tripped madly at the certainty of his purpose as quietly he said, "Very well, then, prepare for a punishment as naughty as yourself. Bend over."

She did not cower or cringe, but defied him with challenge clearly etched in her face, posture and voice.

"Make me." She laughed seductively.

"Ah, Lucia, when will you learn? That just earned you a worse spanking." He grabbed for her and she slapped at him. But now it was he who laughed. A foot taller and a hundred pounds heavier, he was smug in his superior strength. He captured her hands easily, bound both wrists with a single huge fist, the other holding the crop which he brought down smartly on her thigh when she aimed a knee between his legs.

"I said, bend over." The whip brushed her neck and he twined hard fingers in her hair. His tug of it was amazingly tender, yet firm and brooking no contention.

Her head pulled back, his breath was on her, smelling of smoke and lust, and mingling with her own halting gasps.

"Mind me and I'll take that into consideration. I can be generous." He rubbed her hip with the source of his generosity and she felt a scintillating sensation spread through

her womb, expanding and making her greedy for the ful-
fillment of his threat.

But suddenly he let go, allowing her to fight him again
if she so chose. He would like that, she knew; a struggle
would amuse him, further distend his already rampant
arousal.

It was a subtle retaliation, and she was sure he wouldn't
forgive it easily, to acquiesce rather than scratch and bite
as he so dearly loved her to do. Her senses pitched to their
keenest measure, she could almost taste the pithy sob of
defeat when she succumbed to the sweet lash of his whip.

"I am not a bad girl," she sniffed, coy in her disdain.
"I'm a good girl, and you're a terrible man to spank me
when I am so well behaved. Obedient I will be, but no
matter how hard the strike of your rod, never will I give
in to you."

His mocking chuckle naysayed her vow, as did the teasing whisper of the leather on her backside once she'd
turned. Heart beating fast and furious, she heard the sound
of his belt hit the hay-strewn floor, the thud of heavy boots
discarded, the shift of his movements as he rid himself of
the riding breeches. And then she felt the grip of his hands
on her skirt, pulling it over her head, taking the muslin
blouse along with it, and tossing them the way of his
things.

"Widen your stance," he whispered. Though her legs
had begun to shake, she did, and felt his knees nuzzle the
backs of hers. Guided by the gentle pressure of his hand,
she lowered her head and was rewarded with his approving
murmur, a word of coaxing instruction. "Bend your
legs…that's good. Your palms, cup your knees with
them." His body heat lapped achingly near and a fine
quiver of anticipation took hold. "Are your eyes closed?"

"Yes."

"Open them. Look on the floor and see what you find while I give you what you've asked for. By lesson's end, you might even discover your heart. You've wounded mine, you know. It's lying there at your feet."

She fixed her gaze on their silhouettes illuminated by the lantern and was held in thrall by the play of shadow and light. His palm slid over and down her belly, then lower to sweep once, twice, light finger-licks that knew just how to stir and make her need.

And then she felt it, the insistent but miserly push of male invasion. When she instinctively bore down, he countered with an equal withdrawal.

"So compliant," he murmured. "Perhaps I was wrong and should spare you the rod."

"No! No, I deserve it. I am the bad girl that you say."

"Shame on you," he scolded her in a low, sharp whisper and dealt her the first velvet stroke of the leather. Hardly more than a brush, he mated it with a small thrust. "But more the shame on me if I don't make you see the error of your ways. Such a pert little ass you have, saucy as that mouth of yours that has a tendency to talk back. Only, you're so quiet now...not even a choice name for me? Or is it that you realize no other man could ever care for you the way that I do? One confession made, are you prepared to make the other?"

At his slight withdrawal, she instantly said, "Bastard. You cocky bastard—" and moaned in delight at the teasing sting between her cheeks, the feel of him entering her with such stunning force she lost her balance. But there were his hands, steady on her hips as he slowly eased out to where he had been before.

"'Cocky bastard,' is it? So far I've been lenient. Too lenient, I believe. Take back what you said, or you'll have to suffer the consequences for your disrespect."

"Never, you son of a—" Her breath rushed out at the caress of his thumb. Then came several light lashes, the twist of his wrist applying equal chastisements to either side of her bucking derriere as he began to hump her in earnest.

"You bad girl. You beautiful, wicked girl. You deserve this for making me love you, need you, and refusing to love or need me back. Sweet Jesus, you're wet. At least you need this much from me. Need it more…more. *More.*"

Even in the midst of his furious possession, some part of her mind wondered how much of his avowed love and need was fantasy, how much was truth wrenched free in the heat of the moment. But the heat of the moment was such, she didn't care. She felt loved, consumed by the magnitude of it, as his mad rutting kept time with the delicate dance of the whip.

Suddenly, she winced. A single snap laid a stinging path across her buttocks and she cried, "Roses!"

Immediately, she heard the whip hit the floor. Just as immediately, he gentled his thrusting.

The password spoken, Chris was sorry to end their game and yet she was stunned by the wonder of the bond she felt with him. It was intimacy beyond her comprehension. A shriek of release formed in his name won his ultimate generosity.

He felled her to the ground and, with a lift of her hips, pressed until she was full of him. Buried inside her to the hilt, she felt his kisses to her hair, heard his ragged groans as he came and came.

Ecstasy gloved by ecstasy, his chest slumped against her back. Her cheek to the floor, her eyes wide open, Chris stared at the silhouette of their joined shadows while the red mist of unbridled passion slowly receded, amazement and confusion stealing into its place.

She didn't understand what had happened, but it was something subtly momentous.

"What have we done?" she whispered.

Greg rolled off her, cradled her in his arms to share the aftermath of a savagery that was strangely bittersweet. He knew what had happened. And though he hadn't won the war, he'd gotten a fair share of the spoils he'd been after.

"You feel good tucked against me like this." Better than good, she felt perfect. Stroking back her hair, he kissed her softly, soundly, then whispered, "Did I hurt you?"

"No. Except for the last one. It stung."

"When I heard you yelp, I was ready to get rid of the crop before you could say 'Roses.' I'd never hurt you for the world. Tell me you know that, Chris."

"If I didn't believe it, I never would have agreed to the fantasy." She went very still. "It was a fantasy, wasn't it?"

"Yes and no. We did what we did and now it's part of who we are."

"But what did we do? You didn't answer me when I asked, but I get the feeling you know something I don't."

"I think I do." Slipping off the condom he had loathed to put on, Greg wondered how much he should say. This was terra incognita for her, but in lots of ways for him, too.

"Well? Are you going to tell me or not?" she pressed.

"You know, babe, I like it when you get pushy with me. You've got that rare ability to go after what you want, once you decide you want it and not come off like a bitch. Just one of the reasons I'm so crazy about you."

"Greg..." she said in that warning tone he found irresistibly cute. He couldn't imagine a kid being sufficiently intimidated by it to straighten up and behave. He'd be good at putting his foot down, balancing discipline with a generous quota of back pats and hugs. Between him and Chris, they could make a fine team of parents; he just needed more practice like he'd had today. The only problem was convincing Chris.

"Okay," he said slowly, painfully aware of his limited time to do much convincing. "It was an object lesson. The whip, or cat, was the teaching tool—for both of us. What it *wasn't* was a kinky bit of S & M, because that's shallow. What happened between us goes a lot deeper than that. We discovered magic."

"Magic?"

"Magic and more," he confirmed. "Your trust in me had to go beyond the ordinary and my protectiveness toward you had to be greater than my desire. The game was a means to an end, a search for a deeper intimacy than most people are comfortable with. I wonder...has this left you feeling uncomfortable or disturbed?"

"A part of me says that's exactly how I should be feeling, but..." He felt her head shake a "No" against his chest, the fan of her breath there as she confided, "But that's not how I feel."

"Tell me," he whispered.

"Close. So very close to you. I guess if anything disturbs me, that's what it is. And to tell the truth, it's beyond me how something so...sexually beyond the pale can seem so emotionally holy."

Holy. To hear her say it, what hope it gave him. She was quiet for a while, but then he heard a catching little sniffle. "I—I don't think I'll ever be able to see a rose again and not remember this."

"Good." He tilted her face up and brushed aside a single tear. "And while you're at it, remember something else. We don't just have sex—we have sacred sex." Swallowing hard, he forced himself to say the hardest words he'd ever said in his life: "When you get back to Lubbock and go in search of that father you don't think I can be, it might be a good idea for you to sleep with another man or two."

Her expression stricken, she said, "How can you talk about our sex being sacred in one breath and push me toward another man's bed in the next?"

"With great difficulty, that's how. It's agony for me to even think about, but I figure it's the surest way for you to realize that what we've got together, no other relationship could ever compete with." He touched her cheek and she turned away.

"Greg. I want you to stop."

"Only if you say the password."

Her watery gaze meeting his, she whispered, *"Roses."*

CHAPTER TWENTY

"OH, MAMA, PLEE-EASE? Please let me have it." Audrey looped her arms around the big stuffed giraffe standing guard at the toy-store entrance.

Chris glanced at the price tag. "Sorry, sugar. It's way out of our price range. Let's go in and see what else we can find for the trip home tomorrow." Her voice caught on the last words. She didn't want to think about it. If she did, she'd totally humiliate herself by giving in to the tears she'd been fighting all day.

"Okay," Audrey said with a sigh. "Maybe we can find some colors and a colorin' book—one with mommies and daddies and flowers and stuff."

Mommies and daddies and flowers and stuff. Chris wasn't sure what bothered her more—Audrey's mention of "daddies" or her easy acquiescence to forgo what she really wanted. She was such an obedient child, so eager to please. Chris had always thought it a positive quality, but now she wasn't so sure. Life could be hard and kids who didn't know how to fight back were at a disadvantage once their overly protective parents weren't there to tough out their battles for them.

God, she was starting to think like Greg, she realized. Damn him, anyway, for putting such ideas in her head. Audrey was perfectly fine just the way she was. Sure, she needed a father, but her mother's love life had no bearing whatsoever on the provision of a stable home. Audrey had to come first, just as she always had, no ifs, ands or buts about it.

Shuffling through a pile of coloring books, Chris pushed aside one with a family on the front, a little girl wearing a big frown and the mother holding a newborn just beneath the heading: Oh, No! A New Baby Brother—What About Me?

"Look, Audrey, here's one with Barbie. Let's get this one, okay?"

"Okay. But can I have this one, too?"

Chris silently groaned as Audrey flipped through the pages of the baby-brother book. And then she groaned aloud when she glimpsed the giraffe loping their way. Guided by none other than—

"Special delivery for Audrey Nicholson," he called loudly when Chris tried to hustle her in the opposite direction. "Is there an Audrey Nicholson in the store? Please come and claim your stray animal. He's loose and eating all the candy!"

"Look!" Audrey shrieked, breaking free from Chris's urgent grip and racing toward the giraffe that reared up in greeting. But rather than wrap her little arms around its neck, she latched on to Greg's as he bent down, smiling broadly. She gave a big kiss to the cheek Chris wanted to slap.

How dare he? How dare he waltz in and try to buy Audrey's affection? She was just an innocent little girl who couldn't possibly realize she was a bargaining chip in an adults-only game.

Marching over, Chris said sharply, "I'm sorry, Audrey, but you can't accept gifts from…from strangers."

"But he's not a stranger," she protested, tightening her hold when Chris attempted to reclaim her daughter. *Her* daughter, damn it. "He's your friend. And he's my friend, too. Aren'tcha, Greg?"

"You bet I am," he assured her, returning Chris's glare with a level stare. "Say, sweetheart, if it's okay with your mom, why don't you call me Uncle Greg? I'm not a member of the family, but I sure wish that I was."

"Me, too!" As Audrey turned Mark's somber eyes on her mother, Chris saw a spark of defiance light up her gaze. "I wanna call you that. And it's okay with Mama...Uncle Greg."

Chris silently counted to ten and told herself that after they left the store—minus the giraffe and the infuriating man who was now the proud owner of it—she would straighten things out with Audrey.

"Audrey...sugar. Mom wants to talk to her 'friend' alone for a few minutes. Why don't you go find a few treats to eat on the way home tomorrow? We'll probably be leaving in a rush and won't have time to stop on the way."

"Can Uncle Greg come with us?" Before Chris could grind out a "No," Audrey put the question to him. "Can you?"

"I wish I could, sweetheart. But I have to get on a plane and fly to where I live. It's a long way from here."

"I've never been on a plane. I've never been anywhere 'cept here and home. Know what? It kinda smells bad there sometimes. Sure wish I could go on a plane and way up in the sky where the angels and birds live." With an oddly secret smile, she added, "But most of all, I'd like to be in the clouds. So close, I could touch 'em."

Greg's smile was an echo of Audrey's as he tweaked her nose. "Tell you what, Audrey. No promises, mind you, but I'll see what I can do to talk your mother into letting you fly way up in the sky from your home to mine and get as close to those clouds as you want."

Audrey whispered something in his ear and he whispered something back. Straining to hear, Chris felt the bite of exclusion. She knew it was childish, but still she resented them sharing a secret that didn't include her.

Neither did she like Greg reaching into his pocket and plopping a load of change into Audrey's palm. And she liked even less the way Audrey scampered off at a single "Vamoose" from Greg, stopping to flash him a grin without sparing a glance her mother's way.

"Okay, she's gone," he said, rising. "Go ahead and let me have it, but try to keep your voice down to a low roar."

"What are you doing here?" Chris demanded between clenched teeth. If she gritted them much harder, she'd probably have two more missing than Audrey. "What are you doing here and how did you find us?"

"I stopped by your place and Rick told me where I could find you. Have to confess I watched you for a while, but I was enjoying myself so I waited until I saw a chance to make points with Audrey. Which is obviously the reason I'm here."

"Well," she huffed, "you certainly didn't earn any points with me. I can't believe you! You—you—"

"Cocky bastard?" He laughed smugly as her cheeks flared red. "What's wrong, Chris? Got some trouble dealing with your little girl hugging the man who put a whip to her mama's bottom the night before?"

"Damn right, I do. What goes on between us is strictly that and has no place tainting my relationship with my daughter."

"'Tainting,' is it?" he returned with a maddening control. "Funny, last night our tainted relationship was holy. Call me stupid, but I just don't get it. Why is it that you believe your intimate life has to be this separate entity that has nothing to do with anything else?"

"Because…" She searched for an explanation but couldn't come up with anything except it was simply how she'd always viewed it. Certain he'd shoot a hole through that reasoning, she said self-righteously, "Because that's the way it is and should be, that's why."

"My, but you sound sure of yourself. Just as sure as I am that nothing could be further from the truth. Especially since once you get hitched to…well…whoever, the two of you will sleep together, right?"

"Of course. But that won't affect Audrey."

"Oh, I disagree. While she certainly won't be privy to what goes on behind closed doors, her parents' private relationship is sure to affect the overall atmosphere at home. Especially if Mama's tense and avoids her bedroom at night. And she just might notice that Mama would rather kiss and hug her than dear old Dad."

Lips thin, Chris said tightly, "I hate it when you do this."

"Do what?" he asked innocently.

"Twist and turn everything around so that you seem right and I'm wrong. How you do it, I don't know. But you do it every time, damn you."

Greg shrugged. "Hey, it's not hard. After all, I am and you are. Right and wrong, that is."

Oooohh. Chris did a slow burn. Thumping the giraffe on its head, she demanded, "So, what are you going to do with this? Something tells me it won't match your decor."

"No, but it'll look great in Audrey's room. And just maybe she'll think of Uncle Greg when she hugs it."

"You can deep-six that idea. Audrey's going to be crushed when she has to leave without this bribe of yours," she snapped.

"It wasn't a bribe," he snapped back, his composure suddenly slipping. "I gave it to her because I wanted her to have it. And I gave it to her because—because I never spoiled Arlene like that. It's too late for me with her and this was my chance to see a little girl's eyes light up the way Audrey's did. And you know what? I loved it.'' His Adam's apple worked up and down. Before she could stop herself, Chris instinctively touched his hand.

''If you're dead set on Audrey not having my gift, so be it,'' he said, kissing her hand softly, then returning it to her side. ''But Chris, you'll have to be the one to explain why she can't have what I gave her. This was my gift to Audrey, and hell can freeze over before I take it back.''

HOW IN THE WORLD did she end up carrying this thing while Audrey was perched on the ''top row''—as Greg had called his shoulders? Chris continued to wonder this as she awkwardly shifted the giraffe through the madhouse, otherwise known as a mall.

''How about a bite to eat, girls?'' In minutes, Greg and Audrey had decided on their choice in the fast-food court. While they ate and talked, seeming not to notice Chris's own absence of conversation, she again felt the nip of jealousy. Those two had something going and she wasn't in on it.

Suddenly Chris wondered if she wasn't falling victim to the same petulance Audrey had exhibited that day of their awful fight. *Grow up,* she told herself, *and be a good sport while you're at it. They're having fun and it won't last long, so don't spoil it for either of them while it lasts.*

Tomorrow she and Audrey would be gone.

And so would ''Uncle Greg.''

CHAPTER TWENTY-ONE

"SURE YOU DON'T WANT to see the New Year in with the revelers in the bar? There's quite a party going on down there and I could impress you with my knack for working a crowd."

Chris's chuckle was strained. "That's okay. I'm sure your social skills are just fine. Heck, if you can impress my brother and parents, the Queen of England probably wouldn't think twice about inviting you to dinner."

He patted his stomach. "I'm still stuffed. How about you?"

"After steaks with my folks and strawberry shortcake with yours, it'll be two days before I'm hungry again." Her own stomach growled, calling her a liar. Spending time with both sets of families while their own inevitable good-bye too fast approached had worn her nerves thin and eating had been the last thing on her mind.

"I, uh, I really appreciate you putting in an appearance for my mom and dad." Pulling her closer on the couch, he tucked her head against the crook of his neck.

Lord, but he smelled good. And the sound of his low voice, so strong and calming...dear God, how she would miss it.

"You know, Chris, they've been real curious about this old girlfriend I've been 'courting,' as Mom puts it. Hope you don't mind all those nosy questions she was asking you. I got the feeling you were starting to feel a little tense. Especially that last half hour it took to get out the door."

Chris mentally rolled her eyes. She'd thought they would never get away and escape to their suite. All that time with their families when they had next to no time left for themselves. Only good manners had kept her where she did not want to be.

"That's okay," she told him. "My family's just as bad if not worse. And besides, this is New Year's Eve and it was only right for us to spend at least a little of it with our folks. I think they were all pretty disappointed that we had plans to go to a party and couldn't share a toast with them at midnight." She pointed to the champagne bottle on the coffee table. "So, ready to party?"

"Ready as I'll ever be." When he turned her in his arms, their gazes met and she wondered if her own was as troubled as his. "But the truth is, I'm not in much of a partying mood. I'm feeling somewhat depressed."

"Me too, Greg. Me, too." She knuckled his jaw. "We're a sight, aren't we? Half an hour to the New Year and here we are, crying in our beer. Wanna make love? Maybe that would cheer us up."

"I'm not sure I can get it up just yet," he said. "If it's all the same to you I'd just as soon settle for some heavy necking and lots of snuggles, cop a few feels on the couch and—ah shit."

"Ah shit, what?"

"I forgot to pick up a box of rubbers. We used the last one last night."

"All the more reason to settle for some heavy necking and plenty of cuddles." Hugging him tightly, she said, "Actually, Greg, I'd rather end it that way. Just enjoying each other's company and not getting into an argument about where you want to go from here. I don't want to remember our last night as being spoiled by a fight. When

I look back I'd like to think of how good it was just to be together.''

"And how good it is, Chris." He kissed her softly, deeply. "Know what? You're the best company I've kept, ever. And I already promised myself that I won't spoil the night by rehashing our differences. You know how I feel about things and vice versa. We'll let it lie for now and I'll just have to gamble on distance making your heart grow fonder.''

"It's plenty fond already, big guy." Touching her nose to his, she gave him an Eskimo kiss. "Did I ever tell you how much I like you?''

"Not in so many words, but you've let me know in a thousand different ways. Like giving me half of your cheesy rags. If that's not love, what is?''

Love. He'd said it again, and not in the heat of a mind-bending fantasy. Chris ducked her head. She didn't want to think about that word and she didn't want Greg to use it. It tugged at that place she'd sewn tight that night in the car and had vowed never to let tear her apart again.

As if he sensed her feelings, Greg busied himself with the champagne.

There was no hurling of glasses into the mock fireplace, no ribald laughter or putting the bottle anywhere except on the coffee table as they saw midnight in with a toast. His simple "Here's to a new year as wonderful as the last week has been," and her, "Hear, hear" pretty much said it all.

After that, they talked about everything and nothing, hugged and kissed and fondled until his watch called it five.

"I should get you home," he said, looking seductively rumpled after all their cuddling on the couch. "You've always been in by two. Sure your family won't think I've totally corrupted you by keeping you out all night?''

"I told them it was an all-night party and we were meeting some old pals from high school."

Laughing wearily, Greg shook his head. "Seems I didn't do a good enough job of corrupting. That reputation of yours is still intact despite my best efforts. Except your neighbors are probably still talking about what happened on your porch."

"Let them talk," she said with a tight little laugh. Their time was up and they were actually leaving. Where was her breath? Why was it so hard to draw one past the constriction of her throat? And her stomach, it was so tied in knots that she'd surely throw up if she had any food in it.

Forcing herself to smile, she said brightly, "See? You have corrupted me, after all. I really don't give a damn about what old Mrs. Howard thinks. If she had a life, she wouldn't have to keep herself busy by sticking her nose into mine."

"Good for you, Chris," he said, pulling her up. Holding her close, all but crushing her to him, he whispered, "Good for you."

Hugging each other by the waists, they walked slowly to the suite's entrance. Greg opened the small closet where their coats were hung and reached inside. He stood there, just stood, his hand poised over the hangers. And then his fist smacked the adjoining wall.

"We can't leave it like this," he said hoarsely, breathing hard. "God, this is tearing me up, babe. It's tearing me up and—and—" He gripped her to him and she clung with an equal desperation. "What am I going to do without you? Jesus, I want you. I *need* you."

"Why didn't we make love?" she whispered, her hands frantic in their search of his chest, his wonderful, strong chest she'd never touch again. "We had all night and we didn't even take off our clothes. All that time and we wasted it talking, doing everything but—''

"It's not too late." His voice urgent, his palms just as urgent as they raced over her breasts with a fever to match her need. And kisses, hungry, eating kisses. His lips memorizing her face, their mouths clinging as she fumbled to release him from his pants, then holding him, stroking him, pressing his turgid flesh possessively against her belly.

"Be inside me," she pleaded while he gave up on pulling down her hose and ripped them with a fierce, savage yank. Her back to the wall, he lifted her up and she wrapped her legs around his waist.

Just before he pushed inside her, he said raggedly, "We've got no protection."

"Thank God. For once, just this once, I want to feel you without anything between us. It should be safe, my period's due in a few days."

"I'll make it safer and pull out before I come. Now hold me, babe. Hold me like you'll never let me go."

She held him as if her very life depended on it and her body accepted his fevered upthrust without resistance. She was wet for him, her womb starved and already weeping at the loss for what she had now. Again and again he thrust, each departure a painful reminder that her body would soon be empty of his presence—and so would her life.

Gripping him inside, and gripping his waist, his shoulders, Chris could feel her back hitting the wall, her head thrashing against it, the desperation surrounding them and closing in while she moaned his name, over and over. She did not want to come. Not her, not him; never did she want this to end.

She fought the inevitable as long as she could but all too soon her body opened up, then closed in a greedy fist around him where he pressed. Her hungry womb sucked at his tip and she bore down, instinct demanding he fill it. A cry of his name ripped from her throat. And then he was groaning, "Oh God, oh God," and jerking out of her.

Warm spurts on the inside of her thigh, Greg pressing hard there while she commanded herself not to force him back inside where they both wanted him to be.

His arms were shaking as he lowered her legs; neither of them capable of standing, they slumped to the floor.

"What's this?" he whispered haltingly, his fingertips trembling as they stroked her cheeks.

"I'm sorry," she said, a sob catching while the tears continued to ignore her demand to stop. Maybe if she said "Roses" they'd listen, she thought with a piercing sadness.

That only made her cry harder.

"Hey, it's okay, babe," he said, his voice a croon sweeter than a lullaby. "You just go ahead and cry until you're all cried out."

"If—if I did that then we—we might be here forever."

"That'd suit me fine," he said solemnly, and Chris struggled not to say that it would suit her fine, too.

It took a while for her tears to recede, but eventually they did. In silence they put each other back together. In silence he helped her on with her coat. In silence he handed her the empty champagne bottle with pretty pink flowers on it.

And in silence, they shared a parting glance at the room filled with the memories they had made. Then left arm in arm, never looking back after the final close of the door.

"I'M WORRIED ABOUT YOU driving home sleep-deprived, Chris. Can you put off leaving long enough to catch a few winks?" It was hard to talk.

"Actually, I'm pretty wired. Don't worry, between some coffee and the radio, we'll make the trip fine. And it's only five, six hours away." She touched his hand, which gripped and ungripped the steering wheel while the car continued to idle in her parents' driveway.

They sat there a few moments longer, neither of them seeming to know what to say. Heaven knew he didn't. But whatever it was, it sure as hell wasn't goodbye.

"I guess this is goodbye," she said, breaking the heavy silence. And then she offered her palm, sideways.

A handshake? She actually thought they could part with a handshake? Greg stared at her in disbelief.

"Don't you think that's a little formal, considering?"

Chris dropped her hand and wiped her palm on her skirt.

"What would you suggest? A farewell kiss?" Her small laugh was dry, brittle. "I don't think so, Greg. You know us. Once we get started, one thing leads to another and—"

"I love you, Chris." There it was, without warning, the one right thing to say. "You don't have to say you love me back, but I do love you and no matter what, I'll always be there for you. I'm as close as a phone call or an e-mail away."

"Greg, please. Please, don't do this. Don't make it any worse than it already is." She reached for the handle and he gripped her wrist.

"Marry me."

Chris wrenched her hand free. "This is horrible enough. Why did you have to ask me something like that when you know full well what my answer will be? I *can't* marry you!"

"Why not?" Damn, but he was losing it, losing the control he had sworn to himself he would keep. And here he was, ready to grovel, get down on his knees without a stitch of pride and beg her to marry him. The third time would be the charm, he wanted to scream. He wanted to yell at her that if she would only give him the chance, he'd prove what a good father he could be.

Screaming and yelling—yeah, that'd convince her, all right. He had to get out of here, get away from the beautiful, tormented face he was dangerously close to kissing senseless, roll down the window and get some fresh air into this car that was so crowded with raging emotions, he was choking on them.

"Never mind." Reaching past her, he flipped the handle and flung open her door. "Go on. Get out."

"Greg, I—"

"Goddamn it! You heard me. I said *get…out.*"

With a sharp cry, she lurched from the seat and ran toward the house.

He told himself not to watch until she'd gotten in safely. But he did. He told himself not to act like an asshole and peel out of her driveway. But he did. And he told himself that tears were for women, and men who cried them were weaklings, and strong as he was, he would not cry.

But he did.

CHAPTER TWENTY-TWO

THE ONCOMING MACK truck's blaring horn mingled with Audrey's scream and the squeal of tires beneath them as Chris swerved from the interstate's middle line and onto the shoulder.

Once the car had rolled to a stop, Chris gagged on the coffee and bile trying to come up. Grabbing Audrey to her, she assured herself they were still alive.

"Are—are you okay, sugar?"

"I—I'm scared, Mommy," she whimpered. "The big truck was coming at us and—and—"

"Shh, shh. Mama's sorry, so sorry." More than sorry, Chris was furious with herself. How close they'd come to being killed and it was all her fault. She should have been watching the road, not replaying that horrid scene with Greg in her mind. Just another sign that getting involved with him had been a lapse into temporary insanity and the sooner she put it behind her, the better.

What was done was done and now it was time to wise up, get her head back on her shoulders where it belonged. Thank God they were almost home. There, she could think clearly.

GREG EYED THE TELEPHONE in his kitchen. He wanted to call Chris and assure himself she and Audrey had arrived home safely. Chris had no business driving after staying up all night, and the state he'd left her in wasn't conducive to alertness on the road. If anything happened to them, he'd never forgive himself.

He picked up the phone. Put it down.

If he called, she'd surely hang up on him. But he'd go crazy worrying about them. He picked up and dialed. After five rings he was ready to hop a plane and go in search. On the sixth ring, she answered with a breathless "Hello?"

Her voice washing over him, he forced himself to say, "Sorry, wrong number."

CHRIS REPLACED THE receiver with unsteady hands. Still shaken from the near miss, she wondered if the raw edge of her nerves had made her imagine Greg's voice. Covering her ears, she screamed in silence, tried to drown the echo of *"I love you.... Marry me.... Get out."*

A tug at her arm caused her to look down. There was a wealth of insight in the somber brown eyes peering at her.

"What the matter, Mommy? Are you missing Uncle Greg?"

"He's not your uncle, Audrey." Kneeling, she clung to the little girl who was her reason for living. The one who hadn't called her "Mommy" in years but seemed as needful of a security blanket as Chris was herself. "We'll talk about it later, okay? Right now, Mommy just wants to be with you. How about a cup of hot chocolate?" A vision of Greg with a cup of cocoa assaulted her. *Damn him.* Even something as ordinary as hot chocolate was riddled with memories.

"I'm not thirsty. Can I go play with Lizabeth?"

With difficulty, she let Audrey go. Out of her arms, then out of the kitchen, out of the house. Though her child was just next door, Chris felt deserted. She needed Audrey to keep her company, to give her a sense of order while inside she was coming apart at the seams.

And what comes of those who build their lives around a child who'll eventually be gone is a pretty sad thing to witness. Insidiously, Greg's words filled her mind. Her gaze fell on the cup he had sipped from, unwashed on the countertop. She lifted the cup and her lips hovered where his had been. Quickly, she grabbed a bottle of dish soap. Scrubbing furiously, she cleaned the cup, then put it in the dishwasher for good measure.

She had to do something, keep herself busy. Seeking to rid her house of his last traces, she mopped the kitchen floor he'd walked on, shoveled out the fireplace, took off ornaments and hauled the Christmas tree out to the alley's trash bin.

Needles pricked her and she was glad for the little jabs of pain; they took her mind off the far worse pain clawing for attention that she was desperate not to give.

She willed the vacuum cleaner to suck up more than dry pine needles, to inhale and devour the memory they'd made in the living room. And then bedroom. *Why had she let him in here? Why had she let him lie on her bed?*

It was still unmade from their lovemaking. Chris jerked off the top sheet and flung it to the floor. But as she touched the bottom one, the one on which they had lain, she hesitated. And then she softly stroked the sheet.

A sob in her throat, her knees gave way. She threw herself on the bed and imagined Greg was there, holding her.

Hold me, babe. Hold me like you'll never let me go.

She had to find the strength to let him go. She had to wash the sheets that had touched him. Tomorrow. Tomorrow she'd wash them. But tonight she'd be weak and remember....

THE HOUSE WAS SPOTLESS, just as he'd left it. God, but it was like a museum around here, Greg thought. Funny, he'd never seen it that way, everything in impeccable order but a lack of warmth in the high-tech decor.

The place needed a woman's touch. Crocheted doilies covering up worn spots on some lived-in furniture, ugly panty hose draped over a towel bar, toys that got underfoot on the floor. What the damn place needed was signs of the living, sounds of laughter and even an occasional fight.

The silence around him pressed in and he continued to stroke the small mitten he held.

"Chris," he whispered, then, gripping Audrey's glove, he yelled, "Hey, babe, let's grab the kids and go get a bite!"

Yeah, lots of fun eating alone. Just about as much fun as torturing himself with visions of Audrey on his shoulders, a minivan, dirty diapers and coming home, roses in hand, to a frazzled wife.

He had to get out of here. Where, Greg didn't know, but anything was better than talking to the walls that didn't talk back and pacing through a house that was far from a home.

NEVER HAD CHRIS BEEN so glad to see Audrey off to school and get back to work herself. For the next eight hours she wouldn't have to field questions about why Mommy seemed so sad or why they couldn't go visit *their* friend. And at work she wouldn't have to remember Greg's visit with every room she entered, or the bed she had yet to change linens on.

But most important, at work she'd be too busy to think about the questions that assaulted her: Had she been too convinced of her own rightness and made the mistake of her life as a result? Could it be that he actually did love her in the ways that counted, lasted? And was it possible that she loved him just as much but was too afraid to admit it?

Quit beating a dead horse, Chris, she mentally chided herself as she poured a cup of coffee in the teachers' lounge. The answers were plain. Cutting things off was the wisest move she'd made since they'd met. And as for love, the kind that lasted? No way. A whirlwind affair did not a workable marriage make.

Marry me. The coffee lodged in her throat and Chris forced it down past the sudden lump there. She had to remember he'd asked two other women before and it must be force of habit, a weakness he had for buying into a fantasy, then wanting out once reality set in. No, she had no intentions of being another divorce statistic, nor of Audrey being a casualty of domestic war.

"The bell's about to ring, Mrs. Nicholson. Why aren't you in your homeroom? I've a good mind to report you to the principal. Or better yet, the assistant principal."

Startled, Chris whirled around and sloshed coffee onto Jerry's coat sleeve. "Oh, Jerry, I'm so sorry," she said, frantically grabbing for some napkins.

He caught her dabbing hand. "If you really want to make amends, say you'll chaperon with me at the school dance this Friday. I'll even throw in a corsage."

"I—I—" She couldn't get past the stammer, nor her gripping urge to turn him down flat. "I appreciate it, but—"

"Look, if you're worried about school policy, nobody has to know we're on a date. As far as anyone else is concerned, you had car problems and I gave you a lift. No big deal."

But it *was* a big deal, she wanted to tell him. It was a big deal that he obviously cared about the no-fraternization policy, and his PC mentality irked her. *Wait. Hold it right there.* What was she thinking? A week ago she would have been concerned about the same thing—their reputations and jobs dictating social discretion.

Greg again. Damn him, anyway. His influence was a bad one and she had to start thinking her way, not his. A date with Jerry, the most levelheaded person she knew, was exactly what she needed to get her feet on the ground where they belonged.

"What time should I expect you?" she asked, managing a halfhearted smile.

"Why don't I pick you up at five and we can have an early dinner. Someplace quiet, you know?"

Indeed she did. He meant someplace where they weren't likely to be seen and recognized. Distaste for such secrecy filled her and she felt a swift empathy for Greg and the feelings he must have had while she prattled on about her reputation and the sterling example she was compelled to set.

At the shrill sound filling the room, Chris could only think, *Saved by the bell.* Saved from her thoughts and making small talk with Jerry.

But as they departed the teachers' lounge, their date made, she found herself thinking more of what she oughtn't. Jerry had a fat butt. Chris blamed Greg for making her take notice of that. She'd never paid attention to a man's rear end until she'd hung over Greg's shoulder and realized what a work of art tight buns could be.

WORK. WORK WAS THE TONIC for all that had ever ailed him before. Only, after four days of work he was ailing worse than ever and he hadn't gotten squat done, even putting in time and a half.

Greg glanced at the clock on his desk. Nine on a Friday evening and he didn't want to stay any more than he wanted to leave. He couldn't sleep. He couldn't eat. And if he talked to the walls in his house much longer, they'd just maybe start talking back.

Clearly, he was emotionally and mentally in a place he'd never been despite his marital disasters. He wondered if Chris would have turned him down if he'd had a clean slate. Or did she think he was one of those Hollywood types who hopped in and out of marriage like other people changed clothes? If she only knew how seriously he took it, his failures making his need to succeed so much more imperative.

Hell, he was a safer bet than that Jerry jerk who surely didn't have near his experience in damage control.

Jerry. Chris would have seen him by now at school and what hell it was wondering if she was seeing him for reasons other than work. And what if she slept with him, took the advice Greg wanted to cut his tongue out for ever giving? And what if they got a hold of a faulty condom or Jerry wasn't as careful as he was and Chris got knocked up?

Imagining another man touching her, putting the baby in her he himself had begun to crave, a red rage seized Greg. Struggling to control it, he asked himself if he'd love Chris as much, still want her for his wife, if she were to become pregnant with another man's baby.

Greg pondered that unsettling question and emerged with a telling realization. Were the baby an accident, he'd blame himself, not Chris, for it. And he certainly wouldn't blame an unborn child any more than he would Audrey for having been conceived. Yes. *Yes.* He'd love Chris just as intensely and still marry her in a heartbeat.

The only thing he wouldn't be able to forgive would be if she *wanted* another man's child instead of his. He'd had his chance to try beating the odds against her cycle and he hadn't taken it, knowing that was one strategy that would be wrong, wrong. But a part of him regretted he hadn't stooped to such ruthlessness.

He'd felt the first jolt just as he left her. Replaying it again, he frowned, trying once more to remember if he'd exited before that initial spurt. At the time he'd been too obsessed with possessing her to record such a minor-yet-major detail. Ah, hell, it couldn't have been more than a drop, and though a drop was all it took to get pregnant, she'd said the timing wasn't right.

The phone rang. Grabbing for it, he prayed it might be Chris come to her senses and as senseless in love as he.

At the sound of Eileen's voice, his heart dropped flat and he damned himself for a fool.

After hanging up, Greg put his desk in order. At least he didn't have to spend the evening alone. And just maybe ex-wife number two would help him figure out how to convince Chris she was meant to be wife number three.

"WELL, GOOD NIGHT, JERRY. Thanks for a great time." Great? It had been *awful*. Worse than awful, she'd never been so bored in her life.

Chris quickly amended that. As he kissed her, a kiss that was dry as dust on her end and way too wet on his, she wasn't sure whether she was more bored or disgusted.

Disgusted, she decided, when he slid a palm down her back and over her behind. Discreetly, of course, in keeping with his furtive glances around the restaurant where he'd forgone a glass of wine and raised a brow when she'd ordered one and lit up. As for his careful survey of the bill and stingy tipping, she hadn't cared for them any more than his kissing and the butt handling that she put an end to with a quick step back.

He made a sound similar to the one he'd made when she

had laid a five on the table for the waitress—one of disapproval mixed with a hint of embarrassment, as if he'd accidentally farted and turned an accusing glare on his dog. Greg, however, would not only claim such a fart as his, he'd probably rank it on a scale from one to ten.

There she went again, Chris realized with dismay. She'd been comparing the two men all night.

"Mind if I come in?" Jerry asked, clearing his throat.

She did mind, but made herself say politely, "Maybe another time." *Not.*

"Then I'll see you at church." With that, he left and Chris breathed a sigh of relief as she let herself in, paid the sitter, and went to check on Audrey.

She was sleeping with the giraffe, the huge stuffed animal taking up most of the bed's space. A wave of tenderness made Chris's heart soften and lurch as she remembered the toy-store exchange between Audrey and Greg.

Audrey had responded with such open affection that, despite her pique, Chris had been a little amazed. Her child was usually reserved with people she didn't know, especially men, and her ready acceptance of Greg was both extraordinary and disconcerting for a mother who thought she knew best.

But did she? He had been so good with Audrey that day. Chris saw that now, looking back with the clarity of distance. Could it be, she wondered, that he had some latent paternal qualities emerging to which she had shut her eyes, her focus narrowed to old, stubbornly held parameters?

A soft kiss on Audrey's cheek, a pat of the giraffe, and Chris went to her own lonely bedroom. For being so empty it felt awfully crowded. The walls closed in and she confronted the conflicts she could no longer ignore.

The answers she'd been feeding herself lacked the substance of truth. "No more lies," she whispered. "The simple fact is he's under your skin and has a hold on your heart. You made a mistake, Chris. A really big mistake. So, what are you going to do about it now?''

Marriage was a possibility, she decided. But they needed more time together, the three of them, to make such a binding commitment. Time was the answer. The distance between them would make things more difficult, but anything worth having was worth working for. Good marriages took work; they could think of it as a proving ground, a test of their mettle.

Chris felt as if a thousand-pound weight had been lifted from her shoulders, blinders lifted from her eyes. Elation and a lilting hope swept through her. She wanted to share it with Greg. Tell him how wrong she had been, ask his forgiveness for the wounds she had inflicted.

That, too, would be a test. True love forgave, and as with the birth of a baby, the pain was forgotten once a beautiful new life was cradled in one's arms.

And how she did want to be in his arms right now! The thought sent her heart soaring.

Chris cut her gaze to the bedside clock. Eleven here, it was midnight in D.C. Even if Greg was sleeping, surely he wouldn't mind if she woke him up to ask when was the soonest they could meet.

Rummaging in her purse for the card he had given her with home and work numbers on it, she grasped it with tremulous hands. Excitement rising, she dialed. Breath held, an immediate apology on her tongue, she heard his receiver lift.

''Hello?'' It was a woman's voice. Into Chris's stunned silence, the woman said, ''Major Reynolds' residence. Hello?''

"WHO WAS THAT?" Greg asked, looking up from the hamburgers he turned on the stove.

"They hung up. Wrong number, I guess."

Just in case it wasn't, he grabbed the phone and dialed. Better for Chris to hang up on him than to think he'd been in the sack with Eileen. Their relationship was too complex to explain easily, but he'd explain her away somehow if Chris had called.

Which apparently she hadn't. Ten rings, no answer. After midnight and she wasn't home. *Who was she with?* And who was baby-sitting Audrey, or was she at a friend's house while her mother was out on the town...or elsewhere?

Greg returned to the stove and slapped the hamburgers onto a plate, hard. Eileen scratched softly at his back.

"I take it she wasn't there?" she said sympathetically.

"You take it right." He shoved the plate her way. "Here, eat both of them. I just lost my appetite."

"Even for—"

"Yeah, even for that, Eileen. Like I told you earlier, I appreciate the offer, but I just can't cheat on her."

"It's not like you're married," she reminded. Again.

"No one knows better than us that there's a lot more to marriage than a legal paper. It's the 'lot more' between me and Chris that's keeping me out of a bed with you to try to forget her." At Eileen's expression of slight hurt and definite disappointment, he softened his rejection. "If anyone could tempt me that way, it would be you. But the fact is, no one's worth that kind of damage. Even if she didn't know, I would. And I couldn't live with that between us."

"I don't believe it," she said, shaking her head in disbelief. "It's finally, really happened to you, hasn't it?"

"God, has it. I'm crazy about her, Eileen. And I'm just as crazy about her little girl."

"Lucky them," she said wistfully. "I wish it could have been that way for us. But I suppose we should be glad that we've been able to stay friends and occasionally enjoy the best thing we had in our marriage."

"That part of it was good," he agreed. Spicy as their love life had been, though, it had lacked the depth and meaning that defined his intimate bond with Chris. Too private to share and better left unspoken to an old lover and ex-wife.

"I'm going to miss our little frolics down memory lane."

"Yeah, but you sure as hell won't miss the rest of the garbage that went along with our 'I do.'"

"Isn't that the truth," she admitted with a laugh. "Once the honeymoon was over and the domestic stuff got in the way of the bed... Well, I guess it's not too surprising we thought it best to keep the bed and forget the rest. Maybe I'll be lucky and meet a man one day who loves me as much as you obviously love her. Not that I'm in any hurry, mind you."

And he knew she wasn't. Fiercely ambitious, Eileen was married to her career. A lot like he had been before Chris and Audrey had come along and scrambled his priorities.

"Let's eat those burgers," he suggested. *Sonic burgers are my favorite.* He could hear her halting whisper in the elevator as if they were still there. The memory seized him in the groin and wrapped around his heart. Both belonged to Chris. All of him did. God, but he missed her.

"Tell you what, while we eat, give me an earful about this amazing woman who did the impossible."

It was all the encouragement he needed. As they ate, he told her about Chris, about the blind spot she had that made her refuse to give him a chance to be Audrey's daddy.

"I want them, Eileen," he said as she nibbled at the

burger he hadn't touched. "More than anything I've ever wanted in my life, I want them both."

"Hmm." She tapped her temple. "Know what I think? If you're smart you'll give her some space, show her you can be patient. It's certainly not your strong suit, but if you can lay off the arm-wrestling tactics, she might start seeing you in a different way. I know that after tonight, I do."

She gave him a quick kiss, then picked up her purse. "Call me if you want to talk...or anything else."

"There won't be 'anything else,'" he said firmly.

"I know. But you can't blame an ex-wife for trying."

They laughed companionably as he walked her to the front door. There, he asked, "By the way, how do you see me now?"

"You're not the man I married, Greg. But you're showing some real signs of being the one I wish I had. If that woman has a brain in her head and a hormone in her body, she'll come around. Just give her some time."

AS DAWN PEEKED THROUGH the blinds, Chris huddled in the fetal position on the floor of her bedroom. Disbelief had given way to outrage, a wrath she'd taken out on the phone she jerked from the wall, the sheets she'd shorn with her scissors.

And then the tears had come, unending streams of them, each one filled with the hurt wrenching her apart and leaving her in so many pieces, scattered and fragmented, she would never find them all. But now, mercifully numb, Chris knew she had no choice but to pick up what was left of herself and what remains she could gather, and put them in place as best she could.

She had to do it for Audrey. She had to do it for herself. She couldn't allow Greg to destroy her. All their memories and her tattered emotions, she had to tuck them away in a sealed place of her mind where she must never venture.

To church she would go Sunday and with Jerry she would sit. And she would look at him with the veil of self-delusion lifted. As for comparisons, he would surely fare infinitely better than Greg after this.

And he did. So did Harvey, whom she didn't hesitate to accept a date with the next weekend. Chris heard herself laughing at his corny jokes, struck by how natural she sounded when she felt so completely detached. She watched their interaction as if she were an onlooker, just as she went through her days at work and her time at home—with a sense of separation from everyone and everything.

Everyone except Audrey. Chris could feel herself clinging with such desperation it was enough to suffocate the poor child. She knew she had to stop it, and would as soon as she found a few more missing pieces. Rationally, Chris believed she was in shock—not unlike what she'd gone through when she had lost Mark. The symptoms were the same: going through the motions of living while inside she felt cold, dead.

Her period was nearly three weeks late, but that didn't really surprise her, either. She had skipped one entirely after Mark's death. Yes, she was a widow again, but she refused to grieve at the grave of lost dreams, lost hope.

It was only after the first week of February came and went without a sign of her menses that Chris became alarmed. Had she miscalculated? she wondered frantically, checking the last X on the previous year's calendar.

But no, there it was and no matter how many times she counted the days, they didn't miraculously diminish. One period she could miss and explain away but the only explanation for having missed a second was inescapable.

The calendar fell from her nerveless fingers and her gaze riveted on her stomach. "Heaven help me," she whispered. Her surroundings zoomed in and out and she thought she might faint. Slumping to the floor she put her head between her knees and breathed deep until the dizziness passed.

But as reality reasserted its hold she wished she had fainted. *What was she going to do?*

Chris had no idea. She only knew that she was pregnant and the father-to-be would never know.

CHAPTER TWENTY-THREE

SITTING IN THE CLINIC'S waiting room, Chris's heart stopped, then started again when the name called was not hers.

She was desperate for this to be over; desperate for it not to happen. But she had no choice, she sternly reminded herself as she closed her eyes and searched for some remnant of strength. She wanted to pray, but she'd been praying for two weeks and God hadn't sent a miracle miscarriage her way.

She thought He would forgive her for what she was compelled to do if heaven's unconditional love was true. But self-judgment was another matter and Chris wondered if she would ever be able to forgive herself.

She believed life was sacred. Only she had been thrust into an impossible situation where beliefs and existing responsibilities collided. She had examined the options and outcomes as rationally as she could. This had been the hardest, most painful decision of her life.

To bear this child would be to subject Audrey to a fate she did not deserve. The taunts from her peers and inevitable snubbing they both would receive would only be a single thread in their unraveling lives. The structure that supported them was frighteningly fragile, Chris had come to realize. This was a moral community and her position in it would suffer a great fall. Her teaching contract was due to be renewed for next year and the school budget had been cut.

She could hear the clip of her job already. An unmarried

home-ec teacher with her stomach out to there would incite an uproar among those parents who felt she was no example for their children to follow. Gone would be the income and gone would be the existing fabric of their lives.

To do that to Audrey was unthinkable. And so was climbing into bed with another man who might or might not marry her, even if she was able to convince him of a desperate lie.

Desperation had driven her here, where she shrank into her chair, into herself, while another name was called.

So desperate she'd been, she had actually considered calling Greg and insisting he marry her, take her and Audrey in until the baby was born. And after that they could divorce, she could return to Lubbock with both children and bear only the brunt of bad judgment for being swept off her feet by an old flame and jumping into a marriage that hadn't worked out.

It was really the most logical thing to do. But Chris didn't think she could survive living with Greg and the equal measures of love and hate she grappled with even now. Lord, how she wanted to hate him, completely and passionately. Yet there was a weakness inside her, making her wake up and wonder why he wasn't in bed with her. How weak she was, longing so much for his touch that she pretended it was him, the traitor whose name she called when she came. And then damned as she cried into her pillow, cursing him for the hold he still claimed over her body and soul.

Yes, she still wanted him despite the brutal damage he had done. And it was that want which advised her to stay far away because she would fall for him all over again and then he would tear out the remains of her heart.

"Mrs. Nicholson?" The call of her name was close, too close, and Chris started at the tap on her shoulder. The neatly dressed woman looked down at her quizzically. "I called your name twice but you didn't seem to hear. Is something wrong? The nurse is waiting with your prep shot.''

Chris glanced from the woman to the open door leading to a nurse who would dope her up, to a room where she would lie on a table while her womb gave up the life inside it. And once that was done she would go home without the baby in the belly she protectively stroked, home in a cab rather than the car she had come in and would have to pick up later.

The car she was leaving in now.

''I can't do it,'' she said haltingly. ''I'm sorry if I messed up your schedule but I just can't—can't do this.''

The woman nodded sympathetically. ''If you can't, then don't. After all, the only thing to be sorry for is going through with a decision you can't take back and regret once it's made. I'm sure that yours is the right one for you.''

And it was, Chris knew as she claimed the haven of her car and carefully drove home. Home with the child she hadn't been able to sacrifice for the sake of her other one.

She would have a lot of explaining to do. Why Mama was having a baby but didn't have a daddy to offer in the bargain. And why it was best that they move away after the school year was over and find a new home, new friends, a new job.

But she'd sweeten the deal and tell Audrey what a team they would be and wherever they lived it would smell lots better when they swung on the porch, sharing jelly beans, lullabies and lemonade.

EIGHT IN THE MORNING and he hadn't slept a wink all night. His plane was due to leave in a few hours and Greg was still debating whether or not to call first. He was having a lot of trouble making decisions lately; had been for the past three months. Good thing he wasn't running a war since he would have had a mutiny on his hands by now.

He was ineffective on the job and had been strongly advised that whatever his personal problem might be, he needed to get it straightened out. Hell, he hadn't needed the general to tell him that—all he had to do was look in the mirror for a reality check. Twenty pounds lighter, his eyes dull and sunken, on good days he looked like a zombie in a horror flick.

Maybe Chris would take one glance at him and have some pity. Only, he didn't want her pity. He wanted *her*. On any terms. It had come down to a matter of survival.

Only an hour remained before he drove to the airport. If he called, she might make herself scarce. Then again, if he didn't, she might have Saturday-afternoon company when he arrived, as in male, and given the state he was in, Greg didn't trust himself farther than he could spit. If he made a scene, he'd blow what little chance he had for a reconciliation. Knowing that, he laid aside the mitten he'd rubbed a hole in from months of stroking, took a deep breath and made the call.

"Hello-wo," piped the pip-squeak voice trying to sound grown up. It was the most wonderful sound Greg had heard in what seemed forever.

"Audrey," he exclaimed with genuine delight. "Guess who this is."

"Uncle Greg!"

"That's right. How's my special girl?"

With a mischievous little giggle, she said, "Which one? Me or Mommy?"

"Both. But you first."

"I got a tooth in but lost two more and the Tooth Fairy only left three quarters under my pillow. Just 'tween us, I think Mommy's the fairy, but don't tell her I said so."

"Cross my heart, I won't."

"Does that mean you can keep another secret?" she asked in a confidential whisper.

"You know I can." Unable to resist, he asked, "Remember our secret at the toy store?"

"Sure do, but I was 'fraid you forgot."

"Nope," he assured her. "I think about it all the time. So, Audrey, tell me your secret before I talk to your mom."

"She's kinda the secret and I don't think she can talk right now 'cause she's throwin' up again."

Everything seemed to come to a stop. His heartbeat, his lungs, even his ability to speak. And then they came back all at once, faster than fast, the room spinning like a top.

Struggling to remain calm, Greg said very slowly, "This is really important, Audrey, so think hard before you answer. Does your mother have the flu?"

"I don't think so, 'less it's a real weird kind and lasts a long time. Mostly she's just sick in the mornin's and eats crackers in bed a lot."

Symptoms, other symptoms. Jesus, he couldn't think. "Uh...what about sleeping? Is she sleeping a lot, too?"

"Almost as much as she cries. I'm worried about her and that's my secret, Uncle Greg. She keeps tellin' me everything's gonna be all right but it sure doesn't seem like it. 'Specially since she said we were gonna move away after school's over and after that she has a surprise."

A surprise? Fourth of July fireworks and Mardi Gras in New Orleans exploding at his feet couldn't compete with this!

"Listen, sweetheart, don't you worry your pretty little head a second longer. I'm on my way and I'm not leaving without you and your mama."

"Is that a promise?" she asked with such hope it assured him he had a formidable ally in Audrey.

"You bet it's a promise, no matter what it takes for me to make it come true. Between the two of us, we'll make

our toy-store secret happen. You'll be calling me something besides Uncle Greg real soon.''

After swearing Audrey to silence and making her a fellow conspirator in a hasty plan, Greg threw on his new
suit, picked out a power tie, and took off with the frayed
mitten in his pocket for luck. Galvanized into action, he
made two stops on the way to the airport and boarded, out
of breath, his checking account considerably lighter.

A while later, arsenal in hand, he got out of the car he'd
rented and breathed a sigh of relief when he saw Audrey
posted at her station, right on time.

She ran into his arms and gave him a great big hug, the
best hug he'd ever gotten in his life, almost crushing the
foil-wrapped roses between them. He pulled one out and
gave it to her with a warning, ''Careful, it's got stickers on
it.''

''Can I call you Daddy yet?'' she whispered in his ear.

''Not yet, but it won't be long,'' he whispered back.
''Did your mother swallow the bait?''

''The bait?''

Oops. Still had some work to do on kid lingo. But he'd
get it down, just like the rest he still had to learn. And this
time he'd do it right. ''Is your mama inside?''

''Uh-huh. She's still lookin' for her keys. I hid 'em in
the garbage can.''

''Good going, sweetheart. Now give me a high five and
scoot over to that friend's house you said you could go
to.''

''How long am I 'sposed to play with Lizabeth?''

''Think her mom will let you stay till dinner?'' Audrey
assured him she did that ''lots lately since Mama's such a
grouch.''

Greg was a little sorry to see Audrey take off. Now who
was the one hiding behind a child, he asked himself wryly
as he let himself in the unlocked door. He didn't want to

scare Chris, but even less did he want the door slammed in his face.

Shutting it softly behind him, he knew a sweet thrill at the sound of her voice, cursing profusely from the direction of her bedroom.

Divine intervention? What better place for a showdown; an even better place to kiss and make up.

Deciding the flowers would meet a kinder fate after the kiss and make-up part, he placed them on the piano bench. And then, his gaze lifting to the wedding picture atop the upright, he did something extremely difficult, but necessary.

He laid the roses beside the picture. In their time apart he had come to realize many things, and this was a symbol of his acceptance of the whole of her life. Just as Chris would have to accept his for them to make a good life together.

Treading quietly to her open bedroom, he watched from the doorway, devouring the sight of her dressed in a chambray shirt and faded jeans. Chris had never looked so good to him, her hair a mess, barefoot and pregnant, banging shut a drawer and yelling, "Damn! Damn, where the hell are those keys?"

Greg dug into his pocket, and lifting his own, jangled them. They sounded like bells and he could only think one kiss from Chris and oh, how they would ring.

"Audrey, you found them!" she said, whirling around. The smile on her face froze. And then she fell back against the dresser. One hand clutching at it, her other went to her stomach. But as his gaze hungrily followed the movement, she quickly jerked her palm from her belly.

"Audrey's gone to play so her mother and I can put our games away." He shut the door and locked it. "Hello, Chris."

CHAPTER TWENTY-FOUR

HELLO, HELLO, HELLO. There was an echo in her ears and it swept through her head, carrying the sound of the voice that haunted her dreams and her days.

"God, you look good to me," he said, walking slowly toward her while she commanded herself to run, to hide, to do anything but grab her scissors and stab him in his heart if he had one. Or worse, rush into his arms and cover his face with kisses.

She had no idea what she was going to say until she said it. "You look like hell yourself. Make that more like a tomcat who's spent too many nights on the prowl. Man can't live on sex alone, Greg."

He stopped short. Only several feet separated them but the heat of flaring emotions ran a mile wide and just as deep.

A flash of disbelief, then anger crossed his face. But he quickly subdued both as if determined to stay cool in a volatile situation. Too bad, Chris decided. Her hormones were on a rampage and she wanted to vent the manic fury of each one on the man responsible.

"I'm afraid I don't understand where you've gotten such a wrong idea," he said evenly. "The only woman I've been hungry for is you and I'm beyond starved. There hasn't been anyone else, Chris." He glanced at her stomach and she instinctively covered it. "I won't ask if the same holds true for you."

No one else for him? *Yeah, right.* The last thing she

wanted to endure were more professions of innocence, lies she was desperate to hear. And wanting to hear them made her more furious than ever, flush with the need to lash out and hurt him as cruelly as he had her.

"Oh, but I do think you should ask," she said with a flippant little laugh. "I didn't waste any time taking your advice. And what good advice it was. But I'm afraid it backfired on you since it made me realize what we had together wasn't nearly as special as I had thought."

His eyes probed hers and she prayed he wouldn't see past her lie and into the longing she was frantic to suppress.

"I don't believe you."

"Then why don't you ask Jerry?"

Chris watched the clench of his jaw with enormous satisfaction. But then, suddenly, he reached for his belt and whipped it from his pants. With a savage flash of movement, he flung it across the room.

"What do you think you're doing?" she demanded, edging away from the dresser, her eyes darting around for the best path of escape.

"Short as your memory seems to be, I'm going to refresh it. Old friends that we are, indulge me with a comparative analysis once we're done. *Blow by blow.*"

"No!" Chris latched on to a vase behind her and hurled it at his nose, dead center. He caught the porcelain neatly and she heard it shatter against the floor as she raced just beyond his reach.

Seconds later, she felt the surprisingly gentle clamp of his grip around her waist. But there was nothing gentle in his grind against her buttocks nor in his tone.

"'No' won't get it, babe, any more than 'Stop.' The password is *roses* and I'll hear you scream it before I'm done with you. And then, *then,* I'm going to hear you say that you love me and Jerry was a mistake. I can forgive a mistake. But I can't forgive you wanting him and not me. And you won't want him after this. Believe me, it's true.''

Knowing just how true it was, Chris struggled to break free. A real struggle, not a pretend one this time. She couldn't let him take her or her fate would be sealed. She'd let him use her again however he wanted while he snuck around behind her back and ultimately destroyed her.

The knee she jerked up to his groin he easily deflected, but her fingernails connected with his face and she was both repelled and riveted by the three thin streaks she raked, making blood bead to the surface of his cheek.

"Such a bad girl you are," he said with mocking approval as he gripped her wrists and efficiently bound them with his tie. "You just earned yourself a worse punishment."

The baby. If he was too rough she might suffer the miscarriage she had prayed for and had come to thank God heaven had refused to give. But, should she plead to be spared for the baby's sake, Greg would use their child against her to get whatever he wanted.

Grasping at straws, she said, "Go ahead, Greg. Go ahead and do whatever you want. Just be prepared to get slapped with a lawsuit. I'll cry 'Rape' before I cry 'Roses.'"

"Rape?" He laughed a single harsh laugh. "No way, babe. I'm going to make you wet and I'm going to make you beg. For me, Chris, only for me. You're going to open your legs wide, wrap them around mine, and take me home. We're picking up where we left off. As in *now.*"

Chris knew there was no escaping the inevitable; he was bent on it and she was no match for his strength. The best she could do would be to cut off her feelings by remembering the woman's voice and remain silent.

And so, she retaliated with indifference—a weapon more powerful than hate. She went still, stood there and let him take off her clothes. No assistance, no resistance. She could have been a pliable statue, movable but cold.

Shutting her eyes, she refused to look at him; made no reply to his alternately sweet and dirty words. But as she allowed him to carry her stiff form to the bed and endured his languorous stroking, she realized his punishment was immeasurably worse than had he taken her by force.

Gentleness. Tenderness beyond belief. Kisses to her closed eyes, kisses to her breasts, kisses and more kisses to her stomach. She felt loved, treasured, her body worshiped. Her body cared not at all that he had betrayed her. And her heart joined in the conspiracy, whispering that no man could touch a woman like this and be capable of betrayal.

It was heaven. It was hell. She was coming undone, her defenses unraveling, her legs spreading wide, hips rising, moans breaking from her throat amid whimpers of "Greg, please, please, hold me. Be inside me where you belong."

When she beseeched him with raised hands, he untied her wrists and she traced his beloved face, swept her palms over his back and urged him closer, closer.

How carefully he lowered himself over her; how restrained was his entry when so easily he could have thrust and met an eager acceptance. Buried inside her, he remained there, unmoving, pressed firm against her womb, their baby.

Their baby. It was then that Chris began to cry.

Licking at her tears, he murmured, "I love you blind, Chris. I'm so blind with it, I don't care whose baby it is if you'll let me raise it as mine."

Her shock was ample to halt her tears. Staring at him, unblinking, she saw the truth of his words in his gaze and knew for a certainty that no woman had ever been loved more than this man loved her.

"How—how did you find out?"

"From the mouths of babes—the other one that I want as much as the child you're carrying."

And he didn't even care if it was his. Her head was spinning, her heart rose and flew on a wing. What more proof of commitment did she need? But that other woman...there *had* to be an explanation, just had to be. One she should have asked for instead of jumping to conclusions without giving him a chance.

No more repeating mistakes. No more shutting him out or letting lies or pride, reason or fear come between them.

Suddenly needful to assure him, to share this miracle of theirs, she said with a tremulous smile, "There was no other man, Greg. The baby is yours."

Forever would she remember the light in his eyes, the slow spread of his grin, the way he threw back his head and shouted, *"Yes!"*

They made love and never would she forget that, either. It was filled with passion and a sweeping tenderness, soft laughter and pregnant tears. He cried some, too. And never had Greg seemed so strong to her as when he shed them openly, his tears of joy and relief mingling with the blood she had drawn.

Their lovemaking was healing, binding, and in the aftermath when he said solemnly, "Marry me," she didn't have to think twice about her answer.

"Yes, yes," she chanted.

"And it's yes because you love me."

"I love you enough to be more afraid of losing you to someone else than to death. I love you enough to hate you just as much. And when you came here, I hated you enough to lie." She told him about the call and though she had trouble understanding the unique friendship he had with his ex-wife, she could understand how any woman would prize him enough to keep him any way she could. Eileen was no threat and that made it easier to accept Greg's wish to remain friends with her. He even suggested that Chris would come to like her, too.

And maybe she would. After all, Eileen had offered temptation when Greg had been vulnerable for that comfort and his refusal had proved something to them both.

Wanting no secrets between them, Chris recounted her ordeal at the clinic, the reasons that had driven her there.

He listened patiently and there was a wealth of sympathy in his gaze, while his stroking of her belly showed a protectiveness to rival that which had reversed her decision.

"In the end, I couldn't do it. I just—just couldn't let the baby go."

"Thank God for that," he said, his gaze lifting to heaven and then lowering to her. "What stopped you?"

"At the time, I wasn't sure. It was an instinctive thing, not based on reason at all. But then, just like it was after I cut us off and realized I'd made the mistake of my life, I did some sorting and came up with the real reason." Tracing the red streaks she had inflicted with the intensity of passion only Greg had ever roused in her, Chris knew how very true the reason was.

"I wanted to believe it was simply my moral fiber and maternal instincts that stopped me," she confessed. "Only, that wasn't true. Had it been another man's child, I might have gone through with it. But the baby was yours. I wanted your baby, Greg. And I wanted to see you in it, so I could always remember what it was like to come alive, to feel all the horrible, wonderful things you made me feel that I was sure were gone forever."

"'Forever' is here," he told her, though she needed no assurance it was true. "Our bond is solid, Chris. We've got what it takes to get us through, no matter what. Our love, it's tough enough to last.''

''A trial by fire,'' she whispered. ''If we survived this, we can survive anything.''

''Even Arlene.'' He laughed ruefully. ''You are marrying me for better or for worse, and worse is due to spend the summer with us. I...I've decided I'm not ready to cut my losses with her. Better late than never, I want to try to make a difference in her life if I can. I'm going to need your help, Chris.''

''Hey,'' she said, knuckling his jaw, ''what are wives for? We'll take Arlene on together, Greg.''

The sound of a light knock at the bedroom door brought them both upright.

''Oh dear,'' she groaned. ''Reality intrudes. I hope you realize kids have a knack for terrible timing.''

''Actually, Audrey's timing is perfect.'' A quick kiss and he called out, ''We'll be there in a minute, sweetheart. Your mom and your soon-to-be daddy are just about through talking.''

A whoop of delight, a ''Yea! Yea! Yea! Daddy, you did it!'' accompanied the sound of excited jumping on the other side of the door. They made it a game of who could get dressed the fastest, but as Greg raced Chris for first dibs on hugs, she stopped him short.

''Your face. Let me tend it first.''

''Tend it later. Here.'' He pulled out a handkerchief and said, ''Spit. You know, the way moms do while their kids go 'Yuck.''' But as Chris followed orders, he winked and said, ''Yum.''

Audrey was waiting, still hopping almost high enough to touch the clouds, when they came to her, arm in arm.

Greg bent down and said formally, ''I have a very important question to put to you and your mother.''

"What happened to your face?"

"I, uh…borrowed your mother's leg shaver for my whiskers and had a little accident. Want to kiss it and make it all better?"

She did, then patted his cheek. "All better?"

Better? Sweet heaven, Greg thought, life didn't get any better than this. He pulled out two ring boxes from his pocket but left the mitten he would forever treasure. "You made it so good, Audrey, that I'm proposing to you first."

Lifting the velvet top and then the tiny diamond ring inside, he held it over Audrey's right ring finger. "Your left hand is meant to be saved for a man who'll have to ask me for it and promise to be as good to you as I promise to be to your mother. Audrey Nicholson, will you be my daughter?"

At her eager nod, he slipped the ring down her finger, then kissed it.

"Mama's turn now," she said, holding up her hand and admiring the diamond just before she licked it.

Greg stood, pulled Audrey next to him, and felt his heart expand until he thought it would burst.

"You said 'Yes' already, but I'd like to hear it again while I put this on." He took her gasp as a definite yes and slipped on the damn gaudiest diamond he'd been able to find in the jewelry store; a rock as big and solid as he felt with Chris by his side.

"Chris Nicholson, seeing that your daughter's agreed to be mine, I'm in big trouble if you're not equally agreeable. Say you'll be my wife. Again. And again and…"

Chris not only said it, she confirmed her promise with an unending kiss that didn't let up until Audrey tugged at his arm and said, "You forgot to give Mama these."

Greg took the roses and extended them like the vow they were to Chris.

"Roses," he whispered. "I give you roses."

"And I share them with you," she said, clasping her hands over his. The scent of roses lifted between them, surrounding them with sweetness.

"I'll never betray you, Chris."

"And I'll never betray you by doubting it. *Roses,* Greg. My trust in you is complete."

He laid the roses at Chris's feet, singing softly, "Yummy, yummy, yummy, she's got my love in her tummy." His palm moved there, and she laid her own hand over his. Then Audrey's joined theirs.

"And now we're gonna be a family," their daughter pronounced.

"That's right, sweetheart." His steady gaze meeting Chris's, he committed himself with a vow as sacred as their sex, as binding as their secret word. "And this family is for keeps."

LOVE PLAY

For Scott.
Always.

A Note From The Author

While *Love Play* is a work of fiction, the sexual content is based on fact, gleaned from two primary sources of research. I highly recommend *The Yin-Yang Butterfly: Ancient Chinese Sexual Secrets for Western Lovers* by Valentin Chu (Putnam Tarcher, 1993) for anyone who would like to know more about the sensual arts. Mr. Chu generously offered his time and assistance in response to my many questions. I also recommend *The Multi-Orgasmic Man* by Mantak Chia and Douglas Abrams Arava (Harper San Francisco, 1996).

I had great fun investigating this holistic arena of human sexuality. Any mistakes in the information are, of course, the responsibility of the author.

Last, my heartfelt appreciation to dear friend and colleague Christine Pacheco, who can always make me smile. Thanks, toots, for saving my sanity on a frustrating day.

CHAPTER ONE

"SO...SO HOW LONG do I have, Dr...." What was his name? He had delivered her, set her broken arm when she'd fallen out of a tree at the age of eight, then ten years later he'd held her hand when Mama had lost her battle with cancer, and he had even gone to the funeral, swiping away tears as her mama had been laid to rest. Only last week he'd given her a B12 shot for the fatigue she couldn't shake. She'd known him all her life. So why couldn't she remember his name?

"I'm sorry, Whitney, but I'd rather not hazard a guess until we run some more tests."

He was stalling. Didn't he realize she couldn't possibly leave this office without knowing if her worst suspicions were true? "In other words, you don't want to tell me because you've already hazarded a guess, haven't you?"

Silence. He dropped his gaze onto the lab report that held the answer he wasn't giving.

The suspense was killing her. Whitney leaped up out of the chair and snatched the report lying on his desk. Before he could stop her, she scanned the page. Three words stood out: *acute myelogenous leukemia.*

The paper fell from her hands and her legs gave way. Sinking back down into the chair, she vaguely realized he was finally talking. Fast.

"These are only the initial results, Whitney, please keep that in mind and..." Dr. Whatever-His-Name-Was seemed to be having trouble speaking. Or maybe it was just that she wasn't hearing well. There was a buzz in her ears making his voice sound muffled and distant.

Some rational part of her mind insisted it was important she have the answer. "Is it a year? A month, a week? Do I have time to pay my bills?"

"Your bills aren't important, Whitney, you are and—"

"The hell they're not important!" Her tone was so shrill she winced. Struggling to stay calm, she managed a brittle laugh. "I mean, I've always been careful to pay them on time and I'd really hate to die with a bad credit record."

His mouth was moving but she didn't catch more than the gist of his response. Something about her being in shock, she shouldn't drive in the state she was in, and he'd have someone take her home. Dammit, she still couldn't remember his name and he still hadn't answered her question.

Not knowing was torture, and so very slowly, distinctly, she repeated, "How…long…do…I have? *Tell me.*"

He plowed a hand through his thinning gray hair and, with a heavy sigh, gave in. "Six months. Maybe." Then he backtracked as if he were trying to erase his words. "But Whitney, new cures are found every day and remember, this is just the preliminary diagnosis. I want to refer you to a specialist, Dr. Goldberg. I'll call him today, get you in to see him tomorrow. He'll want to do a battery of tests to verify it is advanced leukemia before starting treatment. The sooner that's started the better chance we have of extending—"

"What?" she demanded, unable to believe this was happening to her and not to someone else. "Just what would I be extending besides some trips to the hospital, the treatments, the pain? That's not a life, it's a pitiful attempt to hang on to what's already lost. If six months is all I've got, then I'm not about to waste one precious minute hooked up to some machine.''

"I know that's how you feel now, but give it a little time and you could change your mind.''

"A little time?" Her voice was bordering on a shriek. Maybe she was closer to hysteria than she thought. "Time is the one thing I don't have! Think about it Dr....Dr. Clark—" yes, that was his name, and crazy as it was she was glad she didn't have to devote another priceless second to something as inconsequential as remembering a name.

"What if it was you?" Whitney leaned forward. "Would you let yourself be probed like some specimen under a microscope, then maybe get lucky and hang on another few months, after losing all your hair and wishing you were already dead? That's how bad the treatments are. And you know they are, Dr. Clark. I saw what my mother went through and so did you. Now tell me and don't you dare lie, what would you do if you were terminal?''

The light that always seemed to dance in his eyes was gone; they were as dull as his toneless reply. "I would get a second opinion, take any course of treatment prescribed and fight the inevitable as long as I could. As a doctor, I know that's what I should do.''

"But as a person, a human being who was living on borrowed time, what would you do?''

Dr. Clark looked away, shook his head, then gave her the unvarnished truth. "I'd maybe subject myself to another test or two, then leave it at that. I'd get my affairs in order, and immediately turn my practice over to a colleague. Then I'd do all the things I never made time for, go for the dreams I never went for, laugh enough for a lifetime, and love with the heart of a fool. I'd live each day as if it were my last and squeeze them all dry for every drop of joy I could.''

"And come that last day?" she asked with a quiet tremble.

"Well, Whitney," he said with paternal kindness, "let's just say that we all die with regrets, but for most of us, those regrets aren't so much for the things we've done, but for all the things we didn't do. I'd want to go with as few of those regrets as possible, knowing that for at least a while I'd lived my life with a rare kind of richness."

"Then I guess that makes me pretty lucky." She gave a small, faint laugh. "I mean, anybody can get hit by a truck and boom, that's it. At least I get the chance to…to, well, do whatever before…" She couldn't say it. God, she couldn't even think it. If she did she'd surely start screaming "It's not true! It's not fair!" and turn into some kind of madwoman that Dr. Clark wouldn't let loose on the streets.

"I need to leave." Whitney reached for her purse and though her hand felt oddly detached, she noticed how smooth the leather was, how vibrant the purple-and-green-and-rust patchwork pieces were. To touch, to see, she'd always taken those senses for granted, but suddenly they seemed like a luxury, as wondrous and miraculous as the life she'd taken for granted as well.

"I'll call Dr. Goldberg first." Dr. Clark reached for the phone while she walked to the door like some zombie moving without will or thought. "Whitney, wait! Just wait a minute while I take care of this and I'll drive you home."

"Thanks, but no," she said with an eerie calm. "You have patients waiting and I have to get some fresh air." At his distressed expression, she gave him a wobbly smile. Not much of one, but it was the best she could do. "Don't worry, I'll be okay."

Before he could protest, she took off. She had to get out of there, walk from the office, through the building, out the exit door, and only then could she escape from this really, really bad nightmare.

As a warm September breeze licked at the heat of her skin, Whitney shivered. Huh. She was outside but she wasn't waking up. She was so dazed and distressed that she felt like she was sleepwalking, not seeing or hearing the cars whizzing past on the road as she crossed the street or the people she kept bumping into on the sidewalk.

She didn't remember reaching her apartment, but somehow that's where she ended up. How long she'd been home, Whitney wasn't exactly sure. She'd suddenly developed an aversion to every tick of the clock and so she'd tossed her watch into the silverware drawer in the kitchen. That's where she'd been when it dawned on her that she wasn't going to wake up.

The bad dream was real.

It seemed a shame to waste what was left of the day and night on things that didn't matter much anymore like balancing her checkbook, doing her laundry, wondering what to do with the $27,565.32 in her savings account since she couldn't take it with her. Maybe she should try to enjoy it, throw some of it around, what with all the pennies she'd pinched and the inheritance she'd socked away, given that she had no family to will it to.

She felt very, very strange. For some reason she hadn't shed a tear. Neither had she called anyone, but when she thought about it, just who did she feel like calling? A neighbor, co-workers at the library, maybe someone from the health club? Health club, hah!

A quick anger surged. How many hours had she spent at that stupid health club, working up a sweat to stay in shape? And just look where it had gotten her!

Membership canceled, as of now.

Just as she reached the phone to inform the YMCA their

services were hereby nixed, the phone rang. Whoever it was, she didn't want to talk to them, not even if it was Donny the Dreamboat from Davidson High, asking her out ten years too late.

The answering machine clicked on.

"Whitney, this is Dr. Goldberg. I've spoken to Dr. Clark and I have you scheduled for an office visit at nine in the morning. You might want to pack a few things and bring them along since I'll be sending you to the hospital afterward. I've already contacted admitting so we can get on to this right away. It'll be a busy day, so try to get a good night's sleep. See you tomorrow."

Well, well, wasn't he the presumptuous one? Whitney swallowed down a knot in her throat and struggled to hang on to her anger. Anger felt good, she could hide in that, so the angrier she was the better. Yes, she hoped the Y went bankrupt without her membership. And as for Dr. Goldberg, she'd see him when she was damn good and ready. To be exact, never. Her time was her time from now on and no way was she going to the hospital tomorrow. Once she checked in, they'd prick her and probe her and keep her until Dr. Goldberg said she could leave.

Only to come back and back and back and...

"I know you mean well, Dr. Goldberg, but nevertheless, screw you and your high-tech voodoo, too." No, she wasn't about to end up like her mother who had endured unspeakable suffering, trying to hang on for her only child.

Children. Love. Marriage. Whitney thought of how she'd been feeling cheated lately since those things had yet to come her way. She was gripped with sudden greediness for them, even while acknowledging it was a blessing to have no one but herself to worry about. No lover, no child to struggle to live for, no family left to grieve over her. Oh yes, it was much better this way.

So why didn't she feel blessed instead of mad as hell? Mad at God, at the world, at Dr. Goldberg, and—

Ring. Ring. The phone. How dare it intrude on her spiteful musings? She suddenly hated that phone, wanted to throw it to the ground and stomp it to pieces. Then she'd go for the answering machine, rip that little box to shreds so this was the last beep it ever made.

"Whitney? Whitney, are you there? Dammit, child, if you're there, pick up the phone.... Ah hell, this is Dr. Clark. Look honey, I don't want you staying by yourself. Call a friend or get your preacher over, you can even page me and I'll be there in a wink. If I don't hear from you tonight, I'll be calling Dr. Goldberg first thing tomorrow to make sure you showed up. Be there, Whitney. Remember, I was the first one to spank your bottom twenty-seven years ago, don't give me a reason to straighten you out again, you hear?"

Whitney glared at the phone. Unplugged it. Her wrathful gaze settled on the answering machine. And then she erased the tape, as if that would make the messages disappear. But the words kept playing in her head, so she snatched out the micro cassette and snarled, "Die, sucker."

Imagining it to be the disease stealing her life away, she vented her rage on the cassette. Snapping it in half, then tugging, twisting, mangling the tape inside to death.

There. There, she felt much better! And what better way to spend her time—her time, all hers—than to celebrate her freedom from all the concerns she needn't concern herself with anymore? Champagne was in order. She couldn't remember the last time she'd skipped like a kid, but the child inside who insisted she was still immortal, skipped over to the refrigerator.

No reason to save the bottle of Andrés bubbly. She hadn't had need of it that last, lonely New Year's Eve when

she'd sat alone in front of the TV, watching the New York
revelers and wishing fiercely for a kiss of her own at midnight. Well, she sure as heck had use for that bottle now.
After today she was fully entitled to get plastered and even
dance naked in the streets if she wanted to. So what if she
couldn't sing worth a hoot? Just let the other tenants bang
on the walls, the hell if she cared.

Singing at the top of her lungs, she wondered why she
was grinning like a loon instead of sobbing out the tears
that refused to come. Lord, she was a terrible singer, her
off-pitch voice hurt her own ears. Maybe Dr. Clark was
right, maybe she did need some company, somebody who
could carry a tune.

To the stereo she went and selected an old CD. "Don't
worry," she told Billy Joel as she upped the volume, "I
like what you have to say, so I won't murder your disc."

Music on, champagne uncorked, she guzzled straight
from the bottle. She'd never done that before, never gotten
drunk except for that once in college, little Goody Two-
shoes that she was. Was, as in the past tense. The rebellious
nature she'd never had was finally getting its due. As the
ever so astute Mr. Joel was pointing out, "Only the good
die young."

"Sing it, Billy!" Whitney took another swig, looked at
the bottle and laughed. Laugh enough for a lifetime, that's
what Dr. Clark had said. Well, by golly, she was laughing.
Some rich life she'd led. Why, she hadn't even downed a
fourth of the bottle and here she was, three sheets to the
wing. Or was it the wind?

Didn't matter, starting tonight she was gonna rip through
life with the gusto she'd never had. After all, she only had
six months to pack in the sixty years she was getting
robbed of. Spend those six months at the library, working
for a boss she couldn't stand? Forget it. One of her most

beloved fantasies would be realized tomorrow when she marched into the Mobile Public Library and told that little weasel to take her job and shove it, along with as many books as he could cram up his you-know-what.

"The word is *ass,* Whitney," she slurred. "Gotta work on your...*hic*...bad language."

With a tipsy giggle, she wove her way into her neat-as-a-pin bedroom and pulled her one nice piece of luggage out of the closet. After sniffing in disdain at the buttoned-down, no-frills wardrobe hanging in there, she rummaged through her dresser drawers, found a couple things, threw them into her suitcase, and deemed her packing done.

There was lots of room left for all the naughty, sexy, daring dresses and nighties she was gonna buy to take with her...where? Someplace...exotic. Yeah, exotic. Someplace where there were lots of guys. Yeah, guys. Not that she needed many, one would be plenty. A hunka-hunka-burnin'-love who would make her feel like a love goddess. That was her other big fantasy and by God, she deserved to have it before...

She'd rather think about her fantasy man—some handsome, mysterious stranger who didn't know she was really a mousy children's librarian who got her jollies by reading books out loud to kids.

At the thought of children, of those she would never read to again, of those she would never bear, Whitney felt her throat tighten. There was a sting behind her eyes that she blinked against as she returned to the dresser, for what she didn't know. Just something to focus her attention on, like the brush she picked up and put to her hair.

She had pretty hair, long and dark and wavy. She had pretty blue eyes, too. They were looking back at her from the mirror, but they were so empty and hopeless and frightened that she couldn't bear to meet her own gaze.

She lowered it to her breasts. The brush fell from her fingers and she worked loose the buttons of her plain white blouse. Then that was gone and so was her bra and she was staring at her bare breasts, and how pretty they were too. So pretty that she touched them, cupped them in her hands, and wondered what she had ever done that was so terrible she would never nurse a newborn babe.

Her hands trailed over her arms, traced the neat groove of her waist, the flare of her hips. And then she pressed her palms to her belly, that place where no new life would ever grow because her own had been cut short.

Despite its flaws, her body was beautiful. Beautiful and *sick*. The care and respect she had always shown for it meant nothing. Her body had betrayed her. God had betrayed her.

She had betrayed herself.

Tears welled in her eyes and spilled onto her cheeks. A sob caught in her throat as she whispered, "Whitney Smith. You're kind and you're decent, but what have you really done with your life? Not much and that's a terrible shame because you're twenty-seven years old. And you are going to die."

CHAPTER TWO

"You're late." Mr. Andrews looked over his reading glasses with a scowl. "One hour and twenty-three minutes late, Ms. Smith. And what might be your excuse?"

She had never been late for work, not once in nearly five years, but did he care why she was late today? Was he even capable of caring that she'd spent the morning speaking to a lawyer and a funeral director, for reasons she had no intentions of sharing with him? Did he have enough of a heart to care that she was wearing sunglasses in the library because her eyes were so swollen, anyone who saw them would surely guess she'd been sobbing all night?

He couldn't care less. He was a cold little man who must have some virtues she'd yet to detect.

"I asked you a question, Ms. Smith. What's your excuse for being so late?"

"What's your excuse for speaking to me like you're my whip master and I'm your slave?" Whitney felt a little thrill at the flippant retort she wouldn't have dared speak before.

"Because I'm your boss, that's why!" he sputtered. "Now I suggest you get to work before I write you up for insubordination."

"Feel free to do just that, Mr. Andrews, but you'll only be wasting your time. You see, the reason I'm late is because..." Her heart raced. This was it, she was really going to do it! She smiled and said, "I quit."

His shocked expression was so comical Whitney struggled not to laugh. But hey, she needed a good laugh, and what was he going to do about it, fire her? So laugh she did before informing him, "The only reason I stayed this long is because of the kids, they're so special to me. You, however, have been terrible to work for, Mr. Andrews. You must be a very unhappy person to treat others as shabbily as you do, and I really hope you can change that. After all, life's too short not to enjoy to its fullest and smile as much as we can. You made me smile today. Thanks."

Whitney strode away and was aware of a euphoric lift, as if she'd just let go of all the rules and responsibilities and resentments that had kept her weighted down. She knew it was a rare liberation she'd claimed, but how she wished it hadn't been won by having nothing to lose.

TWO DAYS LATER, Whitney marveled at the peace she felt as the plane bound for Dominica kissed the clouds and promptly hit a pocket of air. Where had her fear of flying gone? Somewhere between Mobile and the layover in San Juan her white-knuckled fists had relaxed and she'd bid her fear good riddance, along with those irksome matters she'd dealt with to simplify her life.

Her insurance, which the library would no longer cover, was paid in advance. The next six months of rent, also was taken care of. Her next residence was secured.

Whitney shuddered. *Don't think about it, dammit, don't you dare. If you do, you'll get depressed and then you'll spoil the moment and the moment is all you have.*

And just what did she have in this moment? That was the little game she'd begun to play with herself, one she wished she'd thought up a long time ago. Better late than never, though, and for now she had a seat by the window in the first-class section, the taste of Wrigley's Spearmint gum in her mouth, a *Cosmo* magazine in her lap, and an attractive man sitting beside her. His nose was firmly planted in a book.

"A room without books is like a body without a soul," she quietly mused.

"Cicero." His low-pitched voice was crisp, and pleasant to the ear. Though she hadn't expected a response, he looked directly at her for the first time—unless she counted a cordial nod when he'd rushed to his seat, laptop and briefcase in hand, the last passenger and probably the culprit for the ten-minute delay out of San Juan. "Of course he also said, 'There is nothing so ridiculous but some philosopher has said it.'"

The man's smile was infectious. Whitney found herself smiling back despite her vow to avoid conversing with other passengers since her last seatmate had been a motormouth.

"You seem to know your Cicero. Do you teach philosophy?" If so, Whitney was sure he didn't lack for students, particularly of the female persuasion.

"Hardly. I had to write a paper on Cicero in college, oh how long ago was that?" He tapped his temple and she noticed he had the most remarkable face. There was an arresting quality to his prominent cheekbones and gleaming black hair, tied back into a short ponytail. His eyes, an exotic, slightly almond shape, were a medley of dark-and-light brown, flecked with amber. The burnished gold shooting from his pupils reminded her of a sparkler dancing against the night while his dark complexion revealed a fondness for the sun.

Guessing him to be a little older than herself, but not by much, he stunned her by saying, "I was a freshman so it's been nearly twenty years. Of course it took me all of two minutes to forget most everything about the class—except for the prof, that is. He was nearing retirement so the uni-

versity kept him on despite this little problem with narco-
lepsy that made him fall asleep in the middle of his own
lectures.''

"That's awful.'' Awful as it was, Whitney giggled.

"Yeah, it is,'' he agreed, chuckling himself. "But at the
time, I thought it was pretty cool since he'd wake up and
say, 'Now where was I?' and we'd all reply, 'You were
about to dismiss us,' and then—''

"Excuse me,'' said a flight attendant, "Would you care
for a cocktail before brunch?''

Though the question was directed to her flying companion, he turned to Whitney and asked with the courteous
finesse of a tuxedo-clad date, "What would you like?''

"Hmmm...how about time in a bottle?''

He smiled that smile again, warm and comfortable as an
old pair of jeans molded to a familiar body. He had very
nice lips. "I'd arm wrestle you for possession if I thought
they had one to serve.''

"In that case, I'll take champagne.''

Another flash of that smile before he ordered a champagne "for the lady'' and an imported beer for himself.
After the drinks were promptly served, he asked, "Now
where was I?''

"Class was just adjourned.''

His expression was somewhere between a rueful grin and
a wince. "And to think the first thing I do on a plane is
open a book so I don't get stuck listening to some stranger
go on and on about stuff I couldn't care less about.'' He
offered his book to Whitney. "Feel free to hide in there
for the rest of the flight, but I will need it back when we
land.''

After glancing at the title, *Volcanology: A Retrospective
Analysis of Earth and Man,* Whitney shook her head. "I

wouldn't dream of stealing your pleasure reading, and besides, I was really enjoying your story. So, did you pass?''

"Can you keep a secret?" he whispered.

"Cross my heart, hope to…" Her smile faltered, but she quickly reminded herself to think only of the moment and in this moment she was with a man whose eyes imparted equal measures of somber reflection and quiet laughter. They held the maturity of one who had seen a lot, and the alertness of one who missed nothing.

He seemed to be taking note of her pause as well as the hand she'd unconsciously laid over her heart.

"Sure you can trust me," she whispered back, aware of a tingling sensation arcing from crown to nape. "So what's the secret?"

"Nothing I'm proud of, believe me." His gaze lifted to hers and what she saw confirmed that indeed he had seen a lot and indeed he missed nothing—her bra size included. But it wasn't a creepy calculation, rather an appreciation for the way she was made. The tingle shimmied down her spine, as she leaned slightly closer.

So did he. "When the prof was asleep," he confided, "we revised some of our grades. Nothing too drastic, but I pulled a B when I should've gotten a D. It was a stupid kid trick and I'm lucky I didn't get caught. As it is, it's one of those things I really regret having done, but not enough to turn myself in and risk losing my reputation. Even worse, they might make me retake that god-awful class and I can't imagine a more fitting punishment than that. Anyway, there you have it, and why I told you, I dunno since I swore silence with my partners in crime and you're the first to hear me spill the beans."

"I'm…flattered," Whitney said. "But really, who better to tell something like that to than a stranger? There's a certain safety in anonymity, don't you think?"

One of his nicely shaped, expressive eyebrows drew up and he tapped his lips with his finger. Generous and firm, she had the wildest impulse to find out if those lips were as kissable as they seemed while he simply looked at her. Looking at…that wasn't quite right. He was studying her, as if he were trying to see what made her tick.

"What I think is," he replied with a confidence she found extraordinarily sexy, "that's an astute observation and I like the way you think."

So, he liked brains as well as her breasts. Though she didn't really know him, she'd bet her nest egg this guy put more stock in gray matter than curves. Maybe it was his choice of reading material telling her that, or maybe it was just the good vibes he was putting out.

Lifting her drink, Whitney said brightly, "Here's to airplane confessions."

"And to charming ladies who listen as well as they think."

As glass tapped glass, Whitney had to wonder just who this woman was, sharing a toast with a handsome stranger who was setting off all sorts of delicious illicit thoughts in her head. As light as her head felt, she couldn't blame it on the champagne she wouldn't have dreamed of ordering a week ago. A diet soda had been more her style—a style which had gotten her nowhere but stuck in the rut she was plowing out of in high gear.

All the more reason to savor a long sip of champagne in the first-class section of a plane flying over the Caribbean Sea, with a delightful man whose sensual half smile prompted her to say, "You have a wonderful smile. It's very sincere and natural."

"Glad you like it since it's the only smile I've got."

"I don't know about that. I've seen at least three different kinds of smiles from you in the little while we've talked.''

''I'm intrigued.'' And he was. Eric couldn't remember when he'd felt so immediately comfortable with a woman, especially one as attractive as his flight companion. Not that she was *whatababe* gorgeous, but that was part of her allure. This perfect stranger, who had somehow got him to share a totally silly yet nonetheless condemning blight on his past, had a natural prettiness that was as unstudied as the tilt of her head, the swish of coppery brown hair over her shoulders, a bit pale but ever so touchable beneath the tropical sundress she wore, and wore well.

A very pretty package on the outside indeed. But there was more to her than that. Just as he was an observer of geographical hot spots, whose expertise had taken him to all corners of the world, he was an observer of its inhabitants and he was drawn to what he had observed so far of this woman.

She radiated a rare love of life in the way she listened, savored her champagne, and made a person feel good on an otherwise awful day. Actually the day had been so awful, he could use the extra lift she'd left herself open to provide.

''I'm waiting,'' Eric prompted.

''For what?''

''To get my ego stroked.'' Oh yes, this woman most definitely had a way of inspiring a man to bare his soul. ''I want to hear your take on those three smiles. If you noticed anything less than complimentary, just do me a favor and lie.''

He'd made her smile again and as much as he liked to make others smile, it wasn't usually for the purpose of imagining such straight pearly whites nibbling on his person. Man, she had great teeth. Unlike his own. They weren't unsightly but he should have had braces as a kid. He'd always been a little self-conscious about his smile, yet here was this pretty stranger, looking closer to beautiful by the moment, who found his smile worthy of comment.

Even if faint praise was the best she could do, Eric was sure he could write a thesis on the inspiration her own smile provoked.

"Okay," she said. "The first time you smiled, my impulse was to smile back. Since I didn't intend to talk to you or anyone else on this flight, consider that first smile to be disarming."

"Disarming. I like that." Her, he liked. A lot. She was made of different stuff than Amy, his hearth-and-home ex. Amy had been a nester. He was a military brat raised on the move and wanting to put his roots in one place, only to learn that he had an unshakable case of wanderlust and a dangerous calling he loved more than a good wife who hadn't been able to handle it.

"Your second smile was even better than disarming." Upon dangling the carrot she took a languorous sip from her glass and sighed in pure pleasure. "This is really good."

Eric hailed the stewardess. "Miss? Uh, Sonja? Could we please get a refill on the lady's glass?"

"Of course."

While Sonja was quick to top off the glass, Ms. Straight-Pearly-Whites with the knockout smile and a personality to match faintly protested, "I really shouldn't."

"Really, you should," he insisted. "After all, if one doesn't carpe the hell out of the diem, what's the use of living, right?"

She stared at the bubbles as if they were a crystal ball, before taking a small but quick drink, then with a short laugh agreed, "Right."

"Good. Now hopefully you're inebriated enough to tell me that second smile could charm the pants off a nun."

She looked over the rim of her flute and grinned. "Nope."

"Damn. And to think I've been practicing that smile since junior high, when the most it netted me was a rap on my knuckles from Sister Eustacia who surely would've been a lot nicer if she'd just gotten laid." Had he said that? Had he actually divulged his heartfelt opinion about the old grouch?

"I can't believe I said that," was all he could say to excuse his totally inexcusable comment about Sister Eustacia. "I don't know what's come over me. First I tell you about the only bad thing I ever did in college, then I foam at the mouth about poor Sister Eustacia who had every reason and then some to put her ruler to my palm in seventh grade. Here, take my book," he insisted. "You can even keep it once we land since I've turned into the seatmate from hell."

He hadn't meant to be funny, it was just the truth, but she threw back her head and laughed. Great as her teeth were, they had nothing on her neck. Her neck was made for licking and kissing. How old was he anyway? Thirty-seven supposedly, but at the moment, sixteen seemed closer to the hormonal count.

"Oh, you are fun!" she exclaimed with a light touch to his wrist. Impulsive, warm, unselfconscious, a touch so frank and frankly arousing he wanted to pull her out of her seat and land her on his lap. "That's actually the second smile I saw, a really fun, easy-in-your-own-skin kind of smile, very inviting and laid-back and...well, you get the idea. Now as for that third smile..." She slyly grinned.

"If you think I'm going to ask after embarrassing myself, no, I won't do it, I swear I will not."

"Okay." Still grinning, she offered him her magazine. While he pretended interest in the contents of *Cosmo*, she began to flip through his textbook.

Literally his textbook. Besides some much needed R and R, the purpose of this trip was to update his research on the Caribbean's volcano activity. Even before it went to print, his findings could be subject to change. Volcanos were unpredictable, fascinating, and potentially fatal when they took man off guard, as they were wont to do.

A lot like women.

The one beside him stirred the same adrenaline rush he got when a mountain heaved up its earthy guts, and lava flowed. Such an intensity of reaction was too rare to ignore. So was the fact that he wanted her eyes—come-hither eyes, soft and inviting and blue—to be on him rather than on his book. It wasn't a long flight and the longer their silence, the less time to get better acquainted.

Fortunately she didn't take long to comment, "What an interesting subject."

"Do you really think so?" he asked, trying not to sound too eager for her feedback. Tempting as it was to shake his plumage, he wasn't ready to give up the anonymity they had connected in. Once formally introduced, she might not return his confidences, and he had her by two. Hell, he didn't even know if she was married. Her ringless left hand suggested not, as did the signals of interest returned, but he couldn't rule out a marriage on the rocks or a free spirit on the make. He'd been both places and knew better than to step foot in that minefield, no matter how enticing the lay of the land.

Having reskimmed the first few pages of text, she confirmed, "A lot of it's over my head but yes, I do find this interesting. Whoever wrote the book is brilliant. I mean, complex and scientific as it is—and believe me, science was to me in school what philosophy was to you—he makes it seem approachable. I like his style.''

Eric couldn't help but puff out his chest after praise like that. She wasn't a colleague or student so her opinion gave a certain validation to his work which professional recommendations lacked.

"I'll be sure to pass that compliment on to the writer the next time I see him.''

"You know him?'' She looked at him with surprise, looked at him with those blue-aqua eyes that reminded him of the ocean beneath. Forget the teeth, forget the neck, yes, the eyes had to be the best of her best features. As for pretty, as for beautiful, no, no, no he had been wrong about that, too. Definitely gorgeous—a catcall, whistle, oooh-baby and more. "I'm impressed. Is he a colleague, a friend?''

"Let's just say we're close,'' Eric hedged, enjoying the unguarded sentiments this anonymity was providing him with.

"Then please tell…'' she glanced at the name of the author ''—Dr. E. D. Townsend that—'' She paused, slowly smiled, then mischievously giggled. "Tell him that if his way with women is as impressive as his way with words, he must have them lined up for miles.''

What a flirt! Only the remark wasn't intentionally directed at him and he did have to wonder if it was the champagne talking, given her little "hic'' and another giggle. Either way this was one hot babe who claimed top billing in that category most prized by men—doable. A woman who hit buttons a cover model couldn't touch because her confidence, humor and intelligence translated into supreme bedability.

His own buttons, still zinging from her earlier touch to

his wrist, were flying in so many directions he was actually tongue-tied.

The delivery of their light meal saved him from making a total fool of himself by murmuring she was the most intoxicating, provocative creature he'd ever met and would she do him the honor of letting him have a go at her feet? A ten-minute massage and she'd be his—for dinner, at least.

"I wish the food hadn't shown up so soon." She sighed. "I wasn't ready to quit reading."

"Tell you what, I can always get another copy from my friend, so why don't you keep it?"

"I'd hate to put you to that bother—"

"No bother, I insist."

"In that case, I accept. I didn't bring many books with me and I could use some extra beach reading while I'm in Dominica."

All right, and he wasn't thinking of airline food. "That's my stop off, too. How long will you be there?"

She paused for a very long chew of her salad. "Awhile."

Blow the horns, throw the confetti, hot damn this was Eric Townsend's lucky day! "Me, too. Where are you staying?"

"The Springfield Guest House in Roseau. What about you?"

Make that, sorta lucky day. "I'll be in the Prince Rupert Bay area." Which meant they wouldn't be getting off at the same airport. Damn. There went suggesting they share a cab and easing into asking her out en route to their destinations. As it now stood, they had a logistical problem and very little time left to share.

The tropical fruit in his mouth suddenly lost its flavor.

"Are you going for business or pleasure?" she asked.

"Both. I haven't seen my brother Adam in a year and

we carved out some time to hang loose. Then it's back to business for us both.'' Eric put down his fork and quit pretending to eat. ''Enough about me. What brings you to Dominica?''

She chewed in a thoughtful silence, then gave up some of the goods he was after. ''I decided it was time to get out of the rat race and take a shot at having a real life.''

''Good for you. Go. See. Do. Be. That's my take on living, too. As for getting out of the rat race, I can't think of a better choice than Dominica.''

''So I gathered from what I found on the net. Not too touristy, not too remote, black sand beaches, rain forests, waterfalls and crystal lakes. That just sounded great to me. Of course, so did the rates on a bungalow compared with other parts of the Caribbean.''

Though he chuckled at her candor, something about her struck him as guarded. Or maybe it was just that he'd been so uncommonly open about himself that he wanted her to be equally forthcoming with some private revelation.

The flight attendant began gathering trays. The Fasten Seat Belt sign flashed on and the pilot announced the plane was descending.

''So, you don't have a lot of plans then?'' he prompted.

''Not really. Just to take it easy, do what I want, when I want, and work on my Scarlett.''

''Letter?'' As in *A* for *Adultery?* She wasn't married, that much he was fairly certain of, but she could be meeting a married lover. Only he didn't get the impression a lover was in the picture. They were clicking like crazy and if she wanted a shot at a real life joyride, he was the man to give her a lift.

Her puzzled expression turned to sudden comprehension. ''Oh, now I get it! I'm one of those people who usually takes five minutes to get a joke and once I laugh everyone

wants to know what's so funny." She laughed a slightly
scandalized laugh and Eric had some of what he'd hoped
for—a small yet intimate insight few were privy to. "The
only Scarlett I'm working on is the 'Tomorrow is another
day,' principle. But I guess that could qualify for a letter,
too—*A* for *Attitude*."

"That's something most of us could work on," he
agreed, pushing up his tray and resenting the plane's rapid
decline. "Including me. Deep down I know the past is just
that and the future's a crapshoot, so the best any of us can
do is take our chances and go for it."

Go for it, he told himself. All he had to say was, "Fly
to the next stop with me? At the rate you're sending me,
we could land on the moon." Ditch that, too corny, even
if it was true. Simple and to the point, that was his best
bet. Then if she rejected him, he could act as if it were no
big deal.

"What's your sign?" What?! Where did that come
from? Duh. He'd spouted nothing but inanities since the
moment she'd knocked him dead with her smile. She was
doing it again, only chances were it came from a vision of
bell-bottoms and a psychedelic shirt. It was too late to wrap
his hands around his neck, and rip out his vocal chords.
He had to save face and hope that she didn't notice his was
turning a bit red.

"Astrology's one of those things I don't completely buy
into," he quickly added, "but there's enough science involved that I think there's something to it."

"Me, too," she agreed as the flight attendant took their
glasses, including the champagne flute he wished he could
keep as a memento of this most memorable flight. "I don't
take it too seriously but I do read my horoscope in the
paper. As for your question, I'm a Gemini."

"The twins." Okay, she'd bailed him out, it was now

or never to make his move. "If the other side of your personality is half as engaging as the one I've met—"

"Could you please fasten your seat belt?" Sonja requested with an inflection, a look, he recognized. Eric disregarded the subtle come-on and took a deep, calming breath, not wanting to roar with frustration.

The moment was lost, their time had run out. He silently damned the brevity of their encounter, cut even shorter by the drone of the pilot announcing their approach to the Canfield Airport. They had landed. She was getting her purse, getting to her feet, smiling as if anticipating his company, at least to the luggage pickup. Perhaps she was even thinking they might share a cab and dinner as he had earlier hoped.

Eric reluctantly stood to allow her access to the aisle.

"I get off at the Melville Airport, next stop." *Stop,* his brain shouted, *stop her from leaving, stop your trite goodbyes, just say something, do something to make sure you see her again or you're gonna regret it for the rest of your life.* Where that thought came from Eric didn't know, but it was a gut deep certainty that caused him to block her path and the traffic behind him. "Even short flights seem to take too long for me, but this one wasn't long enough. I really enjoyed talking to you." He extended his hand.

"Same here. Thanks for the book." She tucked it under her arm and met his grip. The fine hair on his nape prickled and his groin, semihard throughout their flight, thickened and fully extended. The connection between their eyes, their hands was electric. Surely she felt it, too. Nonetheless she let go, glanced at the crowd behind him before saying in a breathy whisper, "By the way, about that third smile?"

"Yes?" he asked expectantly.

"That was the smile that could charm the pants off a nun." The smile she gave him was so simmeringly sensual, it left him speechless. As she moved past him, time ceased to exist. All he could feel was her shoulder breezing against his chest, her hip lightly brushing his erection.

Was that her sharp intake of breath he heard as she walked on, or was it his own? He was only vaguely aware of the passengers pushing past him, urging her closer to the exit. And all he could do was watch as she paused, turned, waved. Desperation to find her again kicked his brain into gear and his tongue into action.

"My name's Eric," he called to her. "What's yours?"

She glanced at the book as if it might provide some inspiration for an adieu befitting their chance meeting. With a wink and the blow of a kiss, she called back, "Anonymous."

CHAPTER THREE

THE BREATHTAKING SCENERY, wrapped on either side of the taxi, was enough to steal her breath away. Lush foliage, an unbelievably vivid emerald-green, contrasted with crystal clear waves lapping against the black sand. The air tasted of salt and blended with the scent of rich, fertile earth that smelled like just cut grass. Even Pierre, the spritely old taxi driver, was a delight to hear speak, a Creole patois flavoring his English.

Despite her vow to exult in each moment, Whitney knew the grandeur of all this deserved a better relishment. It made her a little sick to think of how often she'd dwelt on the past and might have beens, rather than simply enjoy the present. But here she was, doing it again, kicking herself over a mistake she couldn't reverse.

"Anonymous," she groaned, "Whitney, how could you say something so stupid?"

"What you say?" Pierre asked, swiveling his silver-haired head to glance at her in the back seat.

Whitney's immediate reaction was to reply, "Nothing," and keep her distress to herself. But why? She could use a listening ear, and chances were they wouldn't see each other again.

A lot like her and Eric.

Whitney leaned over the front seat, not wanting Pierre to take his eyes off the road. Short as her life expectancy was, she didn't want to give up what she had left with a plunge over the cliff the taxi was hugging.

"Tell me, Pierre, have you ever done something you thought was clever at the time and realized after the fact that you'd give anything not to have done it?"

"Sure," he admitted. "We all think we so smart sometimes then see we not smart at all." He took a dark, weathered hand off the wheel long enough to give a pat to hers, draped over the beat-up vinyl upholstery. "What you do? You tell Pierre and he won' tell nobody, he swear."

Sympathy from a stranger. Before today she'd tended to shy away from people she didn't know, and wasn't quick to open up to those she did know. How many friends had she failed to make because she hadn't reached out or met someone halfway?

"I screwed up, Pierre." His understanding nod was all the incentive she needed to go on. "I met this man, this incredible, wonderful man on the plane. There was something between us I can't even describe and—and he felt it too, I know he did."

"Ah, *frappé par le foudre*," Pierre said knowingly. "Struck by the lightning."

"That's exactly how it felt. I looked in his eyes and my head started to tingle and we were talking and laughing and I felt like I'd known him all my life. I thought he was getting off the plane with me, but it turned out he was flying to another part of the island, someplace called Prince Rupert Bay. I could tell he didn't want to say goodbye, either, the way he kept standing there until I made myself go on…"

A shiver went through her. The sensation when he gripped her hand—she could still feel it. And then, the brush of her arm to his chest, the press of her hip to his erection. He had been hard, hard for her. Just thinking about it created that hot sensation all over again, a primal pulse reminding her that she was still very much alive.

Her breathing quickened and she could feel her cheeks heat up when Pierre observed, "This man, he touch you."

"Yes," she whispered.

"And his touch, it like fire, no?" At her nod, he concluded, "You have the magic. You must see him again."

"If only I could. The problem is, we'd had this conversation about feeling safer with strangers sometimes than people you know and so when he asked me my name, I didn't tell him." *Why?* Whitney could only shake her head at herself. The answer was beyond her. Pierre seemed pretty sharp about such stuff; maybe he had some insights. "What would make me throw away a chance to see him again?"

"The heart," Pierre tapped his chest, "it know only two things." The taxi slowed as they neared the main guest house made of stucco and wood. It nestled cozily in the shadow of a mountain and near the river where her private bungalow should be. "Love and fear. That all the heart know, just love and fear."

"Then you think I was afraid?"

"Could be."

"But what's to be afraid of?" Besides death, that was. And Eric posed no threat there.

They rolled to a stop and as Pierre turned to her, she saw the wisdom of the ages in his brown, brown eyes. "Love."

Whitney considered that. For all of two seconds.

"Love takes time, Pierre. It doesn't happen in an hour or even a month. I don't love this man. It's impossible."

"With love, anything possible. Could be your heart know something the head say 'no' to and it make you so scared, you run away."

This conversation was starting to exhaust her. She felt

so tired. Much too tired to think beyond getting checked in and hitting the sack.

Ready to bring this Dear Abby session to a close, Whitney wound it up by claiming, "I left the way I did because I wanted him to remember me. I wanted to be one of those women who enter and exit a man's life with their mystique intact and live on forever in his mind." It had been a form of immortality she couldn't resist. Made sense.

After a shrug that seemed to imply "So you say, but sounds like bullshit to me," Pierre opened her door. As he retrieved her suitcase from the trunk of his seen-better-days cab, Whitney couldn't help but wonder how much wisdom he'd dispensed to other riders like herself, heading to a new destination while seeking some guidance as to which way to go.

Despite her need to rest, she was sorry when Pierre deposited her bags in the terra-cotta tiled entry, and with a simple farewell, he turned to leave.

"Wait," she called, reaching into her purse. "I need to pay you." From the looks of his cab, she needed to pay him double.

"No charge," he said, waving aside the bills she held out. "Ride is free. Tip included. Prince Rupert Bay, not far away. I take you there and you find him, no problem."

"I can't go chasing after him!" she protested.

"Why such a big no?"

"Because..." Because maybe he was right, maybe she could fall in love with Eric. But even if such a crazy thing was to happen, there was no way for it to last. An affair she could have, but never love. That was for the living, not the dying, even if they needed love the most. "Just because," she said, in a defeated voice.

"See?" Pierre drawled with a shake of his finger in the direction of her chest. "You scared. Look into your heart, you know why. Be brave and I take you to him. Till then, no charge. Okay?''

It wasn't okay, but rather than argue, Whitney stuffed the bills back into her wallet.

Fatigue washed over her and she wasn't certain which was the more to blame—the illness itself or the deep sense of loss she felt for the second time today. She said "so long," checked in, then went on her way, alone to her bungalow.

Too tired to unpack, Whitney just headed straight for the bedroom where she collapsed onto the bed, and fell into a deep sleep.

She woke up to the swish of her heart racing in her ears, her chest. Or maybe it was the sound of waves, rhythmically beating out two words:

Love. Fear. Love. Fear. Love...fear...

The image of a golden-eyed man surrounding her with warmth and laughter, and an erotic pulse between her thighs still lingered, as did the echo of love...fear...

It was dark. She realized she was on a bed with the remnants of an arousing dream still lingering in her half-conscious state. She and Eric had been locked together in an embrace when suddenly she'd been wrenched from his arms and spit into a cavernous darkness where she'd tumbled blindly, so alone, so afraid—

"It's okay, you were just dreaming," Whitney told herself trying to calm down. Yet her voice shook. So did her hand as she reached for the lamp on the nightstand.

The bedroom was bathed in a soft glow, illuminating the breezy, Caribbean interior of her bungalow. A ceiling fan overhead stirred the fragrant air, as well as the pages of an open book. Eric's. She'd fallen asleep with it, perhaps driven by some silly notion that she might learn more about him by osmosis.

Perusing the pages she'd conked out on, Whitney flipped through a section on seismic shifts and laser beam technology, then went for the pictures. They left her marveling at nature's most awesome force. One in particular caught her attention. Not because of the smoke rising out of a crater, but because the person who'd struck a pose nearby looked familiar.

She recognized him.

The caption beneath confirmed it.

She read his name again, just to be sure, and yes, there it was, Dr. Eric D. Townsend, the author himself, a leading expert in the field of volcanology.

Her gaze settled on his face and she felt a delicious little shiver at the sight of the man who had tapped an awesome force of nature buried within herself.

Fire. That's how it had felt when he touched her. Pierre was right. She had been afraid. Afraid to play with fire. So little time left, she couldn't squander it on fear.

Somehow she had to find the courage to go after him and chance a dance in the flames.

After freshening up, Whitney left the bungalow, book in hand. She had to eat, take good care of herself, to give her body all the strength it needed to defy the leukemia for as long as possible.

The path leading to the villa was enveloped by all manner of wildflowers, tangled vines and reaching trees. Exotic. Untamed. And spooky at night.

Love and fear. Much as she loved the idea of treating herself to whatever she wanted on the menu, she had a healthy fear of walking dark, creepy paths alone.

"Everyone comes into the world alone and they die alone," she reminded herself. "Think of it as practice." She made herself take the first step, then the next, fantasizing that Eric would be waiting for her at the end.

He wasn't, but the tiki torches and reggae music were a nice consolation prize. The true reward, however, was in achieving a simple yet courageous act. She kept surprising herself by taking risks she never would have dared before, like ordering *crapaud* instead of shrimp scampi.

As she dined on mountain frogs, which was surprisingly delicious, Eric's book proved good company. The passion he brought to his text made Whitney wonder if he was an equally passionate lover. Her guess was…yes.

She plucked the little umbrella from her mai tai, stuck it between the open pages, and closed the book with a wistful sigh. Eric had been all over the world. Handsome and personable as he was, he'd surely had women throwing themselves at him from every corner of the globe and picked up all kinds of bedroom tricks along the way.

She wasn't worldly or successful, and as for sexual experience, she was embarrassingly limited—thanks to her mother drumming it into her head that nice girls didn't and bad girls did. Her mother had been wrong and now the good daughter was on a mission to find out what she'd been missing.

Still, Whitney knew she'd feel cheap if she slept around, but one lover wouldn't trouble her conscience and if she was relegating herself to one, then she wasn't settling for less than the best. Eric Townsend made her hot. She'd made him hard, and, ohhh, there went that catch of her heart again coinciding with a heavy pulse between her legs. Then and there, she made up her mind.

She would go to Prince Rupert Bay. Since Eric was visiting with his brother, she'd wait a few days and work on a plan of seduction in the meantime. And a tan. Tanned skin and white dresses definitely looked sexy, especially with a French braid.

"Hi. I noticed you were sitting alone and I wondered if you'd like to join me in the bar for an after-dinner drink."

Whitney made herself smile at the man who was trying to pick her up. He wasn't bad looking, but something about the flashy rings on his fingers and the tight black clothes he was wearing reminded her of Tom Jones in his heyday.

"Thanks for the offer, but I'm calling it an early night."

"Then maybe tomorrow night?" he persisted. Before she could inform him she didn't accept dates with strangers—at least not this one—he said, "My name's Richard Kincaid. Dick to my friends, and to you, too. And you would be…?"

"Julia Roberts." It was the first name that popped into her head that wasn't remotely close to her own.

"Nah, get outta here!"

"It's true," she insisted, amazed at her own audacity by coming up with such a far-fetched lie. "Really, it is."

"Hey, I can't go back to Miami and tell my pals I let Julia Roberts get away. Since you won't join me in the bar, mind if I join you at the table?"

He pulled out a chair and Whitney sprang to her feet. Gripping Eric's book to her like some talisman to ward off a tropical snake, she quickly said, "Have to get my beauty sleep, bye!" and made her escape.

Whitney was halfway out of the restaurant when she realized she'd left her mai tai behind. She really wanted to finish it, maybe while she soaked in the tub. Normally she'd just cut her losses rather than return to a table where she had probably come off a little rude. Then again, if anyone was rude, it was Dick, sending her running from her own table.

With an assertiveness she'd always longed to have, Whitney squared her shoulders, returned to the table, and retrieved her glass from Dick, who apparently intended to dump the remains in his mouth.

"I believe that's mine," she told him, realizing she sounded pretty ballsy. It felt good to stand up for her right to drink her own drink and spend the evening as she damn well pleased. Forget calling it a night, she wanted her table back.

Sitting back down, she said with a crisp politeness, "Actually, Dick, I'm not ready to leave, but I would appreciate you doing so yourself. The truth is, my name is Whitney and while I thank you for your interest, you should hit on someone else. I'm meeting my lover soon and I'll bide my time until then."

Dick held up his hands in defeat. "Hey, no problem. But if he doesn't show up, I'll pull out the stops until you agree to an evening out just to get rid of me." He gave her a thoughtful look. "Know what? I wish more women were as honest as you. It sure would save men a lot of second-guessing about what's really going on in their heads. You're okay, Whitney. Later."

Well, Whitney thought as he left, what a revelation! Not only did Dick seem to respect her more, she felt better about herself. The positive changes she'd made in her life in a matter of days were no less than amazing. Seducing a worldly man had once been the stuff of fantasies, but her growing lust for life wanted nothing to do with that. Fantasizing wasn't enough. She wanted, needed the real thing, and Whitney Smith was going after it....

Day after tomorrow. Her schedule had just moved up due to a major incentive: if she didn't snag the lover she wanted and soon, Dick would be back.

CHAPTER FOUR

"ARE WE having fun yet?"

"Huh? Oh sure, this is great, Adam." Eric hoped his reply didn't sound as distracted as he felt. Despite evidence to the contrary, he was still on yesterday's plane rather than chilling out with his brother whom he hadn't seen in nearly a year. "Ready to do some more snorkeling? The scenery's beautiful down there."

"It's not bad up here, either." Adam nodded toward a topless sunbather, lying on her stomach, her breasts partially visible from the sides. "I think I want to come back as a beach towel in my next life. To be exact, that beach towel in this one. She's hot, isn't she?"

After a glance at the babe in question, Eric shrugged. "She's okay."

"Okay?" Adam repeated, his perfect features reflecting curiosity. Though he made his living as a model, and a good living at that, Eric knew his younger brother thought such physical perfection to be more of a liability than not. Perhaps that's why he'd never been envious, despite his own peculiar draw of the genetic mix and a wound from the line of duty which compelled him to keep a tank top on, even when swimming.

As Eric reached for his goggles, Adam stopped him in his tracks by casually asking, "So, what's her name?"

Gazing into the horizon of endless sky and sky-blue sea, all Eric could see were her eyes, her unforgettable face; in the gentle lapping of the waves to shore he heard her lilting laughter. The reactive clutch in his groin and the unfamiliar tightening in his chest left no doubt as to the mystery lady's ongoing hold.

"I wish I knew," he replied with a heavy sigh. "She got off in Roseau and wouldn't tell me when I asked. Maybe because I had foot-in-mouth disease practically the whole time we were together."

"You?" Adam scoffed. "I don't believe it."

"Believe it. And the funny thing is, I was having the time of my life hearing her laugh, so I didn't even care if I was making a fool of myself—until she walked off." Eric lifted a handful of sand and watched it trickle through his fist like so much time in an hourglass. "She worked some kind of mojo on me. I can't get her out of my mind."

Adam wiggled a pinky in his ear to unclog whatever must be affecting his hearing. Had such a statement come from someone else, he wouldn't think much of it, but this was Eric, not one of those hopeless romantics who lost their hearts along with their heads. Eric was too analytical for that, the brain of the family whose thirst for knowledge extended from the back of cereal boxes to subjects that wouldn't even come up on *Jeopardy*—not the least of which was his fascination with their Chinese ancestry, including the hanky-panky practices of emperors a kazillion years ago.

As for Eric's own love life, who really knew? He'd never been one to kiss and tell. Too bad, too, since there was bound to be plenty to tell. Eric was a lady's man. He was also a man of action, a man of his word. A man whose courage bordered on stupidity as far as his brother was concerned. Even after taking a hit that had left his back looking like a strip of fried bacon, Eric preferred getting blown to Kingdom Come over the trappings of marriage, family, nice house, a nine-to-five job and sex on a regular basis, even if it did get to be predictable. Whatever Eric was in search of, it didn't include the mundane or a woman to tie him down. For that reason, Adam could hardly believe this was his brother, staring dreamily into the distance while the sand he kept sifting through his hand was landing in his beer bottle.

The kid brother in Adam couldn't resist raising his own in a salute so Eric might follow suit. "She must have been something else to make such an impression on you."

"Something else? I'll say. A goddess." With a tap of bottle to bottle, Eric took a swig, choked, and spit the gritty foam out. Swiping the back of his arm over his mouth, he demanded, "Did you put sand in my beer?"

"This is too much," Adam chortled, gathering his gear and packing up the cooler. "Get off your ass and get going." Imitating their father when they got out of line as boys, he added firmly, "Hop to and that's an order!"

Eric sprang to his feet, put up his fists and did his best De Niro, *"Are you talking to me?"*

They feigned a few punches before Eric slapped Adam on the back. "Sure you don't mind me taking off so soon? I can wait a few days."

Adam quirked a brow. "Okay," he agreed. "Wait."

Shoving a hand through his hair, thick and sleek and Oriental as the mother he had inherited it from, the scientist in Eric bowed to a greater force than he'd ever encountered. "Can't. Sorry, Adam, I know we've got lots of catching up to do, but I have to find her. Today."

"Then do it. Call if you need me. I'll be around for another week before I take off for the next assignment."

"Paris?"

"Oui."

Since Adam didn't mention Jolene, Eric didn't ask. Theirs was one of those turbulent on-again-off-again relationships he'd never understood. It was as if they were hooked on the chemistry between them—never mind it kept going bad. Which it obviously had, again, given Adam's offer.

"You take the Jeep and I'll introduce myself to the babe. I'm sure she won't mind keeping me company while you find that goddess who makes her look just okay."

ERIC PULLED UP to the Springfield Guest House. He'd been so eager to get here that he'd even asked for directions after taking a wrong turn that put him half an hour behind and arriving past dusk.

The whole time he'd driven, his heart had been racing. His need to see her was a little frightening. He felt compelled by some inner dictate, guided by instinct, not reason.

He went in, certain of nothing but the description he gave the desk clerk. Yes, she'd checked in yesterday. And yes, she was alone.

Eric was elated. And so disturbed by his ease in securing a bungalow next to hers that only a fool in supreme denial would tell himself this woman didn't matter to him in some significant way. The attendant was too trusting; for all she knew he could be a stalker who was or was not telling the truth about how he had met this lovely lady on a plane who'd recommended these accommodations, which were a far cry better than where he'd stayed the night before. He owed her a thank you, but how embarrassing, he couldn't remember her name. Miz Smith? Yes, of course, Ms. Smith, that was it.

Eric's protective instincts rose another notch upon being informed that river bathing was a local custom and if Miz Smith wasn't in her bungalow she might be behind it, bathing in the river. Dr. Townsend might also give it a try. Later. They wanted no complaints about invasion of privacy.

After giving an assurance that no such complaints would be forthcoming, Eric checked out the restaurant. She wasn't there. But the hostess did have a reservation for Smith, party of one, in an hour. He took the liberty of changing it to party of two, in a couple.

As he walked down the path to their separate bungalows and whatever fate they might share, Eric could only hope his beloved Grandmother Ming—who handwrote messages of advice in parables and placed them in the fortune cookies she served after dinner in her restaurant—had been right about the universe throwing open all sorts of doors once one took a step of faith, and knocked.

THE RIVER at night was a tad too cool, but it felt good against the heat of Whitney's skin. Time, which she'd become all too aware of in her determination to ignore its march, had ceased to exist as she'd basked in the sun earlier in the day on a deserted stretch of sand, engrossed in her reading.

The outing had been a tonic for her; she felt better than she had in ages, she thought as she leisurely swam. Of course it had been ages since she'd taken a day off to do nothing but pamper herself. Reading, resting, eating without a care to calories or fat grams, and thinking of Eric. That was her whole day.

And what of him? she wondered yet again. Had he thought of her even half as often? Lord, she hoped so. The closer she came to putting her grand scheme into action, the more nervous she was getting. Dealing with Dick was one thing; seducing a man as dauntingly impressive as Eric was another. But she wouldn't let herself think about that now; she'd stick to her new philosophy of living in the today, instead.

That's right, tomorrow was another day and a potentially auspicious one at that, so she'd better haul her shriveled-as-a-prune butt out of the river, and act as if she strutted around naked outside on a regular basis.

Though a glance in all directions assured her no one else was around, Whitney fought the urge to race to her robe and throw it on in case a straggler came along.

"Who are you?" she asked herself. Was she a scaredy-cat who hid inside storybooks and see-Jane-run clothes or a hot tamale who knew how to shake her booty and get her man? Okay, maybe that wasn't her—not yet, anyway. But if she couldn't show her body to the night, how would she ever get her clothes off in front of Eric?

"C'mon, Whitney, whoever you are," she said defiantly. "You can do this. Think of it as an un-dress rehearsal and imagine he's watching you now."

Moving with a quiet grace, she refused to let modesty steal the pleasure of a warm breeze whispering over the chill of her flesh. She pretended it was a human touch rather than the balmy air caressing her, imagined that the touch belonged to a man who had bewitched her senses.

And how she would love to cast some siren spell of her own over him, see him there on the sandy bank, bedazzled by the water nymph emerging from the river and raising her arms to the night sky.

The breeze licked the droplets of water from her skin and she pretended it was his mouth sipping at the moisture. Her robe absorbed the rest as she slipped her arms through the sleeves and tied the sash at her waist....

Whitney's hands froze there.

A lone figure stepped out of the shadows behind her

bungalow. Some instinct insisted she knew this person. A man.

He came nearer and nearer, and though she discounted her instincts as fantasy gone amuck, her heart sped up, her palms went wetter than the river, and her inner thighs clenched.

She could smell the scent of citrus and spice he'd worn on the plane, carried on the light breeze. She could hear the sand shift as his feet stopped mere inches from her bare toes.

And then there was silence. A silence so absolute that the world seemed filled with the catch of her breath as his hands slowly lifted to her face and touched her as if she were made of the most delicate porcelain and might break should he apply the slightest pressure.

Somehow her hands found their way to his face as well. They spoke in silence, sharing some language that went beyond the explicable and translated into tongues unknown.

A yearning so intense it was a hunger to touch and be touched swelled between them. Without hesitation or even awareness beyond the rightness of how he felt, her palms slid over the sloping plane of hard muscle and crisp cotton covering his shoulders. The amber flecks in his eyes disappeared into the dilated blackness of his pupils.

He gripped the lapels of her robe.

Had he been there, watching? Did he take her stillness as assent to reveal what he had already seen? And would she let him if he tried? Would she?

She would, Whitney realized with no small surprise. She would gladly let this man undress her and touch her however he wished here and now, that's how right this felt.

His eyes said he wanted to even as he closed her robe tighter and pulled her against him with a quick, little yank.

It was an aggressive move from a man who then paused before gently placing his lips upon hers.

Is it all right that I'm doing this? was what she heard in that tentative, first brush.

She answered with a deeper press of her own lips, slightly parting, breathing him in. He tasted of peppermint and lemon, tasted divine. The tip of his tongue introduced itself to hers and after a leisurely greeting, then a heartfelt hello, their kiss became an earnest search of just who they were getting to know.

Never had she met a man like him. A playful tease, a curious seeker, thoughtful of his findings while urging her to do some exploring herself. The interior of his mouth was as warm and inviting as home, yet had an exotic taste, a chameleon texture that was alternately sleek and rough and made a woman feel as if she were flirting with danger. His patience was unlimited and he proved a gracious host, so gracious that her own patience ran out and she wanted to do more than flirt with whatever danger might lurk beneath the still waters of his courteous surface.

Was she ravishing him? Oh yes, Whitney thought she was. And he was letting her do as she pleased, even making a low, rumbling sound of excitement when she twined her fingers in his hair—so thick, so soft, so lustrous—and grabbed blindly at his back.

He was suddenly quiet. Had she done something wrong? Whitney eased up on her kissing and began to stroke his back, only for Eric to prove he was her match and more when it came to pillaging and plundering intimate stores.

She could feel the quick, steady beat of his heart pressed against her breasts. And his hips, flush against her belly, imparted the assurance that he was very much a man. One who was hard. Hard for her.

Too far gone to care if anyone might happen upon them,

she fought the urge to drag him down to the sand. Fire, pure fire engulfed her as he slid his lips to her throat and with a slow, lazy lick, declared their first kiss over and done.

How much time passed as they stood there with her arms around his neck and his hugging her waist while he breathed deep and she gasped for air, Whitney had no idea. It didn't matter anyway since she would gladly stay in this moment for an eternity and beyond.

"Since I met you on the plane," he said quietly, "I've gone through all the motions of eating, sleeping, trying to pretend I was having a good time. I wasn't. All I've been able to think about is you and damn myself for letting the most unforgettable woman I've ever met get away. I must've thought of a thousand different things I wished I'd said or asked, but for the life of me I can't remember what they were. Except for just one question."

Whitney cupped his cheek, stroking the shadow that had lightly abraded her skin. "And just what would that question be, Dr. Townsend?"

A flick of his tongue to the center of her palm, then he gave her that smile that could charm the pants off a nun.

"Besides Anonymous and Smith, have you got a name?"

CHAPTER FIVE

THE WOMAN who had haunted his thoughts for nearly two days now had a name.

"Whitney," Eric murmured. The vision across the small table appeared more ethereal than real. He sure didn't feel very real himself at the moment. He was euphoric, entranced by the sight of satiny smooth bare shoulders atop a heart-shaped white bodice. She sat like a perfect pearl in the middle of the villa's private courtyard, a generous slice of paradise with the fragrance of wild orchids blowing gently through her hair.

Studying her over a flickering taper candle, Eric sipped an after-dinner cognac. His mouth still tasted more of Whitney than the meal he'd consumed. All he could think about was their kiss—oh man, that kiss—and wonder why he hadn't filled his hands with more of the luscious body he had watched emerge from the water.

Conscience had dictated he not steal more than a glance but he'd been held in thrall, consumed by a rush he could only liken to a full body orgasm, circulating around vein and muscle and rocketing through his brain.

"Penny for your thoughts," she said with a melodic lilt.

Eric chuckled. "You'd have to pay me a million to incriminate myself like that." And what was going on in Whitney's intriguing mind? He had a need to know more than the fact she was living off an inheritance, had been in the book biz in some vague way, nuked a mean frozen pizza, loved old movies and hated politics.

"I'm no millionaire myself," he continued, "but I'd ante up what I've got to get inside your head." On impulse, Eric laid down all the money he had with him. There was plenty more in the bank and stashed into investments that he'd be tempted to fork over if he could buy her for that much. But not even Donald Trump could buy a woman who wasn't for sale.

Whitney pushed the money clip back at him. "A fool and his money are soon parted and you're no fool, Eric. Neither am I. I'll tell you what I was thinking. For free."

She sounded more amused than offended. Unlike Amy, Whitney didn't seem to take life or herself too seriously. A quality he greatly admired.

"I was thinking," she continued, "and still am, that I feel like I'm windsurfing on a cloud. I'm with a man who made even dinner seem bland and, for the record, that was some of the best cajun cooking I've ever had."

"I didn't taste a bite. My mind was elsewhere. Still is."

Whitney walked two tapered fingertips around the candle and slid her hand over his. "And where would that be?"

Eric studied the contrast of their skins, hers soft and light, his dark and roughened by laboring outdoors. He raised his hand and she did the same, meeting him in a parallel connection, fingertip to fingertip, palm to palm. He felt such intimacy in this simple touch, a deeper intimacy than he'd ever felt, even in the throes of sex. Maybe that was some of the difference with Whitney. She'd captivated his mind, his imagination and a part of his heart that had eluded even himself before their paths had crossed.

He had a strong premonition they wouldn't be parting any time soon.

"My thoughts have been on you, Whitney. In a way I can't explain, I feel like I've known you for years and yet I can't stop wondering who you are." Leaning forward, he asked the one thing he was burning to know. "Who are you, Whitney Smith?"

Who are you? How many times of late had she asked herself that very question? No answer so far and finding one for Eric sure wasn't easy when he made it so hard to think. All he had to do was touch her with his hand, and her heart felt as if it had sprouted wings. It begged to fly wherever this romance might take her, to soar beyond some hot, sweet memories to warm herself with when her life dwindled to an end and his continued on.

She could tell Eric many things, but not this. If he knew she was sick, he wouldn't see her as the healthy, vibrant woman he thought her to be. And for now, that's who she was. It made no difference who she had been. That woman was gone. Unfortunately she'd gotten a little carried away in creating the glamorous new Whitney and bent the truth about her job, made it sound as if she worked in book distribution—a half lie—and lived out of a suitcase—a lie, pure and simple. But the part about quitting and planning to live a Bohemian life until her money ran out was true.

And honest she would continue to be while keeping him guessing about who she was.

"Who am I?" Whitney repeated, having found an answer that might or might not satisfy Eric, but it certainly suited her. "I am becoming."

He tilted his head, studied her with undisguised fascination. "And just who or what are you becoming?"

"I am becoming who I want to be and doing whatever feels right to get there," she proclaimed.

Eric stroked his chin as if puzzling a brain teaser and that brain teaser was she. Earnestly, as if her answer were very important, he asked, "Do you know where 'there' is?"

"Not really but I suppose I'll know if and when I arrive.

But if I don't, so what? It's the journey, not the destination that counts, anyway."

"Amazing," Eric said with such awe that Whitney saw herself becoming…brilliant. Yes, she felt brilliant! "What you just said, it's amazing. *You* amaze me."

Whitney proceeded to amaze herself with what popped out next. "If you think I'm amazing now, stick around and there's no telling what I'll become."

"Oh, believe me, I'm sticking around," he assured her with a grin that was somehow both wicked and sweet. "Whenever I get impatient, my grandmother Ming always reminds me, 'It is the journey, not the destination.' Her very words. I've heard that phrase from the time I spent summers with her as a kid to just last week on the phone. To hear you say it, is…well, pretty incredible."

Circling her wrist, he pulled her hand his way and quietly informed her, "You, Ms. Smith, are a very sexy woman who's got one helluva sexy brain. Watching those delectable lips of yours move could drive any man to distraction, but it's what comes out of them that really turns me on. C'mon, say something else and do it to me some more."

One of her fingertips disappeared into his mouth. The image, the motion, looked as indecent as Eric made her feel. Her heart hammered.

Whitney drew in a sharp breath. "Where does your grandmother live?"

"San Francisco. Chinatown," he answered between licks.

"Is she Chinese?"

A nod.

"Is that where you get your eyes, your hair?"

She was suddenly sorry she'd asked. Eric stopped what he was doing and gave her a sly smile.

"I'll tell you on one condition."

Considering the condition she was in, she was ready to agree to anything. "Name it."

"For each piece of information I give up about myself, you match me."

The stinker! Eric knew she couldn't claim not fair. What he didn't know was that she couldn't match him at all in interesting tidbits about her background. Unless she lied. Her earlier fudging aside, she was a terrible liar and had no intentions of developing such an awful skill. Other skills, however, she was more than eager to expand. Perhaps they could work a deal that would leave her mystique intact in exchange for intimate favors.

"What if I match you with something besides biographical data?"

His gaze lowered to her breasts and moved slowly, suggestively back to her flushed face. "Such as?"

"A kiss," she said breathlessly, unable to bring herself to be more specific than that. When Eric tapped his lips, appearing to debate, she urged his assent with an emboldened forward lean, a whispered, "Touching me, that's okay, too."

Oh dear, what had she gotten herself into? A single finger dipped into her cleavage and such was the jolt that she nearly came out of her chair. His touch was light yet seared a path from between her breasts, up her neck, to her chin.

Eric tilted it up.

"I can touch you anyway," he said knowingly.

No use in refuting him and she didn't have time to play games. "Yes," she admitted. "I want you to touch me, Eric. And I want to touch you."

"Oh, but you have." The sexual edge of his tone softened to the consistency of warm butter and the slow burn of his eyes became suddenly gentle. "You've touched me like I've never been touched before."

The change in him was as unexpected as the melting sensation that came over her, making her feel as if he had slipped a very warm hand between her legs and was sliding it ever so slowly up her inner thighs. They were quivering now, making her realize that Eric was dangerous, all right. And the danger he was went way beyond the taste of his kisses.

The remnants of good judgment she'd always exercised in the past insisted she switch subjects and get on safer ground fast. But she didn't want to use good judgment. She didn't want to play it safe. Whoever she was apparently liked a little danger. Maybe even a lot of danger, considering the personal turf she boldly joined him on.

"And you touch me, Eric. I feel you touching me now and you don't have a hand on me. How you do it, I don't know, but you do and it makes me feel..." She sighed voluptuously.

"Excited?"

"Oh, yes. So excited, in fact, that..." She shivered.

"It makes you a little afraid?"

Whitney nodded, knowing she had cause to be afraid of these strange feelings and not just a little, especially since she found this fear to be a bit exciting itself. Who was she? The fact she was no longer sure was rather exciting. The new and improved Whitney was more interesting, fun and daring than the too-good-for-her-own-good Whitney she'd left behind. And good riddance to the poor girl since Eric wouldn't be attracted to her in the least, much less be hearing him say:

"Know what? I'm a little afraid, too. It's only natural to fear what we don't understand and that's okay as long as we don't let that fear keep us from confronting the unknown. Ignorance might be bliss but it's really the coward's way out. I'm not a coward, Whitney. And neither are you."

"How can you be so sure about that?"

"Because you would've changed subjects before now and I wouldn't be telling you that I've always considered myself a man of reason but with you I feel things I can't explain." He tapped his temple. "In my brain it makes no sense, but in here—" he put a hand over his heart "—it's like I have this other knowledge inside, insisting we're kindred spirits and were destined to meet on that plane. I'm a scientist by trade and nature, but I've never discounted the possibility of unseen forces at work. If anything could make a believer out of me, it's meeting you. I've even found myself wondering if it's really for the first time."

Was there such a thing as reincarnation? Only heaven knew if she and Eric were picking up where they'd left off in another lifetime. If so, their timing in this one was lousy and she could only hope they'd get another chance down the line.

"There's no way to tell, Eric, but who's to say? Maybe you were Napoleon and I, Josephine. Or if we really want to get fantastical, how about King Arthur and Guinevere or Romeo and Juliet?"

"They didn't have happy endings," he pointed out.

Neither would she and Eric. But that was too much of a downer to contemplate so she suggested, "Then what about Elizabeth Barrett and Robert Browning?"

"I can go for that, even if you're a lot easier on the eyes and the most poetic sentiment I can come up with is, Babe you're one hot number. When I look at you the last thing I want to do is slumber."

"Best line I ever heard." She laughed and he joined her

as if they both knew better than that, when Whitney knew full well she hadn't been joking.

"Enough about poets and poetry," Eric said. "I'd rather talk about you. Tell me what I don't know and I'll take your secrets to my grave. I give you my word and my word is unbreakable."

Of that, Whitney had no doubt. Disregarding his *grave* turn of phrase, she decided her so-called mystique wasn't nearly as important as fostering a relationship with a very, very special man who could indeed touch her if he so pleased. Which apparently he did, tracing her lips, then tapping them until she took a decisive nip.

"What do you want to know?"

"Everything. From your first breath to where you want to go and who you're becoming."

"That could take longer than—" *I have.* All too aware such thinking was a poison that could steal her happiness, Whitney wrapped her mortality up, put her future into a box, sealed the box tight and banished it to a nook in her brain she willed herself to forget existed.

"Let's just say that becoming is like being a work in progress and I'd rather not spend the time speculating. Instead, I'll tell you that I can't compete with your accomplishments, but I did place first in the national spelling bee in grade school. I didn't fare as well in high school since I didn't make cheerleader and ended up on the pep squad. I took piano lessons for eight years and my teacher said I could be a concert pianist if only I had the discipline instead of preferring to play by ear. Bored yet?"

"Hardly." Eric cupped his ear. "Tell me more."

"Okay. I never knew my grandmother but according to Mama she was a spitfire who had several divorces, when even one was the kiss of death for any woman who wanted to be respectable. I think that had a lot to do with being raised on the merits of respectability, going to church three times a week and wondering what made me so sinful I needed to get my head dunked in order to be saved. I've finally quit trying to figure that out and now I'm hell-bent and determined to commit all the sins I've already been saved from.''

''Amen to that,'' Eric said with such conviction she half expected him to throw in a ''praise the Lord!'' Instead he propped an elbow on the table and put chin to palm as if settling in for the rest of the story he could hardly wait to hear. ''I want to know more about this mother of yours. She must be special to have raised a daughter like you.''

''She was a good woman.'' So good that Whitney felt a pang of conscience. Mama had worked her tail off for those piano lessons because she'd always strived to give her child all the things her own mother had never provided. Like security. Like a home that stayed put and didn't change from lover to lover, husband to husband. Unimpeachable morals were right up there with the work ethic when it came to the foundation she'd been raised on.

''A good woman,'' Whitney repeated, hoping Mama couldn't see her now since work had gone the way of the strict morals that were also getting the heave-ho. Still Whitney refused to feel guilty in what little time she had left. For now she was alive and the living was easy. As for Mama, she continued, ''She worked too hard and didn't play enough. But she always had time for me and there's not a day that goes by that I don't wish she was still alive.''

''I'm sorry.'' Eric's expression was sincere, as if he truly felt her loss. ''How old was she when it happened?''

''Only thirty-six. I was eighteen. She had cancer.''

''Thirty-six, that's about my age. I can't even imagine—'' He stopped short, then amended, ''I've had a couple of close calls in the field, so I've more than imagined losing my life early. But cancer? With a young daughter involved? That's tragic. It must have been a horrible time for you."

"Worse than horrible." For some reason Whitney felt like crying. Eric really seemed to care. She'd been alone for so long, had nursed her grief in private. That had been her mother's way and she'd tried valiantly to emulate her mother's strength. But opening up to Eric, letting him in, accepting his sympathy, what a comfort it was turning out to be.

Maybe Mama's way wasn't always the right way after all.

"What about your father?" he gently persisted. "Did he help you get through it or was he too torn up to be much help?"

Whitney stared into the candle flame, wondering what to say. When it came to her father, Mama's judgment had faltered. He was her only real weak spot and she'd done a terrible disservice to herself and her child by trying to hang on to a man who didn't want them.

Though it should have faded into the distant past long ago, it hadn't; though the memory shouldn't hurt anymore, it still did. She never talked about this part of her life. Maybe if she got it out, she could let it go.

"He deserted us when I was still pretty small," she began, her gaze fixed on the descending flame. "But I was old enough to keep hoping he'd come back since my mother missed him. She cried for a long time and for a long time I thought it was my fault." Looking up, Whitney saw no pity in Eric's gaze, but she did see an echo of the anger she felt. "It took me awhile to realize he was an irresponsible jerk and we were better off without him."

"Bastard." Eric's jaw clenched. Then came his next

question, so blunt it caught her off guard. "Do you distrust men because of him?"

Did she? Was that part of the reason she'd never had a hard time keeping her hymen intact when a boyfriend wanted proof she loved him? She not only didn't love the few who'd tried that line, she'd known they didn't love her or such an ultimatum wouldn't have been issued. That was always the end of that relationship because the jerks couldn't be...

Trusted. They would use her then lose her, just like her father had her mother.

"No, I don't trust men," she admitted. "At least, I haven't in the past when it came to the flavor of the month I dated." Flavor of the month, yeah right. But it wouldn't hurt for Eric to think she'd had more romantic entanglements than she could legitimately claim. Besides, the woman she was becoming would've had all the dates and affairs she wanted.

"Forget the past," he told her. "What about me? Do you think I'm more trustworthy than those flavors of the month?"

"I do." She also thought his directness was irresistible, as was the sexy curl of his barely there grin.

"Good. Because I have no interest in being your next flavor of the month. As far as I'm concerned, I'm a veritable Baskin-Robbins and you're more than welcome to sample the store."

Whitney licked her lips. "I always did have a weakness for ice cream. My favorite's Rocky Road."

"Plant one on me and I'll see what I can serve up."

CHAPTER SIX

THEY ROSE slightly, met in the middle. Whitney teased his lips until Eric went for more. It was such fun to play the tease and how heady the thrill of being so wanted by a man that he seemed hard pressed not to leap across the table when she pushed him away and settled back into her seat.

"Uh, uh, uh," Whitney lightly scolded with a shake of her finger. "A deal's a deal. You owe me, so dish."

"With a kiss like that, all you get is the Cliff's Notes version," Eric grumbled. Pulling a band from his ponytail, he shook out his not-quite shoulder length hair and angled his gaze at her. Her own beheld a majestic man, tall in his boots and sure of where he stood.

"The eyes, the hair come compliments of my grandmother," he explained. "I'm one quarter Chinese and three quarters you-name-it thanks to both grandfathers having a diverse pedigree. As for growing up, I was a military brat. Lived in seven countries and ten states in as many years and changed schools just as often. I have one brother, Adam, three years younger and the only friend who moved when I did, so we've always been tight. He's a model and women adore him so don't plan on my introducing the two of you any time soon."

Palms down, arms braced on the table, he leaned in. "I keep an office and apartment in Portland, but spend as little time there as possible. Divorced once, no kids. I don't smoke, though unlike Clinton, I did inhale more than once in my wilder days. Interesting experience, but I'd rather get high on white-water rafting, skydiving or sex, all of which give me the kind of rush I feel just looking at you. If you want any other stats, you'll have to persuade me to talk.''

"I have a better idea." Whitney reached for his shoulders and pulled up on the hard slope she could feel flexing beneath her palms. "Why don't I persuade you not—"

He swallowed her remaining words in an openmouthed kiss. Talking, she thought, who needed it when there was so much more to learn about this man in the torrid yet tender way he took her with his slanting lips and fencing tongue. As for his hands, they were on her as well and well he did use them to stroke her throat lightly and discreetly circle a breast.

He was hard, hard for her. This he expressed in an eloquent groan that called out to a woman who was learning to let go and give in to the ache he created. An ache so terrible it was wonderful, making her want to feel him in her hand, making her so hot she burned. She could even hear the crackle, smell the singe of—

"Your hair!" Eric jerked back, clasped the crackling strand in a fist while gutting the candle with his thumb.

Startled, but not overly upset since Eric had smothered the fire before any real damage was done, Whitney couldn't fathom why he seemed so concerned.

"Are you all right?"

"Sure." She laughed, ready to pick up where they'd left off. "Except for the smell. Pee-uuu!"

Eric wasn't laughing. "Flesh smells even worse. Fire isn't anything to mess around with. I should've thought of the candle but obviously I wasn't thinking past getting what I wanted. I'm sorry, Whitney. That was irresponsible of me."

What was this about burning flesh? Whitney wanted to ask about his comment and find out why he was taking this minor incident so seriously. Any details about burning flesh, however, she'd rather be blissfully ignorant of, even if it was the coward's way out. *Ashes in an urn, go away, go away, I won't let such thoughts spoil my day.*

Wanting the fire back, minus the actual flames, she assured him, "No apologies needed. But if you packed a pair of scissors, I'll be glad to—"

"This should work." Eric pulled out a pocket knife before she could suggest they head to his bungalow on the pretext of searching for some scissors he had no need to possess, given the blade he whipped out. "Mind if I do the honors?"

Whitney's gaze fixed on the sharp, gleaming metal. She'd had an aversion to knives since needing stitches after slicing off a fleshy hunk of her thumb.

"I don't like knives." Whitney held up the crescent moon on the back of her right thumb. "Ever since I carved more than an orange while Mama was working and the baby-sitter had her ear glued to the phone, I've been afraid of knives."

"But you were a little kid and I'm anything but."

"True."

"And you do trust me, don't you?"

"Yes."

He gripped the charred strand and pulled it away from her face. Her scalp tingled from the tug to her roots; apprehension swirled in the pit of her stomach.

"Then close your eyes and don't think about it. Just relax and let go of your fear of knives, along with any fears of getting involved with me that might be less than exciting."

Peeking beneath her lashes as he severed what he held with a quick, clean slice, she felt something overtake her. An exciting, savage something that contrasted with Eric's gentle fingering of her spliced hair. Dangerous? Oh yes, he was as dangerous as any man came. A drug she could get hooked on if she wasn't very, very careful about controlling her potential addiction to him.

"I cut off an inch more than needed. If you don't mind, I'd like to keep it."

"Mind?" Where was her mind? She had to be crazy, getting so aroused that she was ready for him to put his knife to her dress and slice it in half, along with her Victoria's Secret lingerie. "I'm flattered you'd want it. But why?"

"I could say it's because I love your hair, that it reminds me of old copper pennies buffed to a sheen." Eric pocketed the knife and took out a small leather pouch. "Or I could say it's a keepsake of a kiss so scorching it could've sent us both up in flames." He opened the drawstrings. "Both of which are true but that's not why I want to add it to the heirloom my grandmother gave me."

He shook out the pouch and into his palm tumbled a dainty gold chain with a circular medallion attached. A lazy S curve divided the middle, one side black, the other white, with a red dot, top and bottom.

"It's a Tai Chi symbol. I'm sure you've seen them before."

Who hadn't? Otherwise known as yin-yang symbols, they were on posters and stickers everywhere you looked.

But the one Eric placed in her palm wasn't cheaply made and it wasn't anywhere near new.

Studying the inlay of onyx and alabaster with a round ruby on each, Whitney asked, "How old is this?"

"Very old," was the best reply he could give her. "The symbol, it's a lot more ancient and meaningful than most people realize." Pausing, Eric wondered how far he should take this. When the student is ready, the teacher will come.

So said the Buddhists, anyhow. Far be it from him to shove the knowledge he'd acquired onto others, particularly since many would find peculiar what he honored as wisdom from the ancients. An extremely sensual wisdom. Much as he longed to share it with Whitney, if she wanted to know more, she'd ask.

"I hate to show my ignorance, but I thought some hippy from the 60's came up with the design and as for yin and yang, I knew it meant man and woman, but I still have no idea which is which." She tilted her head and peered up at him, a woman with an inquiring mind who was inspiring all sorts of ideas in his. "Care to educate me?"

"Love to." Not only was Whitney giving him the opportunity he'd hoped for, she'd just opened the door to a rare intimacy only a very special partner could share. "Yin is female energy, yang, male. They're opposite, but complementary. When they're opposed, the world is off-kilter. But when they mate, all is in harmony. The Tao was created by their mating."

Watching closely for a reaction, Eric was pleased by the way she touched his prized possession. Passed down in the family for generations, his grandmother had given it to him for luck in love after he'd deemed himself an abject failure at it.

"If this Tao was made by yin and yang getting together, was the result a girl or a boy or some mix of the genders?"

"It wasn't RuPaul," Eric chuckled. "More of an insight into the balance of nature, humanity, and the spiritual. The Way that can't be charted, the Name that can't be described, the Truth that is unknowable—that's the Tao. Guess you could say it's a pretty good metaphor for the way men and women relate, Mars and Venus as it were. We're mysteries to each other, yet there's this drive that keeps us searching for that perfect complement to our opposing natures.''

"Ah, yes.'' Whitney sighed, a bit sadly it seemed. "The proverbial search for Mr. or Ms. Right.''

"It's as old as time,'' Eric agreed, wondering if by some miracle he had found her. Never had he asked a woman for a lock of her hair and never before had he freaked over a minor accident. True, fire to a body part cut too close for comfort, but he'd been seized by the need to protect her. Good thing Whitney bore little, if any, resemblance to Amy. He was bad news for the nesters of the world and should Whitney be a nester, the kindest thing he could do for them both would be to hightail it home. Wherever that might be.

"Have you ever been married?'' he asked, wondering if she, too, might be remembering a grave error in judgment and the emotional toll it took on those who threw in their lots with an incompatible mate.

"Never have been and don't expect I ever will be,'' she declared with authority. Such a statement of fact didn't mesh with her stroke of the amulet as if she were rubbing an ancient lamp and hoping a genie would appear despite believing in no such thing.

"Life is full of surprises, Whitney. It could change your mind yet.'' And who knew? Maybe he would be the man who slammed her expectations into reverse. He wasn't looking for a wife, but looking at Whitney didn't provoke thoughts of an affair. She had too much substance to qualify for the transient sort of liaison he'd had his fill of, including his marriage to Amy. Funny thing about marriage, a legal license might make a union legit and if it was blessed by the church, supposedly all the more binding. But neither amounted to more than words on paper and a self-deluded few out of the mouth, unless the commitment was fully there and what was in the heart was forever and true.

I do, he'd said to Amy. For better or worse, for richer or poorer, in sickness and in health, he'd vowed all that to her. Being a man of his word, it grieved him sorely that he'd broken his vows and the impetuousness of youth didn't excuse his failing.

Neither was his regretful failure an excuse to be a Peter Pan who would rather hole up in Neverneverland than learn from his mistakes and take a chance at love again.

"I don't see marriage in my future," Whitney insisted with the certainty he'd felt himself until now. "But you are right about life being full of surprises."

Was that a hint of bitterness in her voice? No, he must have imagined it, given the pert flash of her smile and her murmured, "Life, what a kick, huh? It's sure thrown some curve balls my way lately, not the least of which was two days ago on a plane."

"Meeting you felt closer to a bat between the eyes. Hell, I'm still seeing stars." A brush of his lips to the small clipping of hair and Eric placed it inside his pouch.

Whitney extended the Tai Chi charm and he felt a sudden desire to see her wear it rather than take back what he felt she should have. But he had promised not to let it out of his possession until he was certain the woman who would eventually wear the heirloom was meant to be his as well.

"I've never seen such a beautiful necklace," its potential wearer remarked as he tucked it away with her hair. "And what it represents, that's beautiful too. Thanks for sharing with me about the Tao."

"There's more," he ventured to say but was quick to add, "If you're interested, that is."

"How could I not be? I'd like to know all about it."

Tell her too much and he might scare her off. Say too little and he'd be guilty of fostering the kind of limited relationship he'd had with Amy—one that was based on deception because they feared to express their true needs.

"The mating of yin and yang," he said carefully, "is more than an ancient take on putting the universe into perspective. The concept extends into, shall we say, personal interactions that are altogether human."

Though they were alone, she whispered, "Sexual?"

Her perfume drew him nearer, nearer, until he inhaled the delicate fragrance at her neck, the scent of wildflowers in her hair and he whispered back, "Very sexual. My ancestors considered lovemaking an art, one they took quite seriously. Want to know what they called this art of theirs?"

He could hear the click of her swallow as he took a small lick and prompted an, "Eric, please."

Whether she meant 'please more' or 'please tell me,' he didn't know, nor did it matter. They both came down to what he wanted from her. Beyond an affair, beyond the physical, no telling where these five secret words might lead:

"The Art of the Bedchamber."

CHAPTER SEVEN

ERIC PULLED back to better view her reaction. Eyes slitted, neck arched, breathing shallow. When the student is ready, the teacher will come.

Whitney was definitely ready and he couldn't wait to roll up his sleeves.

Just as he started to suggest they take this conversation to more secluded quarters, another voice broke in. Male.

"Yo, Whitney! I was hoping I'd see you."

Eric tore his gaze from her and settled it on the intruder. One who seemed far more familiar with Whitney—his Whitney...wait. His Whitney? She didn't belong to him. Yet some deep, territorial instinct insisted she did and nobody better try horning in on his turf.

"Uh, Dick. Hi!"

Dick? Stick those eyeballs back in their sockets if you value yours, buddy. Eric drew himself up to tower over the shrimp and stated, "I don't believe we've met."

Dick stopped ogling Whitney, and instead looked over at him. "You must be the boyfriend Whitney said she was waiting for."

A boyfriend? Eric gazed over at Whitney who looked as if she wasn't sure whether to clobber Dick or crawl under the table.

Before he could consider the wisdom of such a presumptuous reply, Eric said flatly, "I'd better be." He extended his hand. "Eric Townsend."

Dick made a discreet swipe of palm to pants before

meeting Eric's firm grip. Eric grudgingly gave the guy points for not grimacing. Dick earned some more by making himself scarce.

Glad to have him gone, but disturbed by his own reaction, Eric took a deep, calming breath. Sure, he had every right to be ticked since Dick had broken the mood. But wanting to tear his head off for giving Whitney the once-over? He'd all but pounded his chest like a gorilla to scare off any competition. That was nuts, crazy, totally irrational.

Whatever Whitney was doing to him, he took this as a sign to proceed with caution.

Eric cleared his throat. "I hope you don't mind that I didn't invite him to join us."

"Not at all." Whitney smiled sheepishly. "Thanks, Eric."

Assured that she wasn't nearly as upset with him as he was with himself, he cautioned, "Don't thank me yet. I could get even nastier if your boyfriend shows up. Is there one I should know about?"

"Would you be jealous if I said yes?"

"Insanely."

"In that case..." Edging around the table, Whitney looped her arms around his neck. "I made that up so Dick would leave me alone. Only I didn't say 'boyfriend.'"

"Then who did you say you were meeting?"

Whitney gave him a look that left no doubt the mood had been recaptured. "A lover," she murmured. "I said I was meeting my lover."

"Your lover," he repeated, his arms coming around her, fingertips pressing into that triangular hot spot at the small of her back, known as the *Ming-Men,* or life gate. "And did you plan to find one somewhere?"

"I was leaving for Prince Rupert Bay in the morning to enlist the candidate most likely, only he saved me the trip and—mmm..." She sighed, then tilted her head back, giving him a full view of the neck he could no longer wait to teethe.

"That feels wonderful," she murmured.

"This?" he followed his small nip with a nuzzle. Breathing her in, savoring her sigh, he asked, "Or this?" and pressed deeper into the erogenous pressure points that won him a halting gasp and the arch of her spine.

"That...this...both," she moaned. "Eric, what are you doing to me?"

"Making sure you look no further than this candidate most likely for whatever it is you need." *Need,* the operative word, and one he didn't speak lightly. Whitney might want a lover and he could certainly relate after so many celibate months, but need went way beyond two bodies in bed having casual sex.

Such exchanges had long lost their appeal for him. As for Whitney, she exuded comfort with her sexuality and femininity, but by no means did she come across as an easy lay. She had dignity and wouldn't sleep with a man she didn't care about or who didn't care about her.

He cared.

"Tell me what you need," he entreated. When she remained silent, except for what sounded like a stifled catch in her throat, he tried again. "I can do a lot of things, Whitney, but I can't read your mind. Tell me. Please."

Whitney couldn't speak. Tell me what you need. No man had ever asked her that before and Eric's wish to provide moved her in no small way. He said it so simply, yet what she needed wasn't simple at all.

Give me hope, Eric. Give me a lifetime of laughter and let me love with the heart of a fool. Make time go away and don't let this moment ever pass because what I feel is bliss. What do I need? I need more than you can possibly give but I'll take what you've got.

Good thing he couldn't read her mind.

Then again, maybe he could. "It's difficult to come out and say exactly what you need, isn't it?"

"Yes." Pressing her cheek against his chest, Whitney suddenly knew why. She would share this part of herself with Eric; her little secret would be safe with him. "I was taught to be self-reliant and not become too dependant on others—"

"Especially men."

"Them especially. Anyway, it's always been a lot easier for me to give than to take. I used to think that made me a generous person who didn't need much from others, but lately I've begun to wonder if such a so-called virtue is really a weakness in disguise." Much as she hated to name it, Whitney confronted the monster that had stolen all the happiness that could have been hers if she'd taken more chances like this. "Fear, Eric. Someone recently told me that the heart knows only two emotions. Love and fear. Do you think that's true?"

He rested his stubbled chin atop her head and she could feel the slight prickle rubbing her scalp.

"I think who told you that is very wise. I also think children live what they learn and it's hard to break patterns passed on by our parents."

"Yes," she softly agreed, loving the ease of speaking so freely together. "And what did yours pass on to you?"

"They ingrained principles like honor, duty, and excellence. Even if it was cleaning the bathroom, nothing less than our best would do. Adam and I, we've done well in life and I think we owe a lot of that to our parents. I also suspect we owe our inability to put down roots as adults to constantly being uprooted as kids. I love to travel but a part of me wonders if I stay on the move because deep down I feel..."

"What?" she prompted, hoping Eric could empathize with her struggle against this lion in her path. "Fear?"

"Yeah," he whispered. "Don't ask me what of. It's not responsibility, that's something I've never shunned. Maybe it's fear of boredom or becoming this boring old fart who runs his mouth about all the exciting, great things he did back when and keeps repeating himself because he's got nothing new to add. Whatever the reason, the very idea of settling down gives me cold feet. Just ask my ex."

Whitney wanted to know more about his ex. Hopefully she was a bitch, then there would be just cause for this keen stab of resentment against her. "I'd rather ask you."

"And I'd rather not talk about it now." He pushed his hips against hers, slowly rocking. Whitney not only rocked back, she rubbed shamelessly against him. Once, twice, then suddenly he was scooping her up and carrying her off and insisting, "Back to the original subject. What do you need?"

"Everything," she answered honestly. "Everything you can give me willingly, gladly and without regret tomorrow. All we have is now, Eric. That's all any of us have. Call me greedy but I want it all and I want it now."

"A woman after my own heart," he pronounced with a quiet passion, somehow all the more intense for his many murmurs of her name as he strode down the path to her bungalow.

And the bedchamber awaiting.

CHAPTER EIGHT

ERIC STARED down at Whitney. She lay on the bed, gloriously nude except for her little silk panties and the cover of moonlight slipping through the venetian blinds. She was just as he'd left her—with one exception. When he'd dashed to his bungalow she'd been awake.

Putting down the satchel he'd returned with, Eric leaned over her and whispered, "Oh, Sleeping Beauty, time to wake up."

Her only response to his waking kiss was a soft puff of air blown through slack lips.

So much for his intention to annoint her feet with oil and work his way up until she was ready to claw her way down his back. An unsightly back he kept covered even when making love. Especially then. Shudders of revulsion had a way of breaking the mood, not to mention crippling a man's self-confidence.

And yet, in the space of time between his hasty departure and urgent return, he had decided to bare himself to Whitney. Finding the scented candles he kept for private meditations didn't take long; they were in a small satchel with the rest of his personal stash—oils, ginseng and assorted herbs from his favorite apothecary in Chinatown. If he'd grabbed the goods and been back in a flash as he'd promised, surely Whitney would still be awake. But he'd procrastinated, trying to talk himself out of an unexpected and very real need.

To have nothing between them, to feel their flesh connect

as completely and directly as they had in heart, mind and spirit.

"Well, Whitney," he said to her peaceful face as he pulled off his boots, "Apparently you need your sleep as much as I need your acceptance of my less than perfect body."

Releasing a button, then two, he confided, "I'd planned on you helping me do this but the only one getting me naked is me and it's my own fault for buying time when you tried to take off my shirt."

He started to toss it on the end of the bed for easy reach, should he change his mind or Whitney change it for him. With a decisive fling, he tossed it on the white sundress he'd earlier dropped with a slow slide of Whitney's zipper.

"Just in case you have second thoughts in the morning about a decision you made when the night was magic and the wine flowed." Except she didn't have much to drink, certainly not enough to pass out. Maybe she was just taking a little catnap.

"Kitten," he murmured into her ear. He nipped a lobe. No response. If only he could turn back the hands of time. Say, half an hour? When he'd left her in a state of ecstatic suspense with the flick of a finger to satin.

The satin had been moist. Was it still?

Savoring the suspense, he watched his hand slowly lower until it hovered over her mound. Energy. He couldn't see it any more than he could an atom or a gust of air but that didn't mean the waves of energy he felt pulse between them were any less there. Make that a heat wave, one so sweltering that it was sheer hell not to close the distance and...

Cup her.

She felt like such heaven to the touch, what would it be like once he felt her more deeply than this? He had to know but he whispered a stern order to himself. "Wait. Remember the cardinal rule." Discipline. Patience. The keystones a man had to master to keep his body and mind in check so he might bring a woman to unparalleled heights of pleasure. As it had been written, a man should kiss and tease a woman for a meal's time before entering her.

There was no such thing as fast food back then, but given the circumstances he did well to wait as long as he did before temptation won out.

Still holding her in his palm, he wedged a fingertip beneath the elastic and delicately stroked what he ached to claim with an impassioned thrust. "You're velvet," he breathed out, "hot, wet velvet. So smooth, so warm and—"

With a sleepy moan, she rolled away.

Eric stared at the hand he'd been sure could stimulate her awake. Not so. As for the bedchamber lore about anticipation being a heady aphrodisiac, he could only hope Whitney was more responsive to an antiquated language for lovers and intimate games. The ancients had a name for that—love play.

"Not so much as an erotic massage and I already wore you out. Better get your rest while you can. You're gonna need it, *yuan-pao.*"

Prime treasure. Not a typical Chinese endearment, but it slipped out as naturally as the erection from his pants. Throwing them on top of the rest of the clothing, Eric joined her in bed. No need for a sheet, they could keep each other warm.

Maybe too warm. Nuzzled against her backside, they were cuddled up like two spoons in a drawer. That was called the nurturing position. The one needing TLC the most lay as Whitney did, facing out, wrapped in a loving hold by the other partner. One hand over her heart, the other on her belly and pulling her as close as he could, Eric tried to feel nurturing.

He didn't. He felt like jumping her bones.

Groaning, Eric flopped onto his back. Such thinking didn't make him proud of himself. And it sure wouldn't make his ancestors proud of him. After all, they had believed in putting a woman's pleasure before their own. Maybe that had something to do with them devising a more poetic vernacular than testicles and penis, clitoris and vagina. Orchid bags and jade stalk; dark garden and moon grotto. Oh yes, those words were far more pleasant to the ear. But Amy had thought such metaphors strange, and no lover since had warranted such sharing.

No lover, that was, until Whitney. Whitney, who turned over and hitched a leg over his, unaware of what she made even worse with the soft feel of her cheek pillowed on his shoulder and the most gorgeous pair of breasts he'd ever seen pressed against his heart.

Eric draped an arm around her and started counting sheep.

It was going to be a long night.

MMM...SUCH A marvelous sensation. Whitney felt as if she were floating on feathers, soaring on the tingles in her feet. They were slick, warm, gliding through a tunnel of rubs. Or was it a tunnel of love? Kisses, husky murmurs, stolen touches in the dark...yes, she must be in one of those love tunnels at the fair. She'd always wanted to ride in one of those boats, they'd seemed so romantic. Only how had she gotten here? And why did the light filter onto her eyelids? Was the ride over already?

If so, the kisses weren't stopping, the murmurs were getting closer, and the stolen touches were becoming bolder as they moved up her legs. Heavens, surely her date wasn't pulling down her panties! But he was and she was letting him, not even a whimper of protest when he slid his palms between the knees she should close since she wasn't that kind of girl.

But it felt so good, better than anything she'd ever felt before and maybe she was that kind of girl because she obeyed his whispered command to, "Open them for me, just like that. Yes. Oh yes, you're gorgeous. Scarlet pearls, *yuan-pao,* your lips are scarlet pearls."

Yuan-pao? Scarlet pearls?

Wherever she was, it was not the Tunnel of Love, though she felt loved by the hands that were on her, parting her folds and blowing into a haven so wet and throbbing, she must be drenching the sheets.

On a bed. Where she had company. And that company was no more a date in her dreams than the tip of his tongue to her cleft was imaginary.

Whitney opened her eyes. Her spine stiffened but her legs were too slippery and the muscles in them too relaxed to do the same. She tried to vocalize her shock but all that came out of her mouth was a long "aahhh" of ecstasy.

Eric responded with a raggedly whispered, "I love the way you taste, the way you sound, so open to me and letting me play as I please."

Considering the intimacies Eric was taking, he viewed play as some very serious business that didn't leave room for modesty. What he was doing, nibbling and sucking and licking her up like ice cream melting down a sugar cone...oh my. He seemed determined to sweep up each drop before finishing off the remains with the whole of his mouth. It felt delicious. And so decadent, she could hardly believe she was actually letting him do this to her.

Dare she look? Would he notice if she did? Surely not, his attention was so focused down there that he wouldn't possibly be watching her expression up here. At least she hoped not. Her face felt contorted from all his lovely tortures. Tease. Taste. Devour. Depart. Making her moan and thrash around, a wild thing who didn't know the meaning of restraint.

Glorying in the freedom of relinquished control, she let herself look and what should she see but the bob of his head, her legs spread wide, hips tilted up and fists clenched into the sheet to keep from grabbing him back when he...

Raised up. His face, flush with a dark passion, had the same purposeful set as his mouth. Wet. With her juices. And his eyes, they were slitted in crescent half-moons. His gaze locked with hers, pinning her in place.

She couldn't move. She couldn't speak.

Eric licked his lips. Smiled. Just barely. Then pushed a single finger up, curved in, and hit a place against her inner front wall that sent shock waves crashing into his soft, sultry greeting. "Good morning, kitten. Let me hear you purr."

CHAPTER NINE

THE WAVES increased in momentum and dizzying velocity as he pressed firmly and rubbed against a spot so sensitive that she felt as if she were imploding.

"Eric…Eric…Eric…" She heard herself wailing an almost inhuman sound she couldn't contain. And her nails were like talons, clawing blindly at his shoulders while her heels pounded the mattress. On and on it went until she was certain there would be nothing of her left but a heap of bones if he didn't stop.

"Enough," she cried out. "Please, I can't take any more."

Eric stopped his feasting and hauled himself up. Taking her hand, he urged it down.

"Touch me," he panted, struggling to control his breathing and the sensations that could push him over the edge. They intensified as she wrapped her hand around him.

"Like this?" She gave a tentative pump. "You want me to touch you like this?"

If she was asking, far be it from him not to answer. "Harder…yes. Now faster. That's it. You're wonderful. So wonderful that—" He caught her wrist, stilled the motions that could trip him into the point of no return. Pulling back even as he gave himself over to the stunning pleasure rippling from his head to his feet, he had a need to share this with her.

"Feel me," he groaned. "Feel what you do to me."

Whitney could feel him contracting in her hand, she

could feel a surging thrill within herself. Power, that's what she felt. It was she who made his eyes close tight, his mouth open up and let out a shuddering cry of her name; it was she who was responsible for his face pinched into a grimace suggesting pain, though it was obviously rapture that she, yes she, was giving him.

She had never seen a man orgasm before. It was truly a riveting sight. One that provoked her curiosity and propelled her gaze down. He was still, very quiet, and his erection was no longer quite so erect. But he wasn't as flaccid as she expected him to be and strangely, no fluids were to be seen.

And then she thought no more of it. All that mattered was the way Eric held her, so close and tight against him that she felt a oneness that neither words, nor touch could capture.

With the sort of awe reserved for the Sistine chapel, he whispered, "I think I just died and went to heaven."

Whitney knew such a statement should depress her, but Eric looked so sublime she was more inclined to savor the moment, albeit with a bit of black humor.

"If that's what going to heaven is like, I can hardly wait."

"And I can't wait at all for a good-morning kiss."

A brief one and Whitney giggled. "You taste funny."

"I taste like you and you taste divine. Nectar from the goddess. Beats the hell out of coffee. If you don't believe me, I've got proof positive it's true."

Even as he said it, the evidence in her hand mounted. Whitney scooted down for a closer inspection. As she looked, an amazing thing happened. Eric was growing before her stunned eyes.

"Like what you see?"

"You're beautiful," she said, tracing the rim of smooth,

plump flesh and causing him to grow even more in girth and length. So large, in fact, that she added, "And intimidating."

"I'll take that as a compliment."

Whitney tried to imagine something so big taking up such limited space. Exciting to contemplate, but sure to be uncomfortable at first, maybe even painful.

She was hesitant to ask but to hell with hesitance, she wanted to know and so ask she did. "Shouldn't you be smaller than this? I mean, that is normal for most men after, well afterward, so…why isn't it happening to you?"

He wound a hand through her hair and pulled until her chin rested on his hipbone and her eyes met his.

"Because, my dear, I'm not most men."

Goodness. It seemed that Whitney Smith, who had never taken a lover before, had outdone herself in choosing the one she had. Beyond being charming and smart and sexy and sweet—though not too sweet, that was for sure—she could only wonder what she'd gotten herself into by getting into bed with Eric. He was a demon lover who should be exhausted, not fully aroused and making her all hot and bothered with an I'm-ready-for-more-if-you-are suggestive hint of a smile.

"It's an old secret from the Far East," he explained. "You see, most Chinese emperors had lots of wives, sometimes hundreds, and they were able to satisfy ten in a night. When I read that, all I could think was, wow. How did they do it? How can I do it? That's what I wanted to know, so I dug deeper until I turned up their secret. It's a mind-body technique that takes patience, discipline, and a lot of practice to perfect."

"And partners to practice with, right?" How many had Eric had? Plenty, no doubt, and she was jealous of them all. Hopefully he hadn't picked that up from the comment that sounded snippy even to her.

"Actually, it's better to practice alone, especially at first. It's easier to concentrate when there's not so much to sidetrack the attention." Softly he milked a breast.

He had a wonderful touch. Soothing, sure, arousing. Though she was obviously having the same effect on Eric by simply running a fingertip over the length of his truly magnificent organ, the image of other women doing the same continued to thwart her.

"But doesn't all that practice have a purpose?" she persisted. "After all, what would be the point if you didn't plan to put what you learned to use?"

"True," Eric said slowly, moving his stroking palm from her breast to her spine, which he seemed to be counting notches on before settling on an upper area that had her arching like a cat. "That's a love point by the way, an erogenous zone that's only a little piece of your body map I'm itching to investigate. As for why I'd want to learn about such things, I simply like to learn and I'd be a liar if I didn't say I've yet to find a subject as fascinating as sex. I've read everything I can get my hands on about human sexuality."

Fascinated as he obviously was with the subject, Eric didn't seem to see much humor in it when it came to his own sexual past. "Getting laid by whoever, wherever, and doing whatever it took to score used to be a high priority. Say, twenty years ago? I was immature enough to use what I knew to my advantage, but the truth is, I didn't know jack. Not about the girls I took advantage of, not about myself, and most certainly not about making love. Sex. Making love. They're worlds apart, you know."

Wanting to appear more sophisticated than she actually

was, she agreed, "A very big difference, Eric. Sex is…sex. But making love? Ooh-la-la."

He chuckled. "Yeah, ooh-la-la." And then he wasn't chuckling. "I don't respect men who don't respect women, men who'd rather count their conquests than count themselves lucky to have a special someone to be intimate with. So if you think for a second you're just another number to me, I won't only be hurt, I'll be mad."

She didn't want to make him mad. Just the way he said it assured her of that.

"Sorry," Whitney apologized, feeling contrite. "I didn't mean to imply any such thing. Still, I can't help but wonder why you'd want to be able to satisfy ten women in a night when you have such a low opinion of scorekeepers."

"Because if I'm able to give ten women pleasure, think of how much I can give one." He held up a single finger. "Just one. A very unique woman who satisfies my particular needs while I see to hers, even those she doesn't know she's got. As it turned out, Amy wasn't that woman and I would've realized that if we'd waited, instead of jumping into marriage when we were barely twenty and didn't have a clue. We split eight years ago and I've had other lovers since but none who compelled more than my ability to perform. Big difference between them and the one I've been waiting for."

His finger arced down and he pointed it directly at her. "You."

This was not an invitation, but a summons and it made her heart race. Eric spoke with the authority of a confident ruler in his domain, certain of his ability to claim what he wanted and able to conquer if he could not persuade. Given the domain in question, the bed on which they lay, Whitney knew the only struggle to be had was in herself. And there was a struggle. Without doubt he could satisfy any and all of her needs, but this wasn't just about her. It was about them. She couldn't forget it was a lot easier to get into something than out of it, and out she would eventually have to get.

"These needs of yours, Eric, what are they exactly?"

His fingertips skated up, down, sideways across her back, stopped, and with a kneading press, an intense simmer of a golden-eyed gaze, Whitney knew she was in trouble.

"My needs, to be exact, are to share what I've learned and explore what I haven't with a partner whose got a mind as open as her legs. And her arms. I need more than sex. I need to be able to speak freely together and feel comfortable when there's nothing to say. I need to laugh and get crazy. I need peace and anything but. I need all this and more." He raised a brow, and her pulse while he was at it. "In bed. And out."

Whitney took a steadying breath. And then another. For all the good it did since she still didn't feel steady at all. Already she cared more for Eric than any man she'd ever known and all these intimacies she longed for as much as he did, were bound to deepen their emotional bonds. Danger. Danger, danger, *danger*. She couldn't put blinders on and ignore the potential risk to them both if she didn't put an end to this wild and crazy thing. Immediately. Yes, that's what she should do. Get up and get out before this went any further.

She tried to force herself to move, but her limbs refused to budge. They were apparently listening to the insistent voice inside her head, telling her that if she left now, she'd never see Eric again. She'd never learn all the bedchamber secrets he had to share. Chances were, she wouldn't even share a bed with another man because they'd all fall short

of him and there she'd be in the not too distant future, full
of regret for all that she hadn't done, not for what she had.

His offer was too enticing and her time too short. With
so little remaining, how could she throw such an opportunity away? She couldn't. She could, however, think ahead
and pack a parachute for when the time came to bail out.

"We need the same things, Eric. Today, at least. But
you never know what tomorrow might bring, so tomorrow's never more than a maybe for me. If you want more
of a commitment than that, then I'm not the woman you've
been waiting for."

Breath held, she released it with a greatly relieved sigh
when he assured her, "I learned some years ago to take
each day as it comes because tomorrow might not. Amy
didn't think that way. But you and me? We're on the same
page. No reading ahead. We'll turn the pages as they come
and not spoil any surprises."

Surprises, life was full of them. So was Eric. And so was
she! She kept surprising herself, taking what were once
ordinary days and turning them into extraordinary adventures.

In bed. And out.

At the moment—and wonder of wonders Eric seemed to
grasp the moment was all that counted—she couldn't think
of a more fitting place to turn yesterday's page and discover
what today had in store.

"You're quite a man, Eric Townsend." She kissed his
thigh. His abdomen. And then she blew a kiss to his lips.
"Sharing this day and this bed with you is more than a
gift. It's an honor."

He shook his head. "No, *yuan-pao,* the honor is mine."

He looked at her as if she were something priceless that
had fallen from the sky and into his waiting hands which

were in her hair, feather stroking her skin, and erasing any thoughts about the consequences her decision might bring.

"What does *yuan-pao* mean?"

"Prime treasure." He put index fingers and thumbs together, making a longboat-shaped sign. "Instead of ingots and bars, it's the shape gold and silver used to be cast into in China."

Silver and Gold. Their time would run out before they could sing such carols at Christmas together. Holidays were something they wouldn't be sharing but spending them alone wouldn't be so bad when she could remember the day when she'd been dubbed the finest riches any man or king could claim. Prime treasure.

"*Yuan-pao*. I like it."

"And I more than like what the shape symbolizes." Bending his knee then rubbing it between the apex of her thighs, he named what he touched. "The vulva. And yours, like the rest of you, *yuan-pao*, is more precious than gold."

There was nothing she could say to express what she felt at his words, and so she kissed the tip of his phallus and let him speak for her in a deep sigh of pleasure.

She wanted to hear more.

"I want to kiss you the way you kissed me." Whitney boldly took a lick, then two. His hips jerked and the sound he made was closer to gritting his teeth than another appreciative sigh. "You don't mind, do you?"

Eric struggled not to laugh, the question was so preposterous. But he couldn't stop himself, his belly began to shake, then laughter, pure laughter, burst from his lips. She was incredibly good food for his hungry soul. Of all the adventures he'd ever had, he'd never had one like this. In bed or out. Perhaps he'd misled them both about taking one day at a time. He already wanted tomorrow.

"Do I mind?" He chuckled. "The only thing I mind is

you turning into Miss Manners when I'm not feeling mannerly in the least.'' He cupped her head and gave it a nudge. ''Forget the napkin, *yuan-pao,* I know better than to spill the vichyssoise.''

It only took Whitney a few minutes to make him reconsider his claim. She was a little awkward and seemed to improvise as she went, but whatever she lacked in expertise was more than compensated for by the generosity of her mouth. She gave so totally, was so earnest in her desire to please, that Eric was seized by the immediate and absolute need to join their bodies and give back tenfold to her.

He had no condoms. He always used them, even though he rarely lost a drop. But a drop was all it took, and the value of safe sex spoke for itself. While he'd never been so tempted to go without, never before had he been so close to losing it. Once he slid inside her he'd be courting the typical results that were no longer typical for him.

''Whitney,'' he managed to gasp. ''Stop. You have to stop now. Right now. *Now.*''

She paused to lick her lips and inform him, ''But I don't want to stop. Don't you like this?''

''Too much.'' Grabbing her by the arms and pulling her into his, he pressed her palm over his racing heart. ''I want to make love to you in the worst sort of way but I'm going to hit the finish line before you even get started unless I call time out for me and spend some quality time on you.''

''What makes you think I'm not started?'' she protested, bringing his hand to the place that assured him she was as desperate as he to forget play time and get to the heart of the matter. ''I'm aching inside. Make love to me, Eric. Fill me up with you and make the hurt go away.''

''I can't do that,'' he forced himself to say. ''I don't have protection.''

"I do." Pointing to the bedside table, she said with an urgency to rival his own, "In the drawer."

Whitney had brought condoms along on her trip? Though he should be appreciative she'd thought ahead, he wasn't. Maybe because his newfound possessive streak didn't like her coming prepared on vacation with a just-in-case purchase made before they'd met. She had every right to wipe out a condom aisle and bring it with her, of course, and he had no right to sit in judgment. But it bothered him all the same, and if he couldn't say so then their lovemaking would be marked by a lack of emotional honesty. And that was perhaps his greatest need of all because without it, as he'd learned, the foundation of any relationship would soon crumble.

Careful in how he approached this, he casually asked, "I don't suppose prophylactics come compliments of the villa, like chocolates on a pillow?"

"Of course not." No lack of emotional honesty in Whitney's response. She archly informed him, "I bought them yesterday when I was making plans to seduce you. It's not the sort of thing I pack with my toiletries on the outside chance I'll hook up with some stranger on a plane. I assumed you realized that."

"Just as I assumed you realized I wasn't a horn-dog on the make. Our relationship is new, Whitney, and we still have a lot to learn about each other. I didn't mean to offend you but the fact is, if it was anyone else I would've gone straight for those condoms without saying a word. That I did say something, and felt that I could, tells me a lot." Sweeping his lips over hers, he murmured, "Hopefully it tells you something, too."

He kissed her until she nodded, kissed her until she kissed him back. And then he kissed her until she broke free and frantically pointed toward the drawer. "Let's see what else we can learn about each other. Quick."

"I said it before and I'll say it again. Lady, I like the way you think." He rolled to his side and opened the drawer. No sooner did he lift the box than he dropped it with a grimace.

"Eric," she gasped, her voice rife with an emotion that was no longer passion. Whitney put her hand to the back he had turned to her. "What happened to you?"

CHAPTER TEN

HE KNEW he should face her so she wouldn't have to look at the ugly scar tissue that had clearly snapped her out of a dead heat and stopped her cold. But he couldn't look at her. Not yet. Not until he faced down his fear that no woman could ever want him so completely that she'd even want this unsightly part of his body because it was part of him.

Whitney had touched him, was touching him still. He took some comfort from that and more than Whitney could possibly know, he did need such a comfort.

"I'd meant to warn you so you could brace yourself," he began, wishing fiercely for his shirt. "As it is, you got about as much warning as I did before Galeras sent one mother of a fireball my way."

"Galeras," she quietly repeated.

He had to admire her poise.

"That's the volcano you mentioned in your book."

"A very pissed off volcano that blew several of my friends away," he confirmed. "And it didn't get much of a mention since it was just too painful to relive at the time. That was nearly ten years ago and you know what? It's still painful to think about, much less talk about."

Eric slung his legs over the bed and was about to bend over for his shirt when Whitney stopped him with a hand on his shoulder.

"You can talk to me, Eric. Tell me what happened."

In that moment Eric knew that if he could share his story

with one person in the world, that person would be Whitney. Whitney would listen. Not out of morbid curiosity, but because she cared about him. Galeras had marked more than his flesh. It had changed how he viewed life, made him realize how transient and frail human existence really was. That's something Whitney understood in a way other people didn't. Why or how she'd grasped such a truth, he didn't know, but she did and that probably had a lot to do with this intrinsic connection they shared.

"Tell me," she whispered again. "Please."

Emotional honesty. Well, this was about as emotionally honest as he could get, telling her outright, "My guts are churning and it's a little hard for me to breathe. Maybe that's why I don't like to talk about a living memory that can still wake me up in a cold sweat. It's been nearly ten years, but it seems like yesterday. I can still feel the bite in the air, still smell the bacon and coffee we cooked over a campfire for breakfast before taking off. There were seven of us on that early morning climb and I can still hear us giving Mike grief. We'd stayed up late playing cards and Mike was nursing a hangover when we started up the trail. Up and up we all climbed, singing bawdy ditties, one-upping each other with bad jokes, just a bunch of guys who happened to be scientists, bound by more than a passion for volcanos.

"The sky was so blue, the view below so lustrous and green, the mountain so quiet as we neared the top. If only this day would never end, I remember wishing. And I remember thinking a day so perfect should be captured in a picture—good friends, good times, life didn't get any better than this. Yeah, I wanted a picture. A picture of all my pals waving or flipping me the bird from the top of Galeras would put the camera I'd brought along to better use than snapping photos of the crater's ho-hum interior.

"I stationed myself about fifty feet below. Looking through the viewfinder, I saw the best friends I'd ever had. Suddenly the camera shifted. For a split second, I couldn't figure out what was wrong. Another split second and I realized it was the ground that was shifting. Then shaking, rumbling. And there was a sound, a terrible, deafening boom I recognized, but I'd never heard it so close that it threatened to explode my eardrums. The explosion was so loud, I couldn't even hear my friends screaming. I saw their mouths open up into great shrieking O's, while their faces twisted into knots of stark terror as liquid fire gushed up and over them...."

For a while he couldn't go on, couldn't get past the horrific image time would never erase. And yet as she lightly stroked his back he found the strength to continue his tale. "And that was the last I saw of them. Gone, just like that, they were gone. I ran, ran knowing I couldn't save what was already lost to a carnivorous monster who'd disguised itself as a sleeper. It had taken us without warning. I ran and ran, thinking all the time, it should have been me who was taken. Not any of them. If anyone should have died, it should have been me.

"I raced for my life while my friends lay dead, blown to pieces like stick figures blasted by a cannon. One that continued to hurl molten rock at meteoric speed while I leaped over boulders and heaving earth— Until I felt a pain so blinding, that I was sure I was going to die just like my friends had. All I could do was pray. Pray that I'd die quickly as well, since the stench of burning flesh and my weak cries for help were a damn pathetic way to go for someone who'd had the arrogance to believe he could outsmart nature and save others from the fate that would be his own."

"But that wasn't your fate."

"No. I was pulled out of the rubble, but I don't remember it and I don't remember being taken to a hospital in a helicopter. Of course I wouldn't be remembering any of this at all if there hadn't been another group camped on safe ground to call for help. They said the eruption lasted less than fifteen minutes."

His voice as faint as he wished the memory could be, Eric shook his head. "But Whitney, it never goes completely away. I can still hear and I can still see that killing bastard. Galeras. If I could play God I'd level it to a heap of crushed rocks and soot, then sweep it under an ocean floor. That's my fondest fantasy."

"No, it's not," she quietly disagreed. "Bringing your friends back is. Then you'd still have them instead of the guilt that won't go away because you're alive and they aren't."

How did she know that's how he felt? And how did she know that part of his self-imposed punishment was never to have friends like that again?

"It wasn't your fault, Eric. It wasn't," she insisted. "You didn't kill them, a cruel twist of fate did. Don't let it steal more from you than it already has. Last night you mentioned that you tend to be a private person, but if you don't let others get too close because you're afraid you might lose them as well, then you're letting Galeras win. Life is a precious thing and it's much too short to waste on regretting what we can't change, my friend."

My friend. Whitney was his friend. Indeed the best and fastest friend he'd made since…maybe ever. He could talk to her in ways that he couldn't with male friends. Men simply didn't feel comfortable expressing themselves. And they certainly didn't go around commiserating quite the way she did.

Something soft, even softer than her palm, pressed

against his back. Her cheek. The tenderness of her touch held a power far greater than any force of nature he'd yet to encounter. It shook him right down to a secret place inside that was ravaged and vengeful and deeply humbled by the knowledge he hadn't been able to save his friends.

On the bad days he told himself everyone had to die sometime and when his time came, he'd choose to be taken the same way. Without warning, too immediate to suffer, preferably in the field so he could be eulogized like some valiant captain who'd gone down with his ship. But as he felt the brush of Whitney's lips—up, down, here, there, all over his back—Eric decided this was a much better way to go.

"You're killing me," he said gruffly. His throat felt tight. So did his chest. "Amy wouldn't even do that."

"Stupid woman, she obviously didn't appreciate what she had." That said, Whitney resumed her healing kisses.

Though he hated to refute her, it wasn't right to lead Whitney to believe he was some kind of hero he wasn't.

"I wish I could say you're right, but I can't. The truth is, Amy deserved better than me and the reason she couldn't stand to look at what you're kissing is because it represented everything she hated about my job. She wasn't too crazy about it before I ended up in a burn unit for three months, but by the time I got home, she was more than entitled to loathe it."

"Why? Was it because she was afraid of losing you?"

"Yes." Yes, if only it had been that simple. But it hadn't been that simple at all. "And no. Mostly no. Before the accident we were drifting apart. Afterward, I pushed her away every time she tried to get close. As far as I was concerned it was too little, too late on both our sides. In the end all I had was guilt, so much guilt I wanted to share the wealth. Which I did. Generously. Not with words, but silence. As I think back, it's amazing Amy didn't slap me with divorce papers, instead of wanting to make a baby as soon as I got out and could get it on again.''

Silence. A good, healthy minute of it from Whitney before he tried to make himself look better by admitting, ''Of course I knew I was being unfair and even if I wasn't talking much, I did feel ashamed enough of myself to give what was left of our marriage my best shot. She'd worked and supported us while I got my post-graduate degrees and she'd always wanted me to parlay that into a professorship. Use my brains to do something stable and admired by the community, like her dad.''

''He obviously wasn't a politician,'' Whitney surmised. ''So what was he, an honest mechanic?''

Even in the midst of this grueling remembrance she made him smile. Made him laugh. Just a little. But a little was more than he'd done in those long, last months of a marriage that had been destined from the beginning to bite the dust.

''Amy's father was a surgeon, highly respected. As for me, I went in with plenty of respect from the university heads and came out with something even better. Respect from my students. And when it came to the old publish or perish adage, I had no problem living up to expectations, writing papers out the kazoo when I wasn't grading them, putting together a textbook in between. It gave me an excuse not to show up while Amy waited for me in bed.''

''To make a baby, right?''

He tried to imagine ten little fingers and ten little toes wiggling in the air at that time in his life when, for all its promise, had held little of it in the ways that really counted. The price an innocent child would have paid to keep his and Amy's faltering marriage together was enough to make him shudder. No need to keep that from Whitney.

Eric chaffed his arms. "Yeah, she loved kids and thought one of our own would make everything just peachy. I didn't agree. Teaching was okay, but not very fulfilling. I felt empty, like I'd lost a piece of my soul. I knew where it was. Galeras didn't just take my friends, it took a part of me and I wanted that part of me back. By then it'd been two years since the big blow and the fever was in me. As if the gods were listening to my silent screams, I got a call. I was needed in Montserrat. But lemme tell ya, they didn't need me half as much for an on-site evaluation as I needed to get back on that horse and ride. Giddy-yup, giddy-yup, I had to go."

"Something tells me you weren't riding double," Whitney said.

"Hardly that. Amy gave me an ultimatum. Either stay and see another marriage counselor or leave, and don't bother to come back. The decision wasn't easy. *Failure* wasn't a word either of us knew. Maybe that's why we spent so many years pretending that we could make things work if we both just tried hard enough. We did try, and we tried hard, I have to give us that. But in the end…?"

Eric could only shake his head at the folly of youth and the pride that could keep adults from admitting to their misjudgments, their needs and failures. "When I got back from Montserrat, Amy was gone. All that was left in our house were my things, half the furniture and legal papers."

Something wet trickled down his back and for a moment he thought Whitney was crying. For him. But then her hands slid over what must be the oil he'd left on the bed. Though tears for his plight would have revealed a stunning capacity for compassion, her soothing ministrations were equally cherished. She caressed him with an acceptance so complete, he felt damn near to tears himself.

"You must have been sad, coming home to that."

Words of sympathy. Yet he heard an edge in her voice that reminded him of offering condolences for the loss of a relative who was a real SOB.

"I should have been sad."

"But you weren't?" She sounded hopeful.

"No. Amy had a real domestic streak and didn't want to move away from her folks. That was enticing at first, all the things I'd thought I wanted growing up, wrapped in a sweet, pretty package. But you see how it turned out. When I took off my wedding ring I shed a few tears, but they were more from relief than anything else. If anything makes me sad, it's admitting to that."

Continuing to massage the skin Amy wouldn't touch, Whitney sank more than her teeth into his shoulder by asking between soft bites, "Do you still love her?"

"Oh, sure. A part of me always will. But it's a muted sort of love, nothing like one of those grand passions that drives a man out of his mind and brings him to his knees." Eric paused. His head turned. His gaze met hers, as straightforward as his statement. "I've never experienced that before. Neither have you."

"How do you know?"

"Because eyes are windows to the soul and I don't see so much as a sliver of a broken heart in there." He licked a fingertip and made a gentle swipe beneath her lashes.

His eyes searching hers, Whitney knew he was looking for more than smudged mascara or the ghost of a lover past. Could she break his heart? Could he break hers? These were the questions she read in his eyes and she didn't yet have an answer.

Whitney looked away. "Did you break Amy's heart?"

"Let's just say that if the heart knows only love and fear, her fear was greater than her love. Or as Amy put it, she wanted a family, not a volunteer for death row."

Whitney's grinding envy turned to a reluctant sympathy for the woman whose fear of losing her husband had ensured exactly that. But was it simply a fear of his death that had instigated the ultimatum? Whitney didn't think so.

"I think she loved you too much, Eric."

He shrugged. "At one time, maybe, but not in the end. A year after the divorce she was remarried and happier than I could ever make her. After all, she was pregnant by a man who wanted a family. While I wouldn't give a child of mine up for anything, I know how trapped I would've felt, how resentful I would have become. Of Amy. Would I have left her? No. I could never desert an innocent child the way your father did you. But I'm afraid I would have deserted Amy emotionally—which I pretty much had by the time she walked."

As Whitney stared at the flesh she stroked, she digested what he'd said. She saw how desperate Amy must have been. Wanting a child, wanting the husband whose vows had surely included "till death did they part." No wonder she hadn't been able to touch his back. Such a vivid reminder of how close she'd come to losing him—only for Eric to make it clear he valued his work more than his life, and therefore, more than her.

It took a lot of courage or desperation for anyone to gamble on all or nothing. Though she didn't know Amy, it was Whitney's guess that she'd been both and that's what the ultimatum was really about. Amy needed proof he truly loved her and ended up having her fears confirmed that he didn't. Whitney also had a sneaking suspicion that if Eric had chosen Amy over going to Montserrat, she would have changed her mind and told him to go.

"You know, Eric, if I were Amy, I would have left you, too. Only sooner."

"Oh, yeah?" He suddenly swiveled around, pushed her

flat on the mattress and pinned her arms above her head. His lips came down hard on hers but when he lifted them, he was smiling.

"Oh, yeah," he said with an approving nod. "You would've left me eating your dust way before she did. You have too much of a sense of self to put up with the kind of garbage I dished out. Amy didn't ask for much, just a white picket fence, a couple of kids and a van in a suburban driveway. But you want more out of life than that and so do I. We're a lot alike, you and me."

Were they? She'd once dreamed of a white picket fence, two kids and a van to shuttle them from school to church to Little League or Girl Scouts. Since such a life was as obtainable as the miracle cure it would take to have it, that dream was hers no more. She'd gotten lemons and was making the most delicious lemonade she could. With a man who thought her lust for life matched his. In that, Eric was correct. She was indeed becoming that woman.

Whitney declared it so with an inviting lift of her hips, a seductively crooned, "Seeing that we're so alike, why don't we commemorate our mutual admiration?"

"I think that's an excellent idea." Eric released her hands and passed his own over her eyelids. "Don't look. Don't even peek."

"Why not?"

"Shhh." He tapped her lips, curved into a kittenish smile. A sex kitten, she was definitely that, Eric thought as he moved away, going for the leather pouch in his pants pocket.

Had he even a smidgeon of reservation, the lock of hair he tenderly fingered would have dispelled it. But his instincts were so certain, he didn't think twice about the next right thing to do.

He laid himself atop her. Kissed her like the grand passion he knew she was. She clutched his back and throatily sighed, "Eric, I want you. All of you."

"And because you do, I want you to have this. Open your eyes."

Whitney did as he bade her and what should she see but his grandmother's heirloom. As he waved it back and forth from the loop of gold it hung on, she stared at it, feeling hypnotized, almost in a trance.

And a trance she must be in to want this treasured piece of Eric's heritage, knowing full well she had no right to accept such a significant part of his past when her own future was so uncertain. Or rather, too certain.

"Oh, no," she made herself say. "I can't accept something this special from you."

"Oh, yes," he asserted, "you most certainly can. It's mine to do with as I wish and I wish for you to have it."

He unhooked the slender chain, looped it around her neck; a click of the fastening and the medallion rested between her breasts. It was warm from his handling but it felt closer to a branding iron searing her skin and imprinting his claim, body and soul.

"Yin and yang, Whitney. Two halves coming together to make each other whole. Today you've made me feel complete in a way I never have. Please honor what I feel by accepting my gift, *yuan-pao*."

Her heart delighted in the most beautiful, treasured gift she'd ever received. And yet she knew his gift was a stolen delight, had by a heart on borrowed time. She didn't want to insult him by giving the necklace back. She didn't want to give up the connection it signified. But she had to give up something to wear his gift with a clear conscience.

"Why don't we consider it a loan," she suggested. When Eric frowned, she quickly revised, "I mean, since we're taking each day as it comes, let's think of it like we're going steady and I've got on your class ring or I.D. bracelet. If we break up, then it's still yours, not mine.''

He lifted the medallion, studied it a moment, then rested it between her cleavage. Pinch of a nipple, bow of her spine, he left her gasping with the wave of his hand.

''I can live with that today if you can live without me tomorrow.'' He chuckled wickedly. ''We'll just wait and see.''

As Eric made a long reach for the drawer and shuffled out a condom from the box, Whitney saw the writing on the wall.

She would fall in love with Eric Townsend; she was half in love with him already. *Dear Father in heaven,* she silently prayed, *save us both from that. Throw some cold water in my face and let me have the distance I need to keep, lend me the help Eric's not giving to stop this wonderful insanity while I still can. So, c'mon, give me a sign, a wake up call to snap me out of this dream that can't last.*

As if on cue, a phone rang. Eric stopped in midtear of gold foil, groaned, then with an expletive that didn't sound nearly as romantic as the love they were about to make, he pulled out a cell phone from an overnight bag.

The moment he profusely apologized to her then said, ''I left instructions not to call unless it was an emergency,'' Whitney knew she should have paid better heed to the old adage about being careful of what you prayed for since you just might get it.

CHAPTER ELEVEN

THOUGH SHE couldn't hear the other end of the conversation, Eric's intense expression and muttered, "Okay...okay. People on alert? Good. No, don't send Fields in to fix it, he's got three kids. Yes, I realize time's of the essence but keep the chopper, you might need it to get out. While I get a charter plane—of course, ASAP—keep an eye on the tiltmeter data and gas readings...." told Whitney something dangerous that had to do with volcanos was going on and that dangerous something was exciting him. Not a "whoopie, oh boy!" sort of gladness, but an anticipation that relayed itself in his voice, taut posture, and jack-in-the-box spring from the bed as he finished with, "On my way. Oh, and Grayson I'll be pissed if you take that smoker on without me like you did at Kilauea," he said, then hung up.

Kilauea. In Hawaii. Where rain hitting the soot mixed up a cocktail so acidic it was between lemon juice and battery acid. Whitney remembered that from his book. She also remembered a picture of a pretty woman scientist whose name had just struck a bell. No telling where Eric was heading, but some potential competition would be there. Even if she had nothing to worry about with this Grayson, there was a chance Eric wouldn't return despite what he said.

"I can't apologize enough about this, Whitney. I'll be back as soon as I can—hopefully tonight." Leaning down, he kissed her, then called the airport.

As he reached for his clothes, Whitney struggled to keep her voice casual. "So, you're going to Montserrat."

"It's only a hop, skip and a puddle jump away—which is why I'm elected despite being on vacation. Unfortunately they don't have time to get someone else in for an emergency repair on the crater."

"An emergency repair on the crater?" she repeated, laying a hand over her throat. She felt as if she were choking.

"That's right. A seismometer shut down and it's crucial to get it up and running so we have a better chance of evacuating in time if that baby decides to throw more than another temper tantrum."

Eric was tossing on his shirt. If the worst happened, she might never again see the back it covered. So horribly disfigured, yet so beautiful to her. How could she let this man go? He'd brought color to her life, called up a wild passion that had robbed her of reason and given her pure joy.

Stay, Eric, please stay. If it would keep him safe, she would get on her knees and beg him not to leave. Had Amy done that? Whitney felt a keen empathy for the wife who had played second fiddle to Eric's calling. He was a man with a mission. And that mission thrilled him.

"You love the rush, don't you?" Did she sound accusing? Hopefully not. She had no hold on him, certainly less than a wife who had lost him because she couldn't let him go.

Eric stopped in the middle of tucking his shirt into his pants. Her gaze was drawn to his open fly. He was aroused. Did the thrill of danger do that to him? Or was it a reaction to the offering of her body, draped invitingly on the mattress in an attempt to lure him away from a jealous mistress who'd claimed him in a way no woman had?

"It's addictive," he conceded. Eyes slitted, he touched

the length of her with his hooded gaze. Hot. Yet cooly assessing. "And so are you."

He would stay a little longer, let her make him late for his plane even though minutes counted. But she knew he was onto her ploy and his volatile mistress wouldn't easily forgive this indiscretion. She would whisper that yet another woman couldn't be trusted and would manipulate him with the weakness of his flesh as long as he allowed it.

Eric would allow it now. But maybe not the next time— if there was one—and she didn't have the time to squander on chewing her nails while he jousted with the Grim Reaper today.

Getting up, she moved on unsteady legs. Her gaze locked with his, she slipped her hand into his pants and fondled him until his eyes closed, his head fell back, and he groaned, "If that's what you want...you win."

Determined to do just that, she zipped up his pants, turned on her heel, and said over her shoulder, "Give me five and I'll be ready. Jeans and a T-shirt okay?"

"Okay for what?" he demanded, coming after her.

"For Montserrat."

Eric swung her around. "You are not going with me."

"Okay," she said levelly, then informed him, "I'll go by myself. It's a free world and the same plane you're taking won't have any misgivings about accepting my fare with yours. If you don't want to sit by me, fine. But you can't stop me if I want to go. And Eric, I am going."

"The hell you are! It's too dangerous."

"Not too dangerous for you, so why should it be for me?"

"Because I'm an expert and you're not."

Though she was sorely tempted to remind him that he bore the proof that being an expert didn't make him any safer than Joe Schmo, Whitney knew that would antagonize him rather than get her what she was after.

"Yes, Eric, you are an expert." She kissed his stern lips then softened him up with the same sort of strategy that caught bees. Honey, not vinegar. "In fact, I have such faith in your abilities, I know you'll make sure I get off the island safe."

"I can't watch after you while I'm working."

"Of course not. Which is why I'll stay out of your way while you do what you do best." With a slide of her hand between his legs, she added, "Well, almost best."

Eric took her hand away and pressed it over his heart. Though the beat went on in his chest, he was sure if Whitney looked down she would find it lying at her feet.

"I don't like this. I care for you, Whitney, and if anything bad happened I'd never forgive myself."

"I'm not asking you to like it. And as for anything bad happening, you're the one most likely for it to happen to. I'll go where the islanders are waiting it out. Maybe I could even do something to help. You think?"

"I'll tell you what I think. I think it's never been so hard to leave. And I don't want you to go. But if you're determined to do it, I don't know of a better way to find out if you've got the grit and the guts it'll take to throw your lot in with me. The Red Cross can always use extra help."

"Good," she chirped, as if she were on her way to a Club Med instead of taking off for a homeless shelter.

Watching her shimmy into her bra and do that little jiggle thing into her cups, it took a lot of willpower not to jiggle her right back out of them. Eric crossed his arms, refusing to let himself touch her. What little time they had to kill before takeoff didn't permit more than a quickie and he wasn't about to mock the integrity of the intimate arts with a wham-bam-thank-you-ma'am consummation.

"The charter I booked doesn't leave for an hour. If you want, I'll order some breakfast and we can eat it on the way."

"Sounds great. I seem to have worked up an appetite this morning." The growl of her stomach concurred.

Eric was ready to do some growling himself, but his own appetite had nothing to do with food and everything to do with her. After calling the restaurant for takeout, he was closer to famished than hungry. For Whitney. Brave, beautiful and so intoxicatingly naive about what she'd just gotten herself into—a test of her mettle that could land her into even deeper cahoots with him.

As she swept her hair into a ponytail, he imagined letting it down and running a brush through it just so his fingers could mess it up. When she slicked her lips with a stick of carmine rouge, Eric knew he had to keep busy or he'd be smearing it off her mouth and onto his.

"How about a cup of tea?" he suggested. "I've got a special brew I down every day, along with some herbal supplements like ginseng and gingko and *huang-chi* that my grandmother swears by. She looks closer to sixty than ninety and she's the picture of health, so it's either in the genes or the stuff really works. Either way, I figure a handful of organic pills and a cup of *ling-chih* a day can't hurt."

"*Ling-chih.* Something tells me I won't find it sitting next to a box of Red Zinger in the grocery store."

"Hardly." After rummaging through his satchel, he pitched her a slender glass tube. "Catch!"

"What's this?" she asked, examining the powdery contents.

"The *ling-chih.* It's a huge mushroom that grows wild in China. Since it's too tough to eat, I buy it ground for soups or tea. It doesn't taste like much, but lore has it that *ling-chih* has healing powers."

Whitney stared at the vial with an odd expression.

"Do you really buy into that?"

"Let's just say I don't discount the possibility. The 'plant of immortality' as the ancients called it, has some modern researchers thinking it helps prevent cancer and does wonders for the immune system."

Whitney winced and he belatedly recalled she'd lost her mother to cancer. Perhaps that's what prompted her to point him toward the kitchenette and place her order.

"I'll have a double, please."

CHAPTER TWELVE

IT WAS ONLY a twenty-minute hike, a mere seventeen hundred feet up that he and Marcia had to climb, but as they stopped to don their protective garb, Eric muttered, "Damn, I wish we were taking these off already and making tracks back to camp."

"You and me both." Marcia zipped up the flame-retardant suit and adjusted a boot—one that made feet sweat but kept them from getting too toasty from the leap of an unexpected flame. "How long do you think this'll take us?"

"Too long." They hadn't even reached the bubbling crater and already the overpowering stench of sulfur was assaulting his nostrils. Wincing at the sting in his eyes, Eric quickly donned the head covering that made him resemble a cross between a beekeeper and an astronaut. Both professions were a safer bet than the one he'd chosen, and at the moment he'd rather be tackling a hive bare-handed than preparing to dig up a broken seismometer with asbestos gloves. They limited his dexterity and would slow down the process, but better to take the precaution than risk losing his hands to a spurt of lava.

"Ready?" Marcia asked.

"Not in a million years." Taking a determined step forward, he wondered where the thrill had gone. He should be zinging from the pump of adrenaline, not feeling a queasy twist in his stomach and thinking about Whitney when a single wrong step could land him in the hospital. Or worse.

Yet even as they neared the crater, seething with activity and gaseous fumes, his mind wandered back to their lingering kiss goodbye. He wasn't much of one for shows of public affection, but it had been impossible not to kiss her and hold her, to fill his senses with the scent of lavender and Ivory soap, fill his hands with the hair he'd tugged free of a rubber band. And he hadn't wanted to stop, didn't want to leave her in the midst of a camp that looked like a little tent city, populated by people who lacked the means to make a fresh start elsewhere.

The camp was depressing. He should have had someone drive Whitney over to Plymouth for a day of shopping in the boutiques that were hurting for business. Instead, he'd made the offer, and let it drop when she insisted on sticking around to help.

Where was she now? Was she having second thoughts about coming? Or was she thinking of him, remembering this morning, touching his gift? He liked that idea a lot better. Especially if her thoughts included some hot imaginings of what the night might bring. Umm, yes, vivid fantasies that made her blush, made her feel a tingle in her breasts, in her jeans and—

"Eric, watch out!" Marcia's sharp warning coincided with the flinging of her arm against his chest, shoving him back.

Though he didn't need to look down to know what he'd nearly walked over, Eric put his eyes to the ground he should have had them glued on. This particularly treacherous area of Galway's Soufrière hid dangerous fissures beneath thin crusts of earth—which he could feel cracking beneath his feet.

"Oops." What else could he say as he carefully backed

off while Marcia shot him a hey-watch-where-you're-going glare?

"Once we're finished you can tell me all about that woman Larry mentioned you'd brought along—and I do feel perfectly entitled to hear everything after saving your ornery ass. Till then, Eric, do us both a favor and keep your head in the game? You know as well as I do that it's closer to Russian roulette than bingo."

"Right," he curtly agreed as they neared the familiar site. He'd installed the equipment earlier on when his head had been in the game, and his life had been devoted to a calling that was so much more than a job.

The winds of change were upon him. He could feel them blowing sulfurous and hot where he stood, but it was the sweet smell of lavender and Ivory soap that was whispering a seductive command to get this job done so he could haul his ornery ass down to the woman who was waiting and the comparative safety of fertile ground.

"WOULD YOU like some stew?"

"Stew?" repeated the little boy who held out his bowl. Sniffing at the ladle she scooped from a vat, he exclaimed, "Goat-water! It's me favorite."

Whitney filled his bowl to the brim and handed it back. "I didn't realize that was goat in there."

"And mountain chicken, too. *Rrribit, rrribit.*"

"That much I know. I had some the other day." Two days ago to be exact, but it seemed a lifetime had passed since she'd eaten alone and taken her mai tai back from Dick. Eric had changed her life, her very world. Dominica was so close, and yet so far away. These islands shared the same ocean but were oceans apart when it came to the people, the culture, the placid mountains there, the smoking peak Eric was on here....

She couldn't think about it. If she did, she'd be fighting an anxiety attack on top of this terrible urge to throw down the ladle so she could race to headquarters and get the latest progress report. Considering she'd been hovering over Larry's shoulder as he tracked a reading just a half hour ago, she didn't want to give him cause to tell Eric she'd been a pest when he got back.

And he would return. In the meantime she would stay calm and focus on the present.

"There you go, buster."

"Me name's not Buster." He flashed her an endearing snaggle-toothed grin. "It's Mickey."

An Irish name, spoken with a brogue by a child of African heritage. Such a great big world was out there, chock-full of people and places she'd yet to see. If only she'd ventured outside her own backyard sooner. If only it hadn't taken a lab report to cannonball her out of it and send her flying here. Here, where she couldn't cry over her own spilt milk when these people had the whole damn cow tipped over in a disaster zone kitchen.

"Okay, Mickey," she said, making herself match him grin for grin. "Enjoy." Thinking of the delicious eggs Benedict she'd scarfed down in the taxi, Whitney's smile faltered. She couldn't help but wish she'd saved some left-overs to share with Mickey. And all the other children displaced from their homes. Given the number, she might as well have a loaf of bread and two fishes to feed the multitudes.

"Thank you, bonnie lass."

"And you're welcome, me handsome laddie." As Mickey turned to go, dressed in raggedy clothes and no shoes for his feet, an idea came to her. "Wait! Have you got brothers, sisters? Friends?"

"Two brothers there," he said, pointing his bowl to a

table. "Three sisters down there." After nodding to some-where in the middle of the line that had snaked outside, he proudly proclaimed, "And lots of blokes. We camp out, just like G.I. Joe."

Thank God for the imagination of a child consigned to a crowded shelter filled with cots. Maybe she couldn't change that any more than she could work miracles, but there was something she could do.

"Do all you G.I. Joes like hearing stories?" At his big nod she instructed, "Sunset. Your campsite. Spread the word."

Judging from Mickey's race to the table where his broth-ers sat, the whisper in one ear, then passed on from there to another, and another, Whitney was sure she wouldn't be lacking an avid audience.

As self-appointed commander in chief of entertainment for the evening, she issued invitations while serving up the grub to the other children who passed by. What kind of future would they have? And their parents, was this the future they had imagined for themselves in their own days of innocence?

The dinner line was long and each bowl served repre-sented yet another person who'd had to migrate to safer ground and desert the crops many of them tended for a living. While she was a visitor, everything these people had—their jobs, homes, families, lives—hinged on the mood of a volcano with a major-league case of PMS. Two volcanos actually. Ever since Chance's Peak had opened up and spewed ashes onto the south end of the island, put-ting Montserrat on Orange Alert—one step away from evacuation—its bitchin' twin had got in on the act.

Galway's Soufrière was its name. It towered over the island like some mercurial lord of the land hurting its own economy with its hissy fits to keep the tourist trade away.

And its subjects, these native islanders, had built their humble homes in the shadow of the tyrannical ruler who threatened to turn their tropical paradise into sinking sand.

"Do you know what time it is?" she asked the Red Cross worker who was handing out bottled water beside her. When it turned out to be only ten minutes since the last time she'd asked, Whitney told herself that being a worrywart wouldn't make Eric any safer or get him back quicker, so the best she could do was to dole out as much cheer as she did goat-water.

After pitching in with cleanup, Whitney knew she should be too tired to think further than the nearest spare cot. But amazingly, she wasn't tired. She felt better than she had in months, almost as energized as the kids she watched dancing to reggae in the dirt streets or playing hide-and-seek.

They wouldn't be hiding behind trees, at least not the ones with a red circle around them. Those trees dripped acid. And when acidic trees were considered safe ground, what kind of danger was Eric confronting on the higher turf he'd yet to return from?

Deciding enough time had passed, Whitney commanded herself to walk, not run, to get any news she could to alleviate her growing anxiety.

"Larry," she addressed the father of three who'd been relegated to keeping track of the data coming in. "What's the latest?"

Looking up from the graph he was tracking, he said distractedly, "The new equipment we ordered this morning, just in case, is on its way. Good thing, too, since Eric threw the old one into the crater and wasn't mincing any bleeps on getting the replacement when he radioed in a little while ago."

"Did he…" How could she say this without sounding like her personal concerns were more important to her than the lives depending on the installation of a new seis-mometer?

"Yeah, Whitney, he sent a message for you." Larry chuckled as if she'd brightened his day with a frivolous bit of romance, albeit unspoken. "I wrote it down...now where was that paper?"

Larry located the message, skimmed the lines, and had the tact to say no more than "Heh, heh" before handing it over.

The island might be safe enough for now but don't think for a second that includes you. Prepare for a private tango that'll make the earth move.

The room suddenly seemed too warm. Whitney fanned her cheeks with the note responsible for their heat. "When do you think he'll be finished?"

"If the goods arrive soon..." He cupped his ear, stuck two thumbs up in the air. "Yes! I do believe that's a chop-per I hear. Assuming that's the new equipment, and know-ing they'll be working like maniacs to get it in before they can't see their way off the crater, I'd give 'em a couple hours to finish up and hightail it home."

"That long?"

"Could be longer if they run into problems and have to pick their way down with only a flashlight and the moon to see where they're going. Whenever he checks in, want me to pass on the point of rendezvous?"

And to think she'd believed scientists to be even more uptight than librarians. These guys were about as subtle as an elephant parading down Main Street. Yes, better to imagine an elephant parade with Eric at the helm than to envision him tripping in the dark and tumbling into a bub-bling vat of lava.

"That's okay, I'll find him once he gets back." She'd make sure the storytelling session was over by the time he returned, something she'd just as soon keep a secret between her and the kids. And thank goodness for them to take her mind off the gnawing apprehension that had her seeking reassurance. "He will be back, won't he?"

Larry gave her a look that implied such answers came from a higher power than himself and if she didn't realize such, he hated to be the one to break the news.

She needed some fresh air to rid herself of this cloying sensation that was making it hard to breathe. "Well, guess I'd better be going and let you work."

As she clutched the medallion and backed away, Larry said with a sympathy she couldn't miss, "I know it's hard, but try not to worry. When he gets back—and he will, you have to believe that, we all do—don't let him see how afraid you are. It's poison to relationships with guys like us. Of course even guys like us can get smart once we have a reason to play it safer than we otherwise would."

"Words of wisdom from someone who's been there?"

"There and back. I'll always be back for more, just like Eric, but you see where I'm sitting." He bounced on the chair. "Close enough to take in the action but not so close I won't make it home. I'd rather catch Leno with my wife than stick around for the show."

The show. Slang for the visual, and life-threatening effects, that could only be had by hanging around to see a pyrotechnic display that made Fourth of July blowouts seem on a par with fizzling bottle rockets. Eric had become very animated when he described some of the shows he'd seen, but much as she'd begun to crave adventure, running for what life she had left was something she could do without.

"I don't think we'll be catching Leno tonight or make

it a habit in the future, but I appreciate the advice anyway. Oh, and Larry, give my best to your wife. I doubt we'll ever meet, but she must be special for you to feel as you do.''

''Special?'' He pulled out his wallet and planted a kiss on a snapshot sealed in plastic. ''Three kids, ten years of marriage and she is still a fox. One who lets me roam as long as I come home and just thinking about her makes me hope my replacement's arriving with the new equipment. Soon as I can, I'm out of here and making whoopie with my wife. That is, if the kids are in bed. If they're not, that's where they're headed even if I have to bribe them with enough candy to keep the dentist in business for a year.''

Kids. Candy. Dentists. Such were the luxuries of parenthood, though most parents probably didn't think of them that way. She did. Those things were denied her and she longed for them fiercely. As it was, the closest she'd ever get was having been a child herself with a mouthful of braces that had to be replaced after sinking her metal-encrusted teeth into a batch of peanut brittle.

Remembering, Whitney had to smile. A rather pained smile that turned into a broad grin. Perhaps all she had was now but as of now she had to find some volunteers to pull peanut brittle duty while she put on a show of her own. Sugar and peanuts were the basic ingredients, plenty of both in the camp's kitchen. It should be ready by the time she took her bows and what better way to leave the kids? With sticky hands and licking their lips while she did what she could to look alluring despite the grime she'd accumulated on an eye-opening day.

An hour later, Whitney knew she'd never had a day better spent. She didn't have a storyboard with felt figures to move around or even finger puppets. But that was okay. Better than okay. Ratty-haired Barbie dolls and dilapidated stuffed animals made fine characters to enact the sort of story the children had voted for. A scary story and one better told with a white sheet around her face and a flashlight Mickey shone on it as dusk decended and goblins moved closer to the tent they sought refuge in....

POURING ENOUGH sweat to keep a rose garden blooming in Desert Valley, Eric stripped off the outfit only an alien would consider trendy threads while Marcia did the same.

"Yes! Yes, Yes! Mission accomplished," she jubilantly proclaimed. "Gimme ten."

As they slapped four palms together, Eric had the satisfaction of knowing they'd done well. They weren't pushing up daisies yet, and the populace of Montserrat didn't have to worry about it either now, thanks to their efforts. So, why wasn't he feeling like a war hero, just like his two-star general dad whose shoes he'd done his best to fill? Not in the military—he was too independent for that; but he had managed to make Dad proud, make himself proud, by waging war against a force more destructive than man.

Such derring-do usually gave him an incredible high, and that was the addiction, but all Eric felt was a deep disappointment since the reason he couldn't wait to get the hell off that crater wasn't around to greet him the moment he and Marcia returned to camp.

"Time to party!" she whooped with a fling of her sooty jumpsuit into the air. Catching it, she spun the thing around in the sort of way he'd imagined doing with Whitney.

So much for his fantasy, Whitney wasn't anywhere to be seen. As for Marcia's expectations to celebrate in their typical blowout fashion, he had other plans and they didn't include hanging around here to party with his pals.

"Sorry, Marcia, I won't be joining you and the gang.

After we brief Larry, I'm finding Whitney and we're outta here."

"Whitney this, Whitney that," she teased. "Jeez, Eric, I said you owed me the scoop but you haven't shut up about her for the last friggin' hour. Remind me to stuff my ears with cotton the next time you get a crush on—"

"It's not a crush," he interrupted. "Have you ever heard me run my mouth about a woman before?"

"No. And lucky for you, otherwise I would've offered you as a human sacrifice to the volcanic gods years ago. As it is, we've got a lot of history between us and I love ya too much to do you in because you're all ga-ga over a woman you met last Thursday. It's Saturday, Eric. Saturday. You've always had a good head on your shoulders, but if you're head-over-heels after three days, that's not the head you're thinking with."

"You bet she turns me on. With a look, a smile. Even a thought will do. But it's more than that. A lot more. Remember how you felt when we got called in here a few years back? You'd just met Luke and as I recall, you said—"

"Don't remind me of what I said after half a bottle of Jack Daniel's when I was nursing third-degree burns. And keep Luke out of this while you're at it."

"No," he told her flatly. "No, I won't. And why? Because if anyone should know how I feel, it should be you. I'm laying my all out here for you, Marcia. For the first time in fifteen years I'm doing it and asking you to be my friend."

"I am your friend, Eric. I always have been."

Eric knew better. There were friends, and then there were *friends*. Thanks to Whitney, he was taking a chance on making up for the ones he'd lost.

"Okay, then tell me you're happy for me."

"I'm happy for you." Marcia pushed up her lips with two fingers. "Good enough?"

"If that's the best you can do, sure." Upon his reply she gave him a real smile, minus the fingers pushing it up. "So, what's up with you and Luke these days?"

Marcia dropped her smile along with her suit, gave it a kick, then muttered, "He left me, Eric. The same way Amy left you. It always comes down to that final ultimatum, and I guess that's why I'm not predicting great things for you and this Whitney who came along to help out."

"It's more than Amy or Luke ever did," he defended.

"True, but people do crazy things to impress each other when they're infatuated. Once reality sets in, lines get drawn. Those lines separate us from what most people can't stomach for the long haul. We're not most people, Eric. Maybe Whitney isn't, either. But you've only known her a few days and I've known you for how long? Almost fifteen years, big guy. I don't want to see you get hurt."

How could he explain what he didn't fully understand himself? He had a shared history with Marcia, yet she would never know him like Whitney did. It was a fundamental understanding of character and essence that time couldn't reveal or conceal.

"As you said, we've only known each other a few days," he slowly replied, "and what can any of us know in so little time? Quite a lot, it seems, and no one could be more amazed by that than me. Meeting her was...like an epiphany. That's it, an emotional epiphany. All these unfamiliar feelings came rushing in and while I've never experienced anything like it before, those feelings are very clear, pure. Certain. There's such a rightness about her, if Whitney's not the real thing, I don't know what is."

"Whew." Marcia whistled. "That's heavy."

"Yeah, so why do I feel lighter than air?"

Waving her hand under her nose, she hitched a thumb in the direction of the shower tent. "The air smelled better before we got here. Better wash off all that sulfur and sweat if you want a kiss from your girl. While you get cleaned up, I'll see to Larry." Marcia winked. "Get trottin', hot stuff."

Eric could hear her laughing as he danced down the street, singing a Donna Summer's hit.

He didn't care who heard him mutilating the song and if he looked as silly as *The Full Monty* blokes trying to imitate the Chippendales, so what? Whitney was the only one he cared about and tonight they would dance and make love until seductive whispers turned to cries of—

A medley of high-pitched shrieks stopped his thoughts of passion and he changed direction. Children screaming inside a dark canvas shelter. Had a wildcat sneaked in, hunting for dinner? Pulling out his switchblade, Eric raced against time. Just as he reached the tent, all became silent.

Except for the eerie sound of a ghostlike voice. A voice that dipped and swayed, along with a stuffed rabbit that seemed to float in the air, held aloft by a sheet-covered phantom who dramatically intoned, "Who has my golden hand?"

Whitney was encircled by a crowd of kids scooting back and shaking their heads.

"You have my golden hand! Give me my golden hand, Mickey. Give me my golden hand!" Whitney snarled, pointing a finger at the accused.

More shrieks. It was the sound of kids scared half to death and loving every second of their ghost story terror. Who could doubt it amidst the wild applause and shouts for "More! More!" when she tossed the sheet she'd been wearing on top of a group huddled together.

Eric clapped along from his post outside. But he didn't

make himself known with a piercing whistle or a ''Bravo!'' It wouldn't be right to steal Whitney away when so many were begging for an encore.

Thus, he kept his anonymity and faded into the dark. As he did, Eric could only wonder how his life had seemed so full before they'd met, only to realize how empty that life would be without her.

Whitney. His bright, shining star.

CHAPTER THIRTEEN

WHILE THE peanut brittle was being handed out, Whitney made her escape. If the kids had their way, they'd keep her all night. Bless Mickey's little heart, he'd even offered to let her sleep on his cot in exchange for one more story. Just one more, he'd begged so earnestly it had been a struggle not to hold him in her arms and tell him stories until he fell asleep. But she'd already stayed much longer than intended, and she wanted to find Eric before he found her.

Hurrying out of the tent lit with lanterns, she promptly collided with a woman.

"Sorry!" Her eyes adjusting to the lesser light, Whitney realized just who she had bumped into. The picture hadn't done the woman justice. She was Amazon tall, a lithe, bronzed beauty who bore a striking resemblance to another Whitney.

That would be Whitney Houston.

"You're Marcia Grayson, aren't you?"

"If you're with the LAPD and looking to collect on those parking tickets, I'm not. Otherwise, that's the name I saw on my license the last time I checked." Cocking her head, she looked Whitney over then said, "I know who you are. You're Whitney. Whitney Smith."

"How did you guess?"

"Doesn't take much guessing after the description I got. Only I don't see those auburn highlights that really come out in the sun and it's too dark to tell if your eyes could actually make the ocean look murky on its best crystal-clear day.''

Though somewhat embarrassed, Whitney couldn't contain her pleased smile. ''I can't believe Eric said that.''

''Neither can I. Which is why I'm glad he's in the shower and we're out here. We don't have long to talk and I know plenty about you already, so I hope you don't mind if we save the getting-to-know-you chitchat. I'd like to speak frankly. While we walk. Jeez, it's loud in there.'' Hooking her arm through Whitney's with a surprising comradery, Marcia's forthrightness was equally startling.

''Are you in love with Eric? After knowing him three whole days and spending more of that time apart than together, can you honestly say you're in love with the man?''

''I...well, I...'' Was she? The answer was in her heart, not her head. Shutting out the clamoring sound of her heart, she heeded the voice of reason that would protect her and Eric from a rash and painful mistake. ''Not yet.''

''But you could be?''

Disdaining a bald-faced lie, Whitney remained silent. And then she wished she hadn't since it only drove Marcia to say more than Whitney wanted to hear.

''That's a yes if I ever heard one. Look, Whitney, I've never seen him happier than he was today and I couldn't help but notice he was more preoccupied than usual, too. You're bad for his health. Then again, you could be good for it. Much as I hate to lose the best partner I've ever had, Eric needs someone who means more to him than this—'' Marcia nodded toward the smoking peak. ''Even when he was married, Eric didn't have that someone. After what he said to me about you, I think he just might have found her. Please correct me if I'm wrong.''

What could she say? Even if she could bring herself to

confide in Marcia, it wouldn't change the state of her health or any impact she might have on Eric's well-being.

"I'd like to be that someone, Marcia. What woman wouldn't want to be? But as you pointed out, Eric and I haven't known each other long and it's way too soon to lay odds on where we'll be a month from now, much less in a year."

Lame excuse? It didn't sound so, but it felt so.

"Eric said he feels like he's known you for years." Marcia stopped walking and let go of Whitney's arm. She crossed her own as if pulling up the drawbridge from a moat. "Maybe you don't realize it, but Eric's one of those people who's fun and friendly on the outside but he doesn't get too close. I've known him for ages and we've been through a lot together, but he doesn't talk much about his feelings or the relationships he's in. For him to go on and on about you is totally unlike him. I'd like us to be friends, Whitney. But if you break that man's heart, you're gonna wish I'd never laid eyes on you."

It seemed that Marcia wasn't just a colleague or the party pal Eric had painted her out to be. She was ferocious in her loyalty to a man whose heart could indeed be broken.

Just above her own, the medallion dangled on a slender gold chain. Many times today she'd stroked it to ward off her fears and take courage. Yet as Marcia waited for some sign from her that Eric hadn't fallen for the wrong woman, Whitney felt unworthy of holding such a significant link to him.

The lump in her throat made it hard to talk. The sight of Eric walking, then sprinting toward her with arms open, made it impossible to say the words tearing her heart apart. *Don't worry, I'll cut it off before he gets too hurt to recover. As for me, I'll never recover from the moment we met and I'm already hurting for us both.*

Keenly aware of the precious little time they had remaining since she had to cut their ties after one—just one more—night together, Whitney raced to him.

His arms closed around her and her feet took to the air she'd been walking on since the first time he'd smiled that smile that could charm the pants off a nun. He wore it now, laced with a longing and a warmth that she clung to even tighter than she did the arms spinning her around.

And all the while he kissed her like a soldier returning to his sweetheart after a long and arduous war. Even after he stopped his spinning, her head continued to whirl. She was so hungry for him, she couldn't get enough of his touch, the taste of his mouth with a nick beside it, the feel of his just washed hair, or the sound of his hot, sweet murmur.

"I missed you. Kiss me again, *yuan-pao*. Kiss me and don't stop."

Every last morsel of this moment she gobbled up, too greedy to stop and too needy to let reality steal him away.

Until Marcia cleared her throat. "I hate to interrupt this Kodak moment, but it's time for me to say my goodbyes." She offered her hand to Whitney, and with a succinct grip, and a significant woman-to-woman glance, said, "I hope we *all* meet again. Good luck to the *two* of you."

Her buss to Eric's cheek was distinctly more caring. "I know you need some time off so I won't be calling again unless it's an emergency. Till then, you've got my number since it works both ways. Ciao, baby," she said, then walked off.

"What was that about?"

Tell him, Whitney ordered herself. Tell him it was fun while it lasted but the game's over. Tell him you're on the rebound or something like that, and you're sorry for stringing him along but you can't get involved. Make something up he can swallow and if it tastes like bile, all the better. Then he'll go lick his wounds and try to forget a few days' insanity while you fade into the sunset and pretend what you're leaving with is enough.

But it wasn't enough. A quick anger surged at the unfairness of it all and Whitney was suddenly furious, madder than hell at the inequities of life and most of all, Marcia.

How dare she play judge? Marcia had no right to guilt trip her into giving up what happiness she could still have. Excluding an accident, Marcia had decades of living ahead. Ditto for Eric. Whitney Smith, however, didn't have that luxury, and if holding on to what she could have while she could still have it made her selfish, then that's what she was. A selfish woman who desperately needed to laugh enough for a lifetime, and love with the heart of a fool.

At least for a few more days. Should she pick a fight, make it worthy of an exit, and simply disappear, they would have only been together for a little more time.

"I have no idea what that was about," Whitney replied. The lie didn't sit well with her, but her dire need justified it—and getting his attention off Marcia and onto her. Sliding a hand into her bra, she plucked out his earlier message. "Now what's this about a private dance?"

"Ah, yes." He placed one hand in the small of her back, and raised her arm high with the other. With a neat twirl, he dipped her. "The tango."

"I've always wanted to learn the tango," she said breathlessly.

"Then the tango you shall learn." Pulling her up and close to him, he decided, "In the Virgin Islands. Say...Saint Croix?"

"Saint Croix?" She tried to hide her excitement, but her bouncing toes gave her away. "Why there?"

"Because Dominica might be beautiful, but come midnight we'll be plunking change into a jukebox. After today I'm more in the mood to celebrate into the wee hours than turn in early.'' He gave her a devilish wink. ''Then again, if you're ready to hit the hay, far be it from me to disagree. The plane I booked takes off in half an hour. We'll go wherever you want to go.''

''You mean we're leaving already?''

''That much of what Marcia said made sense. My work's done here for now. If the gas readings go up, the water supply turns to sulphur or they register some tremors that spell trouble, they might have to evacuate but they don't need me to do that. I, however, have a need to take my lady to Saint Croix for a dancing lesson. Unless she'd rather tap her ruby slippers elsewhere, that is.''

Whitney clapped her hands, then showered him with butterfly kisses between exclamations of, ''The tango! In Saint Croix! Eric, you make my wildest dreams come true.''

As he absorbed her outpouring of affection, Eric knew an even wilder dream was coming true for him. He was being embraced so wholly he had no reason to hide his feelings, watch his words or be torn between the love of his work and his love of a woman. Did he love Whitney? It shouldn't be possible, yet this incredible, awesome thing that had overtaken him seemed determined to change all his preconceptions about what love was, how long it took to happen, when to express it, and all manner of hooey that reduced the most powerful and inexplicable emotion known to man down to the equivalent of a data sheet.

Yep, there went the needle right off the register when Whitney beamed up at him. All his past blips put together couldn't compete with this. It stood to reason he might be in love. It also stood to reason that he never had been before.

''Uh-oh, I didn't bring any other clothes with me, Eric.''

"What about the condoms?"

She blushed, ducked her head, then looked back up. Still blushing, she whispered, "They're in my purse."

"Then you packed the only real thing of importance. We'll buy some new clothes once we need them." Was he in love? If so, it gave him the craziest ideas. "Tell you what, let's forget about hitting a club tonight and practice in a room—make that a suite. Then tomorrow—or the next day, or next week, whenever we decide to leave the room— we'll go shopping. I'll pick out what I'd like you to wear and you can do the same for me."

"A shopping spree? Together? Neat!"

He'd suggested a shopping spree. Incredible. Insane. He had to be mad. Or madly in love.

Suddenly Whitney's animation faded. She glanced at the tent he'd watched her transform from a shelter for the destitute to a magic kingdom that was hers to command.

"It all sounds so wonderful, Eric. But it seems awfully indulgent when these people are going without. I feel like I should stay and help."

"Whitney." He gripped her shoulders with the madness that was in him. For her. Only for her. "There's always a need for help. I see that need everywhere I go, and it meant a lot to me, what you did today—"

"But I've never seen anything like this in my life. And I didn't do all that much," she insisted. "Handing out bowls of stew—I mean, goat-water—and washing a few dishes seems so paltry. Like one of those token efforts at Thanksgiving to slap some dressing on a plastic plate to feel good about yourself and better appreciate your own full pantry for the next year. Makes you look good, feel good, but how much good did you really do? Not much. And that's how I feel."

So, she'd been pulling kitchen duty, too. And the fact

she wasn't mentioning the true good she'd done those kids, only increased Eric's admiration and respect for her beautiful soul whose inner light deserved to be shared. But another time. Another place. Tonight she would be his, all his.

"If that's how you feel, then you're selling yourself short. You supported me with your presence today, Whitney. And despite what you think, you made a big difference for these people. Yes, they need you, but so do I. You see, I'm in something of a crisis situation myself and while others can help them, only you can help me."

Whitney's concern immediately shifted to exactly where he wanted it. "Eric, what's wrong? Tell me what the problem is and I'll do anything I can to help."

Okay, so he'd exaggerated and didn't really deserve her sympathy. But that didn't lessen his need and the unvarnished truth should be persuasion enough to get them out of here.

"Here's the problem. I've been burning a candle at both ends for a long time and I'm so close to burning out that I have to take care of myself before I'm no good for anyone. Which is why, barring another major emergency, it's *adios, amigos* for the next six months. When I planned this trip, it was on the pretext of updating my book. An excuse, pure and simple, to chill out while pretending to work. Work, that's all I know how to do anymore. I've forgotten how to relax and simply enjoy life. But when I'm with you, it's so easy. That's why I need you with me."

"Six months." Whitney seemed to be making some calculation in her gorgeous head as she rubbed her temples. "I never knew anyone who could take six months off unless they were retired. I'd rather not think that far ahead, especially on vacation."

"Exactly," he readily agreed. "And that's just what I

need from you. Living for the day, let tomorrow take care of itself. You keep reminding me of how important it is to relish the moment, instead of jumping at the chance to sign up for a lecture tour in Europe when I'd rather have a root canal than speak in public. Save me from myself, *yuan-pao*. Give me tonight, give me tomorrow, and if you're ready to dump me after that, so be it. I ask no more of you than the gift of your time, as long as you're willing to give it.''

Whitney clutched his grandmother's amulet. She rubbed her thumb over it, over and over, as if certain the genie would appear despite her lack of belief.

But perhaps she did believe after all, because it took some measure of faith to let go of the medallion and loop her arms around his neck.

''If you put it that way...''

''I can put it any which way you want it, kitten.'' He bumped his hips against hers, pressing home his meaning. *Home.* The word struck a chord in that elusive place Whitney had touched and was helping him discover.

The Way that can't be charted, the Name that can't be defined, the Truth that is unknowable. The Tao was starting to sound a lot closer to home—and love—than he'd ever imagined it might be. He had never imagined that what he'd been in search of all these years, as he traveled from pillar to post, might suddenly appear right under his nose.

Whitney's tilted up impishly. ''Any which way, huh? Does that possibly include some bedchamber secrets you'd be willing to share?''

''More than willing. I'll give you one now to think about until we get to where such secrets won't be secrets anymore.'' Into her ear he whispered, ''According to the Mystic Master—the Tang dynasty's answer to Dr. Ruth—there are thirty positions and fifteen coital movements, which comes to 390 variations of intercourse. Love play—otherwise known as foreplay which sounds a lot more like golf than fooling around to me—not included."

"Three hundred and ninety? Mercy."

When the student is ready the teacher will appear.

Ah so, and voilà.

"Mercy. I like the sound of that. Especially if you're crying for it. I might even be generous enough to give it to you—if you beg half as prettily as you look." Remembering her absolutely beautiful abandon that morning, Eric was inspired to add, "And how prettily you do beg. Meow, that was some purr. Can't wait to hear what kind of sounds you make when I treat you to a Peacock Tease."

Whitney pulled back and he nearly laughed aloud at her expression of avid curiosity.

"What's a Peacock Tease?"

"A game. With a feather." Should he spike up his enticement? Oh yes, he should. "Then there's the Spring Butterfly. We'll need an artist's brush for that. Assuming, of course, that you're interested in playing the games."

"You'll teach me?"

"I can't wait."

"And all those variations of, um, what that Mystic Master said. You'll teach me those, too?"

Most interesting. And promising. Connoisseurs of the intimate arts were always open to something new but they'd tried so many things already that feathers and brushes and a variety of positions wouldn't merit more than a shrug. Whitney had a thirst for sensual knowledge that could only come from a neophyte.

"I'll gladly teach you everything I know," he assured her, and what an assurance it was to have so much to teach. Maybe she didn't want to think too far down the road, but she would have no thoughts of leaving as long as she shared his bed. And share it she would, even in Europe. A few months away, but by then she'd rather die than relinquish the exquisite pleasure he gave her. Such pleasure, in fact, that after tonight she'd realize their little romp this morning was but a pleasant tête-à-tête compared with what he had in store.

With a swat to her behind, he ordered, "Get your purse and let's go. The sooner we're out of here, the sooner I can feed you the best room service has to offer. We'll dine and we'll dance and make love till we drop. The first time you beat me to the door before I can drag you back in, we'll pick up a few game pieces and I'll buy you a new wardrobe."

"Wait." Whitney stalled halfway to the main shelter where they'd parked what little belongings they'd come with. Despite several people milling about and the fact he was considered a top dog around here, she tapped a finger to his chest as if he had about as much clout as a schnauzer. "Correction. You pick, I pay. As for transportation, the hotel, etcetera, we'll split it down the middle. No arguments, Eric. Please."

While he didn't want to waste time arguing, much less sour the evening, they had to get this settled once and for all. Starting with the fact that just because it made him feel more manly to foot the bill didn't make her any less his equal. Only he wouldn't say it like that.

"Look, I appreciate your need to be independent. In fact, I adore how independent you are. It's one of the qualities I admire most about you, but—"

"Don't patronize me, Eric. You're only trying to butter me up to get your way. It won't work. So please let's not disagree. Let's kiss and make up, put this behind us, and hit the road."

As they did exactly that, Eric had to wonder just who was teaching whom.

CHAPTER FOURTEEN

"Time to wake up."

Snuggling deeper into her big cuddly pillow, Whitney asked groggily, "Where are we?"

"Saint Croix. The plane just landed and we need to get off. I'd carry you if I could but the cabin's too small."

Waking up more fully, she realized her head was in Eric's lap. One of his hands cupped a breast, the other was stroking her hair. "Sorry, Eric. I didn't mean to fall asleep on you again."

"That's okay, you needed a nap after putting in such a long day. Besides, I enjoyed watching you sleep." His lingering squeeze to her breast accompanied a rise of the wedge beneath her neck. "And I did manage to entertain myself in the meantime."

Feeling amply refreshed to get frisky, Whitney pressed a kiss to her major means of support and suggested, "Let's find a taxi to the nearest hotel so you can entertain yourself some more."

Though it wasn't the nearest hotel, it had to be the most impressive one she'd ever seen—an elegant, sprawling, Caribbean-style grand villa.

As Eric carried her over the threshold with the sweeping aplomb of a groom wanting to give his new bride only the best, she squealed in delight at the exotic spray of flowers in the marbled entry, ran a thumb down the keys of the grand piano which took center stage in a living space filled with plush furnishings. The room opened up onto a large, private veranda where lights twinkled in the vista like diamonds and the moon rose above the cresting ocean waves.

"It's beautiful, Eric. So beautiful I can't believe it's real."

"No dream," he murmured. "It's as real as you and me. And from where I stand, it's not half as beautiful as what I see."

Their eyes met and in his she saw truth. He really believed what he'd said. How many women had ever had a man gaze upon them this way as if they were the most exquisite beauty? Perhaps movie stars and super models, but real women like herself didn't look in the mirror and see that. They saw their flaws and resolved to fix them. But what was there to fix when one saw oneself as Eric was regarding her?

"You're glowing."

"You make me glow." Pressing a kiss to his cheek, she could feel her own radiance. What magic was this? She didn't need a mirror to know Eric saw her clearly, and at this moment, so did she. She was as beautiful as what was inside her, and inside her was a thing too beautiful to describe.

The bedroom he carried her to was no less dazzling. White flowing drapes and white pillars and a white bearskin rug accentuated the centerpiece—a huge heart-shaped white bed. And beside that bed was a basket overflowing with ripe, tropical fruit.

With a sexy grin that would have convinced Eve if the serpent hadn't, Eric tempted her with his offering.

"Care for a mango? I know you must be hungry."

"I'm hungry," she confirmed and reached down for a banana. Peeling it suggestively, she closed her lips over the fruit's tip then pulled back, leaving it intact. "For you."

Eric's gaze sombered, pupils dilating until they were almost fully eclipsed.

"How brave you are, tempting me with an invitation like that." He pulled off a generous chunk of the banana and gently pushed it past her lips. "I could be more than you've bargained for, Whitney. If you're afraid you might have bitten off more than you can chew, better say so now. Otherwise, it's me, all of me, you're going to get."

With the banana on her tongue and a breath lodged in her throat, she couldn't utter a word.

"In that case..." He tossed the banana into the basket and as she braced herself to be similarly tossed onto the bed, Eric asked with the confidence of one who was certain he wouldn't be turned down, "Want to play?"

The unknown made her suddenly tingle with apprehension. Dare she risk a walk on the wild side with Eric? She did. He would never hurt her.

"I'd love to play with you, Eric. Just name it."

"How about 'Heart and Soul'? It's the only piece of music I know but I can play both ends."

"Heart and Soul," she repeated. "Don't tell me you want to play the piano right now."

"Why not? I saw the way you looked at it when we came in, like a long lost friend you'd forgotten how much you missed. You do want to tinkle those ivories, don't you?"

"Well, yes, but I—well, I just thought—"

"That I'd want you to play my instrument instead?" At her glance south, he chuckled. "You're more than welcome to have at it, but I did promise you dinner and dancing first."

"And a bath," she reminded him. "With bubbles."

"And a bottle of bubbly while we take turns scrubbing backs."

They moved from a kiss and a fondle to the piano where heart met soul in a companionable duet that ended with a splash in a heart-shaped tub for two.

"Ever had your hair washed with champagne?" he asked, tilting the bottle over her head and working the shampoo into an effervescent lather.

"Nope, but it's definitely something every woman should try at least once in her life." Whitney savored another bite of caviar spread on a cracker. Why had she waited so long to discover such a tantalizing taste? And why hadn't she before tried strawberries dipped in chocolate, so rich, juicy, bittersweet?

Yet even these delicacies were as nothing compared to the feel of Eric's fingers massaging her scalp, the curve of her spine next to his chest, so big and strong and dusted with dark, silky hair brushing her skin. His thighs rode hers and their kneecaps peaked through the white foam, swishing up and over her breasts.

He palmed one. "Did I mention I love your breasts?"

"Feel free to repeat yourself."

"I'd rather help myself to what bears repeating." And help himself he did, stroking and kneading until her sighs turned to moans as he pinched their tips and whispered the most decadent request in her ear. "That is, if you're open to the idea."

Whitney slid his hand down and down, past her breasts, over her belly, and to her resounding response to such an idea. "What does that tell you?"

"Bath time's over." After a quick rinse of her hair, Eric pulled her out of the tub. Before either could dry off, they were on the floor, both of them wet and slithering all over each other as they licked and kissed their way from smooth hard tile to soft, plush carpet, and then onto the bearskin rug.

It was there that he made love to her in a way she'd never imagined being made love to before. On her back, Eric straddling her torso and looking down at her with those exotic almond eyes and hers looking back, full of wonder that she felt so free yet so bound to this man making hot, wanton love to her breasts.

She pushed them closer together, sealing the tunnel through which he slid back and forth. The faster he went, the more intense his expression grew, and all the while his eyes burned into her, even as he groaned on a final thrust.

She could feel him shaking, hear the heave of his breath, the ragged utterance of her name. There was no doubt of his coming, though yet again, no fluids to suggest it.

There was only Eric slumping over her, whispering *"yuan-pao,"* into her ear. "I'll never get enough of you. Not enough of your taste, your touch, your voice. You're an incredible woman. And incredibly generous, giving me that release without a thought to yourself."

"The incredible part I'll take. But generous?" She shook her head. Just remembering the fever in his eyes, the ecstasy she'd brought him, quickened the hot rush within that had by no means subsided. "What you did excited me."

"How excited?" he asked.

"I think you already know, considering what you're—" Gone were his stroking fingers. But not his stroking. Or his erection, which slid between her but not inside, making her finish with a gasped "—touching."

"Tell me anyway," he insisted. Even more insistent was the slight push he gave against her. "Tell me how much I excite you."

"More than...more than I can say when you're doing that."

"Then maybe I should stop what I'm doing."

"No!" She grabbed him back, wrapped her legs tight around his. "I'll say anything, just don't leave me."

He didn't try to move away again. In fact, he didn't move at all. Eric stared down at her, perfectly still, in a way that made her shiver. And then he shook her. In a still, quiet voice he shook her with the force of his demand.

"Say you want me like you've never wanted anyone before. Ever."

"More than anyone before, I want you."

"And how much is that?"

"Too much, Eric. I want you too much."

"No, *yuan-pao,*" he said in a silken whisper. "You don't want me enough. Not yet, anyway. But you will," he promised with a gentle rock forward, then a swift retreat when her hips rose up, up in a desperate attempt to capture what he refused to let her claim. "Oh yes, you will. Just wait and see."

"But I don't want to wait. Eric, please, I—"

"Shhh." He laid a finger to her lips. "Lesson."

He said no more than that and Whitney surmised the lesson had begun. Only, what kind of lesson was this? It was torment, sheer torment she endured from the body he offered, then promptly seized back each time she tried to accept his teasing bait. And each time she whimpered a protest he swallowed it up in his mouth, only to pull away, and lick his lips as if her frustrated pleas were the tastiest morsels he'd ever devoured.

She couldn't stand it a moment longer. Ready to mount him and take what she damn well wanted more than enough, Whitney tried pushing him off. And then she tried again. Again and again until she nearly wore herself out.

Eric was unmovable. No longer plucking at the tips of her breasts, his chest bore down on them, and his hard thighs anchored hers to the rug. He gripped her wrists and spread her arms like the span of wings felled to the ground, then notched himself against her copious wetness.

"What do you want from me?" she demanded.

"What do you want from me?" he countered.

"Do I have to spell it out for you?"

"Please do."

Since any idiot could figure that out, and Eric was a very smart man, Whitney knew the obvious wasn't what he was after. Maybe this was some kind of question-and-answer session to determine what she'd learned from a lesson she hadn't learned anything from. Nothing, that is, but Eric's uncanny ability to stay cucumber cool while he turned her into a burning inferno that would bring the roof down around them if he didn't hurry up and put out the flames.

"I want your body, Eric. I want it inside me and I want it there now."

He raised a brow and twitched his lips, apparently digesting what amounted to…not much. "That's all?"

"You've got a great body. I want to feel it move."

"A lot of men have great bodies. If that's all you really want, you don't need me. Any great body would do and I can assure you that most of them wouldn't hesitate to step in while I'm taking a break."

Forget the question-and-answer session. Eric was turning this into a Mensa debate when she didn't have a thought in her head beyond the hormonal messages bombarding her brain. She was weeping and grasping for…him. Eric. So much more than a lust-inspiring body, he made her long to embrace all that he was.

All that she couldn't have. Not in the long run, anyway. But if she told him what he wanted to hear, he'd give her what she couldn't live without tonight. Maybe not ever.

Give him what he wants, she told herself—*your heart,* and worry about it later.

"I don't want any other man, Eric. It's you that I want. So deep inside me I can feel you where I've never been touched before."

He pulled one of her hands to his heart. She could feel it beat fast yet steady against her palm. "This is where you've touched me. It's where I want to touch you."

Whitney hesitated only slightly before placing his palm over her own heart. It beat fast but not steady at all.

"You already have. Touch me deeper?"

Eric rose above her, looking for all the world like Atlas, thoroughly capable of carrying the entire globe on his shoulders. He swept her up from the floor with amazing ease and carried her directly to the bed.

There, he put her down. Her heart was palpitating when he didn't join her.

Standing beside the bed, Eric glanced at the box they'd laughingly tossed on it earlier. When he didn't pick it up, Whitney could only wonder what he was holding out for. She'd offered him her body, extended her heart. All she had left was her soul, the very essence of who and what she was. She'd give him even that if she could, but it was impossible to give Eric what she still struggled to grasp herself.

"'When two hearts aren't in tune…Love and pleasure can't be elicited. But if the man woos the woman and the woman woos the man, their sentiments and minds will merge, and they'll delight each other's hearts.' So said the Arcane Maid to the Golden Emperor in a fable that modern lovers can learn from."

"Was that the lesson?"

He nodded. That's all. A nod and nothing more.

What was going on here? She'd known from the get-go that Eric wasn't an ordinary lover but never had she imagined him to be a bard who got into Chinese torture. That's right, despite all their wooing and shared sentiments and mind merging, he seemed to take his greatest delight in torturing her. Driving her into a frenzy only to pull back, leaving her all hot and bothered on the bed he wasn't joining her on.

Well, Whitney decided, enough was enough. If Eric thought making her wait only made her want him more, he was correct; if he thought she'd wait another minute, wrong.

Too needful to be subtle, Whitney shook out the box. When the foil wouldn't tear between her fingers she ripped it with her teeth, took out the condom and...

Wasn't sure what to do with it next.

She felt silly, dangling a squishy round of flat rubber less than an inch away from where it belonged while Eric made no effort to secure it there. Greatly aroused as he obviously was by her forwardness, he seemed almost equally amused.

"You're smiling," she said accusingly.

"You make me smile." Pushing his hips slightly forward, he lightly teased, "Well, what are you waiting for? Surely not permission after the way you tore into that wrapper."

As Eric watched Whitney's determined efforts to sheath him, his gaze narrowed on what he observed. Her hands were shaking. Her brow was furrowed in fine lines of concentration as she kept her eyes on the task, never once glancing up at him.

Maybe it was just as well since she'd see his dawning awareness of what she apparently didn't want him to be aware of.

"It must be faulty," she declared with a flustered toss of the condom.

Before she could reach for another, Eric swept the packets aside. Her gaze remained on the scattered squares of foil.

"Look at me," he softly commanded.

She shook her head.

"Why not?"

"Because..." Her voice wavered and she shook her head again. "Because you don't think it was faulty, do you?"

"No." He tipped up her chin and in her eyes he saw a painful flush of embarrassment, saw the flush of her cheeks. The last thing he wanted to do was make her feel worse, but dammit, she shouldn't have tried to hide something this important from him.

"You've never put one of these on before, have you?" Another shake of her head. "If you'd told me, I would've shown you how to do it. I thought you trusted me, but the fact you didn't say anything makes me wonder if you really do."

"It's not about trust," she said defensively.

"Everything's about trust. *This* is about trust." He turned, showing her the back that he had exposed to no one but her. Sitting down, he patted the mattress beside him. Whitney scooted over and he pulled her onto his lap. "It's all about trust, Whitney. And if you can't trust me enough to honestly admit what I now know for a truth, then I'm going to be very disappointed in you."

"You're chastizing me."

"Damn straight." He pinched her bottom. More than a tweak, he made her jump. "C'mon. Tell me your little secret. It's safe with me."

"But you already know what it is."

"I don't care." And he didn't. "Like I said, this is about trust and I need some reassurance of yours. From your lips to my ear, I want to hear it."

"Oh, all right. I'm..." She ducked her head and he could

feel her cringe. Suddenly she looked up and with a note of defiance announced, "I'm a virgin. I didn't say anything because I was hoping you wouldn't notice."

"Why? Why wouldn't you want me to know I'm the first?"

"I'm hardly at the age where it's considered normal, that's why. It almost makes me feel like a freak, holding out for..." Her voice trailed off.

"Holding out for what?"

Whitney hesitated, wishing with all her might that she hadn't made mention of what was better left unsaid. They were already more involved than she'd ever intended. Their relationship was progressing at warp speed; she had to get some control of the wheel and stomp on the brakes before they spun out on the rubber they'd yet to burn.

Snuggling deeper into his lap, she cooed, "Well, I suppose I was just waiting for a lover as mysterious and skilled as you, Eric." There. That should get them back on a safer track.

"No, you weren't." He sounded sure of himself. Equally sure was the skill of the fingers he brushed between her thighs, the tongue he adroitly put to use around the ear he whispered in. "You were waiting for the right man. Admit it."

Damn. Did he have to go and say it for her? Didn't Eric realize she was trying to protect them both from a heartbreak just waiting to happen? Of course he didn't. She hadn't told him her biggest secret of all. And before she did that, ruined her chance for an affair of a lifetime with a marvelous man who thought her well and whole, she would admit to what she had no business admitting to.

"Yes, Eric," she whispered, taking a lick at his neck, then nipping at the chin she'd shaved for him in a tub filled with bubbles and champagne shampoo. "I was waiting for the right man. And I can't imagine anyone righter than a man who doesn't consider a twenty-seven-year-old virgin to be a freak of nature or a prude.''

''A prude?'' He laughed heartily and rolled her onto the bed. ''You're no more that than a freak of nature, *yuan-pao*. Just when I think you can't amaze me more than you already have, you do. And for the record, it takes a lot to amaze me.''

She didn't doubt that for a second. Still, she had to ask, just to be sure, ''Then you don't have any reservations about my lack of experience?''

''Are you kidding?'' Rising above her, he gave a small bow. ''I'm honored, Whitney. I've never been anyone's first before. Now out of nowhere, here you suddenly are— the most magnificent, intoxicating woman I've ever met in the world, making a fantasy come true that I gave up on a long time ago.''

Wow. Such heady words of praise, how could she ever forget them? They sang in her ears, demanding celebration.

Scooping up the condoms, Whitney threw them into the air. They rained down upon their heads, as she and Eric laughed.

Until he nudged a wrapper to her lips.

With a deeply sensual half smile that froze her own in place, he told her, ''The way you opened the last one really impressed me. How about putting your teeth to this and impressing me some more?''

Whitney considered the condom she spilled into her hand. She considered the organ it was meant to sheath and decided...

''I'm nervous, Eric,'' she blurted, deciding if it was honesty he wanted from her, then this was as honest as she could get. ''Don't ask me why, but I'm starting to feel a little nervous about this.''

"Hey, I know how you feel. Believe it or not, I was a virgin once myself." He chuckled and relieved her of what trembled between two fingers. With nails. "I'll hang on to that. Won't do us much good if the dam's got a leak, will it?"

"Right," she squeaked.

"Want me to show you how to put it on?"

Yes, she did. And no, she didn't. Once Eric got that thing on, he was bound to be doing all the pouncing and plunging and pumping she'd been salivating at the mouth for when he hadn't been offering any help.

The roof of her mouth felt like cotton. She licked her dry lips. "Sure, Eric. Show away."

For some reason he seemed to find this funny. So funny that he unrolled the condom and puffed in enough air to make a balloon even more intimidating than what was meant to go in it. He gave the balloon a hard punch.

Pop!

Knowing that Eric could have popped more than the balloon by now if that was his intent, Whitney giggled. "Am I that obvious?"

"No more than I was when I was in your shoes." He winked. "Tell you what. Since you're nervous and I'm in no hurry until you are, why don't I let you in on another piece of my past? Adam's been waiting to hear about this for over twenty years and I've yet to let him in on what I'm about to tell you. If you promise not to tell another soul."

"This is between you, me and God. I swear."

"No need for that. I trust you, remember?"

Eric's trust was the last thing she needed reminding of. Preferring not to think about the trust she didn't totally deserve or the guilt his total trust in her elicited, Whitney snuggled against him and urged him on with a kiss. But not a long one; she wanted to hear this bedtime story that was for her ears only.

"Okay," she prompted him. "Once upon a time..."

"Once upon a time," he continued, "There was a curious young lad, fifteen years old and sprouting more pimples than whiskers, who dreamed of becoming a doctor so he could study more than the anatomy of a frog. That boy was me. I'd been saving up my allowance for a year and doing extra chores but still didn't have enough to do the only thing I wanted to do in France. So I borrowed the balance from my brother and instead of going to the cinema on a Saturday evening, I went to visit a Paris brothel...."

CHAPTER FIFTEEN

"HER NAME WAS Danielle. This being France, and the crème de la crème of local brothels, fathers often took their sons to be initiated into a certain rite of passage. I found out that was Danielle's specialty from a friend who couldn't wait to brag about how he'd spent his birthday."

"You mean your father took you to see her?" Realizing her jaw had gone slack, Whitney shut it.

"God, no." Eric grimaced as if the very idea revolted him. "No way, no how. I could've been thirty and my father wouldn't have taken me to a place like that. He and my mother have a good marriage and raised their sons to believe that once married, always married, through thick and thin. I'm sure that had something to do with my sticking around to make Amy miserable for as long as I did. But that's beside the point. The thing is, those fathers were regulars and had a different take on raising their sons than mine did. As an adult, I'm grateful. As a kid who had no business being there, I was wishing my dad was springing for the bill."

"A hefty bill if it took a year's allowance, extra chores and a loan from Adam. So, was it worth it?"

"Let's just say..." Eric smiled at the memory "...Danielle more than earned every franc I paid her."

"Then you kept her longer than expected and turned out to be such a fabulous lover, she didn't charge you for going overtime."

"Hardly." He laughed ruefully. "I was awkward. Worse

than awkward! Fumbling and grabbing and managing all of three frantic pokes before it was over. The sensation was like defying gravity and reaching the moon without a shuttle, but once I came down, I hit ground zero with a crash. We'd been given the room for an hour and there was another forty-five minutes to go. I knew everyone who saw me leave would realize I was no Don Juan, just this horny kid paying for some fine Chardonnay and downing it like Boone's Farm. I didn't want to show my face downstairs but I couldn't stand to face Danielle, either, since she'd see my eyes welling up.''

"How terrible for you."

"Beyond terrible. I'd never been so humiliated and I was desperate to escape with some dignity intact.''

As if she were there, sharing his plight, Whitney felt the angst of a teenage boy who wanted to be a stud, only to end up a failure. Terrible as it must have been, she couldn't help but feel better about her own situation. She didn't have to face anyone downstairs or hide any tears from Eric. And she certainly didn't have to hide her curiosity about how he'd gotten out of the jam he'd found himself in.

"What did you do then? Climb down the fire escape instead of the stairs?''

"There wasn't a fire escape. I checked while I picked up my clothes and started jerking them on without a word, like Danielle was nothing but a two-bit whore I was finished with and never wanted to see again. Fortunately, she was a lot more sensitive to my feelings than I was to hers.''

He opened his palm and Whitney placed her hand in it. Eric's fingers folded over, insistent and sure.

"She took my hand, just like that. And she kissed it, just like this.'' One by one he kissed her fingertips. "And then this wonderful woman led me back to the bed.''

Eric lifted her from his lap and onto the bed. They lay

side by side, face-to-face. He lightly ran a blunt nail down her interior arm and up again, then traced delicate circles around each breast. Whitney had shivers by the time he continued his story.

"'Like this,' Danielle said, and I can still remember her voice, patient and sexy as hell, coaching me, telling me what to do while she ooohed and ahhhed when I did it right and correcting me with another 'Like this' when I got it wrong."

"Ooohhh," Whitney assured him. A roving kiss from her collarbone to her navel then veering to her throat had her further assuring him, "And aaahhh."

"Ah, yes," he mouthed from the neck he nibbled, "by the time I left that room two hours later, I was still no Don Juan but Danielle had me believing I could service the entire female population of Paris and they'd all be clawing each other's eyes out to see who took me home."

Whitney had no doubt those same women would resort to guerilla warfare to take a man like Eric home now and do whatever it took to keep him there.

"So there you have it," he concluded with a lick and a kiss. Leaning on his elbow, Eric looked her up and down as if trying to decide what was his favorite part and where he wanted to venture next.

"Like this," Whitney said, deciding for him with a lift of his hand to an area just above her navel she'd had no idea could be so deliciously responsive to a touch. Eric's touch. It was magic. "She taught you well. No wonder Adam wanted to hear all about it. And you never told him."

"Never," Eric confirmed. "He was willing to forget the debt in exchange for the juicy details but I paid him off— with interest—and to this day I'm glad I bought back my right to silence. There's something so special about that memory and the woman who made it so special, I'd feel like a prostitute myself if I'd coughed up to satisfy the loan. You're the only one who knows, the only one who ever will. Only you, *yuan-pao*. Only you."

Who said the days of chivalry were dead? Whitney wondered. Even as a teenager Eric hadn't been one to kiss and tell. It seemed in keeping with the man he'd grown into. A man of integrity and inner strength. A man who toiled to save the lives of many, then turned around and made her feel as if she were the only one who mattered. This was no ordinary man she lay with. Who knew? Maybe he had a red cape and a blue suit with a big *S* emblazoned across the chest stashed away in a nearby phone booth.

"Can you really leap tall buildings on a single bound?" she quietly mused.

"What?"

Smiling at her own whimsy, Whitney asked, "Did you ever see Danielle again?"

"Once. I passed her on the street. She was holding a little girl's hand. I had my arm around a date whom I would have never asked out if Danielle hadn't given me the confidence to do it. I stopped dead in my tracks, unable to move, not knowing what to say. And just like she did in the brothel, she made everything okay. For me, at least. I'm sure life was anything but fine for her, selling her body to support her child. Anyway, she walked on with that little girl, and as she passed, she turned her head and blew me a kiss. Leaving me to remember and to wonder."

Eric turned somber eyes on her. Something hidden and a little dark simmered beneath their surface. "I remember that when I climbed into bed with Danielle, I wasn't thinking much further than getting to the best part of growing up. I did quite a bit of growing up that day, but it went beyond losing my innocence. When I left, I realized Danielle had given me a sense of self I'd lacked before and it came from this very private thing we'd shared. That's when I started to wonder.''

Eric picked up a foil packet, unwrapped it. "You were trying to put it on inside out before,'' he explained, turning the condom from one side to the other then fitting it on.

"What did you wonder?'' Whitney prompted when he circled thumb and index fingers together and rolled slightly down. Her heart beat faster, then faster still when he placed her hand where his had been.

"I wondered what it must have been like for her—you're doing good, just keep rolling it down—and I wondered if I would ever have the chance to find out. They say most of our fantasies spring from things that we associated with sex in our younger years. There must be some truth to that since I still fantasize about... Perfect. Well done, *yuan-pao.*''

He wrapped his hand around hers as she reached the base of what he'd called a jade stalk during their intimate soak in the tub.

"I'll get even better with practice,'' she said, pleased by his compliment and even more pleased with herself. Whitney Smith had once felt uncomfortable with the forbidden desires she never would have spoken to another. Now here she was, so intrigued by Eric's fantasies that she wanted to come up with some of her own that weren't limited to the confines of her newly liberated libido.

Letting it run a little wild, she boldly asked, "Since you wondered what it was like to be in Danielle's place, does that mean your fantasy is to be a male for sale?'' She hitched a thumb toward her purse. "If that's the case, I'll gladly pay for your services, the way you did hers.''

He cast an I-don't-think-so glance at the purse and Whitney wished she'd kept her thumb to herself, given their earlier argument. But then he eased the tension with a wry concession.

"Actually, it sounds like a role-playing game I could get into and I can't think of a better way for you to spend your money. But that's not my fantasy." Removing her hand from the spear she stroked, Eric laced his fingers with hers and rested their hold over her mound.

"A lot of men fantasize about taking a woman's virginity and claiming a hymen like some trophy they've mounted, minus the wall to tack it on. I don't want to take anything from you, Whitney. I want to give you what Danielle gave me. Wings. Self-discovery. Understanding, accepting, exploring your own sexuality. And I don't want you to feel any more pain than I did while it's happening."

Whitney wasn't sure what surprised her more. That the sexual innocence she'd tried to hide made her quite a prize for all those men who fantasized about it, or that Eric had given so much thought to a fantasy that wasn't self-serving titillation. Not that she didn't find it titillating herself. All this talk about brothels and secret fantasies and deflowerings was very exciting.

"You sure know how to put a girl at ease," she told him. So much for her earlier jitters, now it was she giving assurances to Eric. "Don't worry about hurting me. I know it's bound to be a little painful but—"

"Not necessarily." He raised his grandmother's Tai Chi charm, leaned down, kissed it. Then softly kissed her. "I know a way to make this easy for you. You'd be the one in control, not me. The problem is, I've never tried this before and if I can't pull it off, I could hurt you. And I don't want to do that, *yuan-pao*. I don't want to do that."

Whitney felt her heart expand until she thought it might come undone from his tender mercies. Eric didn't want to be a conquering warrior, spearing into her while she tried not to cry out for a reprieve from the pain of his invasion. And yet he had already invaded her so sweetly and completely that it was a pain in itself not to feel his body joined with hers, consummating the bond they shared.

"I hurt without you, Eric. Show me what to do."

"Like this." He rolled onto his back and lifted her over his hips, bracing her knees on either side so that she hunkered above him but didn't connect with his flesh.

"And like this." He licked one of her fingers then placed it on her clitoris. "This is your dark garden and it's yours to tend. So are your breasts and any other part of your body that responds to your touch. Pretend it's me touching you while I try very hard not to think about what you're doing."

"You mean you can't touch me?"

"No." He shut his eyes. "And I can't look at you. Even your voice could shatter my concentration and if I lose it… I can't think about that either."

"Then what—"

"Shhh. Don't talk. Just listen. Once I'm totally relaxed, very carefully, and quietly, lower yourself onto me and put me in. The more you move, the faster I'll grow, so please, move as little as possible. That way, I'll extend slowly and your body can gradually get accustomed to mine. If there's any discomfort, stop. The more leisurely we take this, the less chance there is of your tearing."

After several deep breaths, he spread his arms out as if in surrender and appeared to go limp all over. Except for his erection, just inches away from the dark garden she explored more freely than she ever had alone. And as she did, Whitney studied this man, who excited her imagination and stimulated her senses as he laid in repose. His lessening arousal only increased her own until she couldn't bear not to touch the pliable flesh he had warned her to maneuver as little as possible.

Whitney soon realized this was easier said than done. Her initial touch caused him to jerk. More deep breaths from him, stifled pants from her. Though he was dry, she was slippery, and without Eric's assistance, she ultimately had no choice but to simply stuff him in, taking care not to dislodge their protection as she did.

She felt his immediate rise but only a small distance. No discomfort where he claimed space, just this terrible ache where he did not. Needing more, she slightly rocked her hips and he responded, giving her all she could take without gasping for breath, and stopping the moment she did. His attunement to her every nuance of movement made her feel as if he truly had become one with her, knowing what she felt, inside her head and under her skin.

Did he feel like a virgin again himself, was that part of his fantasy? She hoped so. He gave her so much now, taking nothing, and it was now that she truly understood the depth of what he'd wanted to give her—an undiscovered part of herself that he could help guide her to, but ultimately it was up to each individual to claim who they were, for until they did, how could another claim them?

Stroking her breasts, exploring the dark garden of her desires, Whitney claimed her own body and in so doing, she felt as if she were taking her own innocence and filling herself up with a wondrous acceptance of what made her a sensual, sexual being, with or without a man. She silently blessed this man she claimed as well, then not so silently as she whispered, "Eric. Open your eyes and see who I am."

As if from far away, Eric heard her summons. He knew if he heeded her call, what Whitney easily accommodated wouldn't be so manageable once he opened his eyes.

"I know who you are. You're my *yuan-pao,* my priceless pearl." Even speaking wasn't wise; the sound of his own voice was disturbing the altered state that was enabling him to safely float between wakefulness and sleep, thus keeping her safe from a total unfurling that could split—

Damn. What was he thinking?

"Oh, yes," she moaned. "Oh, yes, much better. I love the way you feel."

"Stop moving," he begged. "Please stop. Don't say anything else."

"Don't move. Don't talk. Don't touch. I'd rather have the pain than this. It's excruciating. Eric, please. Please look at me and see me as I've never seen myself before."

Were he a saint he might have denied them both that. But he wasn't a saint. Just a man. A very human man who was very much in love with the woman whose gaze met his as she slid her hands over her breasts, down to her belly. She caressed herself there then dipped lower, to the place of their joining.

"God, help me," he groaned. Heaven lended not an ear and neither did Whitney on whose behalf he prayed as he surged upward and out.

He tried to pull back while pushing her up but she bore down, refusing his attempts to save her from what she apparently didn't want to be saved from. Her head swung from side to side. Her hair whipped over the face he did see as never before, leaving him to wonder at this marvelous creature joined with him.

She made love to herself even as she made love to him, showing no mercy whatsoever in taking him as she pleased. Which apparently included a teasing that no feather or scarf or brush could come close to. He let her play, he let her tease, but there came a point when a man couldn't just lie there and do nothing.

He'd reached that point. Eric turned her over and on he went, ready to expand the fantasy that wasn't over yet.

"You took yourself, you took me," he said, his breath hot on her face. "Now we take each other."

There was a rawness in his voice, and in the way he swiped his mouth over hers, that Whitney knew she'd find alarming were she still an innocent. Any naiveté she'd had about her sexual self was gone, leaving her free to fully embrace what she felt, what she wanted, what she might think or say or do.

Indeed, Eric had given her wings. She flew on them, spreading her legs wide to invite him further, hooking them tight around his thighs to insist he come in, all the way in, then opening her mouth to demand, "More. I want more."

He answered her with an endless kiss.

Probe. Push. Swirl. Shallow, too shallow, then a quick, aggressive thrust, leaving her gasping. Pulling away, pulling out, what was too full, now too empty and—

"Eric, please, come back."

And what should he say to her repeated pleas as he parried and jousted between her shaking legs?

"It's the journey, not the destination, remember? Let's savor getting there instead of rushing what we can't repeat. This is a first for me, too, *yuan-pao,* and I'm in no hurry to end what's just gotten started."

On and on he went, taking her at his leisure, until she couldn't stand it a second longer and demanded, "Be there. All the way there. Take me. Take me..."

He pulled out. "Where?"

Desperate to have him back, she searched her heart and emerged with a daunting truth she couldn't withhold.

"To that place where I'm empty and hurting and I need you to feel complete."

Stillness, utter and absolute, above her. Writhing beneath

him, raising up, her hips arched toward the sky, and then, his soft command.

"Hold my hand." Both of his spread over hers and she felt their palms meet, their fingers lock. Tight. "Now look in my eyes and don't look away while we both go there together."

A pause, then *whoosh.* Her breath rushed out on the stunning force of his thrust. It vaulted her over the edge he had repeatedly taken her to, only to raise her fever higher each time he pulled away, leaving her stranded, alone, pleading for his return. And now she was airborne, suspended above that place she was falling into. Falling...falling....

Falling in love and into his hold, being carried to a place she'd never been before.

It was a place too beautiful to belong to this earth, yet grounded in the warmth and nurture of...

Home.

Did he see where she went? Did Eric go there with her?

She searched his eyes and knew they had arrived together. No need to name the destination, they were intimate companions on a path leading to a destiny unknown.

She climaxed again. A climax so intense that she felt in the grips of a seizure that nearly tore her apart before reducing her to tears with the knowledge that the most wondrous experience of her life was over and though they might yet have others, she and Eric couldn't last.

"I made you cry after all." He cupped her face, sipped up her tears. "I'm sorry I hurt you."

"Never that, Eric," she assured him.

"Then why are you crying?"

"Because I want..." She couldn't say it.

"We've shared something beautiful and rare, and what I feel is a closeness I can't even describe. Tell me what you want, what you feel. You know you don't have to hide anything from me.''

How she wished that were true. Then she could tell Eric what she really wanted. Him. All of him, now and forever. But to say such a thing was to mark the beginning of the end, if not the end itself. That left her needing something to explain the leaking tears she dashed away with an impatient swipe at her eyes.

''You made this so wonderful, I wish I could turn back the hands of time and relive it all over again. Only maybe reverse our positions and imagine what it was like being you. I'm sure it wasn't easy.''

''Torture.'' His chuckle mingled with a pained grimace. ''Sheer torture. Some of those bedchamber secrets my ancestors came up with should probably remain secrets and this is one game I can honestly say doesn't bear repeating.''

Given his ancestors' penchant for naming body parts and the recreational uses of them, Whitney was sure this particular exchange had a title to go with it that sounded more romantic than volleyball.

''And just what did they call this game we played?''

''Dead Entry.'' He prodded her hip with the remains of his own game piece, then swirled a finger into her grotto, making it weep for her inevitable, ''Live Exit.''

CHAPTER SIXTEEN

THREE DAYS LATER they'd yet to leave the suite and Eric could only marvel at his reluctance to take the Do Not Disturb sign off the door once he and Whitney got dressed. Granted, indoor surroundings didn't get any posher than this, but rooms had a way of closing in on him and so did the people he shared air space with.

Amazing, he thought, just amazing that he was the one who didn't want to leave so Whitney could explore Saint Croix. And if anyone needed some room to breathe, it was her, too. He kept catching himself crowding her a little, pushing for more than the immediate. Each moment with her was so memorable that he kept wanting more.

More than this afternoon to make good on his offer of a shopping spree that already had him swallowing his pride since Whitney insisted on going dutch. More than tomorrow's plans to go parasailing and dancing someplace more elegant than a club. More than their agreement to head back to Dominica the day after that to visit Boiling Lake, maybe get their things and go wherever the wind took them. Then again, maybe not, since Whitney wouldn't commit further than a "We'll see."

Eric saw just fine. He wanted next week. He wanted next month. He wanted Whitney with him on the lecturing tour in Europe after the ritual New Year's Eve party at Grandmother Ming's.

Simply beholding her sipping a cup of tea on the bed made him think he wanted forever.

"Another cup of tea, darling?" he asked. And how darling she did look with her hair a mess, a rumpled bedsheet tucked around her waist and the shirt she'd pranced around in yesterday, on the floor. His shirt.

"Only if it's *ling-chih*. With a ginseng chaser."

At the rate Whitney was going through the stuff, he'd soon need to wire his grandmother for more. Better yet, take Whitney to meet her before the holidays and do Chinatown, starting with a visit to his favorite apothecary, Uncle Liu.

"After tea, how about something to eat that's not from room service? I did promise you a day on the town."

Whitney pouted prettily. "Rats. I was hoping to try their conch omelette. I'm starved."

"Sorry to disappoint you, but it's closer to lunch than breakfast." Nothing to munch on besides each other, maybe he should order another fruit basket for their suite. Their suite. How he did like the sound of that. Just as he took satisfaction in knowing the smallest habits of his lover. She brushed her teeth first thing in the morning and after meals. Colgate toothpaste was her brand. Baths, not showers. Reading over television, but reruns of Ally McBeal were a close second to The Simpsons when she watched. One thing she didn't watch at all was the clock.

"Who cares what time it is now?" she retorted with the passion of Scarlett shaking her fist at heaven, proclaiming she'd never go hungry again. Which wasn't likely given that Whitney ate whenever and whatever she wanted. He loved the way she dug into her food, relishing each bite as if it might be her last. She valued every second of life in a way few people ever did—which had a lot to do with why they were so perfect for each other. Yet while he'd had an experience to drive such a truth home, he still didn't understand how Whitney had managed such a grasp of it herself.

"Is it because of your mother?" he asked. "Was it her unlived life that makes you so determined to live yours with the kind of abandon that you do?"

Whitney's animated expression immediately disappeared. She suddenly had that look he saw whenever her mother was mentioned—like a schoolgirl caught in the lunchroom with a copy of *Lady Chatterly's Lover* masked between the pages of a grammar book.

"It's not her, is it?" he said, forgetting all thoughts of a cosy lunch for two and any vows he'd made to himself not to push for more than she freely offered. "Then who or what is the reason you quit your job, decided to blow your inheritance, and take up with me instead of investing in bonds and hooking up with some M.D. or accountant who'd make good marriage material?"

"Actually, Eric, I think you make excellent husband material."

"You do?"

He sounded surprised. And hopeful. And glad! Eric wasn't supposed to be glad about what she'd said. And he wasn't supposed to start smiling or looking as if she'd just confirmed what he wanted to believe himself.

All of a sudden his inquisitiveness about her freewheeling existence seemed a much safer subject than discussing his marriageability. That came too close to her dream of a princess bride dress, Eric her dashing groom, walking down the aisle together, a fairy tale come true. Fantasy pure and simple. A fantasy she knew better than to even entertain because to think about it was to desperately want what she couldn't have.

Eric was a dangerous lover. He was doubly dangerous outside a bed. She had to tell him some bit of the truth, even if she did dress it up. A partial truth that would cover the tracks she didn't dare leave behind.

"If I were shopping for a husband, Eric, I just might set my sights on you." His smile broadened and promptly faded with the disclaimer she forced out. "But as I mentioned before, I don't see marriage in my future."

"Why not?"

Softly spoken, but she thought she detected an edge of steel. Surely Eric wasn't imagining more than his grandmother's heirloom around her neck, which she would eventually have to give back. But not yet. Not yet.

"Because like you, I was raised to believe that marriage is meant to be binding, not something a person walks out on like my father did when things get tough. Or boring. While I can't imagine that living with you could ever be boring, that doesn't lessen my aversion to commitments." Taking a deep breath, she plunged. "I wasn't that way a year ago, or even six months ago. But something happened to make me realize I simply didn't want to be tied down. Not to work, not to a relationship, not to anything that imposed expectations or limitations on me or my life."

"Okay," he said slowly, "now we're getting somewhere. What happened to make you decide the very thing that has me wondering what it's going to take to convince you to be my wife?" He nudged up her dropped chin and winked. "Just kidding, kitten. I've got too low a threshold for rejection where you're concerned to send you running with a question like that. Now tell me what happened in your life to make you decide to get one, minus any expectations or limitations beyond your own."

Be still my heart. Despite her inner command, the rat-a-tat-tat against her rib cage rose up and filled her ears, making it hard to continue to make a convincing argument for her new way of living life.

"I had this friend, Eric. A very good friend." Thinking of herself in the past tense helped bring the reality of their relationship...home.

"This friend of mine worked hard, paid her taxes, never even parked illegally. But then she got some bad news. Turned out she didn't have long to live. She told me that her biggest regret was that in all the years she'd existed, she had never really lived. She'd been too chicken to stick her neck out and take chances. Too concerned with other people's opinions about her to say 'screw what anyone else thinks, all that really matters is my opinion of myself.' Too late she realized that herself was all she had—that, and a load of regret for never becoming all that she could have been. When my friend told me this, I swore to her and myself that when my number came up, I wouldn't go with the same regrets she had."

As she'd spoken, Eric's gaze never wavered from hers. It was direct and empathetic; his eyes were filled with an absolute understanding that echoed his unstinting approval of her vow.

"Good for you, Whitney." He put his palms together and quietly applauded, making her long even more for his presence in a life without end. "Good for you. But how sad for your friend. Is she still alive?"

Whitney considered this gorgeous, virile man sprawled over her on a heart-shaped bed. He toyed with a strand of the hair he'd washed in champagne while giving her a lesson in what had become an intimate language, uniquely their own. Was her friend still alive?

"No, Eric," she told him, knowing that the woman she had been was definitely gone, along with all those years she'd wasted. "I think of her often and when I do, I can only imagine her shock at the guilty pleasures I've taken up."

Reaching over to their near-empty fruit basket, he plucked the last grape from a lengthy strand of bare twigs. "There's one left from last night if you'd like to treat me to an appetizer before we head out for lunch."

Whitney leaped from his reach and onto the floor. Her index fingers forming a cross, she laughed out a stern warning.

"Back boy, back. If you want an appetizer put that thing down your throat and don't get another one near me again."

Flipping the purple orb into the air, he caught it in his mouth with the sort of grin that had her eyeing the bathroom door for whatever safety could be had behind it with a quick order for two bolts and a dead-lock.

Despite the lure of safety, Whitney didn't want to leave. Each moment they shared held the promise of another memory and another bedchamber secret to treasure.

CHAPTER SEVENTEEN

"YOU MEAN foot-binding was really an erotic practice?" Massage, now that was erotic. Feeling her arches plied with a firm rub that had her toes curling in and her feminine juices flowing out, yum. But foot-binding? "I don't get it. Why would anyone think it's erotic to suffer for the sake of having three-to-five-inch feet?"

"The same reason European women wore corsets that damaged their hearts and lungs," he retorted. Though Eric wasn't defending either practice, Whitney knew he'd defend his Eastern roots before sympathizing with the Western world that had called his ancestors barbarians.

"Talk about the pot calling the kettle black. What a bunch of hypocrites," he continued, warming to his subject. "China had nothing on those Victorians who got off on whipping and thought their queen was some kind of fashion diva. Ugh. What a dog. But Yao Niang? Man, she must've really been something on those dancing toes to have the king wrapping her feet in ribbons and getting such a fad started."

"Are you telling me that a dancer actually had that kind of impact on an entire culture?"

"Not just any dancer, she was the king's favorite consort and he wanted to make her feet look prettier when she performed. It didn't take long for it to become a social status symbol, and from there it just grew into this total fetish for what they called 'golden lotuses.' Such a fetish that nothing could get a man more excited than fondling a woman's tiny foot—which makes some sense when you consider the binding did more than make them wobble when they walked. It forced certain muscles to work extra hard and the stronger those muscles were, the more prowess a woman had in bed.''

Whitney knew what muscles those were and felt her own tighten and squeeze in reflex to Eric's kneading of her not-so-dainty feet. Eric then began to soothe her with soft caresses, massaging her all over until she was deliciously limp.

Care. That's what Eric was giving her. The deepest of care for her feelings and her body.

"Such a feast you are," he pronounced. "I'd rather live without food for a week than give you up for a day."

"The feeling is mutual," Whitney said blithely, ready to toast the new day with the last sip of Dom Perignon from the bottle they'd ordered to celebrate the night before.

Passing it from her lips to his, they were finished with the champagne long before they were finished with each other.

After going in search of a condom, Eric said between clenched teeth, "Guess what time it is?"

"Time to go shopping for more than a change of clothes, a feather and a brush."

"I'll drink to that—once I get the tea made." Hoisting himself off the bed, he suggested, "Maybe we can pick up a keepsake while we're out and about today. Something to remember our stay in Saint Croix by."

While Eric made the tea, Whitney thought about what she might be able to buy that would keep these unforgettable moments alive. And then, she had it!

Postcards. Maybe even letters on the prettiest stationery she could find. All addressed to Whitney Smith. Or whoever Whitney Smith might be once she returned from her wanderings and all the discoveries she recorded along the way from here to...there.

"How's the tea?" Eric asked.

"Perfect," she pronounced. "And I feel grrr-eat!"

"Tony the Tiger could take lessons from you, kitten."

"And I could take lessons from you," she purred into his ear. "Thanks for the one last night. How'd I do?"

"You earned a bravo. Now what about an encore?"

A tango and a cha-cha later, Whitney whirled on her tiptoes to the bathroom door. There, she curtsied.

"Give me ten minutes alone then I want to watch you do that sexy thing you do every day." Mmm-mmm. Watching Eric shave just drove her wild—especially when he had a towel riding low on his hips. "I'll get the water going so we can take turns scrubbing backs in the tub. Meet you there."

"Yes, ma'am." Eric clicked his heels and gave her a neat salute. "I'll report as ordered, razor in hand."

She no sooner claimed the bathroom than a look in the mirror confirmed the worst: even with her hair sticking out all over and her mascara smudged, she'd never looked better in her life. Her face bore the unmistakable glow of a woman in love. She was radiant, beautiful, energized.

Whitney couldn't figure it out. She should be exhausted. Shouldn't she? Lovemaking took a lot of energy, but it seemed she had energy to spare. Of course when they weren't all over each other, she was either sleeping or eating. Could it be her body was responding to the attention lavished on it? Or were the *ling-chih* and ginseng kicking in, along with the potent healing powers they just might possess?

A third possibility emerged, and not for the first time. It was a thought she kept trying to push away because to even think it was to take hope, and hope was a very dangerous commodity. But just as she'd taken risks she'd never dreamed of taking before, dangerous thoughts and the deeds they spawned had become more tempting than frightening.

If the heart only knew love and fear, then her fear had bowed to the love she bore for Eric, and the love she now bore for herself.

"Whitney Smith," she whispered to her reflection, "You are a good, decent person who's finally found all the joy and laughter and love you deserve. What you do not deserve, is to die. Maybe God finally realized that, too, and decided to cut you a break. Miracles do happen, so why can't one happen to you? Remission. Maybe the monster went to sleep and won't come back for years. Maybe it went away forever."

There. She'd voiced her greatest hope. Was hope really so dangerous? She knew hope didn't automatically make anything so, but it sure did give a person some relief, as if there were a possible alternative to a totally unjust and cruel fate she found so painfully difficult to accept.

A soft knock on the door caused her to jump.

"Yes? Come in," she called, turning her back to the mirror.

"I gave you an extra five minutes—" Eric looked at her with the alertness of a man who missed nothing. A chill went through her. Eric closed the small distance and swept his hands over the gooseflesh prickling her arms.

"Are you okay?"

Was she? On the surface all was well. And inside, where she had dared to hope, things were definitely looking up. Yet, she couldn't hope too much, and her deepest emotions still had to be guarded from Eric. He didn't make it easy.

"I'm fine, Eric."

"No, you're not. What's wrong?"

Silently she damned his ability to pick up her smallest habits, intuit her slightest change of mood. It was starting to drive her a little nuts, this refusal of his to let her hide anything from him while she struggled with her conscience and the constant urge to tell all.

"Nothing's wrong, it's just that I was thinking about some things and I could use a little more time alone to think about them."

He let go of her arms.

"Everyone needs privacy and it's been awhile since you've had some. No need to hole up in here, I'll go for a walk."

As he turned to leave, she suddenly didn't want him to go. "When will you be back?"

"Can you get all your thinking done in an hour? I can take longer if you need me to."

"Half an hour, that's plenty."

"As keen as you are on going halves for everything—" he gave her a sound kiss and a pat on the fanny "—we'll split the difference. Forty-five minutes. See ya, kitten."

As the door shut, Whitney knew he'd done it again— left her wanting more of him, of them together. Every time she tried to get some distance, he lured her closer. Her paltry defenses were no match against the battle she was losing.

Are you okay? No, Whitney decided as she turned once more to the mirror. No, she was not okay. The face she saw was proof positive. She looked vulnerable, wistful, full of hopes and dreams, love and...

Fear. It clouded her eyes and made her vision murky. Though several tears spilled out, she knew tears would solve nothing. Nothing would be solved until she could let go of the secret wedged between them.

Would it ever happen? If she continued to feel better and

had cause to hope more than a little, perhaps she could bare her soul. Only then would she feel truly free to simply be.

Whitney summoned a brave smile and allowed herself to imagine she was reaching out to Eric instead of going for the tissues. Miracles, she told herself, miracles did happen and one might yet come her way. It was just a matter of wait and see...but how long would she have to wait? How many weeks or months would it take before she could let Eric see all that she kept hidden inside?

Hope, it seemed, made it harder to live only for the day.

CHAPTER EIGHTEEN

Dear Whitney,

Just a quick note to catch you up on the latest. As you know, we extended our stay in Saint Croix where I lost my heart—along with my you know what—and we decided to put Dominica on hold while we trotted off to beautiful Bonaire where flamingos outnumber humans. We're still here, but plan to leave tomorrow for Dominica, unless we change our minds again. As Eric says, go, see, do, be. And there's so many places I want to go!

Including San Francisco. Eric wants me to meet his relatives. Never did I believe I'd meet a man and two weeks later he's wanting to take me home to his family. I haven't agreed because I know it's impossible—then again, anything's possible, isn't it?

After all, I did get reeled out from that boat on a harness thingamajig and floated from a parachute a thousand feet in the air. Parasailing, what a trip! It looks scary as hell but I gotta tell you, that's as close to heaven on earth as a person can get. Especially when you're riding double and hoping no one's got a pair of binoculars to see what's making that parachute swing!

By the time we left Saint Croix I was so hooked that Eric convinced me we should make plans for an entire week devoted to my two greatest passions—parasailing and island hopping.

Of course he's my greatest passion of all. He wants to show me the world and I'm so hungry for it, for him, it's just not in me to refuse.

Oh, Whitney, what have I gotten myself into? I'm over my head and getting in deeper by the day. As for the nights—and nooners—they're just too incredible to describe. I can feel myself blushing, too shy to commit such memories to paper. But never fear, I'm sure I'll get over that eventually and have even more to write about than getting tied to a bed with silk scarves and being made love to by a man who sure knows how to use a peacock's plume.

Lord, I'm burning up. And shivering. Sometimes I wonder what's come over me but when I look in the mirror, I like what I see and what I see is me. The me I never was. The me who's becoming more than I'd ever dreamed. As for who "me" is, I'm still finding out and having the time of my life doing it.

Each day's a new discovery, so who knows who I'll be by the time we finally get back to Dominica? And if we don't go there tomorrow, who knows how much money I'll have left once I do? Truth of the matter is, I'm going through the dough so fast I almost wish I hadn't given as much to Mickey as I did before taking off from Montserrat.

Wait, X that out. I wouldn't take anything back from him, not a single penny, but I do have to face facts. After insisting on buying Eric a new wardrobe—gosh that was fun, picking out his outfits and getting him to model them for me—and paying my half of the hotel bill—ouch, ouch, ouch!—I dropped an easy five grand in Saint Croix. I hate thinking this far ahead, really I do, but I could end up staying put in my prepaid bungalow long before I'm ready to.

Unless. I take Eric up on his offer of a job.

He says he needs an assistant. It's an offer no sane woman would refuse but so far I have. Maybe because I'm crazy about him. So crazy in love with—oops, here he comes and I can't let him see this. He gives me an hour alone every day and this one's up.

Later, W.

WHITNEY QUICKLY folded the stationery, added a few pictures of her and Eric on their various adventures, then stuffed the contents into an envelope.

A lick and it was sealed.

She tossed it into her big woven handbag just before he arrived with two tall, icy drinks and a fresh bottle of suntan lotion.

Sitting beside her on the pool lounge, he glided a palmful of oil onto her legs while she sipped.

"You're spoiling me, Eric."

"No, I'm spoiling you rotten. With any luck you'll turn into a brat who deserves a good spanking."

Whitney couldn't see his eyes behind the dark lenses but she was certain she'd glimpse a hint of the satyr if she could. As for herself, she was glad to have on some shades. They concealed her wary glance toward the envelope sticking out of her purse. The Alabama address would provide Eric with information she wasn't ready to give. As for sending mail to herself, how could she possibly explain that?

Discreetly she pushed the envelope to the bottom of her purse. Silly as it might seem, having this mail to greet her when she returned home was very important. These pictures, these words laid down, were tangible proof of how richly she'd led her life—and how dearly she would need those to hang on to as that life drew to an end.

Correction. *If* it drew to an end.

Was she in remission? Had she been miraculously cured? The fatigue was gone. No symptoms had appeared that would point to even a cold. She could be a walking advertisement for the health benefits of surf, sun, sex and piña coladas. Oh, and Chinese panaceas that didn't taste like much, still she was downing them like a chocoholic on a Godiva binge.

Unfortunately, she couldn't know her prognosis without a medical examination. And she wasn't willing to risk the growing hope that her postcards and letters would simply be priceless mementoes to share with Eric once she took him to another residence where another woman had lived without ever really living.

"A call came in while you were sleeping this morning." He shrugged out of his tank top and splashed some oil onto his chest; his back was on the lounge so no one could see. But she knew what was there and how it had gotten that way.

Whitney felt the tendons in her neck tense. She willed them to relax and tried to ask casually, "So, what are we doing out here? Shouldn't we be on our way to Montserrat?"

"Actually it's Japan and I'm just on standby."

"You mean *we're* on standby." Before he could protest, she made sure he wouldn't. "If I'm your assistant that means I have to go along and take notes and help with your research and sleep my way to the top."

Eric pulled at his chin, appearing to reconsider. "Are you sure you want the job? You'd have to be able to take off on a moment's notice and you could get tired of seeing me so much. I might even turn out to be one of those types who want personal services on company time. If you want to change your mind, I'll understand. I can always get another assistant but I've only got one of you, *yuan-pao*. I don't want work to interfere with the good thing we've got."

"It won't," she assured him. A downward trend in her health, however, would put an immediate end to her impromptu new career. She had to keep some means of escape. "Still, it's probably not a bad idea to do this on a trial basis. If for any reason things aren't working out, you get someone else and we'll shake hands, no hard feelings."

"If that's what you want to do, that's what we'll do."

"It is," she asserted before tapping her glass to his.

Eric took a long pull of his drink to mask the twitch of his lips. Though he could get an emergency call at any time, there had been no call. A stretch of the truth, perhaps, but it had enabled him to put Whitney on the payroll before her mad money ran out.

"When do I start?" she asked eagerly.

"How does tomorrow sound? Or day after? Even next week's fine with me. Just whenever you're ready to head back to Dominica. I want to do some updates on Boiling Lake and you could help navigate us there."

"Tomorrow it is and I'd rather drive."

"You want to drive through a rain forest? Those roads get pretty rough, Whitney."

"So? I can give it a try, can't I?"

The determined set of her jaw assured Eric that not only would she try, Whitney would come, she would conquer, and those roads would eat her hell-on-wheels dust.

"Consider the wheel yours."

"Yes!" She raised her glass high.

Eric caught her by the wrist and felt the trip of her pulse. "Either your adrenaline's pumping over a Jeep or your new boss gets you so hot and bothered you can't wait to start climbing up that ladder."

"I always was an overachiever," she whispered.

"Of that, I have no doubt." A light snap of her wrist and the cold drink spilled onto her bare stomach, causing Whitney to gasp. Leaning down, he added, "In fact, I wouldn't be a bit surprised if you're up for a promotion soon."

As he sipped up the pooling beverage, Eric recalled the affectionate title his father had given his mother—the boss's boss.

"HANG ON!" Whitney gleefully yelled as she took a hair-pin curve that nearly landed Eric in her lap.

Gazing at her profile, listening to her lilting laughter, he wondered if she would ever cease to amaze him. Not only had Whitney taken on the road with a vengeance, she'd mastered a stick shift and right-hand drive in next to no time.

Time. Forever wouldn't be long enough to get his fill of her. The more they were together the more living without her seemed unbearable. He'd packed a lot of living into thirty-seven years, but always there had been something missing, something that kept him on the move while he searched for...her. With Whitney he was complete, seam-lessly intertwined with the other half of his Tai Chi whole.

His grandmother's medallion bounced between her breasts as she flew over another rut and hit a bump that sent her several inches in the air.

Glancing over at him, she exclaimed, "I love this!"

"And I love you!"

Their eyes locked and time seemed to move not at all and then, as they nearly careened into a tree, it sped for-ward with the screech of brakes.

Silence. Except for the squawk of a startled parrot, the rustle of wildlife scurrying into the protective cover of rainforest vegetation. And the tick of his heart waiting… waiting…

Waiting for more than the shallow wisp of her breathing and the slight shake of her head, which he countered with a decisive nod.

"I do love you, Whitney. I thought I'd say so in a more intimate setting, when the time seemed right. But it just slipped out. You know what, though? I always thought that's how it should be. I've never felt anything as right as we are together."

"I…" She gripped the steering wheel as if it were a life preserver that would keep her afloat in the midst of an emotional undertow that threatened to suck her in and down. "I don't know what to say, Eric."

"You don't have to say anything. Do I want some assurance your feelings for me are just as deep? Sure I do. But I can wait. Because Whitney, if you say you love me, I want it to be because what you feel is so strong you can't keep it in, not out of some sense of obligation to me. That's not love. It's a mockery of love, and no better than what I had with Amy."

He covered her hand and squeezed. "So, do us both a favor and don't say anything unless you're ready. As for me, I stand by my words but I won't be repeating them until you let me know that's what you want to hear."

Whitney's heart painfully contracted. It hurt to keep in what begged to be let out—love. Unbridled, unleashed, untamed. Her love for Eric was a wild thing that had grown rampant, like this rain forest surrounding them, like the hope she clung to, despite the diagnosis of leukemia. Now she faced a turn in the road once more, and only she could decide which way to go. Since that day in Dr. Clark's office, she'd thrown caution to the wind, knowing she had nothing to lose, and no one to worry about but herself.

With Eric's words still singing in her ears, she chose the most loving and difficult course—prudence. It might not last long, but in this moment she found the strength to keep her silence—while confirming more than she should in a reckless kiss.

"If actions speak louder than words," he said raggedly, "then I've got all the assurance any man could possibly need."

CHAPTER NINETEEN

My dear friend,

He loves me! I knew he did, he shows it in so many ways, but to hear Eric say those three magic words was like being spiked with a nirvana high. I'm addicted. Addicted to him, his touch, his love. It's only been three days since he shouted ''I LOVE YOU!'' to the world—okay, the jungle—but I'm going through withdrawal already, waiting on pins and needles to hear him say it again.

He won't, though. Not until I vouch the same. He doesn't want to pressure me, but I know that's only part of it. Eric is a proud man and until he gets the word from me, he's not about to wax poetic or get down on a bended knee.

I saw a ring, a breathlessly gorgeous pearl ring with two gold hands clasping it like a globe between them, in a jewelry store window yesterday. Eric suggested I try it on and I forced myself to decline. It's the first time I've seen him sulk. I wish, I wish, I wish, I didn't have to fight this constant battle of saying no, when my heart is saying yes.

Not only to rings, but to the love that consumes me. The words keep trying to burst out, and they will unless I leave. Yet it would be easier to swallow poison than to tear myself away from Eric. He is everything to me. My joy. My life.

He's been gone awhile this morning, said he had

some errands to run. I miss him, but it's probably good to have a little distance. I can't think beyond wanting him when he's near and I need to think clearly.

I'm trying hard to live just for the moment, but the moment's not enough anymore. I want a future with Eric. I try to tell myself otherwise, that the perfection of today can't stop the could be's of an eventual desertion. Still, my love is growing stronger every second, beating down my fears and resistance.

Enough of that. While Eric's still gone, I should pay a visit to the doctor and see about getting some birth control pills. Extra insurance against an accident that I simply can't risk.

Will get pictures developed while I'm out. Enjoy!

Love, Whitney

P.S. We just finished updating Eric's research on Dominica and, barring a call to action, we're taking off tomorrow for Jamaica. From there, who knows? Who cares? As long as I'm with Eric, I'm home. And as for working together, so far it's a gas!

AFTER READING Whitney's letter, Eric began to tap it against his lips as he considered what he had just learned. His curiosity about the letters and postcards Whitney kept stashed away in a tote bag had finally gotten the better of him, and he'd stolen one from her bag when temptation had won out over...trust.

Yes, he trusted Whitney, implicitly. It was her secrecy he didn't trust. He had told himself that Whitney's correspondence was her business and if she wanted him to know who she was writing to, she'd tell him. But she hadn't. And much as he hated to admit it, he'd been insecure enough to imagine she might be staying in touch with an old flame.

Until Whitney, he'd never been jealous in his life. Now here he was putting the evidence of how misplaced his jealousy had been back into the unmarked envelope. No clues there as to whom she was spilling her guts to and the greeting didn't even offer a name. Didn't matter. He had violated Whitney's privacy, thus breaching the trust between them. He wouldn't stoop so low again.

Still, he felt fantastic! *I'm addicted to him…the love that consumes me…he's everything to me…I want a future with Eric.…*

All the words he'd ached to hear had been spilled onto a page that assured him the ring in his pocket wouldn't be refused when he proposed. Hell, he might even wax so poetic Robert Browning would want to puke.

As for birth control pills, that was an issue that could wait. He, however, couldn't wait to chuck the condoms. It wasn't a bad idea for Whitney to take extra precautions. It was too soon to risk a pregnancy, but that hadn't kept him from imagining Whitney's belly protruding, their love filling her womb. His ancestors had regarded a woman's baby palace as sacred. He bowed to their wisdom. Babies were miracles, and no man had any business sowing his seed where they grew if he didn't cherish the mother and adore the child.

With Amy, he didn't have the love to give. With Whitney, he had plenty to spare. When the time was right for them both, he'd be ready to seriously discuss making babies. The life-style they now enjoyed would need some altering but by then…

"Eric? Eric, are you here?"

Eric quickly shoved the letter back into Whitney's tote, and strode to the doorway separating bedroom from parlor.

Elbow to frame, he struck a cocky pose, past ready to bull-
doze his way over any resistance that remained.

"Not only am I here, I'm waiting."

"Waiting?" Whitney eyed him uncertainly, not knowing
what to make of his mood. "Waiting for what?"

"You." He crooked his finger. "Come here."

"And since when do I come with a crook of your finger?"

"Since early this morning if memory serves."

His wicked half smile left her blushing. He was referring
to her G-spot, of course, which he preferred to call her
Sacred Spot; call it whatever he wanted, it was a hot spot
that sent her into an orgasmic frenzy whenever he touched
it. "You're impossible," she charged.

"And you're impossibly delicious. Now get your sweet
little butt over here and don't make me come after you."

Eric seemed to think he was calling the shots today and,
though she shouldn't, she rather liked it. After her unsettling visit to the clinic, it was a comfort to come home to
a man who thought her butt was little and would no doubt
move it for her if she didn't hustle it his way.

"Well, here I am," she said, having obeyed. "Now
what?"

"Now this." His mouth fell upon her neck and feasted,
eating her up with nibbling bites and melting kisses. "And
this," he murmured, sliding his hands through her hair,
then wrapping the length of it around his wrist. Pulling her
head back with a firm tug, his lips curved into a sexy, sly
smile.

"And this." He placed a small, red velvet box shaped
like a heart in front of her eyes.

Her throat constricted. Eric had bought the ring. She had
wanted it, desperately, but to accept such a gift was to
signal her readiness for a deeper commitment. How she

wanted to give him that; how she wanted it for herself. So much it was pure torture to stand here, gazing at the unopened box, shaped like the heart that she could feel twisting in her chest.

The urge was strong to seize the ring and all that it signified. Even stronger was the memory of the crowded clinic, the smell of antiseptic and illness that had made her skin crawl so bad that she had run out of there. She wouldn't be going back to that place or anywhere else for the birth control Eric would have to continue to be responsible for. Nothing could be more morally wrong than to conceive. Unless she got a clean bill of health, she couldn't have a baby.

Neither could she have the ring that she was bracing herself to decline. Eric's gaze, filled with devotion, made her want to weep. And his slow lift of the lid, it made her feel like a starving soul taken to a banquet she was forced to watch and forbidden to eat.

"A love gift." He exposed the contents. "For you, *yuan-pao*."

Earrings. Why did she feel so disappointed? She should be breathing a huge sigh of relief.

"Oh, Eric. They're beautiful."

"They're yours. Try them on for me?"

"I'd rather you do the honors."

"My pleasure."

His hands, large and adroit and sure, went from one ear to the next, freeing the gold studs she wore. His slight tug on her earlobes as he replaced them with a pair of pearls was subtly arousing and overwhelmingly intimate. So was the way he framed her face, tilted her head from side to side.

"Perfect," he pronounced. "Let's see what you think."

At the vanity mirror, Whitney divided her attention between the most elegant earrings she'd ever worn and Eric's image behind her.

"Yes, perfect."

"As perfect as we are together," he said, echoing her thoughts.

And then the one thought that refused to be contained a moment longer escaped the last fragments of her resistance.

"I love you, Eric. More than I've ever loved anyone or anything in my life, more than I could ever say in words, I love you."

"One word would say it all. Three simple letters. You know what I want to hear, don't you?"

"Yes."

"That's the word." His face moved closer until she felt his cheek brush hers, felt his chest against her back, his groin pressing into that triangle known as the *Ming-Men,* the lifegate. "Will that be your answer if I ask you to—"

"Eric, please, don't ask me that." Unable to bear her own look of distress, she turned from the mirror and put a silencing fingertip to his lips. She couldn't say yes. She couldn't force herself to say no. Her body trembled and so did the hope on which she'd hung her most beloved dream. A dream that refused to die despite knowing she very well might.

Shunning that knowledge and the hurt she could see in his face, she tried to kiss him, make everything go away that was between them. He pulled back.

"No," he said firmly. "It's not that easy anymore, Whitney."

Whitney. He didn't call her that very often. Kitten, that's what he called her when he felt affectionate or was kidding around. *Yuan-pao* she heard the most since it was his greatest endearment, used in moments of torrid sex, sweet romance or deep emotion. Her given name had somehow become relegated to discussions of splitting the bills and other disagreements, exchanges, and any matters that pertained to business.

He meant business now. The way he extricated himself, flung the emptied jewelry box onto the bed, then crossed his arms, left no doubt about it.

"I can understand your reluctance to make a commitment because of your sorry father. I can understand how your friend's death affected your own life. But eventually you have to get past all that, Whitney. Time goes on. People have to make choices about how they're going to spend that time. I've made mine and I chose you. You, on the other hand, say you love me in a way you've never loved before—then turn around and back off instead of backing up what I want to believe is the truth. Why?"

He was demanding an answer she couldn't give him. Whitney rubbed her arms against the chill that had settled in; she tried to clear her throat, but it was clogged with tears she dared not shed. To cry was to feel his arms come around her, to hear an apology for the outburst he was fully entitled to.

Then again, maybe that's not how he would react. Eric had begun to pace. He appeared too agitated to be contrite anytime soon, which gave her no recourse but to swallow hard and try to act tough. But tough was next to impossible, so maybe her best approach was—

Logic. Logic would speak to him.

"Eric, let's be reasonable about this—"

"I don't want to be reasonable. What I want is an answer. Why are you so afraid of a permanent commitment if you love me as much as you say?"

"I'm not afraid." That wasn't true. Eric was a little scary when he got mad. Love was even scarier. It was consuming and making her wish he'd haul her over his shoulder and down the nearest aisle before she could convince him to wait. Which was exactly what she had to do if she really did love him. "You want too much, too soon, Eric."

He stopped in mid pace and turned.

"Do I?" A single, dark brow lifted. "And this from the woman who told me she wanted it all and she wanted it now the first night I carried her to this very room."

"That's still true," she hastened to assure him. "But I also said that now is all we have, all that any of us really have. And you agreed, said I was a woman after your own heart."

"You've got my heart, Whitney. Lock, stock and barrel, you've got it. I love you. Fiercely and completely, I love you. You know how to live for the moment and I can't deny that's one of the things that made me fall in love with you to begin with. But a lot has happened, a lot's changed since that night and I can't pretend that the moment's enough because tomorrow might never come." He held out his hand. "Tomorrow does come, *yuan-pao.* I believe in tomorrow. I believe in us. Can't you believe in us, too?"

He'd called her *yuan-pao.* That's all she needed to hear to meet him halfway. She took his hand.

"Of course I believe in us, Eric. And I do want every tomorrow we have to be together. But..." She ducked her head, fearful he might see the lie in her eyes. "But what's the hurry if we're destined to have forever? We've only known each other a few weeks—the best weeks of my life—and that's only a drop in the bucket of time I'd love nothing better than to share. We need more time, Eric, before making a hasty decision that might seem right at the moment, but we could both end up regretting later."

"Like I did with Amy, right?" He tipped up her chin and shook his head. "I made a bad call when I was too young to be making the most important decision anyone can ever make. I learned from that mistake and have no intentions of repeating it again. As for my intentions where you're concerned, they're as honorable as any man's can get."

"I know." She sought his lips and then the buttons of his shirt. Casting it aside, she went for his zipper.

Eric caught her hand. His eyes held her still as the heartbeat on hold in her chest.

"You *will* think about it?"

She didn't want to think. She didn't want to argue. All she wanted to do was forget everything and make love like there was no tomorrow. But as Eric had said, tomorrow would come and good as her health seemed to be, they might have many, many more tomorrows ahead.

"I will," she promised.

"That's an answer I can accept. For now."

Clinging to her hope and coveting the ring he hadn't purchased after all, Whitney prayed she wasn't setting them both up for a terrible, fatal fall as she whispered back, "I've got a lot to sleep on but eventually we all have to wake up. The sleep's still in my eyes but that doesn't mean I can't smell the morning coffee. And Eric, there's not another soul on this earth who can make a better cup of java than you."

CHAPTER TWENTY

Dear Me,

Oh, dear me. What am I going to do? It's been two weeks since our argument in Dominica, and we haven't had a cross word since—which is part of the problem I'm struggling with today in Barbados. I continue to feel physically strong—went hang gliding this morning, move over parasailing—but emotionally I'm not doing so good.

I mean, here I am surrounded by absolute beauty and tranquility, but inside me it's mayhem. I find myself wishing that Eric and I could have a really nasty fight that would let me get some of this bottled-up anxiety out, and maybe even convince me it's time to pack my bags and go. Not back to Mobile, I can't bear to even think of returning there. But somewhere that I feel safe from my feelings and the man who touches them more deeply by the day.

Oh God, I'm so confused. I confuse myself. Eric confuses me. He's yet to mention marriage again, seems to have forgotten he ever mentioned it at all. I think he's trying to give me space but all that space is making me realize I don't want it.

The man drives me crazy. I drive myself crazy. I can't think about this anymore or I'll go stark raving mad and propose to him myself, which would be the craziest thing I could possibly do.

Okay, I've got it together now, I'm in control.

"READY TO GO?"

Startled by Eric's voice, Whitney slapped a hand over the page she'd been writing on, and sat up straight on the lounge.

"You snuck up on me."

"I did not sneak," he informed her. "I called out to you, and gave you plenty of time to put away whatever it is you were so engrossed in that you didn't hear me." He leaned down and tugged at the edge of a page. "So, what have we here?"

"I'm sure you wouldn't be interested."

"I'm sure that I would be." He grinned. "You wouldn't be writing to yourself, so it must be to a friend. Man or woman?"

"Woman."

"Is she cute?"

"You betcha." Behind her shades, Whitney rolled her eyes. "Almost as cute as me."

"Yeah, you're cute." He forgot the letter and stroked her cheek. "Cute as a kitten. Especially when you're spitting and hissing."

"I don't spit and hiss all that much."

"I know." He kissed her soundly and she wrapped her arms around his neck. Once she did, he drew away. "Now that I think about it, you're not really all that cute. Beautiful, yes. Gorgeous, yes. And so intriguing that you keep me guessing about what tomorrow might bring."

Okay, here it was. Eric wanted to talk about their future tomorrows. Though she knew full well she shouldn't be leaving the subject open, she replied, "Your guess is as good as mine."

He glanced down at the page no longer covered by her hands, still looped around his neck.

Apparently the letter wasn't totally forgotten.

"A wild guess—you're sending that letter by courier to invite your friend to join us and sending along a ticket so she can meet me day after tomorrow."

"No!"

"What, you don't want her to meet me? You don't think she'd like me?"

"She'd adore you."

"Sorry, I'm already taken. But I do have a brother who's available and they just might hit it off."

"Stop it!" Whitney giggled. Then giggled even harder when Eric goosed her ribs. The pages she'd written fluttered onto the sand. Before she could pick them up, he did.

He stacked the pages. Folded them in half. Print on the inside, blank on the out.

"I believe this is yours."

She hesitated to take what Eric was returning. Her earlier urgency to conceal was suddenly a wild impulse to reveal. "Don't you want to read it?"

"Only if you want me to."

She wanted to end the charade she was trapped in. A trap of her own making; only she could undo it.

"Eric, I..."

"Yes?" He started to unfold the pages.

She snatched them away fast.

"I prefer that you not read this." Rifling through her beach tote, she pulled out an envelope, slipped in the letter intending to pick up where she'd left off later.

"I have no problem with that," he said. "Just as long as you're not taking someone else into your confidence because you don't feel you can do the same with me. That, I would have a problem with."

Since she was sharing her most private thoughts with no one but herself, Whitney felt perfectly justified to tilt down her shades, look him straight in the eyes and say, "Then we don't have a problem."

Eric chuckled, and paying no heed to the beach joggers passing by, he wedged a hand between her locked thighs. His eyelids drooped seductively. Bedroom eyes. She knew where they'd be going from here and it wouldn't be to dinner.

Feeling over warm already from the heat he generated with the stroke of his fingertips between thighs that refused to stay locked on a public beach, she suggested, "Let's get out of here so we can compromise our morals some more."

"Excellent idea." He pulled her up and into his arms. Dipping to her ear, he whispered, "And it just so happens that I received an overnighted package that had more than tea and herbs in it. Uncle Liu made a special trip to a bookstore so I could try my hand at calligraphy. Bless his heart, he even sent some ink along. Maybe I'll use it to write him a thank you note since I found some other paints to put to the canvas I can't wait to get my hands on. Should be sinfully exciting once I do."

"He sent you the brush!" It wasn't just an ordinary brush they'd been searching for—and without success since Chinese brush-pens weren't exactly a staple of art shops in the Caribbean. "Can I see it?"

"As soon as we get back to our room. Or should I say...our private studio?" He scooped up her beach tote, adding, "If my model's ready, I'm feeling inspired."

Half an hour later, Eric surveyed the room he'd done his best to transform into an artist's loft and decided it looked...not bad.

Though it was late afternoon and the sun had yet to meet the ocean, he'd drawn the venetian blinds to create the illusion of dusk. A dozen candles burned around the bed he'd stripped down to a fitted white sheet. In the middle lay the object of his affections and deepest desires, ready to be transformed into an object d'art, crafted by the skill of his hands.

He held a Chinese brush-pen, with a soft, pointed end, set in a thin, bamboo tube. Beside the pen was a pallet dotted with shades of red, cobalt-blue, yellow and white. Edible body paints, they could be washed off with a swipe of his tongue. Not so the permanent black ink that filled a small, glass well. This he would use to mark her as indelibly his—after he cleared a shadowed area with the other items he'd placed beside the bed: a basin of water, a towel, French milled soap, tiny scissors in the shape of a stork whose beak clipped open and shut, commanded by the snip of a thumb and finger, his razor.

"Now where should I start?" he quietly mused.

"At the beginning?" Whitney coyly suggested.

Watching her lips move, Eric felt the stirrings of creative genius at work. They guided him to the small pool of red and the dip of fine sable hair into the paint.

"In the beginning, there was a man who began his day in his usual way, thinking no further than getting up alone, skipping breakfast because he was tired of eating alone, and despite leaving in plenty of time, racing to catch a plane since his cab got stuck in traffic. Little did he realize that a fateful meeting was about to change his life. He sat beside a woman who pretended not to notice him while he pretended not to notice her. Then suddenly, she said something that took his eyes off the book he wasn't really reading and brought his attention to her mouth."

Tipping the brush into the cupid's groove of her upper lip, he arced up then down. Repeated the motion on the other side. Then outlined the bottom swell he was already hard-pressed not to lick clean of the paint he applied.

As he filled in the lines, Eric continued, "She had the most kissable lips he'd ever seen, but it's what came out of them then that turned his world upside down. Less than an hour later, he was a goner."

"Gone your way while I went mine," Whitney reminded him, smiling.

"Not for long since a day without you seemed like eternity and the ones ever since go much too fast." He swished the brush in the basin of water, then the color yellow beckoned. Transferring it from the pallet to the circumference of an areola, he plied the brush from the outside in until he put the finishing touches on a golden peak. But something was missing. Ah, yes. Rays.

Darting the sable tip up and down, he drew the sunshine of his life that she was. Scorching him with heat; warming him with the intensity of emotion he felt between them—

Except for those moments when she drew away. When she did, his internal urgings insisted that he seek and find; then coax, cajole, or bully her out of hiding if those ploys didn't work. He still fought those urges, but somewhere along the line he'd learned to bite the bullet and wait her out. His patience was always rewarded, but in the meantime he had to weather an unpleasant affliction.

A virus called the blues.

Over her heart he drew two butterfly wings. They signified her reluctance to be tied down and for that, only cobalt would do. A beautiful color, but as his gaze settled on the taut, creamy abdominal flesh guarding her baby palace, he rid the brush of any traces of blue.

"The days continue to pass, *yuan-pao*. They go so quickly that I could swear we just met yesterday. And yet, the life I had before I met you seems more and more unreal to me. Like a distant piece of the past that must count for something but doesn't seem all that important to remember. Have you ever felt that way?"

"Only always," she whispered.

"Always," he repeated, drawing the shape of a cradle where he imagined the full expression of their love residing. He painted it white. White was pure. Their love was pure. So too, any children which came of it.

"Mmm, that felt good. What did you draw?"

"The future. As I see it."

As Whitney raised up to look, he leaned over and erased the cradle with his tongue. The last bit of evidence licked away, Eric decided he was done with his transient painting; what he wanted was permanent and better suited to indigo ink.

"And how do you see the future, Eric?"

"I see the future as...a collection of memories we've yet to make." Dipping an end of the towel into the wash bowl, he stroked the cloth over the V-shaped shadow between her thighs. Rubbing the soap between his palms, he spent several minutes fluffing her pubic hair and filling it with miniscule bubbles. Yes, tomorrow would come and when it did, Whitney would have a reminder of the claim he made on her today. It would be there for her to see, as evident as his shearing of short, curly locks that fell away with the delicate snip of scissors.

"I'll always remember this moment," he said solemnly, placing his newest keepsake inside the pouch where another memory resided. With the greatest of care, he lightly scraped over the shy mound that could no longer hide behind nature's dressing. "Forever and always, I'll remember you laying here, making this unforgettable memory with me. And you, *yuan-pao,* will you remember it, too?''

''Always,'' she said with a catch in her throat. ''Even death couldn't rob me of all that you make me feel.''

A chill went through him at the thought of ever living without her. Death was a Grim Reaper that took loved ones away and left the living wishing they were dead themselves. That's how he'd felt when he'd lost his friends. But life had gone on and so had he. Whitney had made him realize how lucky he was to still be alive. She was his grand passion; the love of his life; his bright, shining star. She made him feel so complete that he could no longer dismiss poets as stargazers who needed to get their heads out of the clouds and their feet on the ground.

He was a scientist, not a poet. But that didn't stop him from dipping the sable brush into a well of black ink and etching his sentiments in Chinese characters on the woman who inspired the verse he penned over her mound:

seasons of my life
they are nothing without you
will you be my wife?

''Oh, that's pretty!'' Whitney exclaimed. ''What did you write?''

''A haiku.'' Sort of. Haikus weren't supposed to rhyme but he had made the obligatory mention of the seasons and kept it down to three lines. Five syllables in the first and last, seven in the middle.

''Read it to me?''

Should he? No, Eric decided; one rejection of marriage was enough. He wouldn't ask again until he was certain she would agree. And so, he put ink and pen to her bared lips, translating the symbols as he went:

"wild orchid are you
who opens my heart and eyes
as I watch you bloom"

Though pleased with his improvisation, he added, "To be exact, a wild orchid in spring."

"But Eric," she murmured, "it's the middle of October and November's just around the corner."

Ah, the sweetest words he'd heard all week. Make that the last month and counting. Whitney was thinking ahead. And if she could do it, so could he.

"Won't be long before Thanksgiving. Grandmother Ming makes some mean dim sum hors d'oeuvres before serving up the best turkey you ever ate. I'm sure she'd like you to join us—just as I'm sure that I won't care to be there for the first time in years if you're not with me."

Whitney got that look again. The one that reminded him of a hungry animal eyeing a baited trap, and pausing to decide if it could grab dinner before the cage snapped shut and turned it into the dinner served.

"We'll see," she finally replied.

We'll see. How many times had she said that? Too many. He was tired of hearing it. Damn tired. So damn tired, in fact, that he was inspired to flip her over and express his feelings on the spine she wouldn't be washing until he let her out of bed. That could be awhile. A very long while.

wait, she says to me
I say how long will that be?
her silence thwarts me

Another rhyme and it was far from being a haiku since seasons hadn't been mentioned on the skin he blew dry with an exasperated puff of air from his lips.

Whitney's puckered invitingly. "The way you dashed that off, I get the feeling you're in a hurry to wind this artist session up so we can try Mystic Master technique number forty-two. With three hundred and ninety variations of intercourse, love play not included, that leaves us with three hundred and forty-eight to go. If we get really ambitious, we could be down to three hundred by the time Thanksgiving rolls around."

Oh, Whitney, he thought, you've missed the point altogether.

Seeking to drive it home, Eric made love to her. Forget every position but the most basic, he made love in the missionary position. He made her come that way. Again and again. And each time she orgasmed, he denied himself the same release, wanting assurance that it didn't matter to her what position they were in and no matter the day or month or year, she would always need him.

Then he couldn't hold back his own need. His body responded to three simple words. They left her mouth, and filled his waiting ears. "Never leave me."

CHAPTER TWENTY-ONE

"YOU'RE SURE about this?"

"Positive, Adam," Eric confirmed. "I've never been more sure about anything in my life."

Watching Whitney frolic in the surf with a child she'd befriended, Adam could understand his brother's decision. What didn't make sense was the rush he seemed to be in. Unlike himself, Eric had never been obsessive over anything but his work.

"So you really do plan to pop the question."

"I do. And I won't take no for an answer."

"And you intend to tie the knot today, right?"

"That's why we're in Antigua. Same day nuptials. Which, by the way, I really appreciate your scooting over here to be my best man."

"Hey, I wouldn't miss this for the world." London to Antigua wasn't exactly scooting, but what was an eight-hour flight to witness something as incredible as this? Eric in a white-hot heat to get married. Incredible? Unbelievable.

Adam looked from Whitney to Eric. His eyes were positively glued on her. It reminded him of their brief get-together six weeks ago, when Eric had stared out at the sea, transfixed by the memory of a goddess who'd worked some kind of mojo on him. That old black magic had cast one helluva spell, all right, and since most of Eric's left brain seemed to have been affected, Adam gave it a tweak.

"The folks and Grandmother Ming aren't going to be happy they weren't invited."

"They'll get over it. Once they meet Whitney they'll understand why I couldn't wait."

"But what about her family? Won't they be upset when they find out she got married before they even met you?"

"Whitney has no family."

Eric glanced at Adam and in that glance Adam saw flint. Shit. Eric would kill for this woman.

"Her dad was a real piece of work who ran out on Whitney and her mother. Her mom? She's dead. I'm not so sure we would've gotten along."

"Why not?"

"Because she had a lot of influence over her daughter and while a lot of that influence was good, she placed too much emphasis on self-reliance and playing it safe. Whitney was devoted to her, and I think that glorious, free spirit playing in the water suppressed a lot of that spirit to please her only parent. But just look at her there—" He blew a kiss and she pretended to catch it on the cheek so hard it knocked her back into a wave.

Chuckling, Eric confessed what he could hardly believe himself. "When I see her like that, so full of life and with her great love for adventure...well, it's a long stretch of the imagination but there could have been a time in her past when she might have reminded me of Amy. Tied to home, afraid to dream or make her own rules."

"There's a divorce waiting to happen."

"Yup. But it won't happen to us." Eric patted the ring in his pant's pocket, confident that the vows they exchanged would never waver.

As ERIC and Whitney walked hand in hand through the streets of Saint John, Antigua's capital, Eric navigated their seemingly aimless stroll in the direction of the Ministry of Legal Affairs. A civil ceremony was only a signature and a license fee away. Simple as that.

Getting Whitney to agree wouldn't be such a piece of cake. He'd ordered one anyway—along with a chapel and all the other trimmings Adam was seeing to while he went about the business of convincing Whitney to be a willing bride.

"So tell me, what do you think of Adam?"

"He's a doll. I wish he would've joined us for lunch."

"Late lunch, long flight. He'll join us later." As their destination came into sight, Eric slowed his pace. "He's a handsome devil, isn't he?"

"Very handsome." Peering up at him, Whitney grinned. "But not half as yummy as you."

"All I can say to that is, either love really is blind or you need your eyes checked."

"Oh, I'm definitely in love but there's nothing blind about it. And as for my eyes..." She laid them on him, taking him in from head to toe with blatant appreciation. "I've got twenty-twenty vision and what I see is a work of art."

"A virile work of art."

"Absolutely virile," she assured him. "And exotic. I know Adam has classic good looks, but that hint of the Orient gives you a lot more mystique. I'd take you over Adam or any other man alive any day of the week."

"Or any week of the month?"

"Yes!" She giggled, apparently thinking this conversation to be heading nowhere but to the stroking of his ego.

"What about extending that to any month of the year?"

Her laughter stilled, and she looked away from his probing gaze. "Why do I get the feeling this is going somewhere that has nothing to do with Adam or my opinion of your looks?''

"Because it's going somewhere that has nothing to do with any of that and everything to do with us.'' They had reached the ministry building. Eric sat on the bottom step leading to the offices and their future. He patted the space beside him. "Sit with me?''

Whitney sat, but didn't take his hand. She clasped hers together with a movement that suggested a subtle wringing.

"What if I modified any month of the year to just three months? Three months you'd vow to take me above any other man.'' He claimed her left hand, brought it to his mouth, and kissed the finger where his ring belonged. "Marry me? Three months, that's all I'm asking for.''

"Marry you?'' she whispered faintly. "For three months? Eric, I...I don't understand. Why?''

"Because I'm crazy in love with you. Because I love you and more than anything I want you to be my wife.''

Be my wife. The words ricocheted through Whitney's brain, echoing through that chamber where emotion ruled and reason struggled to be heard. But she had to listen, listen very closely. Not only to what little reason she had but to what Eric had to say.

"As for the three months,'' he continued, "I believe the odds are a lot better of getting you to agree if you feel you have a way out and don't run the risk of falling into a bad situation like your mother. Do I want a lifetime commitment from you? Of course I do. But I've come to terms with the fact that I might never get it. I'd rather take my three months and my chances over holding out for a lifetime that could end up being an indefinite string of maybes.''

His reasoning held up. There was no trap here that Whitney could perceive. All she saw was a miracle, an answer to her prayers. She could have her dream, marriage to the only man she'd ever loved or wanted. And all he wanted was three months. She could safely accept that, couldn't she? If she got sick, she could cite irreconcilable differences or something and bail out, Eric none the wiser. Unless…what? What, she had to think, had to make sure there wasn't a hitch she was missing in her eagerness to throw her arms around his neck and shout yes.

Trying hard to remain calm, Whitney gripped his hand and demanded, "What if it doesn't work out? Will you let me go without a fight? Legally or otherwise?"

Eric looked deep into her eyes and in the directness of his gaze she saw he spoke truth. "I can't hold you if you don't want to be there. For three months I'll claim the right to be your husband—along with any fights we might have along the way. But I won't fight you if you don't want me in the end. Legally or otherwise. Any other questions?"

Questions, questions, surely she should have some, after all this was a really big step. Yet as she nearly knocked him down on the one where they sat with a lurch into his arms, all she had was an answer.

"I'll marry you." Kisses, kisses, showered on his face, the hands which cupped hers. "When, Eric? When?"

"Now."

"Now?"

At his firm nod, a question belatedly emerged that could throw their grand, wonderful plans into a tailspin.

Whitney licked her suddenly dry lips. Her voice was barely a croak. "But what about…" Deep breath. "Blood work? Don't we have to do that and whatever else people have to do before they can get married?"

"Not here." Pulling her up with him, his broad smile banished the last traces of fear that when something seemed too good to be true, it was. "And here we are." With a sweep of his arm toward the building, he ushered her in and before she knew it, they were back out.

"That's it?" she asked, horribly disappointed that her cherished dream of a wedding had consisted of nothing more than appearing before some official called a Marriage Coordinator, their signatures on a declaration paper, and a license fee paid.

"If that was it, I'd still be kissing my bride." He gave her a peck. "I'll save the real one for the ceremony."

"You mean there's more?" Please, let there be more.

Eric shook his head at her. "Ah, *yuan-pao,* you know me better than anyone but apparently there's still more for you to learn. I'd rather be thrown to the lions, kitten, than give you such a paltry excuse for a wedding."

He checked his watch, looked up then down the street, grumbled something about Adam being late, then suddenly covered her eyes.

"No peeking till I say so."

"What is it?" she asked excitedly as the sound of *clip-clop-clip-clop-rattle-rattle-rattle* drew nearer, nearer...

Then stopped.

Eric removed his hands and she blinked. And blinked again, unable to believe what had appeared before her eyes:

A white horse with gold plumage sprouting from its crown like a unicorn followed by a glossy white carriage that would put Cinderella's coach to shame. It had cans trailing from behind and ribbons and streamers and a pouf of white netting affixed to its door. And there was Adam, transformed into a liveryman, extending a huge bouquet of tiger lilies and white orchids.

"M'lady." Eric bowed. "Your chariot awaits."

CHAPTER TWENTY-TWO

"HOW DID YOU DO THIS?" Whitney asked as she waved back to the pedestrian well-wishers they passed along the way.

"How?" Eric snapped his fingers. "Magic."

Magic, Adam thought with a roll of his eyes in the front seat. More like Eric enlisting the hotel's concierge for the matrimonial best of everything Antigua had to offer, and a jet-lagged brother running around like a chicken with its head cut off for the past few hours to ensure all was ready and set for the bride's arrival.

Giving Eric a thumbs-up to assure him it was a go, Adam couldn't help but envy their happiness. Whitney was beaming; Eric, oblivious to everything but her. Just to look at them was to want some of what they had. Life in the fast lane had gotten old. He wasn't getting any younger, either. His glory days of *GQ* photo spreads were trickling to an end, and what would he have then? What did he have now?

Anyone from the outside looking in would probably think he had more than his slice of the pie. Sexy cars. Sexy women. Sexy moves and clothes with an Adonis face and build that made those sexy women think of sex. Fantasy, pure fantasy. In reality, cars could be crashed, he could lose his perfect body and face in the second it would take to have a wreck, and those sexy women would evaporate the moment he needed them for the kind of loyalty, love and support that Jolene didn't have the capacity to give.

Amazing how the sex could be so good and the relationship so rotten.

"Adam," Whitney called to him. "Love the outfit. Where did you get it?"

"This old thing?" he scoffed with a flash of his trademark smile and a dismissive wave at the Armani gold brocade vest. "It's from last year's collection. Not the sort of accessory anyone would want to sport on a daily basis but nice to have around when the need arises. Sort of like Jolene."

"Eric mentioned her. She's your girlfriend, isn't she?"

"Was," he corrected. "And if I have any sense, I'll keep it that way. We're..." How to say this? "We're great in the sack together but lousy once we crawl out of it. We just don't have the stuff it takes to build a real future." He winked. "Unlike you and Eric."

Was it a trick of lighting or did Whitney's brilliant glow suddenly dim? Adam glanced at the sky. Some clouds were rolling in. When he looked back she averted her gaze and buried her face in the crook of Eric's neck. But not before he glimpsed something troubled and evasive in her eyes and in her smile.

She had secrets.

Whatever she was hiding, Adam could only hope the soon-to-be Mrs. Townsend wasn't carrying some deadly ammunition that could blow a hole into the happily-ever-after his brother was counting on.

As the storybook-picture wedding chapel came into sight, heralded by the pealing of bells from its small tower, Whitney burrowed deeper beneath the protection of Eric's arm.

The stuff it takes to build a real future...like you and Eric. Adam's words had spread through her brain like a malignancy since he'd uttered them. She couldn't help but resent the innocent remark that threatened to spoil her reign as queen for a day.

And what of tomorrow? The day after that? Would she be dogged by thoughts of a future she was about to pledge, knowing full well a desperate deception fueled her vows to have and to hold in sickness and in health from this day forward?

Eric could hold her in health, whether it be for three months or thirty years. But she would not bind him to her sick bed if the tides of fate turned that way. And who knew better than she how quickly those tides could turn.

The horse stopped, and the driver tipped his hat to an elegant, dark-skinned woman dressed in a chic royal blue sarong with a matching turban.

Whitney couldn't help but notice the bride was underdressed for the occasion in comparison.

Neither could she help noticing Adam's scrutiny as he played liveryman once more and assisted her out of the carriage.

"Eric's got a big heart," he whispered into her ear. "Don't break it, okay?"

Direct hit. She hadn't seen it coming. Whitney summoned a stiff nod and an equally stiff smile. In the short time it took for Eric to hop out with the buoyancy of a pogo stick from the carriage, memories of Marcia in Montserrat rolled in. Along with it came a wave of guilt, tainting her dream come true with a swift, hard kick from her conscience.

Eric offered his arm. "Shall we? The Marriage Officer's due to be here soon and that doesn't give you much time to change into the new dress that's waiting."

Eric had bought her a dress. One that would surely be as special as him and the wedding of her dreams. Only in her dreams she wasn't shaking her head and stalling outside the chapel doors. They swished behind Adam and the woman who tactfully joined him after it became apparent the bride wasn't going in and the groom was concerned.

"What's wrong?"

"Eric, I...I don't know if we should do this."

"Why not? Did I say something, do something to give you second thoughts?"

"No," she assured him, clasping his hand and wanting to bawl her head off. Or scream her frustration and outrage at the top of her lungs. But more than anything, she wanted to tell him the truth. "The Truth isn't all that's unknowable," she heard herself say. Then earnestly, "Eric, the future holds no guarantees."

"I'm not asking for guarantees. I'm asking you to be my wife. For three months, no more, no less. From there it's up to you as to which path we'll be charting."

"But it's not up to me!" Stay calm, she ordered herself. Say what you have to say even if it means giving up the most important moment of your life. Eric deserves this much from you. "My—my friend, the one I told you about, well, when she found out she was going to die it seemed to her like a blessing that she wouldn't be leaving behind a grieving husband. And—and I can understand how she'd feel that way. Life is so fragile, you know. It makes me afraid, Eric. I'm afraid of my own mortality."

"Aren't we all," Eric said quietly. Much as he empathized with such a statement, how odd that their impending marriage was eliciting it. Still, his primary concern right now was getting a jittery bride into her wedding dress and down the aisle so he could wed her, then properly bed her. Which meant he needed to make the right noises to put her at ease.

"Look, sweetheart, if it makes you feel better we can have the 'Till death do we part' part deleted."

"We can?"

"Sure we can."

"I'd like that," she said, sounding relieved.

"Now that we've got that settled, let's go in."

As they neared the small changing room where the dressmaker who'd be doubling as a witness waited, Eric imparted a final reassurance.

"Remember this and never forget it. If I had to choose between having one day, and one day only, with the woman who completes me or a lifetime with someone else, I wouldn't have to think twice about choosing you."

SHE FELT AS IF she were in a dream. A lucid dream in which a fairy godmother named Celeste fussed with her hair, touched up her makeup, and voilà, there was *The Dress.* A flowing white gown made of soft silk and running streams of seed pearls. An empire waist and sheer bell sleeves lent a touch of Renaissance romance. The veil, attached to a garland of white roses and baby's breath, crowned her head as if she were a princess bride in King Arthur's court.

Strains of *Ode to Joy* filtered in from the chapel proper. Celeste kissed her cheek. She said, "This man, he loves you very much," and then she was walking from the room and toward the aisle. Alone, Whitney cradled the bouquet in her arm and sent a prayer to heaven that God would be merciful, that one day she might sing a lullaby as she held a babe just so.

Quickly, she sent the plea up and let it go. Feeling as if she had angel's wings upon her feet, she floated toward the music, down the aisle and past ten marching pews, all the while gazing with adoration at the man who met her halfway, tucked her hand in the crook of his arm and murmured, "You are a vision."

"And you are a prince amongst men." Beholding him, she was in awe that fate had brought such a man into her life. With his almond eyes doing a slow burn, his sleek black hair raked severely back from his dark, chiseled face, and his tailored black tuxedo cloaking his magnificent frame, he could have been a raven who had assumed human form.

Indeed, he was the raven and she was the dove, feeling both consumed and protected as he took her to be his lawfully wedded wife with a voice that rang clear and strong.

"I do."

Adam produced the ring. His eyes never leaving hers, Eric slid onto her finger two golden hands holding a pearl like the balance of life, the earth suspended by the joined forces of woman and man.

"And do you, Whitney Smith, take this man to be your husband?"

"I do," she vowed and wished dearly for a ring to give him.

"By the power vested in me, I now pronounce you husband and wife. You may kiss the bride."

Eric lifted the veil. And as he did, she saw his eyes glitter with a foxlike intelligence. The brilliance of his mind was familiar; the slyness of its workings, not. His lips were inclined to smile often, and while she'd seen many variations on the initial three, this was a smile that had yet to emerge. Self-satisfied; minus the tenderness, it would have been smug.

And his kiss, it was different too. So soft she could scarce bear the gentleness pouring from his mouth and into hers, then, his lips slanted and he pressed hard, imprinting on her mouth and her psyche that she was his. Never had he kissed her with such possession, such passion, that she felt hurled into the eye of a tornado that had sucked her into its orbit and wasn't about to spit her out.

With her head reeling, Eric swept her off her feet and into his arms. They were halfway out of the chapel when she realized music accompanied their departure.

"Heart and Soul."

Flower petals rained on them as they exited. It was a beautiful touch. She asked Adam and Celeste to please join them for a celebration.

Adam had to fly to New York. Celeste had to close shop.

She threw the bouquet. Adam caught it. A brotherly hug and a wave later, she was back in the carriage with a ring on her finger and a husband who'd made her wish fiercely for some company on their wedding night.

Eric had her heart. But with a look, a kiss, he'd made it clear he wouldn't settle for less than her soul.

CHAPTER TWENTY-THREE

"MORE CHAMPAGNE for my bride?"

"Yes, please."

There was an emphasis on the please that gave Eric to think Whitney was actually nervous on their wedding night, and perhaps she had cause to be. Whitney would always be her own person, but that person was now his wife and that's how he meant her to stay. Legal vows couldn't hold her; a husband who claimed her heart, body and soul, could.

And that he would—once he got rid of the obstacles in the way. He had three months to win her absolute trust and obliterate any ideas she might have about leaving once his time was up.

Wasting none, Eric took off his watch. He tossed it beside the wedding cake Whitney had barely touched—unlike the champagne.

His watch hit the villa's glass dining table with a clatter. She gave a startled jump.

"Guess what time it is, Mrs. Townsend."

Whitney felt a shiver trip down the notches of her spine as Eric rose from his chair with sudden purpose.

"What time is it?" she asked while his casual tug of a loosened bow tie from around his neck seemed more ominous than a ticking bomb.

"Time to slip you out of that dress and into nothing."

"You mean you didn't get a negligee to go along with the dress?" She laughed as if making a joke but the sound

was as uncertain as she felt about getting naked with Eric.
His shirt was nearly unbuttoned. Down to the tuck of his
pants.

He stopped at the waistband his fingers were poised to
unfasten. "I find it odd that you never had any qualms
about going to bed nude with your lover, but now that your
lover is also your husband, you want to cover yourself up.
Why?"

No use in pretending otherwise, he'd call her bluff. "I'm
nervous, that's why," she blurted. "Ever since the wedding
you seem different, almost like a stranger."

"And is this stranger...scary?"

"No, not scary exactly, just a little dark and unnerving."

"A dark stranger. Hmmm." He tapped his lips and as
her eyes followed the movement, his tongue sneaked out,
snakelike and subtle as a subliminal message. "I understand being taken by a dark stranger is a common fantasy
for women. Is it one of yours?"

What kind of question was that for Eric to be asking on
their wedding night? He'd never asked such a thing when
they were only lovers and yet, here was the spouse she had
wed, asking if she'd ever had a fantasy about being taken
by a dark stranger. He looked like one, the sort of night
rider who emerged from the shadows to ravish his unsuspecting prey, then disappeared before daylight....

Leaving her satiated yet wondering if the phantom lover
had been no more than a lusty figment of her depraved
imagination.

"Well?" Eric prompted. "Have you imagined it or
not?"

"Maybe."

He fixed her with an enigmatic stare. "There's a stranger
in all of us, *yuan-pao*. We like to hide that stranger, not
only from others, but from ourselves. I'm no exception but

if it's the dark stranger in me you want for your wedding night, that's what you'll get. All I ask in return is that you give me what I need.''

He rounded the table and stood behind her chair, so close she could feel his body heat, then his hands lightly plucking the pins out of her hair.

''And what do you need?'' she asked breathlessly, struck by the sexual energy coursing from him and mightily stirring hers.

''I need to be your every fantasy, the only man you could ever want in your life or in your most shameless dreams.'' His hands splayed through her hair and he buried his face in it. His voice sifted through the strands and seduced her ears. ''I learned a lot from my first marriage and one of the most important things I learned is that marriage should never be constrictive or limiting. It's a place where people should be safe to express themselves because there's a trust that's unbreakable that allows them to grow together, not stagnate and drift apart.''

He kissed her neck and chills mingled with heat. ''Now why don't you relax with another glass,'' he suggested with a smoothness befitting James Bond.

Then like that master of intrigue, Eric moved from her reach and toward the light in the adjacent bedroom. He was at the open door when she found her voice.

''Where are you going?''

The bedroom light flicked off. And with no more answer than that, Eric disappeared into the dark.

Her throat was dry and her palms moist. His suggestion that she relax with another glass suddenly seemed like a very good idea.

There's a stranger in all of us. Sip. *We like to hide that stranger, not only from others but ourselves.* Sip, sip. *If it's the dark stranger in me you want, that's what you'll get.*

And just what would she be getting? Would her tender lover turn into some kind of beast she'd yet to meet?

Gulp.

The champagne tasted sharp, as if she'd swallowed down a healthy dose of fear with the bubbles. Yet it wasn't some potentially deep, dark side of Eric that slowed her steps toward the door. It was knowing that some stranger in herself might emerge should he lure her into a place where they forged a dark secret. Secrets, the kind you'd never dare share with anyone else, bound the souls of those who kept them with a pact of silence.

It was only a feeling, but the premonition was too strong to ignore as she paused at the doorway. Some mystery was about to unfold and that mystery resided in herself.

One step divided her from the light and the dark unknown. She took the step. Only to discover the bedroom was empty. The French doors leading outside to the veranda were open. A breeze fluttered the flowing white curtains. They had a spectral appearance, like ghosts chasing their own shadows.

One of the shadows moved. Deciding it must be Eric playing cat-and-mouse, she quietly approached the open doors and stepped onto the veranda.

Deserted. No sign of Eric on the tiled portico that fronted a sparkling swimming pool. Perhaps he was hiding in the water, waiting for her to investigate so he could grab an ankle and pull her in. While he might not think twice about getting her wedding dress soaking wet, she wasn't about to risk ruining her princess bride dress.

Whitney slipped it off, leaving it resting on a chair on the veranda. Then she took off her hosiery and shoes, unconcerned that anyone but Eric could have seen her undress. The villa he'd rented for a week was private, a tucked-away piece of paradise that had a rather pagan appeal about it. The swimming pool had been designed in a soft, diamond shape. From its middle sprouted a large sculpture of Aphrodite, spewing water from her nipples and mouth.

Yes, a perfect place for Eric to lie in wait.

Clad only in a thin, full-length slip, she tiptoed to the water's edge, fully expecting Eric to assume the guise of a sea monster springing from its depths to drag her in.

What she hadn't been prepared for was to find the pool empty. Whitney chafed her arms. Goose bumps prickled her skin. Eerie.

A rustling sound from the courtyard gardens intensified the feeling.

"Eric?" she called, moving cautiously toward the sound.

Another rustle. The dart of a shadow. Her pulse picked up speed. So did her feet.

"Eric," she said, louder this time when the courtyard turned out to be as empty as the pool. "Eric, where are you?"

Her demand was met with the low rumble of a growl that a predator might make. It came from the edge of the terrain the villa backed onto. Palm trees guarded the tropical interior.

The fine hair on her nape rose with each step she took.

"Eric, this isn't funny," she informed him, certain he was the predator the trees were camouflaging from sight. Five steps into the untamed surroundings, she stopped.

The absolute stillness surrounding her gave her the creeps and made up her mind.

"That's it, I'm going back inside and if you—"

A hand clamped over her mouth, muffling her scream.

"Silencio," commanded the roughened voice from be-hind her. *"No digas nada."*

The language was Spanish and though she didn't know what the words meant, the tone carried an unmistakable warning. Unable to see his face and assure herself it was Eric dragging her deeper into the forest, Whitney knew she should be frightened. And she was. Only what frightened her was the forbidden thrill she felt upon being manhandled by stern, greedy hands that were devoid of the finesse and delicacy Eric always displayed.

These hands didn't feel like his. They were demanding. Savage. As uncivilized as the woman who struggled against him and bit at his silencing hand. And as she did, Whitney had to wonder just who this woman was. She wasn't in-censed or terrified by an assailant far stronger than she. No, this woman enjoyed the struggle, the adrenaline rushing through pumping veins and thrashing limbs. She was ex-cited by the feel of dank air and hard muscle, the sound of harsh breathing on her neck, the deft, determined hands gripping hers and binding them with a silken material be-hind the smooth trunk of a tree.

Who was this woman? The one who should be demand-ing her freedom instead of spurring her captor on.

"I'm not afraid of you, but you must be afraid of me. Otherwise you wouldn't be hiding behind that tree. Either let me go or let me see if you're to my liking."

A pleased smile touched the dark stranger's lips. *No di-gas nada.* He'd told her not to say a word but now that he had her where he wanted her—defenseless, unable to es-cape the barbarian he was discovering he could be—he very much wanted to hear a reaction to the form he had assumed.

"Sss," he hissed as he slinked around and faced her.

Her mouth opened. A startled gasp emerged.

"Rindete. Rindete a mi, solamente a mi." Surrender. Surrender to me, only to me. His command carried a note of coercion he was sure she understood. Just as she must realize the short nails raking down her throat and lightly pawing at her breasts belonged to a stranger who could better reveal his hidden nature if he were masked.

The carnival mask he'd bought on a whim from the dressmaker's costumery fit over his forehead and down to the bridge of his nose. Gold spikes extended like sunrays and he could see Whitney's gaze trip from their tips, over the smooth bronze surface covering his face, then peering into the two holes edged with sequins. He could see out, but he doubted she could see in. Perhaps that's why her gaze lowered to his lips, seeking some familiar part of him.

It was a futile search. He didn't feel familiar with himself. It was strange, not knowing exactly what he meant to do or how this stranger might react. Strange and liberating.

Deciding he couldn't wait to liberate her from the slip, he pulled out his knife and flicked it to one strap, then the other, delighting in the defiant tilt of her chin. Even more delightful was the sound of her astonishment when he slit the silk from bodice to hem.

The slip slithered to the grass and he clamped a hand over her mound with a blunt possession he'd never allowed himself to exhibit before.

"Tu eres mia." You are mine, he told her, leaving no doubt this part of her was his and only his to palm, to touch, to take with a sliding finger insistently pushing up. Her walls squeezed around him and he felt her watering.

Despite the slight shake of her head, her body responded to his unrefined courting of it. Her nipples peaked and he teethed them until she moaned and her thighs parted, giving more than his hand access to what lay between them.

A gutteral sound of victory rumbled in his chest and

stranger greeted stranger as she joined him with a distinctly primal noise. Savage yet feminine, like a cat in heat. He licked her up. She tasted like wild nectar, intoxicating and addictive; no wonder she had him on his knees.

"Get up," she demanded. "Get off the ground and give it to me. Hard and fast."

It excited him to hear her speak with such carnal frankness. This was what he wanted. The two of them stripped down to their marrow, revealing who and what they really were beneath the layers of their civilized masks.

She was the one bound to the tree and yet he couldn't deny her command. His captive had turned captor. Indeed she held claim to every emotion he possessed, every desire she stirred.

"Yo soy tuyo." Yes, he was hers. All of him, even this stranger who gave thanks for the dark and her incomprehension of anything but the urgency of his hoist, her legs wrapped around him and riding his hips, then the plow of those hips as he put his body inside hers. Hard. And fast.

Skin to skin. Nothing between them. Unsheathed as the polished veneer they had discarded, the raw power of soul emerging with all those trappings gone. And she was with him, with him all the way, taking him and him taking her, both of them frantic, no restraint.

"Nos pertenecemos el uno al otro," he rasped, willing her to know that they belonged to each other. And surely she knew it, too.

"Yes, yes..." she whimpered as she writhed against the tree and he pumped into her without any thought to depth, timing or technique. There was only them, her inner walls clamping tight, the pressure in his testicles surging, about to explode.

"Tomame como yo a ti," he cried. And she did take him as he took her. All of him, even this ungodly stranger rag-

gedly tearing between her thighs like a mad dog rutting, panting, compelled by the instinct to plant himself up and up and up to her womb. He could feel her clenching, quivering, convulsing around him then letting go with a keening wail.

Her rapacious climax triggered his own. It ripped through him so fiercely that had he been wearing a condom it surely would have burst.

His knees gave out and he slumped against her for support, whispering, *"Te a-mo...te a-mo..."*

"I love you, too," she softly sobbed against his shoulder. "I love you, too. Untie me so I can hold you."

He obeyed. They fell to the ground and he pulled out before he withered. She reached down to touch him and he caught her hand, kissed it, pressed it over his heart.

"Who do you love?" he asked, toying with her hair. "The stranger who took you?" He touched the mask. "Or that other man you call husband, lover and friend?"

"That's an easy one." Whitney slipped off the mask and framed his face with still-trembling hands. "Both. Because both of them are you. I have to admit, though, I had no idea you could be such an animal."

"Makes two of us."

"And I liked whatever it was you said." She peered up at him, curious. "By the way, just what did you say?"

He told her and she enjoyed his recounting almost as much as the finger he swirled around their mingled juices. Ah, it had been heaven. And after this, putting on a condom would be hell. He could only hope that he could ditch the damn things for good.

As of now, there was no wet spot on the sheet to give his knowledge of her little secret away. And as of tomorrow, it was back to the raincoats until she trusted him enough to admit she feared even his desertion and didn't want to risk him getting her with child. It was something they had to talk about. One day. The operative words. That day would come a lot sooner if she could learn to trust him completely and tell him anything. Tonight was meant to lead that way.

"Any last words?" she asked, burrowing down.

"How about...*Es bueno que estes tomando la pildora. Sino adentro se estaria cociendo algo.*"

"What's that mean?"

It's a good thing you're on the pill or we could have one in the oven.

"It means there's a certain safety in anonymity, don't you think?"

She smiled the sort of smile that said this was their line and nobody else could have it. "What I think is, that's an astute observation and I like the way you think."

Whitney looped the mask over her face and seemed to consider what it felt like on the other side.

"Maybe next time you'd like to wear the mask and find out what kind of dark stranger's in you."

"I found her already, Eric. And I have you to thank for that. Just like the night when you helped me discover myself with a game your ancestors played." Removing the mask, she tilted her head. "Does this one have a name, too?"

Laying his head over her heart, he cherished its beat.

"Not that I know of but we could give it one of our own."

"How about...Dark Stranger, Shared Secret?"

"Perfect," he decreed, knowing The Art, as well as the game they'd played, wasn't nearly so much about a libidinous thrill as an intimate bonding. And what was true intimacy but a baring, a sharing, of souls.

CHAPTER TWENTY-FOUR

Dear Whitney,

I have big news! I'm married to Eric. I agreed to a three-month trial run and after a week I'm so deliriously happy it scares me. No one can stay this way forever. Reality is bound to intrude. What happens after our time is up? It's too distressing to even contemplate.

Eric insists that I meet his family over Thanksgiving, which is only a few weeks away. I spoke with his parents and Grandmother Ming on the phone. I was really nervous at first but they were all just wonderful and made me feel genuinely welcome and accepted, even sight unseen. I worry that once we make that face-to-face connection the ability to leave Eric, should the worst happen, will become even more impossible. I was so alone before we met and now my life is so full. He's given me everything I've ever wanted. He's made me a part of his family and no one, not even Eric, could possibly know how much that means to me.

I've gained so much; I have so much more to lose.

Reading this over, I realize I sound like a real worrywart, more like the old me. Stop that, Whitney, and think only of the moment. And the moment, dear friend, is very very good.

We decided to extend our stay at our honeymoon villa and I'm wondering if we'll ever go back to

work—not that doing a little research between all sorts
of fun stuff ever seemed like work. All we want to do
is love and play—which reminds me, we're going to
a play tonight—my treat!—and I need to get ready.

Hopefully Eric won't want to dance the night away
after it's over. I'm a wee bit tired today. Nothing I'm
concerned about since even Wonder Woman would
be pooped after a week of Eric "claiming his husbandly rights." Love it when he says that, it makes
me feel so…wifely. You should see me smile!

Guess that about wraps it up. Oh, and did I mention
that I'm happy? So happy I have tears in my eyes.

Love, W.

SHE SENT THE LETTER. A few days later, she followed it
with another, detailing her joy and only that since she had
to believe everything was all right, that she was well. But
after three brief postcards, Whitney could no longer ignore
the fact that all wasn't right because well she was not.

Eric wanted to go ahead with their plans to spend an
entire week parasailing from one island to another. How
could she tell him that she wanted to, desperately, but she
just didn't have the energy to swim to a boat and step into
the apparatus that would allow her to be heaven-bound?

Heaven, that's where she feared she might be bound for
and soon—unless their secret sin and other carnal indul-
gences sent her elsewhere. Of course lying was a sin, too,
and if lying to oneself didn't count, then lying to others
surely did. She had lied to Eric about her true state of
affairs; a lie of omission but a lie nonetheless. And she had
lied to him even more blatantly to cover up the unspoken
first.

She'd told him that she was tired—all too true—of traveling so much, which wasn't true at all. She'd also said

that parasailing had lost its appeal since she'd read about someone whose parachute had collapsed and they'd fallen to their death in shark-infested waters.

She hadn't read any such article, but death was very much on Whitney's mind as she lifted a pen. It shook. Her hands were unsteady and her stomach gave another lurch while she tried to summon the strength to write what she feared would be her last missive.

MY DEAR FRIEND and confidant,

I'm trying very hard not to cry. Not long ago I wrote at some length about my dream come true but in a frighteningly short time, I've become alarmed. Something is wrong, terribly wrong.

Remember my mention that a week of honeymooning had left me a little tired? I no longer believe that's the cause.

Eric's been pampering me for the past few days, ever since he decided I must be coming down with a bug of some sort that's to blame for sapping me of my usual high energy. I'm going along with his reasoning and taking it easy but no matter how much *ling-chih* or ginseng I consume, no matter how much sleep I get, the fatigue won't go away. It's a struggle to wake up and once I'm awake, all I want to do is sleep.

I'm trying so hard not to freak but the questions keep coming and won't go away. How could this happen to me? How could fate be so cruel as to let me have everything I could ever want and then threaten to take it away overnight? Was three months so much to hope for? Dammit, we deserve those three months and more. So much more.

Like going to San Francisco and then leaving for

Europe together. Eric's lecture tour starts in about six weeks, just after the first of the year. Imagine, me, hopping from country to country with a big shot in the science community who's also my devoted hunk of a husband. Amazing, isn't it? Almost too amazing to believe. And now my faith wavers and I begin to fear what I do believe.

That belief is too heinous to put on paper. I don't dare even whisper it to myself. But it's there, like a guillotine over my head, ready to fall at any time. And all the while I paste on this happy face to keep Eric in the dark. Only he's no stranger and it won't be long before he knows something's not quite right in paradise.

What will I do? What will I say? I can't bear the thought of telling him the truth, of subjecting him to the agony I went through, watching Mama endure all that pain, watching her die. No, no I can't do that to him. All I can do is pray for a miracle. And if it doesn't come to pass? Then I must do what is right. Leave. Leave him with all our beautiful memories before they're tarnished by a future I shudder to envision.

Must go. So tired. Need a nap while Eric's off shopping. Hope he doesn't cook another big dinner. Food doesn't taste too good. Even my sexual appetite's down. Eric blames himself for wearing me out and contents himself with lots of hugs. I can't get enough of them.

If only it were possible to save them up and take one out whenever I might be in need of such comfort. But I won't think about that now. Instead I'll hope that come tomorrow I feel more like Scarlett and less like the horse that dropped dead in the road. Ha, ha. Bad joke. But sometimes ya just gotta laugh to keep from crying.

Love always,
Me.

P.S. If you don't get another note soon, might I suggest investing what little you have left in Kimberly-Clark stock? It's sure to go up after all the cases of tissues I'll be needing for a homecoming to a place that's no longer my home.

CHAPTER TWENTY-FIVE

"WHITNEY? Whitney where are you?" Eric called with increasing urgency as he searched the villa he'd reluctantly left, minus Whitney, a few days before.

He'd been needed immediately in South America. Whitney wasn't feeling well, so tired and sleepy, no appetite, he'd gone from mildly concerned to truly worried and why on earth had she been so dead set against seeing a doctor? If for nothing else to put his own mind at ease.

Easy it was not. He'd see to it that she'd keep her promise to see a doctor if she wasn't feeling substantially better.

Yesterday he'd called repeatedly to check on her, tell her he loved her and would be back asap.

For the first time in his career he'd left in the middle of a crisis situation to tend to personal business—a wife who wasn't answering the phone and had him no longer just worried, but worried sick.

Where was *she?* Eric stared dumbly at the open closet. Empty. Except for her wedding dress.

"What's going on?" he whispered. Then, as the reality of her disappearance clicked, "What the *hell* is going on?"

His voice, a jagged roar, splintered the silence before fading into the nothingness of dead air. There was no lilting laughter to be heard, no words of comfort, just this awful churn of his breathing, the hard thumping of his heartbeat echoing between his ears, and the pounding of his feet racing from room to room, seeking some clue.

Then his breath was sucked right out of him; even his

heart seemed to cease beating. No, it couldn't be. There had to be something wrong with his eyes, making him see things as if he were trapped in a Salvadore Dalí canvas, life twisted into melting images and skewed perception.

On the gilded entry table he'd rushed past in his hurry to make sure Whitney didn't lay unconscious on the bed, or worse, he saw the medallion.

The feeling left his fingertips. They were amazingly steady as he lifted the medallion made of onyx and alabaster with two small rubies, dangling on a chain that was no longer around her neck. He laid it down with the care reserved for a delicate figurine easily shattered. Then picked up the symbol of his eternal fidelity to a woman who had discarded it.

His hands felt as still and lifeless as two golden ones holding a pearl between them. Eric stared sightlessly at the pearl, shaped like the world that had suddenly tilted on its axis. He laid the ring down before he dropped it.

As it was, he could hardly lift the envelope with his name on it, his hands were suddenly shaking that bad.

If the heart knew only two emotions, Eric wasn't sure which was the greater. His love for Whitney or his fear of what resided in the envelope, which would possibly shed some light on why her own love wasn't great enough to battle whatever fear had driven her away.

Ripping open the seal, he read the contents. Or at least he tried to read the swirling words, filling his vision like so much spilled black ink.

My dearest Eric,

It grieves me to write this letter, yet I owe you this much. And more, much more than words can ever say. You have given me so much. Love. Laughter. Friendship beyond measure. And what have I given you in return?

Lies. Conscience dictates I belatedly confess the truth.

When we met I wasn't free to make a commitment beyond the day and what pleasures that day might bring. My life was, and is, far more complicated than I led you to believe. Those complexities don't bear mention. All you need know is that I married you under false pretenses and no marriage built on hidden agendas can last.

You are a good man, Eric Townsend. You deserve a happy, wonderful life and someone who can share it fully. I cannot. For this reason I urge you to have the marriage annulled on grounds of desertion.

I won't be back, Eric. And please, please don't waste your time trying to find me. The airline has assured me that my destination is privileged information they won't give out, and given that I'll soon be going only God knows where from there, you have very little chance of succeeding in finding me. But should you manage to do so, it would be devastating for us both. I've already brought you so much pain, don't be a glutton for punishment. Trust me on this, Eric—if you can. After all, I've proven myself to be less than trustworthy and for that, I beg your forgiveness.

If the Fates are kind, perhaps we'll meet again in another lifetime. I pray so. More than anything I want the chance to get it right the next time around. Till then, carpe the hell out of the diem as you continue on the path you'll have to chart without me. Indeed, certain truths aren't meant to be known, Eric.

Just as some names are better left undescribed.

Love always,
Anonymous

CHAPTER TWENTY-SIX

WHITNEY FELT SICK. Sick in her heart. Sick to her stomach. Acid churned around what little she'd made herself get down for breakfast today. Or was it yesterday that she'd last eaten? Since returning to Mobile, her time had been spent alternately sleeping, weeping and staring at the walls of her perpetually darkened bedroom.

She didn't want to go outside, didn't even want to open the curtains to see the sunshine. Those things of nature had once given her joy, but there was no joy to be had in her anymore.

Life held no meaning beyond the memories that wouldn't go away. They beat at her relentlessly, whether waking or asleep, making serrated ribbons of her heart. It was broken. All of her was broken. She felt like she was on the verge of a nervous breakdown. At least she didn't think sane people crawled on all fours in the dark to heave into a toilet without the vaguest idea as to the time of day, day of week, or week of the year. Had New Year's Eve passed? Had Christmas?

She'd had no choice but to run away from Eric. She loved him too much to stay. She had deceived him with her silence and once broken, she would have dragged him down with her.

Instead he would remember her as she had been, not what she was now—a ghost of her former self. Though who that self was, Whitney was no more certain of that than she was of the time.

Time…time…time. If only she could turn back the hands of the clock and make it stop, she'd be forever young and vibrant, the lusty, great adventuress Eric had admired, loved, adored. Turn the clock back a little further and she'd be alone but self-sufficient, capable of dealing with the nightmare she was trapped in now.

How she longed to be the old Whitney again. Not this mewling lump of nothingness without a spine, who whimpered, "Eric, Eric, Eric. I need you to hold me, to love me, to make it all go away and tell me I'm the most beautiful thing you've ever seen even if I look like hell."

She had his number. She even had Grandmother Ming's number. If she called, he would come. How desperate she was now to cling to his strength while she wasted away. Mind, body, spirit, they were slipping from her fast. Yes, she must be losing her mind, she was actually tempted to plug her phone back in, and undo the last good deed she had done.

The temptation was so great that she hooked a hand over the sink and pulled herself up. For a moment she was so dizzy she feared she might pass out. Leaning against the porcelain for support, she waited until the dizziness passed. Her head slightly cleared. Not much but enough to know she had no right to make that call without confronting the image Eric would see should she make it.

She fumbled for the light switch. Suddenly her eyes stung as if torched by fire after being cocooned in a dark, dank cave.

Slowly, ever so slowly, Whitney raised her eyelids, letting her eyes adjust to the light above the mirror.

One glance and she shut her eyes. Tight.

Is this what she had become? How proudly she had once asserted she was becoming who she wanted to be and getting there by whatever means felt right.

Oh, she had become something all right. A ghoul, according to the mirror. But could it be the mirror had lied? Surely she didn't look that bad.

Whitney forced herself to risk another look.

The mirror hadn't lied. Her cheeks were sunken, dark circles rimmed her eyes despite the sleep she couldn't get enough of. Her tan was a memory of the past. Like her and Eric. Never, never could she let him see her this way with an ashen complexion, her hair a rat's nest of matted tangles, and her lips cracked.

She touched them and tried to imagine Eric wanting to do the same. All she could imagine was revulsion. She disgusted herself. Her breath tasted foul. Sniffing, she decided the rest of her smelled no better.

Had she actually come to this? Dying was one thing but to die with such little dignity was less than pitiful.

She had to snap herself out of this stupor and scrape together a smidgeon of self-respect.

She felt too weak to pick up a brush, bathe herself or put on some lipstick. Tough. She was doing it. Starting with some cold water from the faucet.

The bite of the water had the effect of a bracing slap. Slap. Slap. She soaked her face with handfuls of it, faster and faster, until it streamed down her throat, drenching the slip she had on. And how long had she been wearing this stinking, stained slip she never wanted to wear or see again?

Peeling it off like a reptilian second skin, she threw it into the trash. This was the slip she had worn as she made her escape and returned to where she had come from. The flight was a hazy memory. Neither did she quite remember getting home. All she knew was that somehow she had arrived and fallen into the bed she'd hardly left since...whenever it had been. And for however long that was, she hadn't cared enough to change out of the slip or put on clean linens.

Suddenly feeling as if she were the embodiment of a neglected nursing home, Whitney filled the tub and congratulated herself on caring enough about her person to pour half a box of bath salts into the rushing water. A small victory, true, but it felt hugely significant to do something for herself beyond wallow in self-pity and ignore the fact her hair had the consistency of starch.

She scrubbed herself clean from her head to her toes but avoided more than a cursory swish between her thighs. The water would simply have to do because to touch herself there would be to invite the image of dark, skillful fingers playing her sweetly, hotly, urging her on to a fever pitch of desire for what she could no longer have.

Eric. Beside her, inside her. Holding her, loving her, filling her up with his spirit, his body, his—

No. No, she couldn't let herself remember, couldn't let herself pretend she was with him again. To do so was to start unraveling the slender thread of sanity she had managed to hang on to.

Quickly, before she succumbed, she finished her bath, dried off, and watched the sheen of filth and despair she had discarded go down the drain.

And now…what? What did she do next? Change the sheets and crawl back into the bed she had consigned herself to with the lifelessness of a vampire in a coffin? The spirit, the fight had been sucked out of her. She still didn't have much but there was ample to get dressed and open the curtains, at least see if it was day or night.

Day. But what day, what month and year? Not that it mattered, but she was a little curious to know. Curiosity, oh that was good. A sign she wasn't comatose despite evidence to the contrary.

There were crackers on her bedroom floor and a half-eaten bowl of cereal on her night table. Assorted other discards littered the floor.

Her legs were wobbly but she made it to the living room. Her luggage stood by the door where she'd left it. She didn't have the strength to carry the baggage or even the desire to. More than anything she wanted to get out of here, get on a bus, a plane, a train, any mode of transportation that would take her far, far away from the walls that were pressing in.

Though she didn't trust her legs to make it down the street, she did feel capable of driving. At least a little ways, maybe to the nearest convenience store.

It felt amazingly good to get in her Ford Escort, twist the key and crank the engine. Not exactly a Jeep careening through a rain forest but—

"Stop it," she snapped. "Just keep your eyes on the road and your mind on the present. Here. Now. You can't go back and you can't afford to remember. Cut it out of your brain, you're not dead yet, Whitney. Make the most of what time you've got left or forget the store and head for the nearest pawn shop. Better to buy a gun and get it over with than sink back into that hellhole you're crawling out of, hand over fist."

Hand over fist, the way she'd spent her money. She'd spent it like there was no tomorrow but tomorrow was now today and there was precious little nest egg remaining in the nest. Five grand should still be in the savings but that wouldn't go far if she lingered on. It was possible. The bath and fresh air were making her already feel better. Not healthy, but sufficiently well to take some pleasure in the sight of wreaths dangling from light poles and Christmas trees decked out in the windows she passed.

"Look on the bright side," she told herself. "At least you don't have to worry about buying presents."

Her mirthless laughter had a hollow ring that echoed through the chamber of her heart. Empty. That's how she felt inside, empty. Like a paper doll some child had put away, tired of animating a pretend playmate.

Such a child she had been and what fun while it lasted. But that time was gone and she had to go on. Each minute was a precious thing and she didn't really want to blow her brains out. Walking into the store, buying a carton of milk and picking up a newspaper seemed a far better option.

December 23, that was the date. Which meant she'd been holed up for nearly a month. A month of madness. Whitney shuddered and her stomach gave a queasy lurch. Only hours ago she'd been crawling around on all fours, having spiraled down so deep that her personal hygiene was non-existent. Of course she might have had the presence of mind to wash off earlier if her period had—

Her period. When was her last period?

Her heart stopped. And then it raced faster than the dart of her mind as she combed it for a time frame that settled on the week before their wedding. November 1, that was their wedding day. And now it was December 23. Which meant...

"No. No, it can't be." Her knees buckled and she dropped the milk to grab hold of a shelf. Milk pooled around her feet but all she could see was the newspaper splayed on the ground, the date staring up at her.

"Ma'am? Ma'am, are you all right?" a voice said.

Whitney couldn't find hers to reply. The best she could do was nod, mumble an apology and get out of the store with the halting gait of a tin soldier minus his oilcan.

She made it to the car, slumped into the seat. Resting her head on the steering wheel, Whitney took several deep breaths and tried to calm herself. Only the harder she tried to stay calm the more frantic she became to assure herself there was an explanation she could live with because she couldn't bear to think that she might have committed a heinous crime against nature.

A nervous breakdown, severe depression, that could throw her cycle out of whack. Couldn't it? And even if not, leukemia was a disease of the blood, an insidious stalker that just might rob her of a menstrual flow. That was a possibility, wasn't it?

Her stomach gave another lurch and she gagged on the bile rising up in her throat. Suddenly she felt sicker than ever. Too ill to drive back to her apartment, much less the drugstore. But she had to. First, the drugstore.

She grabbed the first pregnancy test kit she saw. Her head swirling in a dense fog, it was a miracle she made it back safely into her assigned parking spot. And then she was at her apartment door, keys in her shaking hand.

"I don't want to go in, I don't want to go in," she chanted, dreading the potential results far more than the squalor to which she was returning.

A white Camaro zipped into the space next to her Ford. That would be her neighbor, Carl. He drove even faster than he talked once he got started, a chatterbox who set her teeth on edge.

She was so close to the edge right now that she'd surely start howling if he said so much as "Hello." Just as his car door opened, Whitney shut the apartment door behind her.

Leaning against it, she slid down. And sat there, just sat there by her packed luggage, head between her knees. She was panting, almost hyperventilating. She had to take some deep breaths and get a grip.

She took what grip she had and the pregnancy test kit

to the bathroom. Her insides were so tied up it was almost impossible to pee into the cup.

But she did.

And then she made herself insert the strip. So innocuous looking, just this small flimsy gauge that would tell her, was she or wasn't she?

The test went quickly though the wait seemed forever.

Then forever wasn't long enough.

Such a simple little test. Such devastating results.

They confirmed the worst: Whitney Smith was a monster. It wasn't enough to break Eric's heart. His baby was in her belly, a child in the making who was innocent of any wrongdoing and didn't deserve the fate she would share.

The thought filled her with self-loathing. The pregnancy wasn't intentional but that wouldn't make her any less guilty of a total lack of moral responsibility—

Unless she could carry it long enough for the baby to survive. Premature infants were born every day and pulled through, thanks to the miracles of modern medicine and the doctors who practiced it.

Dr. Clark. She had to call him. Explain her condition. It didn't matter if he thought her a horrible person for it, all that mattered was doing whatever it took to keep breathing until her unborn child was capable of picking up where she left off.

That's right, she had to take charge again. Do what was necessary, responsible, right. The woman Eric had fallen in love with had lived for the day with no thought to the future or the repercussions of her actions. That wildcat had put her in this position, but thank heavens for the old Whitney, she knew what to do.

Greeting her old self like a long lost friend she could

depend on in a time of need, Whitney went directly to the phone, plugged it in and made her call.

"This is Whitney Smith," she said without pause. "I need to speak to Dr. Clark. Immediately, please."

CHAPTER TWENTY-SEVEN

"WHERE THE HELL have you been, child?"

Dr. Clark's bark of greeting triggered a wince at his shout and a protective hug of her stomach at the reference to *child*.

"I need your help, Dr. Clark. I need to see you—"

"A day late and a dollar short, young lady. Do you realize I've been calling every damn day and keeping the post office in business with all the damn letters I sent and you never bothered to open? Now where the hell have you been?"

What could she tell him? Oh, no place worth mentioning, just hanging out by active volcanos, high diving off cliffs, having a whirlwind affair and getting an education in the intimate arts. Falling in love, getting married, telling myself I was in remission when I was really in denial, getting pregnant, running away, and having a nervous breakdown.

"Let's just say that I checked out of reality for a while and now I'm back with a very big problem. How soon can I see you?"

"Now's not soon enough to suit me. Get yourself over here lickety-split and we'll discuss your problem after we draw some blood. We need another test, Whitney, and we need it now. We needed it months ago."

The urgency in his voice made her grip the phone tighter. "Why?"

"I'll tell you after the test."

"If you want me over there now, you'll tell me now."

After a thick silence, he cautioned, "I don't want you to get your hopes up."

Even as they sparked to life, she answered, "Of course not."

Palms sweating, knees shaking, she hardly breathed lest she miss a single syllable of the words that came out in a rush of excitement tempered by a heavy note of warning.

"There's a chance your initial tests were incorrectly diagnosed. No way to tell until we take another sample. You have to be prepared since the results could be the same but I do have cause to believe otherwise."

"You mean...I—I...Dr. Clark, are you sure?"

"I won't be sure about anything until—"

"I'm on my way."

HALF AN HOUR LATER she was in Dr. Clark's office, feeling like a prisoner on death row praying for a stay of execution. The last time she sat here she couldn't remember his name; now she was anxiously awaiting the results of the new blood test he'd immediately taken, and expressed to the lab. Whitney tried to follow what he was saying.

"A few weeks after you took off, I was at one of these gala things. You know, a banquet, boring speakers and beepers going off all over the place since there were a lot of doctors around. Anyway, me and my better half got put at a table with a fine young man I taught awhile back in med school. Turns out he was upset that night and it wasn't because his wife was making eyes at me."

Dr. Clark slapped his thigh and chortled. A little too heartily. Whitney knew he was trying to take her mind off the life-or-death balance that hung on the ring of a phone.

Her heart hammered, her muscles twitched. Nonetheless she forced a stiff smile and wagged a trembling finger at him.

"Now Dr. Clark, tell the truth. She was making eyes at you and her husband was upset because she dumped a bowl of soup in his lap to get rid of him so she could make a play for the handsomest doctor in town."

"You're a flirt, Whitney. And a very brave young lady. The truth is, I nearly choked on my overdone filet mignon when Cam—that's Dr. Cameron Lark, as in Dr. C. Lark—started fretting about a certain patient of his. Seems she'd been diagnosed with anemia, a pretty bad case of it but nothing that couldn't be fixed with a hefty dose of iron, a sensible diet, rest and exercise and all that other good stuff that makes for healthy living. Odd thing was, she was living healthy already. Even odder, she collapsed and wound up in the hospital a week after her initial blood tests came back. Which would you rather know first, the day those tests were done or the results of the second testing?"

"Dear Lord," Whitney whispered. Something wet was on her cheeks. Hope seized her and wouldn't let go though she tried to break its hold. She couldn't hope too much, not yet, because if the phone rang and the news was bad then she'd be back in the ranks of the living dead and once she got out of this horrid, horrid place she couldn't bear to go there again.

"That's right. The two of you were tested on the same day. As for the results of that second test... Needless to say, Dr. *C. Lark* was beside himself when his patient, *Whitney Smith,* expired from acute myelogenous leukemia. She went fast, there was nothing he could've done to save her, but it really did upset him to lose a patient like that. Of course, he wasn't the only one upset. I tore out of that shebang and wanted somebody's head. After I got ahold of you and made sure my suspicions were confirmed."

He stared at the phone as if by staring he could make it ring. Whitney laid hands on her concaved stomach. She wanted to demand assurances but Dr. Clark didn't have them to give. As for wanting somebody's head, if she had been put through all this for nothing then she was in the market for an ax.

"How could something like this happen? I mean, if there was a mix-up and our tests got switched."

"Plain and simple? Human error. The lab could transpose the results. Or the transcriptionist could accidentally do the same. With two identical names and two similar ones, even a careful recorder might have made a mistake."

"And you think that's the case here," she prompted, wanting that much assurance at least.

"I think there's a very good possibility. I think that possibility is increased if someone was distracted because they were having a bad day, had a fight at home before work, or was maybe under the weather. I'd like to lay blame on someone if there is blame to be had, but the fact of the matter is, we're all capable of making mistakes so I hope you'll keep that in mind before getting sue crazy like everybody else, and that said, I think this damn phone better ring before I stick my neck out further than I already have."

He slapped the desk and barked, "Ring!"

As if obeying the orders of a higher command, the phone did ring. Dr. Clark grabbed it up, said urgently, "Tell me what you've got, Susan."

Whitney's gaze froze on Dr. Clark. Her life depended on this call. The life growing inside her depended on this call.

Though the conversation didn't take more than a minute it seemed like hours, days, weeks before Dr. Clark hung up and shouted, "Glory be and hallelujah! Congratulations, Whitney! Negative. Not a trace, you're clean as a whistle."

Whitney didn't remember falling to her knees but the next thing she knew Dr. Clark was helping her up and patting her back while she sobbed, "Thank you, thank you, dear Father in heaven, thank you."

"There, there now. It's going to be all right, child. Everything's going to be all right."

Laughing and crying for joy all at once, she blew her nose on the handkerchief Dr. Clark pulled from his pocket.

A baby on the way. A baby! A baby! She'd gotten her life back and a baby to go with it. A sweet little bundle of love she would hold and rock and kiss and never, ever desert the way her father had deserted her.

The way she had deserted Eric.

Her laughter trickled to a halt; her smile faded. She turned somber eyes on Dr. Clark.

"What's wrong, Whitney?" he asked kindly. "Now that we've got this crisis out of the way, maybe you want to talk about that big problem you mentioned earlier."

"I'm pregnant, Dr. Clark," she answered bluntly. "I'm not sure how it happened but it did and thrilled as I am to be expecting, I'm appalled to know I conceived when I could have killed my own child if the test had turned out differently."

"Only one way I know of for something like that to happen and it takes two to do it." Dr. Clark pulled at his chin and had the good grace not to stand in judgment. Not of her, anyway. "I don't mean to pry, but I can't help but wonder who got you in this condition, Whitney. After all, raising a child is a tremendous responsibility and any man who would shirk his duty toward his own child isn't much of a man."

"He's very much a man, Dr. Clark," she asserted, quick to rush to Eric's defense. "And he would never shirk his duties."

"Then why isn't he here with you?"

"Because he doesn't know where I am."

"And why is that?"

Though she wasn't proud to admit it, there was no way to dress up the truth and it was high time she started telling it. Not only to Dr. Clark but to herself.

"Because I loved him, I always will. But I was afraid to tell him I was dying because I knew he would have stood by me until the end. I couldn't bring myself to put him through that, but even more I was afraid to let him see me so vulnerable, dependant on him to take care of me. So what did I do? I ran away."

"Ran away?" Dr. Clark shook his head at her. "Whitney, that's not like you. I've never known you to run away from anything in your life."

Whitney snorted in self-derision. "No," she had to agree. "It's not like me at all. It's not like me to be deceitful or to endanger the life of an unborn child. But I did and all I can say is, I acted out of character. Eric didn't. Unfortunately, that means I know him but he doesn't really know me. The woman he fell in love with is someone I don't even recognize myself."

She stroked her belly and silently wished their child to take after Eric. But no matter how their child turned out, she couldn't give it less than a happy, stable home. Very possibly without the father she refused to tie down for the sake of keeping him at a distance he didn't want to be.

Dr. Clark squeezed her left hand. "Give him a chance and don't underestimate yourself. From what you say, this Eric would make a good husband and father. I'm sure he'll do the right thing by you."

It was an assurance meant to comfort but it left Whitney uneasy.

"Yes," she softly replied while clenching a fist of determination. "But Dr. Clark," she vowed, "I won't have any man who stays with me out of duty."

CHAPTER TWENTY-EIGHT

LAST-MINUTE Christmas shopping should be a drag. *Au contraire*—what a delight!

Au contraire. Eric spoke French. German, Italian, Spanish, Chinese, and no telling what else, too. Her?

All she knew was English. And the universal language only the heart could speak. How it did speak now, alternating between disturbing whispers and joyous shouts.

Ignoring the whispers of uncertainty and niggling fears, Whitney gave a soft whoop of jubilation upon finding a darling pale green diaper stacker, embroidered with yellow-and-white daisies at the top, on a seventy-five percent off clearance table at JCPenny's.

Whether boy or girl the diaper holder would be perfect for itsy-bitsy diapers—disposable preferably but only if finances allowed. No use in concerning herself with that now, she'd deal with it when the time came.

Time. She had time and never, ever would she take it, or life, for granted again. As for love, while she'd never taken it for granted, there was a price for loving with the heart of a fool and it wasn't just hers to pay.

Was it really better to die with regrets for what one had done rather than for what one hadn't? She was no longer sure. One thing she did know was that a baby didn't leave room for making hasty decisions or using poor judgment. Hard, so very, very hard not to call Eric, tell him the whole twisted truth, beg his forgiveness, then pick up where they'd left off if at all possible.

And there was the hitch. It wasn't possible.

The reasons why were many but they all coalesced into the simple fact that he loved a woman who no longer existed.

Whitney Smith had developed a taste for risk, adventure and white-hot passion. Eric shared that thirst and drinking from the cup of such a life had been their communion. Now knee-deep in the consequences of her recklessness, she no longer had the right, nor the inclination, to partake.

Life was such a grand adventure, but one better observed from the safety of a rocking chair when a tiny silver brush on a clearance table made the heart leap, and a cup of hot chocolate on Christmas Eve was a far better treat for mommy and baby than a glass of Dom Perignon.

Perched on her couch, Whitney hummed "Away in a Manger" along with the stereo. After a sip of steaming hot cocoa, she sat it on the coffee table and put the finishing touches on the small, artificial Christmas tree that she kept stored for holidays. She'd always longed for a big fir dripping with bows and ornaments and candy canes and filling the air with that heavenly scent of evergreen but the apartment was small and she simply couldn't justify such an expenditure when there was no one around to enjoy it but her.

"Maybe next Christmas," she told the baby. "After all, it won't be just me anymore. You'll be here and..." Her gaze drifted to the pile of mail she'd picked up after leaving Dr. Clark's office yesterday. She hadn't sorted through it yet, hadn't even taken off the thick rubber band holding the stack together. Just looking at it made her heart pound, her palms sweat. Her other life was in there and seeing Eric again, only a snapshot away.

"Well," she said shakily. "You have your presents and Mama has hers. Should we save them all for Christmas morning or open one apiece tonight and unwrap the rest tomorrow?''

''Joy to the World'' played in the background and she suddenly wondered how Mickey was spending his own Christmas Eve. He would be grateful for a gift of shoes—and thrilled to receive a box of peanut brittle. Why hadn't she thought of that before now? Because while everyone else was sending cards and presents, she'd been on the threshold of insanity and wallowing in the muck of misery in surroundings that would make a pigsty look fastidious.

That had been only yesterday.

Today she was going to live. She was going to have a child and be the best mother ever, even if she had to raise it alone. That would take a lot of wisdom and strength.

Was it wise to open a letter, even just one? Was she strong enough to indulge in a single memory without breaking down and curling into the fetal position, reduced once more to the equivalent of a bawling newborn?

With trembling hands she lifted the mail from the end of the coffee table and placed it in her lap, close to the child her body housed.

''Okay, baby, that's your daddy snuggled up against you. His face is in lots of pictures and his name's on probably a hundred pages. I hope you get closer than this and he holds you one day, but...we'll have to see what the future brings. For now, it's just you and me, kid. And since the kid in me can't wait to tear into the goods, let's each open a present tonight. You first.''

Closing her eyes, Whitney picked a gift beneath the tree, pretending she didn't know what she'd wrapped less than an hour ago. After carefully slicing a nail beneath the tape to keep the paper intact so she might press it between the pages of a baby book, she exclaimed, ''A rattle!''

Shaking it in the air like a maraca in an island band, she

had a flash of dancing feet, a strong arm coming around her and bending her back; a passionate kiss.

The smile left her face. She laid the rattle down. Folded her hands over her stomach and pressed the letters as close as she could get them to her skin.

Did she dare? Did she dare risk even a peek at the memories she needed to put behind her so she could get on with her life?

Come, they told me, Parrump-a-pum-pum....

"The Little Drummer Boy." Her favorite Christmas carol. She loved the sound of those drums, but the thrum of her heart was drowning the music out. With the blind pluck of an envelope, the careful opening of it, a remembrance emerged. One so immediately close and real that she could smell the salt air, the citrus of Eric's cologne; she could see the moon smiling down on them as they laughed up at it, and their hands were clasped together, swinging between them. Yes, she could feel it still, the warmth of his palm to hers, the lace of their fingers, the—

Longing. It was a physical pang, trenchant and sharp. Whitney tore her gaze from the letter. Looking around her, she saw a baby rattle and the furnishings that had once belonged to her mother; she heard Christmas carols.

Quickly putting the letter back, she told herself she couldn't look at it or the photo enclosed. She saw things more clearly now; a glimpse of Eric could only cloud her good judgment.

And vision. Tears sprang to her eyes the moment she weakened and peered at his face, frozen in time. She touched him with a fingertip, then nearly choked on a strangled cry.

In self-protection, she grabbed the tape she'd wrapped the presents with and sealed the envelope, consigning both letter and picture to a past she couldn't go back to again. The rest of the letters and postcards joined the one she never should have opened in a shoe box. She put it on the upper ledge in her closet, pushed it as far from reach as possible.

"Pandora's box," she said feeling very fragile. Her heart was fragile. And unruly. She couldn't let it mess with the head she had to keep firmly on her shoulders. There was a baby to consider now and it was up to her to protect it.

Whitney stroked her belly with all the love she felt for what resided safely in her womb. And safe she would keep it, she vowed, as she turned away from the closet with a tender smile on her lips.

CHAPTER TWENTY-NINE

MUTED LAUGHTER trailed behind Adam from the less-than-upbeat New Year's Eve party going on in Grandmother Ming's living room. The reason for the damper on everyone's spirits was slouched in a chair on the darkened back porch. Adam approached him warily yet with firm intent.

"Eric?" he called softly. "Hey, bro, why don't you come join us? It's almost midnight and the champagne's flowing—along with the sake, for those who prefer it."

"Thanks but I've got my own bottle of preference," came the slightly slurred reply. A sliver of moonlight glinted off the bottle, the amber liquid at low tide. Eric raised it in a mock salute before tipping it to his lips. "Want to see the New Year in with me and my pal?" he offered after a guzzle. "Allow me to introduce you. Jim Beam meet Adam. Adam, this is—"

"This is not going to bring her back, Eric."

"Maybe not, dammit!" he exploded. Then his voice dropped to a broken whisper. "But it's all I've got for the comfort she's not around to give anymore."

Adam dropped to a crouch and put his arm around the brother who had always been the logical one, the strong one, the brave big brother he'd always looked up to. Man, was he worried about him. Everyone was. Haggard, dishevelled, Eric had been looped ever since the family had gotten together over a week ago. Not that their presence had done any good. Eric, usually so gregarious in their midst, had been remote, unapproachable, disdaining any and all efforts to lend a hand or a shoulder to cry on.

There were no tears on Eric's hollow cheeks but Adam could hear the click in his throat as he swallowed them down.

"I trusted her, Adam."

"I know, but..."

"But what?"

"I'm sorry, Eric. Maybe I should have said something before. Then again, maybe I shouldn't be saying anything now. The truth is, I didn't trust her as completely as you did."

Eric glanced at him sharply—or as sharply as his bleary eyes allowed. He felt offended that Adam would ever question Whitney's integrity...despite her own written confession of misleading the man who had trusted her with his heart, his very soul.

"Heart and Soul." They'd played it the night she'd given him her innocence and he'd reclaimed his own, feeling like a virgin again himself. And it wasn't just coincidence that "Heart and Soul" had marked their exit from the chapel as he carried his blushing bride down the aisle.

Heart and Soul. Yeah, right. He'd given Whitney his heart and she'd ripped out his soul. How could he have so misjudged her? He had let her in where no one else had gone, not even himself before she'd brought out the best and deepest parts of what was inside him. And he'd done the same for her. Oh sure, their relationship was intensely sexual, but all those lessons in bed were about intimate bonding, not sex....

"What are you going to do with that scarf?"

"Tie you up. And tie you even closer to me. Consider it a lesson, yuan-pao, *in the ties that bind."*

He had bound her to the bed, spread-eagle. And given

her stretching wings even more room to fly with the brush of a peacock's plume. First, dusting shut her eyes. Then tickling her lips into a smile. Her throat deserved much attention; so did the breasts he cascaded down to. By then, she was no longer smiling but panting.

"Breathe," he coached her. "Breathe slow and steady. Remember, our breath is the essence of life and 'chi', our life force."

"But Eric, I can't catch my breath when you're doing that."

"Then maybe I should do this." Stroking the feather lower, then lower still, she not only caught her breath but expelled it on a plaintive wail.

"You're torturing me!"

"Torture you? Never. I care for you. Deeply. All I want to do is give you pleasure and take my own in the trust you've given to me. You do trust me, don't you?"

"What kind of question is that? Look at me!"

"I am." The picture of trust, she laid splayed on the bed, writhing and moaning and begging him to come to her, touch her with more than the feather he discarded.

He unbound her legs, her arms. She reached out to him and he filled her. Just as she filled him.

The Peacock Tease had been the name of the game and may the best man or woman win. He'd gladly called this one a draw. While Whitney cashed in, he claimed his own winnings. They'd both gotten off on an enticing bit of love play, but the real object of the game was trust.

Trust. He had trusted Whitney until she'd left him with nothing more than that goddamn letter, her wedding ring and the Tai Chi heirloom he now wore around his own neck.

"Let's just think of it as a loan…like we're going steady and if we break up, I'll give it back."

Eric fingered the medallion. He'd never expected to get it back. Neither had he expected the ring she so loved to end back up in the velvet box he kept in his pants pocket. His pants were loose; he'd lost weight. And there sure wasn't any sexual desire filling up the vacant space while he mulled over Adam's distrust of Whitney, which he still couldn't summon up, despite every reason to.

"Why didn't you trust her?" Eric made himself ask. Hell, maybe Adam knew something he didn't. Maybe he had a clue, which was more than the private investigators had been able to turn up.

"It was while we were riding in the carriage on your wedding day. I'd made an offhanded comment about me and Jolene not having what it took to make a real future together, unlike the two of you. For a split second she cringed and I saw guilt written all over her face. I thought I might've imagined it at first, but when I asked her to be as good to you as I knew you'd be to her, she did it again. That's when I decided Whitney had secrets."

His mind less than razor sharp, Eric silently damned the forget-about-time in the bottle he took another swig from anyway. Something was trying to emerge from his memory about the conversation he and Whitney had before entering the chapel and it had overtones he didn't want to acknowledge. Still, the tap against his brain came, sounding more like a death knell than the ringing of wedding bells from an ivory tower.

"I'm afraid of my own mortality, Eric."

"Aren't we all?" Whatever, *he'd thought,* let's just get this show on the road. *"If it'll make you feel better we'll take out the part about till death do we part, how's that?"*

That had made her feel much better. That had sealed her decision to go on with the wedding and take him as her husband for three months, no obligation beyond. That was more than he wanted to remember but now that he had, much too much else was starting to fall into place.

"All we have is the day, it's all any of us have."

"We'll see...we'll see...we'll see..."

Dozens of other seemingly innocuous comments came back to him, all suddenly taking on ominous hues. Like a haiku penned in black ink, he saw what love and hope had blinded him to before.

my bright shining star
you lived only for the day
no thought of winter

Somewhere in the distance he heard Adam saying, "If you find her, what will you do?"

"Love her more than ever and make as many memories as we can before it's too late." He could feel himself choking up. "If it's not too late already."

"What do you mean?"

Eric turned haunted eyes on Adam. "At first I couldn't imagine what had happened. But what you said about our wedding day knocked something loose."

He took another gulp from the bottle, swiped at the trickle on his chin with the sleeve of a wrinkled dress shirt. Adam was right, drinking himself into a stupor wouldn't bring Whitney back, but anything that promised oblivion over clarity was a better way to see the New Year in. Alone.

Without Whitney he would forever be alone.

"Eric. Eric, talk to me."

Adam was shaking him. Not that he could feel it. He'd gone numb. Nothing seemed real. Good. Real was bad. Numb was good.

"Look, bro, you can take a swing at me for me saying

this—actually, I wish you would, that'd be the brother I know—but if I could get my hands on Whitney right now I'd be up for murder one. I'd like to kill her for what she's done to you.''

"Don't say that." Eric gripped his brother by the shirt and would have punched him out if his other hand wasn't latched onto a bottle and so unsteady that he'd probably miss his target anyway. "Don't ever say that," he growled putting the bottle down. "Whitney had this friend she told me about, a friend who was supposedly dead and made her rethink her own life. Then with no warning—just all of a sudden—Whitney was sick and she wouldn't go to a doctor."

"Are you suggesting...?"

"Yeah. I think Whitney was that friend and she went away to die." Eric buried his face in his hands. "I can forgive her anything as long as she's alive. But Adam, if she cheated me out of sharing what time she had left, if she didn't trust me to love her to the very end and be there for her when she needed me the most, I'll never forgive her for that. Never."

CHAPTER THIRTY

By MID-JANUARY, Whitney had more dilemmas than solutions. The urge to call Eric was unceasing. The urge not to call had grown in proportion to the problems she faced. Like a tight job market and hoping she would get a call from Winn-Dixie to check groceries. If that fell through, she had an application for Burger King. There was an opening on the late shift and she could at least make enough to support herself until something better came along.

She did have other options. Such as legal grounds for a lawsuit for the personal suffering the misdiagnosis had put her through. A part of her wanted blood and at least a return of all the savings she had squandered.

But what price vengeance? Dr. Clark would be implicated and she couldn't do that to him. Besides, if she hadn't taken it upon herself to grab the report off his desk and refuse to see Dr. Goldberg, the mistake would have been caught, she would have been put on vitamins, told to get more rest and exercise and eat right—all the things that had gotten her healthy in the first place before she'd emotionally caved in. As for the savings squandered, she couldn't blame that on anyone but herself.

Option Two. Go to the library and appeal to Mr. Andrews' sense of humanity. Her old position was surely filled but they often needed part-time help with cataloging, reshelving, things like that. However, considering Mr. Andrews' lack of humanity and her lack of professionalism in leaving, chances were slim to none of getting rehired for even maid duty.

The third and final option was the most tempting. And the most untenable. It was the option she contemplated now with one hand hovering over the phone, the other clenching a marriage license from Antigua.

The lines were all rehearsed in her head. *Hi, Eric. It's me, Whitney. I'm really sorry for hurting you and running off the way I did, but you see, I thought I was dying. Since then I found out that I wasn't ill, just pregnant. With your baby. Don't worry, I'm not asking you to honor a marriage to someone you don't really even know, but you have a right to be part of your child's life and I need your help because I'm out of work....*

That's as far as she'd gotten with her speech. She kept trying to say it aloud but the words always got clogged in her throat, staunched by love and fear and pride. All the things that kept her from venturing into Pandora's box. Too much resided in there that she didn't dare unleash on the tenuous control she kept over her emotions.

How she ached to see him again, to hear his voice, feel his touch. Such a yearning was terrifying when the basis of their relationship had been a dream, and in reality she couldn't live up to the image he had fallen in love with.

Oh yes, Whitney Smith had slipped into her old skin with amazing ease. The devil-may-care insouciance that Eric adored had disappeared and been replaced with maternal instincts, and a sedate nature that was a lot safer, wiser to accept in herself than another identity which no longer fit her needs, her life-style, or would be good for a baby.

Eric's baby. One that would compel him to stay put, even if he wanted out. That's how he'd felt about Amy; it would be ditto for her.

Whitney turned away from the phone. She replaced the marriage license in the dresser drawer where a rattle shared hallowed space with a silver brush, a diaper stacker and a skein of pastel-hued yarn, destined to be a blanket. Though she could ill afford any of it, she simply hadn't been able to resist the call to nest.

As for Eric, there would be no call today, no plea for help. She had to find a job. Once on her feet, she would contact him. It had to be soon, before she started to show. Because if Eric couldn't love her as is, then they had no future and their baby wasn't going to be a bargaining chip.

SHE DIDN'T GET a call from Winn-Dixie. The job at Burger King lasted all of two nights. The smell of burgers on the grill had been more than her heightened sense of smell and sensitive stomach could take. After gagging into a bag containing someone's order of a Whopper and fries, the manager had taken her aside and tactfully suggested she apply at McDonald's.

Since she could cry at the drop of a hat—just browsing the card section could do it—she had burst into tears and only dire necessity had sent her back for the paltry paycheck after disgracing herself like that.

The situation was not good. She was nearly three months pregnant. She had no job in sight, and soon there would be no insurance, no place to live. Time was running out and she felt trapped, desperate.

She was desperate to call him, desperate to undo her sins against him, desperate to be held and loved for who she was, even if she didn't know herself half the time.

But to reach out to Eric now would be the next wrong step to take. So where did one go when three options had dwindled to one? The choice was easy when there wasn't a choice.

She would swallow her pride and plead with Mr. Andrews to take her back, no matter how menial the position.

THE LIBRARY had never looked so enticing. Or so formidable. Still gathering her courage to climb the palatial stairs up to the grand, old structure, Whitney sat on the bottom step. How many times had she climbed these stairs as a child, then as an eager assistant fresh out of school with a master's degree in Library Science? She'd only been twenty-three, plowing straight through from undergrad to graduate degree, then applying the same workhorse mentality to her profession.

All that overtime had netted her a big promotion and the added responsibility which came with the title of Children's Librarian. At twenty-five, she had been extremely young to assume such a demanding position. It had been such an honor that she had worked even harder—so hard that her body had finally rebelled against the long hours, fast-food diet, stress and more stress, and lack of downtime.

It had taken an in-her-face wake-up call to stop and smell the roses.

Whitney sniffed the small bouquet she'd brought as a peace offering. As she had bought them, it occurred to her that Mr. Andrews might not have been so unapproachable before had she thought of him as a person with his own needs, instead of a dictator who set the standard of the time she put in. Could it be he hadn't expected her to match him hour for hour, that maybe he simply didn't want to go home? Too bad she had seen him as the enemy rather than a human being she might have more in common with than she had thought.

Of course she saw a lot of things differently now. Life was too short, too precious, to hold grudges, to blithely ignore its beauty and nature's riches and too short to beat herself up for past mistakes. So she got off her duff, and marched up the stairs, flowers in hand. When she reached the top landing, she ran smack into Mr. Andrews.

Noticing the small brown bag he held, she said, "Mr. Andrews, I was just coming to see you. But I guess you're off to lunch. Mind if I join you?"

His stunned expression reminded her of the moment she'd quit. Whitney didn't laugh now. He was brown-bagging it and probably planned to eat alone on a park bench. That's how he usually took his lunches in nice weather and she felt a little ashamed that she'd never asked to join him before.

He pushed up his reading glasses and glanced at the flowers suspiciously, as if he thought she might have a trick daisy amongst the blooms to squirt him with.

"If you came to gloat, Ms. Smith, you may not. If you came to bring me flowers, you may."

From the way he said it, she knew he didn't believe for a second she was here to bring him flowers. As for gloating, it bothered her greatly that he thought her capable of smiling on whatever his misfortune might be.

"These are for you, Mr. Andrews. Along with my apologies for leaving you in the lurch the way I did. It was very unprofessional of me. I can't excuse my actions, but if you can spare me the time, I'd like to explain why— which is what I should have done before I left."

He didn't immediately take the flowers, but his expression said he wanted to.

"You left because of me, Ms. Smith. And it seems you set a trend. Your assistants were quite loyal and followed your lead. They liked working for you, but refused to answer to a slave driver like me. Or should I say, 'whip master?' Either way, we're still searching for replacements, the children's department is a shambles and my position as branch manager is shaky. Happy?''

"No," she whispered, those damnable tears springing to her eyes with embarrassing ease. "I'm so sorry, Mr. Andrews. I never meant to do you harm. The truth is, I didn't quit because of you, I quit because of a serious personal problem.''

"How serious?" He seemed genuinely concerned.

"Very serious.''

"Then why didn't you tell me?''

"Because it was easier to walk away than explain something I couldn't bring myself to talk about—especially to someone who I thought wouldn't care.''

His small flinch assured her that Mr. Andrews most definitely had the capacity to care; he just had a hard time showing it. He cleared his throat and asked awkwardly, "Would you tell me now?''

"Only if you take the flowers and call me Whitney.''

He took the flowers and shared his lunch. As they sat together on a park bench, Whitney wasn't sure who was the more amazed. Mr. Andrews as she related her story— minus her pregnancy and affair with Eric—or her, since the man she had once detested proved to be a truly sympathetic soul.

Apparently inspired by her frankness, Mr. Andrews admitted, "I considered you a rival, Whitney. The more you worked, the harder I had to so you wouldn't outshine me. I thought you had designs on my job and because of that, I wasn't very pleasant. Not that I was ever on anyone's party list, but with you, I showed my worst colors.'' He ducked his head. "I hope you can forgive me for that.''

Whitney touched his hand. He looked up, and she saw his isolation, his longing, his loneliness.

"There's nothing to forgive, Mr. Andrews. If I'd made

more of an effort to get to know you, I would have realized you not only belonged at the top of my party list, but that we could've made a good team.''

He raised a brow; the sides of his lips followed suit.

''We still could, Whitney. That is, if you're interested in a certain position I'm racing against the clock to get filled. I believe you more than meet the requirements: A team player who can whip the children's section back into shape and dispel the doubts that have arisen about my ability to oversee the library.''

''Mr. Andrews?'' She offered her hand.

They shook on it and parted with a brief hug and big grins on their faces. They had high hopes even if it wasn't yet a sure deal. As branch manager, Mr. Andrews could hire and fire, but he still had to go through the appropriate channels.

True to his word, he spoke with the library's director who gave the go-ahead to get her back ASAP. She was rehired with full benefits, and was to start Monday.

After profuse thanks to Mr. Andrews, who called with the news Saturday morning, Whitney hung up the phone with a huge sigh of relief.

The insurance was almost as important as the job itself, considering the baby she should have mentioned but was afraid would complicate matters. Once she had the department back on track, she would tell Mr. Andrews.

Strange that she didn't dread that revelation half as much as the call she had to make to Eric. She'd sworn to do it as soon as she was beyond the desperate stage and had a job to depend on, instead of just him.

Do it, she ordered herself.

Whitney picked up the receiver. Her palms were suddenly slick. Her breath was barely a wheeze.

She punched three numbers. Stopped.

Look, if you call him now, you won't be able to concentrate on your job and Whitney, you can't afford to screw up. Wait a week, then call him.

She continued dialing. She had to call him now, she'd waited too long as it was and, she was dying to hear his voice, to see him. Soon she'd be showing, so there was no time to lose.

Ring. Ring. Did he still have her wedding ring? Or did he decide to get rid of it after the way she'd left him, no explanations, not even a kiss goodbye?

"Hello, you've reached Eric Townsend. Please leave a message, and I'll return your call. If this is regarding the reward offered for information leading to the whereabouts of Whitney Smith-Townsend, please state your name, where you can be reached, and…"

The plea in his voice ripped the ground from beneath her feet. Whitney bowed her head in sorrow, in shame. How could she have done this to him? To hear him sound so weary, frayed, hollow…

Beeep. Her cue to respond.

"Eric," she began tremulously. "This is—this is Whitney." What next? Had her voice even made it on tape? She could feel her vocal cords moving, but she couldn't hear anything beyond the roar in her ears.

"This is Whitney," she repeated. "I'm very, truly sorry about everything and—and there's so much to say, only I have no idea how to say any of it. Except…" *I love you like crazy, I miss you like mad, and I'm so, so scared you won't feel the same way once you know who I really am.* "We need to talk, Eric, and after we talk you can decide if and when you want to see me. You might not want to, Eric. I'm not…me. I mean, I'm not the me you know."

Did that make sense? She had to be honest with him, honest with herself. In truth she couldn't yet handle a face-to-face meeting, not when she could hardly form a coherent thought or put together an intelligent sentence.

"What I mean is," she tried to explain again, "I think it's a good idea for us to get reacquainted on the phone— maybe a chat or two—and then take it from there." Now what was her number? Oh yeah, that's right, area code 251, the rest came by rote. Time to sign off, try to come up with something warm but cautious, hopeful but not too.

"I know I've caused you a lot of pain and Eric, I'm deeply sorry for that. I think of you often…" *Constantly, except for when I'm thinking of the baby, but the baby's part of you.* "And, well, take care. Hope to hear from you soon."

Whitney replaced the receiver. Softly. With trembling hands, she stroked her slightly rounded abdomen and whispered, "I tried, baby, I swear I did. I tried to tell your daddy where to find us but once I see him, I'm afraid I won't be able to let him go, that I'll tell him about you so he'll stay, but that would be wrong, so wrong for all of us. That's why it's better this way. First we'll talk, that's what we'll do. A conversation or two and in a couple of weeks, I'll be settled back into work and be ready to risk—"

The sudden ring of the phone stopped her cold. Palms still sweating, they were closer to drenched in the three rings it took to gather the strength to haltingly answer, "Hello?"

"Whitney? Is that you?"

That depends, Mr. Andrews. Just which Whitney did you want to talk to? The good Whitney, the bad Whitney, or the Whitney who thinks she's back on track only to fall apart at the sound of Eric's voice, who's too much of a chicken to tell him where I am when he's offering money to strangers to help find me.

"Yes, Mr. Andrews, it's me."

A pause, then Mr. Andrews continued, "Sorry to call you at home again, but I forgot to mention a storytime is scheduled for Monday. I've been pinch-hitting but if I have to deal with those antsy little rug rats one more time, I'll pull out what's left of my hair. Besides, I'm sure the, uh, tykes will be as glad to have you back as I am."

"Thanks," she said, "I'll come up with something special. No problem."

"Good! Then I'll see you first thing Monday morning."

"Nine a.m. sharp," she promised.

The expected goodbye on the other end didn't come. After a small silence, Mr. Andrews asked quietly, "Are you all right?"

"Of course," she lied. Making sure he bought it, she added, "You just caught me in the middle of planning some activities for next week. Behind as I am, I wanted to get a head start."

"Sounds just like you. But could you do me a favor and not burn too much of the midnight oil? You know I don't need you showing me up from the get-go," he kidded, their inside joke.

Whitney managed a companionable laugh.

Managing to get through the day was another matter. Important as it was to get some plan of action together for work, her concentration was zero. Her gaze kept wandering to the phone that wasn't ringing while her mind refused to budge past the person who wasn't calling.

Why? Was he busy in Europe with that lecture tour she'd agreed to go on, so he could show her Paris, Rome, Munich and more? Or could he be as close as San Francisco, seeking some wisdom or comfort from his dear Grandmother Ming?

Whitney had her number. Eric had wanted to make sure

she had access to his family should anything happen to him.

Had it? By Sunday, she was pacing the floor and several times came close to calling a sweet, old lady who had every reason to hate her guts after the grief she'd dished out to number one grandson. So why didn't she call to make sure Eric was all right, even if he wasn't picking up his messages?

Cowardice. Shame. A growing fear that the worst had happened.

All too soon, and yet not nearly soon enough, Monday morning dawned, clear and bright—unlike her spirits that were anything but. The dregs of her nightmare last night lingered: Eric, in the field, preoccupied with a runaway bride he was on a manhunt to find, then *boom.*

Gone. Gone from her and returned to the earth he so loved, scattered into a million pieces.

"Stop it," she wept into her pillow. "You have to put him out of your mind and focus on the moment. He's probably perfectly fine but the same won't be true for your job if you can't stay on task. And you need that job, Whitney, need it like never before. Not just financially, but if Eric decides he doesn't want you, if something as horrible as that nightmare ever came true, that's all you'll have to hang on to besides the baby."

Eyes puffy, nose red, she spent the next half hour alternately reprimanding herself and applying enough makeup to disguise the fitful sleep that had left her more tired than rested.

She got dressed in her best suit—a nicely tailored navy jacket and skirt just below the knees, complemented by a white silk blouse buttoned all the way up and Mama's cameo brooch anchored at the top. After doing her hair into a French twist and slipping into dark dress pumps, she surveyed her image from top to bottom in the full-length mirror anchored on the bathroom door.

Perfect. Almost. Something was missing. Earrings.

Without warning, she experienced a flash of memory that nearly buckled her knees. Another mirror. Another face beside hers.

"A love gift...for you, yuan-pao.*"*

"Oh, Eric. They're beautiful...perfect."

"As perfect as we are together."

"No," she whispered, turning away from the mirror and the past she couldn't let herself remember. If she did she'd never get through the day. As for the earrings stashed away with the marriage license and baby things, if she wore them, she would come undone every time she touched them. Which meant she'd be a wreck since it would be impossible to keep her hands on a book, instead of her ears.

Returning to her bedroom, she went to the dresser and literally slapped her hand away from the drawer it was reaching for.

"Oh no, you don't," she scolded herself. "Get what you came here for, and get going before you mess up the makeup you just put on."

After a quick search through the small jewelry box on top of the dresser, she chanced another look in the mirror hanging over it.

The dainty gold hoops were discreet and suitable for...

"A librarian. It's an identity you can hang your hat on—not to mention your paycheck. Remember that and make this day count. Do your best and you'll do fine. For you, Whitney Smith, are a darn good librarian."

And proud of it, she reminded herself while glancing at her old watch, the one she'd rediscovered in the cutlery drawer.

It was 8:20 a.m.; she was due at nine. Oh well, better to

show up ten minutes early than two minutes late. She and Mr. Andrews had resolved their differences, but the tardy issue cut a little too close to the bone to take any chances. Not only that, work would take her mind off Eric, so the sooner she got there, the better.

And if he called while she was away?

Whitney sent up a prayer that she'd have more than a baby blanket in progress to return to when she came home. Dog tired, no doubt. But maybe that would be a blessing, too. Especially if her answering machine wasn't blinking.

She grabbed her purse, along with a sack containing a can of soda and soda crackers in case she became queasy. Fortunately, her stomach felt fine this morning.

A step out of her ground-floor apartment and her stomach bottomed out.

A car was parked in the slot next to hers. It wasn't Carl's Camaro which had a compulsive tendency to peel in and out even faster than he talked. And the man emerging wasn't an irritating neighbor coming home after a night on the prowl.

His gaze locked with hers. He said not a word.

Whitney dropped her purse, the sack, and hugged herself, her baby, as this man, gaunt yet never more beautiful, slowly, then more quickly, then quicker still, came to her, until his hands were on her, cupping her face, stroking her arms, gathering her to him.

In silence his lips descended as her own parted to breathe his name.

"Eric."

HE COULDN'T get enough of her mouth, the taste of her, the scent, the feel of her in his arms. All assuring him that Whitney, his Whitney, his soul mate and true companion was alive. And for that, he could forgive her anything, no matter what her answers might be to the questions that could wait.

"It's you, it's really you," he said raggedly between hungry, eating kisses that never stopped as he moved them back into her apartment. Booting the door shut, he claimed this moment he'd lost hope of ever claiming....

Only in his fantasies, Whitney had come running to him, wasn't rooted in place, her face immobilized by shock. And the kisses he'd showered on her had been ravenously returned, not given back with hesitant reserve.

And in his fantasies, she'd worn a long, cool dress made of muslin; her hair the way he loved it, flowing wild and free.

The pins had to go. He had to get his hands in it, pushed through his fingers and wrapped around his wrists.

"Eric." She caught at his hands. "Eric, what are you doing?"

"Not half of what I'm aching to do," he assured her while pulling loose the blouse from her skirt to needfully palm a breast. Not close enough. He pressed his cheek to her chest, listened to her heart beat.

"I gave you up for dead," he said. "My mind just went wild and all I could imagine was that your friend who died young was really you and when we met you were making the most of what time you had left.'' He gripped her closer to him and she cupped his head, still hesitantly it seemed.

"You imagined right, Eric.''

Just like that, his world crumbled again. "Oh, God,'' he groaned. "Oh, God. Why didn't you tell me? All this time we lost together, gone. But I'm here now, *yuan-pao*. I'm here and I won't leave you.''

"If anyone leaves, Eric,'' she whispered shakily, "it'll be you. I found out I'm going to live but like I said in my message, I'm not the same person you thought me to be.''

The tears he'd been fighting abruptly receded.

After months of a fruitless search, getting her message late Saturday in Equador, searching her out with nothing to go on but a phone number, then jaunting from plane to plane to get here, Whitney wasn't welcoming him with open arms, she was offering him his walking papers.

Maybe in some twisted way, she thought she was being kind. He'd give her the benefit of the doubt, and let her know where he stood on such nonsense as she'd suggested.

He straightened, and his eyes met hers. Clear and to the point. "You let me be the judge of that. By no means did I come here to assure myself of your wellness just so I could say 'hi, bye' and leave without my wife.''

Her light stroke of his neck, which he needed so much, veered away to clutch the schoolmarm brooch at her throat. It was her left hand. Ringless, of course. He had her wedding ring in his pocket. His fingers itched to shove it immediately back on, but given the way this reunion was turning out, he'd have to bide his time—long enough to kiss her more senseless than he apparently had, soften her up with some wine and roses, then reclaim those nuptial rights that belonged to him solely.

"I don't know how to say this, Eric, so I'll just say it.

The woman you married, she doesn't exist. If you'd met me under any other circumstances, chances are slim to none that we ever would have had a date. Much less an affair, and all the craziness that went along with it.''

Garbage and more garbage, that's all she was spouting from her mouth! Lipstick smeared, her hair all mussed, she existed all right, and that existence belonged with him.

"Crazy?" he repeated. "If loving you at first sight and marrying the woman of my dreams is crazy, then I'm a certifiable lunatic. I want to be with you, laugh and cry and sleep with you. If you really think that's so crazy, then one of us is delusional and belongs in the nearest padded cell. Say it's me and I'll call for a reservation.''

Her eyes welled up. The strained set of her mouth softened. Just as he was certain his coup de grace had struck home, the phone rang.

Whitney turned to get it.

"You aren't actually going to answer that, are you?''

"I'm sorry, I have to," she said, suddenly running for the phone and glancing at her watch. "Oh no, it's almost 9:30. It's probably—''

In disbelief Eric watched her snatch up the receiver.

"Hello? Mr. Andrews? Mr. Andrews, an emergency came up and…yes, yes I'm okay…. Yes, I know the reading's scheduled in half an hour…. Of course I'll be there. I'm on my way.''

Whitney slammed down the phone and glanced frantically around the room, her eyes lighting on him with each pass, as if seeing a ghost from her past and not knowing what to do with him.

It hurt to have her look at him in such a way, so he did some glancing around himself.

For the first time, Eric took note of his surroundings. An afghan and doilies were on the serviceable furniture. Needlepoint and craft fair decorations on the wall. Heaps of books, some kind of knitting project, even a crystal candy dish with peppermints on a Duncan Phyfe coffee table.

Put it all together and the room seemed to scream, "Nester."

Hmmm.

"My purse, where's my purse?"

"Probably on the sidewalk where you dropped it."

She raked a hand through her hair. "Oh no, I don't have time to fix it. It's a mess, isn't it?"

"Looks gorgeous," he pronounced, pleased with the mess he'd made of it. Her lipstick and blouse were in similar disarray. He liked that even better than her hair.

What better way for her to nearly rush past him in her urgency to leave. "Work. I have to get to the library. I'm late, so late, and Mr. Andrews said the kids are already coming in and—"

Eric gripped her arm. "You're a librarian?"

"Head librarian of the children's section," she explained, her eyes darting uncertainly from him to the door.

So, her involvement with the book biz wasn't exactly what she'd dressed it up to be. Ah well, variation on a theme. As he anticipated any other revelations would be...

Interesting. Especially that knitting project on the coffee table. He'd like to get a closer look at just what her talented hands were working on.

And how talented they were when her attention was more on him than the goddamn purse she was in such a hurry to get at that she broke away to open the door and swoop it up from the sidewalk. Along with the bag she stuffed in it, just like those letters she used to conceal.

"I have to go." Her tone was insistent yet plaintive.

She wanted his understanding on this?

"I don't think so," he informed her, catching up in two aggressive strides. "Not without me, anyway."

Whitney shut her eyes, unable to bear the censor in his. It was justified, she couldn't blame Eric for being upset with her. But he wasn't the only one upset. Her head was still reeling, her heart still palpitating, and what in the world was she going to do? She longed beyond longing to wrap herself around Eric, shut the door and make the world go away. But how long before reality intruded?

It already had.

Mr. Andrews was depending on her and she was depending on this job. Control, that's what she had to get, some control of herself, of the situation, do what she must to get through the day, then deal with her personal issues tonight. As for Eric, he was right. She couldn't leave him here alone, not after what she'd put him through, and not with her knitting in the living room. Once he got a gander at the baby blanket, he might get curious and poke through her drawers.

Whitney met his gaze. She felt as if a fist had landed in her middle, such was the impact.

"If I'd known you were coming, I would have welcomed you better than this. But Eric, I have obligations and responsibilities that have to be seen to. It's part of my life, part of who I am. Please try to understand."

He gave a nod, laid his palms on her shoulders. A jolt went through her at the contact and she jerked in reflex.

"What? Part of who you are doesn't want me to touch you anymore?" He sounded as hurt as he looked.

"No, it's not that. Not that at all," she hastened to assure him, determined to be as honest as possible—minus the baby—from this point on. "It's been so long and when you touch me it's so intense—"

"Well, thank God for small favors. At least that much

hasn't changed.'' He chuckled, though there wasn't much humor in it. "If you want, I'll keep my hands off you while you're working.''

"Thank you, Eric.''

"Save your thanks for later. Once we get back, we're picking up where we left off when I walked in unannounced.''

He touched her then. To tuck in the blouse that strained at her bosom and fit no better than the skirt she'd struggled to button. She'd gone from being a scarecrow to barely fitting into her clothes in six weeks, despite her bouts with the nausea. Eric, on the other hand, had dropped a good twenty pounds. Yet he'd never looked stronger, and certainly never better, to her hungry-for-him-and-only-for-him eyes.

"You're late so we'd better get going.''

His reminder nudged her back into the frantic present. She made a dive into her grab bag of a purse, and couldn't put her hands on the keys.

Eric dangled his. "Want me to drive? If we take my wheels at least that'll keep my hands off you—though I won't promise to do the same with my mouth if we luck out and hit a stoplight.''

He was doing it to her already. Making her smile when she wanted to curl up in a ball of shot nerves and frustration to weep.

A glance from her dependable Ford Escort to his rented BMW made up her mind. Not only was she too embarrassed to point out her own mode of transportation, she didn't trust the sudden wild impulse to drive straight to the airport for the first flight out to somewhere, anywhere, just to get away from reality, rather than the library where Mr. Andrews and a bunch of rambunctious children were waiting.

What presence of mind she'd had to lock her apartment was gone by the time they arrived. Eric, wearing a most satisfied expression as he opened her door; she, struggling with an impossible mental leap from an extended stoplight a few minutes before to making a composed entrance.

The small composure she'd gotten together fled the moment Mr. Andrews urgently waved her to the front desk.

"The kids are going nuts in there while most of the moms are taking a break in the paperback section. Not only that, the director wanted to welcome you back personally and he's cooling his heels in my office. You deal with the kids and I'll deal with him until..."

His eyes darted from her to Eric, standing so close behind her she could feel his body heat. Suddenly, Mr. Andrews looked at her funny. He seemed to be scrutinizing her hair, her face—especially around her mouth.

"I hope you don't mind, but I brought a guest with me," she ad-libbed while fighting the urge to wipe away what evidence might be smeared around her lips.

"Uh, of course I don't mind. Everyone's welcome at our library." Mr. Andrews appeared to be doing some ad-libbing himself. It was all so awkward, Whitney wanted to cringe.

Then cringe she did as Eric moved closer, proffered a gentleman's grip to her boss, and introduced himself. "Eric Townsend. Whitney's husband, and the reason for her delay."

Mr. Andrews shook hands with the gusto of a dead fish. Whitney gave him credit for that much, considering he appeared so stunned that smelling salts seemed more in order than her hastily improvised, "Now that we've got the introductions taken care of, I'd better be off to see to the children."

CHAPTER THIRTY-TWO

THIS WAS USUALLY her favorite part of her job, where she always shined, enticing them with illustrations and props while playing the actress who could assume the characters' voices in the tales she was reading out loud.

Not today. She was still so shaken by Eric's sudden reemergence into her life, shaken from his touch, his kisses. Then disaster heaped upon disaster on this, her first day back at work, no wonder her stomach churned and her voice trembled.

So did her hands. She held the book no better than she did the children's attention. From the back of the semicircle he'd helped get formed around her, Eric was watching, listening—unlike the restless audience who'd begun to fidget and make noises they thought to be more entertaining than her.

About halfway through, he snapped his fingers at the little rowdy boy beside him and commanded them all to "Hush."

His voice of authority ensured their silence for the remainder of the reading. It also increased her painful awareness that she was making a fool of herself in front of him. It was humiliating. Nerve-racking. She couldn't wait for the once-upon-a-time favorite part of her job to be over.

And once it was, her lackluster performance received an honest evaluation from the kids who were discerning enough to mention, "Gee Ms. Smith, you didn't do too good today."

Whitney was relieved when Eric removed himself from hearing range, perhaps embarrassed for her, and trying to spare the tattered remains of her pride.

Though she was glad to see them go, it stung to see the children in such a hurry to leave—except for a little girl with big doe eyes. She tugged at Whitney's skirt and up flashed a toothless grin.

"Hi, my name's Mary and I don't care what the other kids said, I liked your story. Could you read me another one?"

"I'd love to." It's all she could say to a little girl named Mary whose head had bowed in dejection, as she waited for Whitney's response.

She read two books to Mary whose mother had joined them for the second. They were avid listeners and she did much, much better for them than she had for the group. When they thanked her, Whitney knew it was really she who owed them the thanks.

"I hope you come back, Mary. I'll be doing another group next week."

"Can't wait!" she chirped. "I just love to get read to."

"Why don't you check out some books? I'm sure your mother would be glad to read them to you."

Mary's animated face sombered, and she shook her head. Her mother squeezed her hand and said, "That's okay, Mary. I'm taking those lessons and we'll be reading together soon."

She couldn't read, Whitney realized, and wished she hadn't put Mary's mother in such an awkward position. Adult illiteracy was a very real problem and how terrible it had to be. Even a menu or page of instructions was a reminder to those who couldn't read that they were like paraplegics without a wheelchair in a world that depended on the written word to communicate.

The only greater communicator was touch. Whitney playfully pulled one of Mary's braids and invited, "Any time you'd like a story read to you, come see me and bring your mother along. Just the three of us can have more fun without all the noise the other kids were making today. You were a very good listener, Mary. And I know you're going to be a great reader some day." She sent an encouraging smile to the other woman. "Just like your mom."

Whitney was sorry to see them go. They had given her back some of the self-esteem she had lost while Eric bore witness to her failure.

"That was a nice gesture," he said from behind her. "What you did was admirable. Reminds me of another time you made someone else's day."

She didn't want to turn and face him. She didn't want to know how much of the conversation he'd overheard. She didn't want to ask him what other time he was referring to since the present was difficult enough without dredging up the past. And she certainly didn't want some token bit of admiration for a small good deed that wasn't exactly on a par with saving lives. Though she was sure he meant well, the most caring thing Eric could do would be to leave her alone while she gathered her bearings so she could deal with the higher-ups who were waiting.

"Just doing my job," she told him and busied herself with the chore of picking up the picture books the kids had left scattered all around.

"Here, I'll help."

When he reached for the books she was about to stack, she said more tersely than she meant to, "Really, Eric, I can do this myself."

"I'm sure you can," he said with such calm it made her realize how close she was to shrill.

More than ever she needed his support, a hug, a massage

to loosen the taut muscles bunched tighter than a fist in her neck. But this was not the place, nor was it the time. Even if it had been, she doubted the ability to simply ask. And why? Pride.

Stupid pride that decreed this was her turf and a giant amongst men was diminishing her stature by his kingly presence in her realm.

As if his powers extended to divining her petty thoughts, he caught her hand en route to a book she was trying to grab before he could, and brought it to his lips for a soft kiss.

"I know you're under a lot of pressure and you don't need me around to make it worse. But Whitney, it's taking all I've got to keep my hands off you and not make demands of your time. Hard as it is, I'll bide mine and stay out of your way. That's the best I can do because I just can't leave and have you out of my sight when you're the best thing I've seen in months." Then he scoffed, "Months? It seems like eternity."

His hungry eyes said it all. All the pain, all the ache, all the need she was no longer sure she could ease.

But oh, how she wanted to, wanted to be everything and more he could ever need.

"Funny thing about thinking you're going to die," she mused. "It gives a person wings. Reality has a way of clipping those wings and keeping our feet glued to the earth—"

"Not mine."

"No," she agreed before admitting, "And a part of me is envious of that."

"No need to be." He squeezed her hand, then felled the pile of books with a quick swipe, as if he could erase their surroundings just as easily, and pulled her up with him.

"Let's go," he urged. "You and me, Whitney, the way

it used to be. The way it's meant to be. We'll get in the car and go wherever the road leads us while we talk about everything and nothing. And we won't stop until we run out of words or gas or pack it in to cuddle up in a hotel, whichever comes first. I don't give a damn, all I want is you. Please, *yuan-pao,* don't give a damn either about anything, but putting us back together again and letting us heal.''

He was reaching out as far as he could stretch. She strained to meet his grip. Where would they run? she wondered. Neverneverland, nirvana, wherever the wind took them, wild and free—until Eric got summoned to his next potential disaster.

That was his job. She had a job, too. And a boss, who was tapping her on the shoulder, bringing her back to reality.

Whitney forced herself to turn around.

Mr. Andrews. Not smiling, but making a valiant effort to be cordial as he explained the director had left for a meeting but had invited them all to lunch.

The polite summons included Eric.

''I appreciate the offer, Mr. Andrews, but business is better conducted without outside company,'' he declined.

Mr. Andrews looked relieved, and Eric bent down to restack the books he had toppled over.

''Outside company, are you kidding?'' Whitney said impulsively. ''After all, what's a library without the people who write the books? Since Eric's got one on our shelves—checked out when I looked last Friday—I think he more than qualifies to join us for lunch.''

''We've got your book? Fiction or nonfiction?'' Mr. Andrews said, his voice rising with amazement.

''Non-fiction,'' Eric answered, then was lost in thought for a moment as he studied Whitney. So what was he going to do? Try to upset her neat, orderly world more than he already had, and hope she got canned before the week was out? Have her come back to him, full of resentment and anger for his calculated measures and greed?

A hollow victory, no thanks. He intended to win, and his eyes were on the prize—Whitney. All of her. Freely given, not taken.

If he had to make a small sacrifice now for the larger gain, then so be it. He'd not only go to the damn lunch he had no appetite for, but he'd do his best to impress those whom Whitney wished to impress.

Standing, he gave Whitney's immediate superior a self-effacing smile. "My work's important to me—as Whitney's is to her—and it really does please me that you'd have a copy of my text in such a fine facility." He gestured to the surroundings that were vast enough and had an undeniable charm but could use a face-lift. "I've been in libraries throughout the world and I have to say this one is…" *Flatter him shamelessly, even if it's a lie.* "…exceptional."

Whatever vanity this Mr. Andrews had was clearly invested in the library he oversaw. The man practically preened.

"It is, isn't it?" he replied with the sort of sigh a Romeo had on reserve for his Juliet.

Ah well, beauty was ever in the eye of the beholder. Though more accolades would obviously be welcome, he'd never been much of a suck up and didn't want to lay it on too thick. Better to spend his energy on the reason for his efforts.

Draping an arm around Whitney, Eric asserted what he did know to be undeniably true. "But just as a room without books is like a body without soul, a room filled with books doesn't count for much without the souls who love them. I'm sure you consider yourself fortunate to have Whitney bring out the best this library has to offer.''

''Of course, I just told her so myself the other day.'' An approving smile at Whitney, and Mr. Andrews turned the conversation back to the last place Eric wanted it. On him. ''Now about this book of yours. What's the title?''

''Nothing you're likely to recognize,'' he replied frankly. ''It's a scientific text called *Volcanology: A Retrospective Analysis of—*''

''*Earth and Man*! No wonder your name sounded familiar. I'm the one who checked that book out! Not the sort of thing I usually read, but I caught a documentary on the Discovery Channel about volcanos and it was just so interesting, I had to find out more. The book was mentioned because one of those scientists on the show had...say! It was you they were interviewing. Well, I'll be darned.'' He gripped Eric's hand and pumped it enthusiastically. ''Dr. Townsend, it's a privilege to meet you.''

Oh jeez, wouldn't you know it, one of the few people in existence who thought being on PBS made a person deserving of celebrity treatment had to be Whitney's boss. Such fawning made him uncomfortable—how Adam continually dealt with it, he had no idea—but for Whitney's sake, he'd grin and bear it.

''Please, call me Eric.''

''And that's Tom, to you.''

Though making points with the boss—and then the boss's boss, who insisted Eric call him Al—was on a par with playing the devil's advocate, he remained on his best behavior at the seafood restaurant and even tossed in a few entertaining anecdotes when pressed to do so by the company he didn't want to be with.

No, he did not want to be here, much less assume the demeanor of a gracious host who kept the conversation running to compensate for Whitney's silence. She was too subdued. Her brief smiles, forced. And when he grasped her hand beneath the table to lend some support, she pulled away.

"So tell me, how did the two of you meet?" Al wanted to know.

Eric stayed quiet, putting the ball in her court.

"We met on a plane. And, well, one thing sort of led to another and..." Trailing off, she fumbled the ball he'd so hoped she would pick up and run with.

"Oh, come on," he interjected, daring her to dispute him. "It was one of those whirlwind romances that suck the air out of your lungs and the oxygen from your brain." A glance at Whitney for a corroborative nod netted him no more than her fork's pick at the plate she'd hardly touched. It made him want to shake her, demand she announce to the table—hell, the whole room—that what they had was so much more than any whirlwind romance could ever be. With a nudge to her ribs, he broke the subtle tension by quipping, "Like you read about."

Big ha-ha's from across the table. Whitney laughed along. Belatedly.

"If you'll excuse me..." She took her purse and went in the direction of a mermaid hanging over a rest room door.

Eric watched her go, watched the glances of other men follow in her wake. He knew they saw what he did. The flow of her walk, the natural sway of her hips, an unstudied poise in the way she carried herself. Alluring and untouchable.

But did anyone besides him notice her fragility? Did they see her spine was so stiff it was ready to snap? Did they perceive that beneath the composure was a proud woman who had escaped before she crumbled in public?

Of course no one else noticed. They didn't know her like he did.

Granted, he still had a lot to learn about Whitney Smith-Townsend. And starting today, learn he would.

CHAPTER THIRTY-THREE

BY WORKDAY'S END, Whitney felt like a punching bag with the stuffing knocked out of it. Listening to Eric dazzle Mr. Andrews and Mr. Richards—of course that was Tom and Al to him—had been an acerbic reminder of their disparate stations in life. The more he shined, the duller she'd felt during that gruelling lunch. Of course it was she who had initially wanted Eric there and it wasn't his fault he was fascinating and she wasn't.

But still, she blamed him for the final blow she'd been dealt a few minutes ago in Mr. Andrews' office.

"What did he want?" Eric asked as he kept pace with her brisk stride out of the building. "To give alms to the goddess who worked her tail off all day, and throw in a raise while he was at it?"

"Not exactly." Her crisp response belied the urge to purge herself with a cleansing, primal scream.

Was Mr. Andrews pleased with the strides she'd made today? She supposed so since he'd tossed her a complimentary crumb before trying to get the inside scoop on how a simple librarian—albeit one he valued—had managed to snag someone of Eric's ilk. Not that he'd actually come out and said it, but that's how it came across.

As Eric opened the car door for her, he seemed sincerely interested in knowing, "So, what did he want?"

Whitney was tempted to give her raving hormones their due by turning into a drama queen who bowed at Eric's feet, her arms going up and down as if he were some great sahib while she chanted, "I am not worthy...I am not worthy...."

Instead, she smiled sweet as saccharine and replied, "Your autograph."

Eric stopped in midlaugh. The request was ludicrous but Whitney's brittle rejoinder wasn't. Neither was her abrupt shut of the door that nearly caught his fingers.

Shit and be damned. He'd been Prince Charming all friggin' day and what was he getting for his efforts? Grief and more grief. The loving reunion he'd envisioned was turning out to be anything but that.

He suddenly wanted to hit something. The trunk of the car got the honors before he threw in his briefcase and laptop, which were suffering from an extreme case of neglect. He hadn't even made a dent, despite all the hours he'd stayed out of Whitney's way as promised. Out of her way but he'd never let her out of his sight and how could he possibly work when all he could think about was getting her alone?

So much for his intentions to kiss her and kiss her some more before broaching the questions he deserved to have answered once he had her all to himself. He could taste the dust his plans were biting as he slid behind the wheel.

What had he done wrong? What could he say to make everything right again? The silent woman staring out the opposite window didn't give him a clue.

"I'm sorry." For what, he didn't know.

"There's nothing to be sorry for," she whispered.

Well that sure told him a lot. To get beyond this impasse, he had to get her talking.

"If there's nothing to be sorry for, why the distance?" When she shrugged, he cranked the engine and took a sharp turn out of the parking lot. Not overly mature but it got some anger out of his system and into the open where their feelings belonged. Laying his own bare, he charged, "So much for Southern hospitality. The Arctic has to be warmer than the cold shoulder you've turned to me. All I want to know is, why? Why wouldn't you hold my hand at lunch? Why won't you look at me instead of staring out that damn window? Why the silent treatment when I need you to talk to me? Why?"

She looked at him then with moist, limpid eyes. That's all it took to turn him from a raging bull into a defeated matador.

"I made a promise to myself, Eric, to be as honest with you as I can possibly be. And quite honestly, I'm too upset to talk just yet. It's been a really hard day and I'm beat."

"I understand." Patience, he told himself, when she returned to gazing out the window. Maybe some wine would help loosen her tongue—though Lord knew he could use something stronger after one bitch of a day and an evening that wasn't boding well, either.

How to turn it around? How to get her easy in the skin he ached to slide into? That's what they needed to dissolve the barriers between them, those intimate, soulful connections forged in the bedchamber, where lovemaking consisted of so much more than seduction's art.

Even so, he couldn't deny that seduction was very much on his mind. Whitney had probably tossed her pills. The letter he'd read, which he shouldn't have but did, now made perfect sense. No wonder she'd taken the extra precaution, thinking she was dying.

Such a cross to bear and she hadn't shared it with him. That hurt. But they'd talk about all that later, maybe over the sumptuous dinner he'd prepare while she took a long, hot bath he would gladly draw for her as well.

As if it were a sign from heaven giving its blessing to his plan of action, a Bruno's supermarket appeared.

Pulling in, he announced, "I'm making dinner and if you've got any requests, now's the time to say so. Otherwise, you get whatever I'm in the mood to cook up."

She smiled at him. But to the eyes that couldn't get enough of her, she didn't look happy. Not the way she had when she'd read to that little girl. Or those children in Montserrat.

"Surprise me, but don't make it too spicy."

If memory served, and he did have an excellent memory, Whitney loved spicy foods. The hotter, the better. Oh well, if she was leaning toward bland these days he wouldn't bother picking up the cayenne pepper.

"You've got it." Then hopefully he asked, "Want to come in with me and help me surprise you?"

She shook her head. "No thanks. If it's all the same to you, I could use a few minutes alone to sort my thoughts."

Please do and once you've got them sorted, how about letting me in on what they are, he thought. He'd even settle for the skinny if that was all she could dish since that was more than he was getting so far.

"No problem. You think, I'll shop."

"AND HERE WE HAVE napa cabbage, straw mushrooms, bean sprouts, chicken breasts, a lemon, saffron, sesame seeds..." Several other items landed on the counter, followed by a bottle of bubbly, as in lavender for the bath, which he placed in her hands.

"Thank you, Eric. What did I do to deserve this?"

"The same thing you did to deserve these." A paper bag folded at the top that didn't appear to have much in it opened and out came a bouquet of bright colors.

The flowers weren't wild orchids but the scent was just as sweet and the tiger lilies among the chrysanthemums had the same impact of wild blooms surrounding her in a tropical paradise where a masked man awaited.

She inhaled deeply, allowing herself to remember that magical moment with a dark stranger on her wedding night.

The memory was too potent, too dangerous, making her yearn for a dream that had been just that.

"I'll put them in water." A brief kiss to his cheek, that's all, since she didn't dare risk more. "Oh good, it's got one of those packets that make the flowers last longer."

As she spilled the contents into a vase filled with water, Eric plucked a tiger lily from its stalk and tucked the vibrant orange blossom behind one ear.

"Some things are worth preserving, you know." He pinged a dainty gold hoop. "Like us."

Us. Two little letters that had once defined them. But she had to remember that yesterday was yesterday, today was just that, and as for tomorrow, there were no guarantees. *Us* was one big question mark she wanted to keep that way as long as she could since the answer might obliterate those small hopes she struggled to hold at bay.

No, she couldn't let herself hope too much. Still, what harm could come from her sheer delight in the flowers, from reveling in his searing yet light touch, or anticipating the luxury of a lavender-scented bath filled with bubbles?

"I think I'll take my bath now."

"You've worked hard today and you deserve it." He gave her a wink, followed by a swat to her retreating behind. "Just don't take too long or I'm liable to join you."

Kidding and yet not, she retorted, "In that case, I'll be quick about it."

"Suit yourself but keep in mind I'm not bluffing if Calgon takes you away."

Her lilting laughter, music to his ears. It soothed the soul of the savage beast who withdrew one of the last items remaining in the grocery bags. With the flourish of a chef in his element he decreed, "And for dessert..."

Condoms.

CHAPTER THIRTY-FOUR

WHEN WHITNEY emerged from the bathroom in a terry cloth robe, the first thing she noticed was the white negligee Eric had given her in Saint Croix, laid out on her bed.

Alarm bells sounded. Eric had been in her closet. What gave him the idea it was okay to go through her things? He had no right to do that—especially if it included the chest of drawers where her secret treasures were stashed.

Her relaxing bath and its calming effects forgotten, she fought a wave of panic and made a beeline for the dresser. After a quick investigation, she breathed a sigh of relief.

No signs of tampering, but she had to find a better hiding place. Only, where? Certainly not her closet. Under her bed was a possibility, but that's where she kept her—

Luggage! Perfect.

And then she noticed. Another suitcase. Parked on the floor, close to the foot of her bed.

A light tap sounded. Before she could tell him not to come in, he did.

"Dinner's ready." His gaze took her in from towel-turbaned hair to bare toes curling into the carpet then traveled back up to linger on the terry cloth she cinched tighter at her waist. "When you are, that is."

What was this? A not-so-subtle hint that he expected her to change into the lingerie he had selected? What Eric apparently thought to be a familiar act of intimacy felt more like an invasion of privacy.

Just as she was about to firmly request that he remove

his luggage and himself while he was at it, he gave her that smile that might charm the pants off a nun but not her—not tonight, no way, no how—and left.

She suddenly wished for a lock on her door.

Quickly, before he decided to breeze back in and take more liberties than he already had, Whitney hid the evidence, along with their marriage license. She didn't need him wagging it in her face as proof of his "husbandly rights" when she refused to let him share her bed.

After shoving her suitcase back under the dust ruffle, she gave a little kick to his own luggage.

"It's not that easy, Eric," she quietly fumed. "You can't just waltz your way back into my life and act as if nothing has changed. It has. A lot's changed, not the least of which is me."

Perhaps he needed her to prove it. Actions spoke louder than words and so far her words of caution had fallen on deaf ears. All the more reason to tumble the pearl earrings into her jewelry box despite the urge to try them on and see how he would react. And perhaps she'd do just that if he was still around in a week.

Refusing the temptress who longed to tease him with the peek of flesh through a gossamer gown, Whitney returned the negligee back to her closet—only to gasp. "No! No, Eric, you can't do this to me."

But he already had, so what was she going to do about it? Confront him? Put her wedding dress back in his luggage? She didn't trust herself to touch the princess bride dress she sorely wanted to caress and slip on, despite knowing it would no longer fit.

Deciding the best she could do was to say nothing, she removed temptation from sight by hanging it at the back. Next, she selected a demure Sunday-go-to-meeting dress and immediately put it back.

Too frumpy. She'd compromise and get comfortable in what she would wear if Eric weren't here.

Jeans and a short-sleeved turtleneck.

A cursory blow-dry of her hair, shake it out, no makeup.

Well, a swipe of lipstick and some mascara wouldn't hurt.

Done.

No sooner did she emerge than Whitney wished she'd gone to greater lengths with her what-you-see-is-what-you-get appearance.

The dining table looked better than she did. So did the elaborate concoctions set out on the white linen, replete with her mother's good china and gold candelabra. The white taper candles she'd kept in them for show were lit. The silverware reserved for holidays was laid out in full service.

And the crystal? Water goblets filled with sparkling liquid, lemon slices floating on top. The yet-to-be-used wineglasses that had come with the set, on ready for the chilled bottle wrapped in a white dish towel. Beside it resided a small bowl filled with fruit.

Eric emerged from a darkened corner, where he'd no doubt observed her unawares.

"You look lovely as always."

"Thank you," she said, self-consciously. A note of disappointment had flavored his compliment. Maybe a hint of disapproval, too, but ever the gentleman he held out the chair at the head of her mother's mahogany table—

And lifted her hair to drop a kiss on her neck. Soft, brief, yet starkly sensual and no doubt meant to tantalize the senses responsible for the prickle that raced from her nape to the bead of her nipples.

"Mmm. You smell good enough to eat." He took a small nibble of her lobe, lightly raked his teeth down to tug at a dangling gold hoop. The prickles turned to arcing tingles of such heady delight that she frantically pulled away before he could do more.

Silence. Heavy and thick. She broke it by announcing, "I'm thirsty," then went for the water she nearly knocked over before gripping the glass with both hands to hold it steady.

The gulping in her throat seemed to reverberate through the room. When Eric didn't move from behind her or say another word, she gestured to the elaborate spread and chattered, "This all looks so wonderful. Can't wait to get started. I'm hungry."

"You're nervous." He left his post and started to take the seat beside her. Pausing, he asked, "Would you rather me move to the other end?"

Actually, she did. Her stomach was already so twisted up from his proximity that staying within his reach would make eating next to impossible.

"No," she made herself say. "That's not necessary."

"Good. I asked to be polite but I'm afraid my politeness doesn't extend beyond the asking since I prefer to sit next to my wife." His warm regard had an edge of challenge to it.

Heart in throat, Whitney shook her head. "I'm not your wife, Eric. The woman you married was someone I created as I went along. She's an illusion, a mirage, a fictional Scarlett wanna-be who flitted along from day to day. I don't flit, and I don't flirt with strange men on planes. You have to realize that wasn't me and we're no more married than two actors playing that part in a movie."

He snorted. "From what I'm hearing, you sound more like a director to me. One who's telling me it's *The End* and I don't need to stick around for the final credits while you edit me out of your life.'' With a dismissive wave, he brushed her claims aside and asserted his own.

"Sorry—actually, I'm not sorry at all—but I don't buy it and I'm not leaving. You agreed to live together as husband and wife for three months and I'm holding you to it. Since the ink was barely dry on our license when you ran away—something we need to discuss and most definitely we will—that gives me two months, one week and a day to live with you.'' He reached for the wine with a polished finesse that jarred with his rip of the foil and stab of the corkscrew into the cork he ratcheted more than screwed.

He poured a sample's worth into her glass and smoothly continued, ''I know you're accustomed to better but it's the best I could do at the store. Give it a try and indulge me in pretending it's some fine stock that suits the mood of an equally fine evening ahead.''

Whitney stared longingly at the wine. A taster's sip wouldn't hurt the baby but the glass to follow might loosen her inhibitions enough for her to make a big mistake.

"I don't drink, Eric.''

"Since when?''

Since she'd found out she was pregnant, that's when. "Before we met I was pretty much a teetotaler. In retrospect I realize I should have stayed that way.''

Eric filled his own glass to the brim. Saluted her with the toast, ''Here's to life. And living it as it's meant to be lived. Fully, passionately, sinking your teeth into it and shaking it for all it's worth.'' He looked as if he wanted to shake her and do some serious nibbling while he was at it.

In lieu of the wine which she wanted and wanted really badly, Whitney lifted her glass of water and feebly echoed, ''Hear, hear.''

A generic "cheers'' would have sounded less hollow.

Hollow, that's how she felt as Eric took a healthy sip of

his wine and did a much better job than she at pretending that this time together was the stuff great memories were made of.

"I noticed you crochet," he mentioned while she spooned up a serving from a steaming bowl of rice.

Splat went the rice onto her plate. *Thunk* went the spoon to the floor. Picking it up, she struggled to make light of his remark and her gaffe. "I'm such a klutz, it'll be a miracle if I finish that baby blanket before Wanda's shower."

"Wanda," he repeated. "She must be a good friend to warrant such a thoughtful gift."

"A very good friend."

"Who's apparently in better health than the other one."

"What other one?"

"You know." He nodded. At her. "The one you told me about who turned out to be you, before you turned out to be perfectly fine. Which you weren't when you left, so please enlighten me on what exactly transpired from then to now."

The small bite she had taken lodged in her throat.

She had to do her best to dress up the truth. Dress up the truth, that sounded a lot better than praying he would swallow her lie.

"When I left, I felt so sick that I was certain the leukemia—what I'd been diagnosed with—had won. I came home and put off going to the doctor because I...well, I just didn't want to be put in the hospital."

He caught her hand, gripped it. "You were so alone. I can't stand to think of you being so alone like that."

Alone and in the dark, no will to live without you, Eric. Shunning the memory of that horrible, horrible time, she glossed over the truth. "As you can see, I got through it. But I should have gone to the doctor sooner since it turned out that I only had some strange kind of flu, which kicked the anemia I should have been diagnosed with back in. So there you have it," she concluded neatly. "Exactly what transpired from then to now."

"Amazing. How you could be so sick and bounce back so quickly is just amazing to me." He didn't look as if he quite believed it possible.

"Well, I did have a little time to bounce back."

"A little time?" He removed his hand. "How little? Or, should I say, how much time since you found out the good news?"

Another tweak of the truth beckoned. Eric wouldn't know if she fudged. But she would. And she had sworn that, except for the baby, she would be totally honest with him, no matter the expense to herself.

Whitney took a deep breath. "Six weeks."

A muscle ticked in his cheek. "Six weeks, that puts it right about Christmas. Nice present."

"Best one I ever got."

He cut her with a glance that could've shaved ice. "Being the season of good will toward men, did it possibly occur to you to send some my way? Did it even cross your mind that I might be half out of my mind, so worried and torn up that I couldn't work, couldn't even think beyond the sheer terror of imagining the worst?" His voice dropped to a seething whisper, more piercing than a roar. "Did it?"

Whitney wanted to shut her eyes, she could scarce bear the censor in his. Worse than that, the pain. But she made herself look through the windows of the soul she had bruised.

"Yes, Eric," she answered him. "It did occur to me to call you." Every day, every night, every minute she pounded the pavement and told herself to be strong, not give in to the weakness of her need for him and go crawling back with her hand out.

"Then why didn't you pick up the phone sooner?"

"Because…" Falling apart had made her learn the value of care for the soul. She had to be able to take care of herself so she could take care of the baby. "Because I was pretty messed up and needed to get my life back together again first."

He chewed on what appeared to be nails. Then decided, "I don't like it but I can accept that. What I can't accept is being relegated to the fringes of the life you've put back together."

The fringes of life, that was just the problem. Eric was like a circus master surrounded by excitement and flamboyant activity, thrilling to the spectacle he commandeered and shared with those around him. He had shared so much with her, but she had nothing new to bring to the table. Every adventure she'd ever had was owed to Eric. Far from the fringes, he was her life. Without him, she didn't have much of one.

She really needed to tell him that, just swallow her pride and lay it all out. But if she did, she'd give up what tiny mystique she might still possess and, unlike pride, that would be a loss she could never regain.

Whitney changed the subject.

"This is wonderful," she told him, forcing down another tasteless bite. "Where did you get the recipe?"

"From my grandmother. Just last week as a matter of fact." Significantly, he added, "I was helping her out at the restaurant when I should have been lecturing in Spain. But I canceled out since other things were taking precedence at the time. Personal things that made me so impossible to live with that when I got a call to oversee a situation in the Galapagos Islands, she shooed me out the door and said, 'Go.'"

"And did you?"

"That's where I was when I picked up my messages.

Off the coast of Equador. If it tells you anything, my colleagues were glad to get rid of me, too. The consensus seemed to be I was distracted to the point of being more a liability than an asset.'' He teased her lips with a bite from his plate and upon the shake of her head, he topped off his glass. ''Don't know where they got that idea.''

Whitney put down her fork. She couldn't pretend to enjoy dinner when this conversation was turning her stomach.

''If you're trying to make me feel guilty, there's no need. Nothing could make me feel worse than I already do, Eric. I'm very well aware of the hell I've put you through and for what it's worth, I'm sorry. So sorry.''

''Save your apologies for someone who wants them. I don't.'' He pushed his chair back and patted his lap. ''All I want is you. Come here.''

When she didn't move, he clenched his hands into fists to keep from hauling her out of her seat and onto his. Force would solve nothing but oh, was he tempted.

''Love and fear, Whitney. Love and fear. If you can't act as if you still love me, even a little, then at least tell me what you're so damn afraid of.''

To her credit she admitted, ''You.''

''Why?'' he demanded. ''Why would you be afraid of me? Never would I hurt you. I love you.''

''Eric, haven't you heard anything I've said? You can't love me because you don't even know me.''

''Then let me know you and quit pushing me away whenever I try to get close.'' Before he could stop himself, he was out of his chair and had Whitney out of hers.

''Like it or not, I am your husband and I need to hold my wife. Dinner's over, kitten. And I'm past ready to get reacquainted.'' He locked her against him. ''In bed.''

CHAPTER THIRTY-FIVE

WHITNEY STRUGGLED against him; he tightened his hold. His lips came down and she turned her head; mistake, mistake, he put his mouth to her neck.

Never had she been so frantic to escape the very thing she wanted with a fury. Such fury belonged to the wild woman inside who screamed to be free and live for the moment without a thought to the consequences her actions might bring.

That woman was trouble. She didn't care about security or keeping a job or putting the welfare of her child above her own. Her needs consisted of raging emotions she thrived on and lived to appease. Love. Longing. Lust.

"No," Whitney denied the man encouraging the mutiny of such needs. "We're not sleeping together, Eric."

He quit tonguing the runaway pulse in her jugular and gave her a little shake when she tried to break free.

"Be still and listen to me. This is where I put my foot down. Sex or no sex, we share the same bed. You can give me your back and there's nothing I can do about that, but try to shut me out of your room and I'll splinter the goddamn door."

Her heart beating in her chest like a rabbit's given chase, Whitney knew she was cornered. Eric was unmovable. She could argue until she was blue in the face, but in the end he would have his way—even if it came down to busting open the door she didn't have a lock on anyway.

At least he'd given her an out. She could turn her back

to him, even sleep in her clothes. What she couldn't do was let him touch her. Should he do that, every self-protective defense she had would tumble like dice. Such a gamble, only a fool would risk it. But how happily she would play that fool if he truly did love her—the real her, not an alter ego she couldn't accept, much less love in herself. If only he could do that, greedily would she welcome him into her arms and between her legs on the bed he was determined to share.

"All right. We share a bed," she reluctantly agreed. Then hastened to lay down the stipulations. "Only we divide it down the middle. You stay on your side and I'll stay on mine. Secondly—"

"Don't tell me. You want to put up a clothesline and drape a sheet between us to make sure that just because it happened one night in St. Croix—make that eighty-six times in assorted locations, I kept count—it won't be happening again. At least not until you're so horny you'll give me permission to tear the walls of Jericho down."

Whitney wasn't sure what stunned her more. The fact that he'd actually kept count of their sexual encounters— pretty romantic for any man who wasn't carving notches on his bedpost—or his final jab that wasn't romantic at all.

"You're being crude."

"No, I'm being honest." He cupped a breast and flicked a thumb over her nipple. Already distended and so sensitive she nearly cried out, it blossomed from a pucker to a hard peak.

He took his hand away.

"I know your body even better than you know it yourself, Mrs. Townsend. I know what buttons to hit, what turns you on and inside out. Deny it all you like, you're a sexual creature. So am I. But what I need from you isn't just sex. I need comfort, release, acceptance. I need to give all that back to you. It's the connection, what we feed back and forth through each other, that I'm after. I won't settle for less. So go ahead, draw the line in bed and I won't cross it. Trust me on that because I'm drawing a line of my own. Until you say you love me, I won't be putting the evidence of mine inside you.''

Whitney stared at him, dumbfounded. How had he turned the tables so quickly?

''Fine,'' she conceded, trying not to sound like a sore loser when, for all practical purposes, she had won. ''I'll clean the kitchen while you go on to sleep.''

''I'm not sleepy,'' he informed her. ''And I'm not about to have you doing the dishes when you look ready to drop.'' Like quicksilver he segued from tough to tender with the press of his palm to her forehead. ''You're flushed and warm. Are you sure you're all right?''

Maybe she should pretend to swoon. Then he'd pick her up and hold her and carry her to bed—without the requisite vow of love on her end. Tell him that and those walls would come tumbling down, burying her too deep to get out intact. Perhaps it would yet happen, once she was certain of Eric's love and knew he would be as thrilled about the baby as she. But until that time, she would make excuses for the vagaries pregnancy visited upon expecting mothers.

''Yes, I'm sure.'' She allowed herself a peck to his cheek. ''The day just caught up with me all of a sudden and when I get upset, I tend to overheat. Sometimes I even break out in rashes.''

Eric absorbed the small kiss, as well as the information imparted. The kiss fell short, way short, of what he wanted, but it was sweet and Whitney's little revelation was exactly what he wanted. To know all there was to know about her, every minute detail.

"Rashes, huh?" At her nod, he probed, "And what could make you so upset to bring that on?"

"Confrontations." She cringed. "I hate confrontations, which is why I'll do almost anything to avoid them."

They hadn't had many confrontations in the past but Whitney had never been shy about giving him what-for. He'd liked that about her, admired her chutzpah. But apparently she hadn't always been one to speak her mind and had reverted to a more placating nature now that she was back in her old digs.

He needed to get her out of here. Out of this restrictive, knickknacky apartment filled with furniture that had probably belonged to her mother; out of this mundane little world she had returned to. The glorious stream of life, that's where she'd flourished. That's where she belonged. With him. The problem was, how to lure her back without strong-arming her into a bath of calamine lotion?

"No more confrontations tonight," he promised, though he could still go for a good brouhaha himself. A passionate fight with equally passionate results once the dust amply settled to make up. In bed. The very bed that no longer had use for the condoms he'd bought since he'd had to one up her on the rules being set. *Duh.* What had he been thinking?

"Then we'll call it a truce," she said. "And on that note, I'll say good-night."

Another kiss to his cheek, as if he were an unthreatening big brother rather than a lover champing at the bit to claim his husbandly rights. He'd been good, he'd been nice, but this was more than he could take.

"Not so fast." Eric gripped her arm and spun her back around. Then proceeded to demonstrate he wasn't as quick to heel as she thought. Her mouth was meant for kissing and so was her neck and everything below it. But he stuck with the mouth, consumed her flavor, the smooth texture of her lips, her evasive tongue. But he got it, got as much of her as he was going to get for now, and stopped short of completely ransacking her mouth.

He had what he wanted, Whitney gasping for breath between throaty moans, her hands clutching his back, his hair.

"And on that note," he murmured, "I'll be saying goodnight." A kiss to her cheek and he went to see to the dishes.

From the corner of his eye he watched her gape in disbelief before turning on her heel with a huff. At the sound of her door shutting just shy of a slam, Eric smiled smugly.

He'd left her wanting him as much as he wanted her. Hopefully she was so frustrated that when he joined her she'd be ready to admit what he knew to be true. Whitney did love him—never mind the changes in her life, she couldn't change that—but he needed to hear it and until he did, he'd tempt her with all she was missing.

The table cleared off, dishes done, Eric strode to the bedroom door. He no sooner opened it than his high expectations took a fall.

A big fall. A rolled-up blanket divided the mattress in half. Whitney, on the far side with her back turned, lay on top of the covers. In a granny gown.

Stripping down to his underwear, a single, insistent thought pumped through his head:

Yep, he definitely had to get them out of here.

Pretending to sleep, Whitney didn't make a single move. Was he coming to bed naked as he always had in the past? She prayed not. She prayed so. And she prayed he couldn't hear the shallow pant of her breathing when she felt the give of the mattress taking his weight.

"*Yuan-pao,*" he said quietly. "Are you still awake?"

More than awake, she was buzzing like a human vibrator minus an off switch. She shut her eyes tighter.

"Guess not," he grumbled, fitting himself as close as he

could get and making her grateful for the lumpy barrier that made her feel at least a little safer from them both.

But not so safe that she could sleep. Especially not with his fingertips stroking the flannel-clad shoulder turned to him. He did it for ten minutes according to the illuminated dial of the clock next to her side of the bed. Another twenty minutes passed with his arm over the blanket and his palm riding her waist. For half an hour after that, he tossed and turned, any body contact brief and accidental.

"Screw this shit," he suddenly growled. Just as suddenly the blanket hit the floor.

A long, muscular leg came over hers, strapping her in place. His arm locked the rest of her against him and his hand took full possession of a covered breast. Neither of them were naked but she could feel the press of his erection, the heat of his body calling to hers. And if she responded, even with the moan she struggled to contain, what then? Then the flimsy shield of her gown would be gone the way of the blanket. Then he would kiss her and touch her all over. And then, he would be on her, but not in her.

Not until she said she loved him. That was the line he had drawn and Eric wouldn't back down. She knew him too well, just as he didn't know her well at all. Oh yes, he would say he loved her and believe it with all his heart. Tonight, anyway. And maybe even tomorrow. But what of next week? Next month? Next year?

He moved against her, thick and hot and full. His hand moved down and he lifted the hem of her nightgown. Slowly he pulled it up, his palm skating over the leg he bared in the process. Her heart hammered.

If she didn't do something to stop this, she would say anything, do anything to have what her body was crying for. She was desperate to have him, heart and soul, but this was too like the moment she'd been afraid to hope her life had been spared, knowing she couldn't bear to go back to death row if the chance for escape failed. Leaving Eric had nearly done her in; if he left her....

Whitney shivered, and it wasn't just from the air hitting the skin he exposed. With the gown above her knees and his leg lifted to pull it higher, it was now or never to make her move before Eric made his.

Still pretending sleep, she rolled onto her stomach and buried her whimper into the pillow.

Eric didn't try to pull her back. He uttered a foul word and got out of bed. She heard him feeling his way around in the dark and for a terrible few moments she thought he was searching for his clothes, intending to leave. Not for good, just go for a drive and hit a bar—where he'd get hit on more than likely. A good-looking man, alone at midnight according to the clock, and so frustrated that no woman could miss the sexual electricity he put out.

Other women would put out. Lonely women who would rather have a one-night stand with a sexy, charismatic man than wait another day for a Mr. Right who'd yet to show. Would Eric bow to temptation? No. But given the state he was in, tempted he would be. She didn't want another woman to tempt him, not even a little.

It was all the incentive she needed to call him back to bed. Just as she opened her mouth, the bathroom door shut. The shower went on. Straining her ears, she heard more than the spray of water. The sound came from Eric. Low, muted, but unmistakable. He wasn't singing. He was chanting her name. Abruptly, he stopped. So did the spritzing water.

When Eric emerged it was 12:18. A very relaxing shower, it seemed, since by twelve-thirty he was under the top sheet, sound asleep. This time it was he who lay on his side, his back turned to her. She made it an hour without touching him, then made the grave mistake of putting her hand to the flesh he had bared to no one but her.

He didn't wake up, but every sense she had did. He smelled wonderful and felt even better. His deep, even breathing accelerated her own and the taste of that first notch on his spine sent shivers down hers. Whitney forced herself away and by the time 3:00 a.m. rolled around, she was considering taking a shower herself.

She never took the shower. Neither did she see the hour or minute she finally fell into a fitful sleep, but before she knew it, the alarm buzzer went off. Fumbling for the snooze button, Whitney hit it and rolled over, searching for...

Something that was no longer there. No, not something. Someone. *Eric.* Her eyes snapped open but with the sleep still in them, she wondered if his return had only been a dream. Frantically, she scrambled out of bed and stumbled toward the living room.

And there was her dream come true. Eric. Sitting on the couch, reading the paper and sipping a cup of coffee. He was freshly shaven and fully dressed—if she didn't count the fact his shirt was casually tossed on and left unbuttoned.

"Want me to fix you a cup of tea or coffee?" he asked, continuing to read.

Coffee didn't smell as good as it used to and her taste buds agreed. She wasn't so sure about the tea, either.

"No, thanks."

"What about breakfast? I can cook something up while you're getting ready for work."

Until recently breakfast had consisted of soda crackers and 7-Up set out the previous night so she could settle her stomach in bed before raising her head off the pillow.

"Maybe something light. Like a piece of toast and a glass of milk. If it's no problem."

"Glad to do it," he said amiably enough but without the delight he'd always taken in her robust appetite. "How did you sleep?"

"Fine." A lie, but one he wouldn't notice as long as he kept reading that damn paper without so much as a glance at the bags he was responsible for beneath her eyes. "What about you?"

"Me?" Eric looked up. Smiled with ill-disguised glee as he took in her bedraggled appearance. Obviously well rested, he stretched, fully exposing the muscles in his chest that she had a sudden urge to smack. "Slept like a baby."

CHAPTER THIRTY-SIX

PERCHED ON the examining table while she waited for Dr. Clark, Whitney whispered to her tummy, "Ten pounds! You can't weigh much yet, so how could I put on ten pounds since our last visit? Another month like this and even my fat clothes won't fit."

How long, she wondered, before people started to speculate if she was pregnant or if she just needed to lay off the milk shakes and start downing Slim-Fast? At this rate, maybe another month before the library staff started laying bets at the water cooler. Eric, however, wouldn't be so discreet, and it was him, not gossip, she had to worry about.

This being Friday, he'd only been living with her four days. In those four days, he'd overtaken her place. Toothbrush and shaver parked in the bathroom; paperwork and graphs, computer and assorted gadgetry to track the hot spots under surveillance, set up in her living room. And then there was his phone that had started to ring at all hours, her heart on hold each time he picked up.

Sometimes she wasn't sure if her anxiety was due to the fear he would return to Equador, or that he wouldn't.

A brisk tap and Dr. Clark entered the room, chart in hand.

"Ten pounds," he clucked, wagging his finger at her. "Either you're eating for three or those Milky Way binges have to go. Then again, we might need to keep an eye out for fluid retention." He gave her a wink. "Other than that, how's my favorite mama-to-be doing?"

"Never better, Dr. Clark."

"You sure about that?" He scrutinized her for a moment before observing, "You've got a pretty glow about you, Whitney, but those circles under your eyes don't do you justice. So what's up? Are you working too hard again or do you have some personal concerns infringing on your proper rest?"

No use denying it, not with Dr. Clark anyway, so she gave it up. "Both. Despite appearances to the contrary, the library's eating my lunch. On the home front, I'm even more stressed. I have a new roommate. Eric's back."

"You don't sound too happy about that. Is it because he didn't turn cartwheels when he found out he's going to be a daddy?"

"He doesn't know. And until I'm certain he'll turn those cartwheels, he won't."

"You're showing early," Dr. Clark stated, as if that needed any pointing out. "If this Eric of yours stays around much longer, he won't need any formal announcements. Seeing that he's the responsible sort, or so you said before, my guess is that even if he's not strutting around like a peacock, he'll be fairly upset about you keeping such a secret from him."

Looking away from the good doctor who made an equally good shrink, she studied a wall poster that tracked the growth of an embryo to birth. At fourteen weeks, the baby had a ways to go to reach the cute and cuddly stage, but already little feet and hands and eyes had formed. So had its heart. Today was the day she would hear it beat.

"Take the chance, Whitney," Dr. Clark urged. "Take the chance and tell him. Could be he'll surprise you and want to go celebrate."

Go celebrate. What? A baby to tie him down when all he wanted to do was go, go, go? *Let's go out to eat, let's*

*go to a movie, let's go hop a plane this weekend and if
you're not up to doing the family thing in San Fran, then
how about shooting down to Equador and you can climb
your first pyramid. No? Then what about scuba diving in
Bonaire? It'll be like old times. No to that, too? All right,
we'll keep it closer to home. Say, Florida. Make that Or-
lando. Kind of ugly but lots of stuff to do. Roller coasters,
bungee jumping…*

No. Why couldn't he take no for an answer instead of
tempting her with a plethora of adventures that involved
some risk to the baby? Of course if he knew about the baby,
he wouldn't be making such suggestions.

Lying back on the table, she imagined his reaction once
again. Again and again she had played out the scenario in
her mind and it always ended the same way with Eric's
stunned silence, then a swift embrace, followed by his profession of gladness. Initially he'd wait on her hand and
foot, ever the devoted husband who would want her to quit
her job and be the pampered wife. One who tried not to
notice that as her belly grew, so did his cabin fever.

The walls were already pressing in on him. He constantly
wanted to get out. News of a baby might distract Eric for
a while, but not for long. New people, new places, new
experiences would always beckon. She'd had a taste of that,
and couldn't blame him for his insatiable hunger. It was in
her as well, in that part of her she didn't trust. Perhaps her
empathy with Eric was the reason she didn't trust him to
be content once reality sank in, and taking off on the spur
of the moment to climb a pyramid—or a volcano—in
Equador was gone for good.

"A few more months and you'll have an outie instead
of an innie," Dr. Clark said with a chuckle as he pressed
a stethoscope close to her belly button. After a nod and a
smile, he fiddled with some contraption that had an ampli-

fier attached. "Listen," he said. "Listen and you'll hear the sweetest music ever put to your ears."

Amidst a swishing sound, she discerned a rapid *badump-badump-badump*.

"I hear it," she whispered in awe. "I can hear the baby's heart."

"Won't be long and you'll feel him moving, too." While turning up the volume, Dr. Clark corrected himself. "Make that, him or her. Damn, I'm fed up with having to be so politically correct these days."

The heartbeat of life, that's what she heard. A miracle of such dimensions that nothing could eclipse it, even if she lived to be a hundred.

She would remember this moment always. And forever would she lay on this hard table with a roll of paper sticking to her back if she could simply stay and listen to the music of life, glorious life, ticking like infinity inside her.

All too soon the moment was over and her lunch hour overextended. Dr. Clark had other patients waiting. She had a date with Mary to listen to her mother read *The Pokey Little Puppy,* a tremendous accomplishment, and not to be missed.

She made it in time and Mary's mother did well, though Whitney hardly caught a word. All she could hear was her baby's heart; all she could hear was her own, racing much faster than the clock while she alternately dreaded and couldn't wait to go home. To Eric.

She left early. Much earlier than usual, anyway, since she'd been putting in at least ten hours a day, not counting the work she was lugging home. It wasn't so much out of dedication as having something to do when insomnia struck. Tossing, turning, hugging her side of the mattress while Eric hogged the bed, sleep had become an exercise in exhaustion.

Standing at the door, she wondered if she could finagle a nap while Eric went about his business. Unless he was in the midst of an urgent consultation, not likely. He'd either want to get a jump on the weekend or engage her in yet another conversation. The topic? Whitney Smith, from childhood on.

"Who was your best friend?"

"Loretta Breedlove, my next-door neighbor—until she moved to Texas. I cried for days."

"Worst enemy?"

"Janet Lakes. She put a tack on my seat in sixth grade."

"Ouch, that must've hurt."

"Not half as much as sitting alone at lunch and recess. She was pretty and popular. I was chubby and won spelling bees but other than that, no one wanted me on their teams—especially after Janet gave the word that anyone who hung out with me wouldn't be invited to her parties."

"Little brat. If I'd been in that class, she wouldn't have messed with you."

Whitney had no doubt he would have been kind to a social misfit like herself, the sort of boy she would have pined for from afar, knowing he could have his pick of the lot, and a pudgy nerd with a mouthful of braces didn't have a chance of getting kissed outside of a kissing booth.

When did she first get kissed? he'd wanted to know. Could he see her yearbooks? His curiosity was so voracious that she found herself dredging up incidents she hadn't thought of in years.

Like getting blackmailed for her Halloween candy by the preacher's son, who'd threatened to rat to his dad, who in turn would tell her mama about the naughty ditty her first-grade daughter had made up: "Wee willy winkle sat on his pinkle. And what did he do? Tinkle, tinkle, tinkle!"

Though Eric had laughed and laughed, he'd hit the nail

on the head when he had told her, "You feared reprisal too much, kiddo. I never knew your mom, but something tells me if that shark with a sweet tooth made good on his threats and his dad backed him up, she would've switched churches before punishing you for hearsay. You had her love and loyalty but you let fear steal your belief in it away. Not to mention your candy. Love and fear, *yuan-pao*. Love and fear. We all get pulled in that tug-of-war, but ultimately we have to dig our heels in on one side or the other. You'll know which side I'm on once you quit straddling the rope."

At times like that, and there had been several, she got the feeling that Eric knew her even better than she knew herself. It made her feel even more vulnerable to those kisses that left her hanging, slow-burning gazes that made her melt, his body brushing hers. The sight of him shaving, the heady scent of cologne on his neck and her sheets—

Rats. If she wanted a nap, she should have checked into a motel. A shower was in order, make it cold. And she'd better make it quick before Eric pushed her precariously closer to saying "The hell with it, I love you. Take me now!"

Bracing herself, she twisted the knob. Locked. Scanning the parking lot, she realized the BMW wasn't in the visitor's spot at the far end, across the midway. A sigh of relief mingled with a sharp pang of distress. Quickly, she unlocked the door.

The living room was empty. But that was okay since she took comfort in the sight greeting her—piles of paper, a fax coming in, a blinking cursor on a screen filled with calculations and a leather pouch next to a ring box.

Whitney's heart caught. She didn't need to look in the pouch to know what was inside. It wasn't the medallion since Eric now wore it around his neck. The delicate chain only seemed to accentuate the manliness of the chest she ached to stroke.

How she longed to have the necklace back. All she had to do was ask. But once she did, Eric would entice her to go a step further and to start wearing her wedding ring again.

She wanted the ring even more than the heirloom that was meant to stay in the family. But until she was certain they could raise a family with all the security and harmony a child deserved, she couldn't lay claim to such things. And just because he wasn't around didn't give her the right to pretend she did.

C'mon Whitney, go for it. You're alone and Eric will be none the wiser if you look at the ring. The temptation was impossible to resist. Whitney opened the small velvet box. But one look, one touch of this beautiful ring she yearned for day and night, wasn't enough.

You know you want it, want it so bad. Try the ring on and remember what it was like to be a princess bride on that magical day of your life.

Oh, that day had been magic, sheer magic. If she had one day to put in a bottle and keep, that would be it. And so she let herself remember...

White horses, a chariot, tin cans rattling in the back. Adam playing a liveryman; Eric so desirous and enamoured with the woman he wanted for his wife. The dress he'd had made just for her, floating like the sweetest of dreams. Walking down the aisle, a fairy tale come true. Taking their vows in front of God and man, his own so certain and true as he pledged, "With this ring, I thee wed...."

She slipped on the ring, exulting in the feel of it on her finger once more. In that moment Whitney knew she never should have put the ring on. Taking it off before had been excruciatingly difficult; it would be no easier now. But she had to do it, before—

The living room door swung open. "Hey, kitten, you're home early! What are you doing...here." His gaze zeroed in on the hands she immediately hid behind her back.

She couldn't move. Eric's eyes narrowed, pinning her in place as he shut the door and came her way. With each step closer she became more frantic to slip off the ring he'd caught her with red-handed.

Danger. It crackled in the silence that stretched between them like a live wire. And then, *zap.* He pressed his lips to the wild race of blood shooting through her jugular.

"Let me see your hands," he whispered coaxingly.

She tried, but she was paralyzed by fear. Yes, fear of what would happen once she obeyed.

"I *said,* let me see your hands." No coaxing whisper; not even a terse request. This was a demand that wouldn't take a refusal.

Whitney showed him her hands. He lifted her left one and she could feel the fine tremble in her fingertips quicken when he bowed and pressed his lips to the ring.

"For better or worse," he intoned. "Now that the worst is over, we can get better. And the road to recovery, *yuan-pao,* starts here."

Before she could refute his assumption, her feet left the ground. Eric carried her to the bedroom, where he slid her down his length and obliterated any thoughts of escape beyond the haven of his arms, the press of his body against hers.

"Do this for me," he urged, leading her hands to his shirt. "The way you used to."

With each button she released, he felt increasingly freed from the prison of isolation he'd been cast in while Whitney shut him out of her life. He wouldn't let her do that again. No more keeping him at arm's length; no more of these cat-and-mouse games they'd been playing. This was where the marriage of inconvenience stopped, and the real relationship began.

"That, too," he insisted when she hesitated at his belt. "Take it off." Her fingers were visibly shaking. It reminded him of their wedding night when she'd turned nervous and shy. He'd rather liked it then; he didn't like it much at all now. He wanted his wife back and he'd had his fill of being a stranger in her bed.

"And the pants."

"Eric…" Her eyes beseeched him. She was trembling.

"Do it." When he'd first returned, he might have felt sympathy and relieved her of the task, but sympathy was something he couldn't afford. Too much hinged on the intimate bridges they were mending, and he wasn't giving her room to back out later on the pretext that he'd forced her into something she wasn't ready for.

As for himself, he was so beyond ready that it took all the willpower he had not to strip her with the urgency of his need once she was done.

"My turn." Yes, it was his turn and he'd waited a damn long time for it. No matter, he made himself stop after pulling free the pins in the hair he buried his face in. And then he made himself ask, "Do you want me?"

"Yes," she whispered, running her palms over his back.

There was a hunger in her touch; hunger in her eyes.

Hunger. It consumed him as well as the restraint he'd sworn to keep. The art of the bedchamber demanded that of a man so he might give his lover many, many pleasures before taking his own.

Art could wait. He couldn't. Whitney was his wife and well he let her know it as he raced against time to return to that place called…

Home.

CHAPTER THIRTY-SEVEN

EACH SWIPE OF Eric's mouth, his hands, his tongue, filled her with an ecstasy as addictive as an opiate. She was hooked all over again.

"Say you love me," he demanded when she claimed the sleek turgid flesh that she was hungrily kissing and tonguing.

"I love you," she said, looking up into his eyes. There, she'd said it and it was true, so true.

"Then love me more."

She did. Eric was hers, all hers, to possess and pleasure while her own juices flowed. Hers to love and adore from the tip of his phallus to the clench of his testicles.

Wait, that wasn't quite right. Jade stalk. Orchid bags. Yes, those were much lovelier words from a language he had taught her to speak.

Would she regret this tomorrow? She didn't know, didn't care. All that mattered was the taste and substance of Eric, the clean smell of his skin, her name chanted repeatedly, falling softly as a rain of rose petals on her ears.

His fingers speared through her hair and pulled back until she tilted her face up. He gripped her upper arms and hoisted her over him. Whitney rose above him as she had the first time they'd made love, only then they'd played a game called Dead Entry, Live Exit. Such a game would be impossible now and she hadn't the patience for it anyway. She wanted him in her, immediately and completely. Poised to fill herself up with him, all the way to her womb and into her heart, she cried out, "No!" when he pushed her onto her back and straddled her hips instead.

"You've kept me waiting too long for this," he raggedly whispered. "Now it's your turn to wait and to want me as much as I wanted you when I'd given up hope of ever seeing or touching you again."

"Eric, please. I can't wait and I don't want to talk about this now."

"Too bad, I do," he gruffly told her, though his svelte slide of a fingertip that tapped lightly against the spot he called sacred was anything but gruff. "I do, you said when you took your vows. I cherished those two words and they followed me everywhere I went once you were gone. And everywhere I went, I looked for you. On the sidewalk, in a store, on a plane—especially on a plane—no matter where I was, I searched through the crowd looking, always looking for a glimpse of your face. I think I went a little mad—no, a lot mad, hanging on to yesterday while time crept forward and all I wanted to do was forget it existed outside of the past. Do you have any idea what that was like?"

He pressed up and in. "Do you?"

"Yes!" she shrieked, coming with the crook of his finger, coming in his hand.

Laying every defense she possessed to waste, he urged, "Come for me again. Heal me with the sound of my name while I feel you shake. For me. Only for me, *yuan-pao*."

"Only for you," she vowed. And then she sobbed out his name. Gripping his wrist, she stilled his vibrations. "Heal me," she implored him. "Be one with me again."

He gave her a fraction of what she'd give her very life for at the moment. Yet almost immediately, he took even that small portion away.

"I...I can't last," he panted.

"I don't care," she assured him, guiding him in. "I need you with me. Now and for—"

Ever.

He plunged. In a single stroke he filled her with him, filled her with bliss. He filled her with a shattering ecstasy and her body clutched urgently to keep him when Eric hastily withdrew.

"No, no, no," he groaned, each denial accompanied by a warm spurt landing on her belly. Coveting each drop, she rubbed his essence into her skin, absorbing the last traces of passion spent.

"I'm sorry," he whispered. "I've imagined this moment so many times, but never like this. It wasn't supposed to happen this way."

"Nothing ever happens like we imagine and I can't imagine anything more wonderful than this," she soothed. And yet, as wondrous as this moment was, she knew it fell short of perfection. If Eric knew about the baby, if he could gladly give up the risks that endangered his life and love her as completely as he did now, then…yes, nothing could be more wonderful than this.

"You're sure?"

He needed reassurance; she needed some of her own. Eric couldn't give it to her until she told all. She had to do it. But…not yet. They had taken a major step forward but she wasn't ready to take the leap of faith required to tell him they'd soon be hearing the pitter-patter of little feet.

Putting her own needs aside, she sought to give him the reassurance he'd rarely asked for before. Remembering a song they'd danced to on white sand while the scent of wild orchids blended with the sound of waves lapping against the shore, she smiled.

"Don't worry, be happy. I am."

"Then so am I. Your happiness, *yuan-pao*, is mine."

Burrowing closer, she inhaled the remnants of his cologne, licked the tart salt of their mingled sweat. It was heaven to have this once more and woe unto her for that because it would tear her apart to ever give it up again.

"This is what I came back for." He pressed her left hand over his chest. "Feeling you in my arms, feeling your heart beat. We're meant to be together, forever and always. Say you know it's true."

"When we're like this…yes." Heaven shook a little and so did her voice as she gave him the larger truth they couldn't ignore. "But beyond this, our lives move in different directions. Face it, Eric. You hate being tied down to one place. I need the security of someplace to call home."

"Home is where the heart is," he countered. "It's not a place but what we carry inside that gives us peace and security, or chaos and discontent, wherever we go. I've watched you and listened closely to everything you've had to say this week. What I've seen and what I've heard haven't convinced me that you're happy here. I don't hear you laugh like you used to and your smiles never reach your eyes. In them, I see a thirst. Not only for me and what we had, but for that rare love of life you found in yourself. I love who you are. And I miss who you were."

"I don't." An automatic denial, it came out with the instinctive reflex of a rubber hammer put to a kneecap. "And the fact that you miss someone I'm not makes me wonder how you can possibly love who I've turned out to be. A librarian who lives within her limited means and gets her kicks out of…"

Suddenly she felt something. Not quite a kick, more like the soft stirring of butterfly wings in her tummy. Her abdomen was pressed against his hip. Had Eric felt it, too?

"Go on. Tell me what you get your kicks from these days besides crochet since I haven't quite figured that out."

The baby had moved. Eric, so close to where his child resided, didn't have a clue. If he did, his mention of the crochet would have been more significant than wanting to find out what else she did for fun.

"I like walking the beach and gathering seashells," she told him with such joy that he couldn't doubt her humble claim. "Long drives in chilly weather with the windows rolled down and the heater on. Staring up at the clouds and making pictures and faces from cotton puffs in the sky. The simple things in life are my purest pleasures."

"But what of your guilty pleasures? Like me." He shook his head. "Since I came back, that's the feeling I've gotten from you and I don't understand it. Neither do I understand why you shun your natural thirst for experience. It's in you Whitney, and why you deny it is truly beyond me. Say what you may, think what you want, but I know who you are and that's a great soul who longs to grow. The world calls out to you, just like the pearl in this ring."

He moved her hand until the ring filled her vision. "When I saw it on your finger again, I could hardly believe my eyes. It's the first sign you've given me that you still want a future together as much as I do. The woman I want that future with is a complex creature I could spend the rest of my life trying to figure out. She frustrates me sometimes but she never ceases to intrigue me. I do love who you are, *yuan-pao*. The fact you want to suppress the part of you I miss doesn't lessen the commitment I've made. If you don't believe me, say so now, because I mean what I say and I'll be thoroughly pissed if you ever doubt my love again."

No woman could doubt a man after such an impassioned little speech, and pissing Eric off wasn't the sort of thing anyone would want to do. Especially not her and not now, when she so needed such assurances to get up the guts to tell him about the baby.

"I believe you, Eric." Tell him. "And I...well, I do want a future together but I'm still worried a couple of months in paradise hasn't necessarily made us prepared for whatever the future holds outside of it."

"Look, we make our own futures by the choices we make today. You know where I stand but I'm still getting a sense of ambivalence from you. Yeah, you've put the ring back on where it belongs and finally we're making love again. And yes, you're right, the sort of life you lead here isn't my cup of tea. But it's not yours, either. You sip at it like castor oil mixed in a bowl of oatmeal you're bound and determined to get down for nutrition's sake, no matter how bland or nasty it tastes. I'm itching to race forward, you're dragging your feet. If you'd just tell me why, I'm sure we can deal with it and move past this deadlock we've been in."

Could they? Could Eric deal with putting a child over his career? And if not, could she deal with the risks he took in the field while caring for a child whose father might never come back? Desertion. The fear of it ran strong in her veins and desertion by death was as absolute as it got.

So went reason. Yet an insistent wail, like that of a starving infant, cried out, *Tell him.* Her pulse raced. Feeling as if life hung on a trip hammer balance and she was poised on the edge of a trigger, Whitney took aim.

And missed the bull's-eye of ultimate risk.

"What's holding me back? Trust, Eric."

"Trust?" he repeated. "How could you not trust me? I've never kept anything from you."

He didn't point the finger, but they both knew who had

kept secrets before. The one she kept now was on the tip of her tongue and stirring against her belly.

Such trust it took in him, in herself, to take a great running leap and pole-vault them both over the top without anything to cushion their landing on the rock bed of reality.

Eyes closed, she took a deep, bracing breath and—

"Never? You've never kept anything from me? Not even some minor something you thought better kept to yourself?"

"I most certainly have—" His quick response, surely meant to be a denial, was followed by a sudden retraction. "Yes, I have hidden something from you. I read one of the letters you were hiding from me."

He'd read one of her letters? Did that mean he'd opened Pandora's box?

Trying hard not to sound accusing, and not succeeding very well, she demanded, "Why did you read it and when?"

"I read it because I'd seen you writing all those notes and trying to keep them out of my sight. I couldn't stand being in the dark, so I snuck a look while you were gone. It was in Dominica. The day I gave you the earrings. Pearls. Not these gold loops I never want to see again once you take them off and put my gift back on." He unlatched a hoop and pulled it free. "Do it for me now?"

Whitney made no move for her jewelry box. Instead, she pushed his hand away when he went for the next ear. How dare Eric go through her purse? Or maybe it had been her beach tote, since that was the day she'd gone to the doctor, only to leave without the pills she'd gone for.

Wait a minute. The pills. Though she didn't have to ask, she did. "And which letter did you happen to read?"

"The one about how much you wanted a future together but didn't want to risk getting pregnant. You were going to see the doctor about some birth control for yourself to make sure you were doubly protected.''

Her blood pressure shot up, she could feel it zoom like a geyser threatening to explode the top of her head off. Not because she was upset by what he'd done, which she was, but because of the perfect opportunity his admission had given her to ask, ''And how did you feel about what you'd read?''

''Relief. Enormous relief.''

Relief. That she wanted a future but had taken extra precaution to ensure children weren't included. Did he love her? Oh yeah. Did he want this marriage? No question. But kids weren't part of the bargain they'd struck.

Had a fist just landed in her gut? No, this was worse. She felt as if Eric had reached into her chest and torn out her heart. He didn't want their love child, he'd just said as much while he had no need to guard such sentiments from her. Even if he tried to take it back should he learn the truth, she wouldn't believe him. Belated assurances he wanted the baby would only be pretty lies, destined to erode once silent resentments and fitful cries in the night turned them into strangers who didn't need a rolled-up blanket to divide them in bed.

''In the letter you said how much you loved me,'' he continued. ''That's what I'd been waiting to hear and I didn't want to jeopardize your trust by admitting to what I'd done. So I said nothing and gave it some time, long enough to be certain you'd marry me. What I did wasn't right and it's disturbed me ever since. It feels good to clear my conscience. Now I can honestly say that I've kept nothing from you,'' he said then paused. ''No, I take that back.'' She wanted to wash out the kiss he placed on her hair. Judas, Judas, Judas. ''I waited for the pills to kick in and on our honeymoon night—that incredible, unforgettable night—I did what I'd wanted to do since our first kiss. I came inside you with nothing between us. You were too far gone to notice and I was flying too high to care if you did. So there you have it, the only two times I've ever deceived you. The only two times I ever will. I swear.''

So there she had it. Mystery pregnancy solved.

Like she cared.

Gritting her teeth against the urge to vomit, Whitney patted his penis. That's right, penis, since ancient poetry for body parts no longer applied to them.

Just like that, he was fully erect. She removed her hand.

''What's done is done, Eric. And while I appreciate your honesty about what you did then, what about today? You weren't using a condom and I'm not on the pill.'' She wanted to leave it at that and stalk away to nurse her wounds in private. But she owed it to the baby to raise the ultimate question before deciding if all of them would be better off if she cut Eric out of their lives.

Clinging to her anger, the only protection she had to shield herself with, Whitney asked sharply, ''So tell me, what if the worst happened and I'm pregnant even as we speak?''

CHAPTER THIRTY-EIGHT

ERIC DIDN'T REPLY right away. Whitney had raised a valid question—one he'd intended to put to her, but in much gentler terms once the most crucial issues impeding their future were out of the way. He'd thought them fairly well tackled, from convincing her of his unconditional love to the higher path he knew she was itching to take once she gave herself permission. But Whitney had turned chameleon on him again, and he couldn't decipher her mixed messages. His confession of guilt had been absolved, but he discerned no real forgiveness.

Accusation, resentment, that's what he'd heard in her voice. And her touch to his groin transmitted even less tenderness than her eyes. They were frosty, not warm. The chill seemed to have spread to her complexion as well. Gone was her aftermath glow; the high color in her cheeks had waned to a shade resembling gray chalk.

Her moods of late were more than he could keep up with. Was she distressed because they'd gotten carried away and one of his tadpoles could have swum to her eggs before he yanked the others out? Didn't make sense, not when they loved each other and she was basically a nester. But it was much too soon to start a family when they'd only begun to put their relationship back together, so maybe that was where she was coming from. That's all he could guess since Whitney was obviously unhappy about the wait-and-see circumstance posed.

"If the worst happened and you're pregnant," he slowly

reiterated, "all I can do is apologize for my lack of control. I'll keep my fingers crossed until we're in the clear and promise it won't happen again unless we're both agreed that it should. Something tells me that could be awhile. I'm in no rush to complicate matters when they're scrambling my mind as it is, so rest assured I'll be more responsible after this."

"Once is all it takes," she snapped. "If I'm pregnant already, what will we do?"

He could try to placate her, if that was possible, and say the decision's up to you. But it wasn't. It took two to make a baby and never would he give a child of his up. He couldn't imagine Whitney feeling any differently. An unplanned pregnancy deserved no less acceptance or celebration—at least not for two mature, committed adults who were able to provide everything a child could ever need—love, security and every advantage possible, including the rare opportunity to be a world student. The world, so grand and diverse, he loved it.

Share that love with a child, and if his genes had any say, the grandchildren to come wouldn't be content with less than walking on Mars. That was part of the romance, he supposed, of wishing he'd gotten Whitney pregnant, despite her troubling animosity at the mere potential of it.

"I asked you," she said tersely, "what will we do if I'm pregnant?"

Given her attitude about it, he was tempted to suggest she see the child to gestation and he'd take things from there. Raise the child himself if need be, but no way was he about to make it feel as unwanted as her tone implied.

"We'll cross that bridge when we come to it," he answered as diplomatically as he was able. A stretch. He did not feel diplomatic in the least about this. In fact, he was so close to an in-her-face confrontation it was a good thing

Whitney sprang to her feet and made a fast trot to the adjoining bathroom.

There she turned, palms planted on her hips. A little wider than he remembered, but never more voluptuous. Her breasts appeared weightier as well but he couldn't be sure. Memory had a way of reshaping things and people who didn't necessarily fit into the present as neatly.

Testimony to that was Whitney's crisp reply. "Bridges are built on trust, Eric. Once that trust is broken, bridges get burned. Sorry, but my trust in you is terribly shaken and it'll take more than another mindless tussle in the sack to get it back."

The bathroom door shut. Softly. He would have preferred a slam, giving him just cause to fling the door back open and demand just what the hell she'd meant by that.

As it was, his erection had gone soft and so had his brain. No matter which way he turned it, there was no rhyme or reason to Whitney's behavior. A clearing of this muddled air was in order once she deigned to reappear, but until then he could use the downtime to—

The phone rang. His, not hers. A minute ago he would have ignored it but now he hurried to the living room, glad for the diversion.

"Hey, Grayson, how are ya?"

"Sweltering and one person short in Montserrat now that Equador's simmered down. Care to guess who that person might be?"

Grateful as he was for the touchstone of the one thing he still understood, Eric knew he couldn't accept Marcia's summons. "Sorry but there's a home fire burning—make that closer to a skyscraper about to be gutted by flames—I have to tend to before I can even think about it."

"You gotta do what you've gotta do," she graciously conceded. "I'll call Larry in again."

"Should you do that? You know he's got kids."

"His decision to have them, his decision whether or not to come. Chances are he will. The situation here is gathering steam and he'll see some action, but won't have to stay for the show. Best of both worlds, you know?"

No, Eric thought, he didn't. More often than not he'd stuck around for the show instead of getting out while the getting was good. So far he'd been lucky, except for nearly getting blasted to kingdom come by Galeras when she was supposed to be taking a nap.

"Even the best of both worlds is a crapshoot, Marcia," he reflected. "You never know what might happen that could turn the world on its head and blow yours off."

"Sounds like the freeway in Los Angeles. Lots more dangerous there than taking your chances here with a chopper on standby."

He knew that. Just as he knew the thrill for danger had lost its appeal, while getting a piece of the action never would.

"Consider me on standby if Larry can't make it."

"Roger," she answered. "Now copy this. Feel free to join us once you put that fire out."

Eric hung up the phone. He felt as if he'd done some surgery on himself and severed an artery, cutting the flow of blood to his veins. But as Marcia had said, he had to do what he had to do. And what he had to do was get back in the bedroom, take Whitney on, and get them both out of this hellhole that was making her act so weird and was damn near suffocating him.

His decision made, he picked up the phone, made two reservations for the first flight out to Montserrat, which was mercifully soon, and returned to the bedroom where they'd get things settled before taking off.

Whitney was still in the bathroom. He could hear her

softly cursing. Hmmm. Maybe it wouldn't be a bad idea to get her into the car and then get things settled. Once on the plane they'd have to be civil and after they were up to their eyeballs in percolating earth, floating soot, and kids gobbling up every word she read, all would be well again.

This Eric told himself, and this he believed with such total conviction he packed his bags, deciding not to give Whitney the chance to refuse packing hers.

Flipping up the dust ruffle, he pulled out her suitcase. It was really pretty and he sighed as he stroked the tapestry of pink flowers and green ferns. Ahh. Such a thrill to have her luggage in hand again. Even a pull of the zipper stoked his nostalgia for those times they'd packed for each other, making a show of dangling undies before kissing the crotch and dropping them one by one into the open suitcase.

He couldn't wait to fill hers up again with the naughty nighties she'd worn—no way was he taking that granny gown—and his favorite silk panties and bras—forget that serviceable cotton crap—and once he did that, he'd top it all off with the medallion that belonged around her neck, not his.

Eric threw back the top.

His mind reeled. His breathing went on hold. His fingers felt oddly disattached as he took out their marriage license. Then one by one, touched the remaining items he couldn't believe he beheld.

A box of disposable diapers. A diaper stacker to put them in. A box of Gerber oatmeal. A small silver brush. A pair of crocheted booties. And a rattle that shook in his hand.

CHAPTER THIRTY-NINE

WHITNEY DRIED OFF with the towel she'd used to muffle her earlier sobs. Softly rubbing her stomach with the terry cloth, she wished for a robe to better cover her nakedness than the too short towel she was wrapping around her torso.

She didn't want Eric to see her stomach, didn't want him to even be in the room she'd left him waiting in. It had been a long wait. Considering her exit, she wasn't sure what to expect. If he wanted to hash things out, too bad, she wasn't up to it. If he thought she just needed some time to cool down after blowing off some steam because he'd read one of her letters, then he'd no doubt greet her from the bed, Mr. Romance primed and ready for his Mrs.

Wasn't going to happen. The baby was between them. The baby wasn't going anywhere and neither was she. Another week in the apartment and chances were, Eric would. He was so antsy that unless her ears deceived her, she could already hear him pacing the floor.

Eric prowled. Eric pounced. Eric pontificated on occasion. But he only paced when agitated or was thwarted by a problem he couldn't figure out.

He didn't pace often.

Securing the towel tighter, Whitney notched up her chin and with all the bravado she could muster, marched out.

Eric stopped pacing. The intensity of his gaze stopped her two steps short of the closet.

"Take off the towel."

An order, quietly spoken, but an order all the same, as

if he were the officer in charge, and she, a wayward soldier, caught in the midst of a treasonous act.

It took her a moment to find her voice. "No."

"Why not?" As he swiftly closed the distance, Eric tapped something into his palm. It rattled. And continued to rattle with each soft strike he made, like a judge's gavel pronouncing her guilty, guilty, guilty. "You wouldn't be hiding something under there would you?"

Though made of plastic, no sword had been mightier than the baby rattle he held up and sliced between her cleavage.

The towel fell away. And there she stood, fully exposed to his view. She shivered. His gaze was on her abdomen; his fingertips followed suit. They lightly stroked the flesh she was more urgent than ever to conceal.

Moving away from the touch that could make her come undone, Whitney sought protection from the closet and the robe she hastily donned.

Eric stared at his fingertips while trying to fathom her retreat. Okay, maybe he'd come on a little strong, but hell and be damned, they were going to have a baby and Whitney had no right to treat him like a sperm donor whose role in the pregnancy consisted of no more than his provision of genes.

He'd never been so angry. He'd never been so elated. And never had he been so taken aback upon being informed, "I get custody of the child, but I'll be generous with visitation rights. If we can agree on that, you're free to go." She pointed a finger, visibly shaking, at his luggage. "I see you're already packed."

His hands itched to grab up his suitcase, along with anything else he could land his hands on, and send it sailing through the window. Better that than seizing Whitney by the shoulders and shaking her or turning her over his knee and giving her fanny a good whack. He didn't dare do either. She was pregnant with his child. Their child! And he had to remember pregnant women could be irrational. According to Larry, his own sweetheart of a wife had actually slugged him in the throes of labor just because he'd told her to forget the pain medicine and take another deep breath with him.

Eric struggled to keep his voice low, his response calm. "Custody implies divorce, Whitney. We're expecting a baby. There will be no divorce. The three months I was holding you to have hereby been extended to the duration of our lives."

"We didn't say 'till death do we part' and frankly Eric, I think that was wise. It's one thing to bicker and argue amongst ourselves but I refuse to put a child in the middle. That's exactly where ours will be when I'm pleading 'stay with us' and you're saying 'Sorry but I've got to go.'"

"Don't put words in my mouth!" He hit the rattle into his palm with such force tiny beads sprayed out of the plastic and into the charged air. Ashamed as he was of his outburst, it had nothing on his simmering rage. Try as he might, he couldn't contain it.

"With a child involved, I never would have said such a thing to Amy, much less to you," he quietly seethed. Tossing the broken rattle aside, he lightly tapped a finger to her chest. "But you, you, the love of my life, the one I hold above all others and believed to be my most trusted friend, have the gall to suggest I'm not fit to be a father and therefore not worthy to be your husband. That's bullshit. Absolute bullshit. I might be far from perfect but I have no hidden agendas here. Never have, never will. And that's more than I can say for you."

He wanted to say a lot more. Like telling her she could prattle on about trust all she wanted, but between the two of them he was clearly the more trustworthy. But why stop there? Why not throw it up to her that nothing could be more crucial in the balance of life than the death of a partner or a child created between them, and her silences about both said more about her insecurities than his ability to overcome them.

Fuming, Eric knew he had to chill before so much smoke came out of his ears the hallway alarm went off. He grabbed his luggage on the way out.

"Where are you going?"

Whitney actually sounded concerned. Good. If she missed him already it wasn't likely she'd serve him with divorce papers the second he returned. It probably wouldn't be long but it wouldn't hurt for her to be the one worried about his whereabouts for a change.

"I don't know," he snapped over his shoulder. "Maybe just for a walk, maybe I'll head for the next plane out to Montserrat." Making her worry was one thing; striking the fear of God in her, another. Too much anxiety wasn't good for the baby. "But I'll probably take five in San Franscisco and check on my grandmother. I'll be back," he assured her.

"When?"

"When I'm sure I won't mouth off and make matters worse than they already are."

Out the front door, which he locked to keep his wife and baby safe, Eric made tracks before he reversed his position as ruler of the roost and let Whitney run all over him. Striding across the asphalt to the BMW parked in a space marked Visitor, he was pleasantly debating whether to go shopping for a football or a baby doll when he heard her yelling his name.

"Eric! Eric, wait!"

He stopped. Cupped his ear. How sweet the sound of her

plea. But he wasn't quite ready to come running home after what she'd dished out.

"Eric! Don't go!"

The sweet sound of her desperation to keep him, that's all he needed to hear to meet her halfway. Yet an image of Whitney flinging herself at his disfigured back and pulling him into that damnable apartment he'd get them both out of yet, froze him in his tracks. He'd been doing all the chasing, all the wooing and even the cooking so far. It was his turn to stall while Whitney played catch up. Once she latched on to him, they were on even ground.

Two seconds, maybe three, went by before he heard her call out to him again. Only his name was a shriek of "Eric" that coincided with the screech of tires.

Jerking around, a sickening thud accompanied the pound of his feet. Too late, too late, he couldn't save her. Because of him, Whitney was the one who got hit, she was the one splayed on the hood of a shiny white Camaro.

And he was the one howling, "Nooo!" as he saw rivulets of blood streaking down her legs.

While her freaked out neighbor ran inside to dial 911, Eric frantically searched for a pulse.

CHAPTER FORTY

"HOW IS SHE?" Eric rushed to his feet in the surgical waiting room, urgently needing to know.

"Have a seat, son." Dr. Clark, the physician Whitney
had asked for when she briefly came to in the ambulance,
pulled up a chair. Though they were alone, his voice was
hushed. "She was lucky. No internal bleeding, no broken
bones, a minor concussion but no damage to the brain.
Physically, she's going to be fine."

"Thank God," Eric whispered. "Thank God." Though
relief sluiced through him, he could still feel himself trembling inside. "What about the baby?"

"There's no easy way to say this." Dr. Clark put a
steadying hand on Eric's shoulder. "I had to do a D and
C. She lost the baby. Fortunately, she can have others,
but..."

"But what?" Eric pressed.

"Strictly speaking as a doctor, there is no 'but.' Man to
man, however, I'm very worried about your wife. A
woman's bound to be depressed after a miscarriage but I'm
afraid Whitney's going to have a harder time than most.
I've known that little gal since the day she was born and I
love her like one of my own. But family's family and ever
since her mama died, she's been without one. Lord, how
she wanted that baby. It meant she'd have a family again.
It's a terrible loss she's suffered and her body'll mend a
lot sooner than her heart. She's going to need your support
to get through this."

Eric's own heart contracted painfully. His attempts to console her in the emergency room had been futile. She hadn't even wanted him to hold her hand. He couldn't blame her. He had their baby's blood on his hands, and no amount of soap could wash away the taint of his actions.

He stared at his palms, empty as the future ahead if Whitney cut him out of her life.

"Has she asked for me?"

"No, but she's still sedated so don't feel too bad about that."

Oh no, he didn't feel bad about that. He felt wretched. He wanted to weep, beat his chest in self-flagellation until he bled like she had onto the grill of the car. He wanted to take a sledgehammer to that car. Hit it and hit it until there was nothing left but broken glass and twisted metal.

Kill the car. Yeah, that's what he wanted to do. Smash it to smithereens with the vigilante justice of a kid who'd wrecked his prized bike on an object that just happened to be in the way when he was too busy looking cool to watch where he was going.

Eric dropped his face into his hands, knowing such destruction wouldn't bring their child back. Wouldn't put them back together again and erase the tragedy he was responsible for. That's right. Him. Not the goddamn car.

"I know it's not my business," Dr. Clark said quietly, "but I do have to wonder what was going on with you two before the accident, seeing that Whitney was outside in a robe when it happened."

"It was my fault." Eric couldn't look at the good doctor. How long would it be before he could even look at himself in the mirror again?

"You mean you were driving the car?"

"I wasn't the one behind the wheel but that didn't keep me from mowing her down after I found some baby things she'd been hiding and got into a self-righteous snit because she hadn't told me she was pregnant.'' Shoulders slumping with the weight of the blame that laid squarely on him, he made himself go on.

''I said some pretty ugly things and broke the baby's rattle, then left to get a grip on my temper—after I got the last word in. Whitney came after me, kept calling out to me. But did I turn around? No. I was feeling too high-and-mighty to do that. I only turned after I heard the tires squeal. By then the damage was done. So much damage, she may never forgive me. God knows, I'll never forgive myself.''

Fond as Dr. Clark was of Whitney, Eric anticipated more coals heaped upon his bowed head. Surprisingly, they didn't come. A gentle pat to his knee did.

''She should have told you. I advised her to do just that when she came into the office this afternoon. I said, 'Whitney, this husband of yours is going to be mad if he figures out what you should've fessed up to already.' Or some such something as that. Fact is, Eric, married folks argue all the time over piddly things that don't hold a candle to what you had every right to be upset about. I know that doesn't make what happened any easier to bear, but there's no rewriting the past and the best the two of you can do is grieve until your tears run out, then turn the page and go on.''

''If only it were that simple,'' Eric said, wishing it with all his heart. ''Takes two to make a marriage work and while I'd break what's left of my back to do it, I'm afraid Whitney will turn hers on me. If she does, I'll still love her. For whatever that's worth.''

''Can't put a price on such a priceless commodity but I do believe yours is richer than gold.'' Dr. Clark chuckled. It sounded strange in a room filled with such remorse and angst. ''If Whitney's got a brain in her head she'll realize how fortunate she is to have the likes of you. She's always been bright, son. And she told me you were a good man. After this little chat, I believe that's true.''

In the elder man's wizened gaze, Eric saw a deep compassion. If Whitney could extend him half as much, maybe they stood a chance.

A nurse approached and signaled for Dr. Clark. After a brief conversation conducted in whispers, she left.

''What's wrong?''

''Whitney's hollering for her baby. The nurses in recovery can't calm her down so I ordered another sedative.''

''If only she'd asked for me,'' Eric whispered. ''If only...''

Reaching into his lab coat, Dr. Clark heaved a heavy sigh. ''Just remember it's always darkest before the dawn. At least that's what my daddy used to tell me when the sun seemed like it'd never come up. He was full of so much advice I started putting cotton in my ears.'' A bottle of Bayer appeared. As Dr. Clark chewed a couple of tablets, he tossed the cotton into a trash can and screwed the cap back on.

''Makes it easier to get to in situations such as this. Of course such situations make me think seriously about taking down the old shingle and going fishing instead. But every time I make such a mention, the wife reminds me she prefers fish in a restaurant over gutting and cooking whatever I might catch.''

Spoken by a man who would do the world a great injustice by retiring before his hands were feeble, his mind no longer quite so sharp.

Eric knew he had a lot of thinking to do about his own calling, where public duty ended and putting family first began. Plenty of time to think about it while he sat alone

and waited an interminable wait for Whitney to leave recovery.

Would she ever fully recover? Would he? And if by
some miracle she could forgive him and let him hold her
once again, how could he possibly leave her waiting for
him while he put his life at risk?

By the time he was allowed to see her, Eric knew he
could never put Whitney through the absolute hell of waiting for a husband who might come back in a box. The
sight of her on a hospital bed with an IV bottle feeding the
needle in her arm was role reversal enough to get his priorities straight once and for all. She was number one. Ditto
for kids. No qualms.

"Yuan-pao," he whispered, touching her ashen cheek.
"Dr. Clark said you're going to be fine, that we can have
other babies. I know it's too soon to talk about having
another one but when you're ready, I'll be there. I'll never
walk away from you again, I swear it."

Whitney turned her head. She didn't want other babies,
she wanted the one whose heart she'd heard beat, the one
she'd felt move before Eric walked away while she begged
him to stop. They'd said she got hit by a car but she had
no memory of it. Just the memory of Eric giving her his
back, blinding pain, then feeling the life inside ebb out of
her.

More than the baby had died. Her spirit had died with it
and left a black hole where things like love and hope resided.

"Doesn't matter," she told him. Him, the man who had
once made her thrill to his touch. The thrill was gone. She
didn't want him to touch her, didn't want him here. "Go
away, Eric. Leave me alone."

He made a sound as if he were choking on tears. Let
him cry, she didn't care. All the tears in the world wouldn't

bring her baby back and well she knew it after the great buckets of tears she had shed. No more left, she was dry. So dry and empty inside that she closed her eyes and drifted off, not even caring if she died.

It had to be the longest night of his life. Catnapping in a chair beside the bed he kept vigil over, waking each time she moved or a nurse came in, swiping at his eyes when Whitney whimpered in her sleep.

He told himself she hadn't really meant what she'd said. Told himself she was drugged up and after she slept it off, Whitney would be glad he hadn't left after her cold dismissal, if she remembered it all.

The sun came up. Vital signs taken, breakfast arrived.

Hard to work up much enthusiasm over a soft diet consisting of a small carton of juice, a little yellow heap of scrambled eggs and a dry slice of toast, but he did his best.

"Yum, looks delicious. Forget breakfast at Tiffany's, they've got nothing on this."

No response. Whitney stared at the plate as if it had no more substance than he did.

"You need to eat." Forking up a small portion of eggs, he made like an airplane zooming toward the landing strip of her mouth. Closed. "Make you a deal, eat the eggs, drink the juice, forget the toast and I'll take you to Tiffany's the minute you're up to it. Hell, I'll even throw in the best of Broadway and whatever your heart desires at Cartier's. No strings attached, all you have to do is open up and it's done."

Whitney lifted her gaze, stared straight at him. He suddenly wished she'd kept her eyes on the plate or looked out the window at the bricks on the opposing wing. Her eyes were flat and lifeless. He felt as if he were staring through glass into an empty room.

"Whitney, you're scaring me. Talk to me. Tell me you're all right."

"I'm fine." Her toneless reply sent chills down his spine. "And I'm not hungry. Now if you don't mind, and even if you do, I want some privacy while I call for the nurse to help me walk to the bathroom."

Tossing the fork, Eric got out before he broke down. As he made his way to the elevator, he stopped at the nursing station to request the help Whitney wouldn't let him give.

"She already buzzed us and I sent someone down."

Funny, he hadn't noticed any passing nurses. Then again, a whole troop of them could have gone by and he wouldn't have noticed anything beyond the green tile, fluorescent lighting and the knot in his throat, blocking a deep, cleansing gulp of antiseptic air.

"Thanks." Seemed the polite thing to say, though he had no idea what there was to be thankful for.

"It's always good news when a patient wants to get out of bed after surgery, even when it's minor."

Minor surgery. He supposed a D and C qualified since it entailed no more than scraping the lining of the uterus. At least that's the way Dr. Clark had explained it before he left to see to another patient in the birthing center. A hasty departure since she was dilated to eight centimeters and the baby could crown before he got there if his creaky old bones didn't hustle down quick.

Dr. Clark had to be nearing seventy. He seemed so much younger than that. As for himself, Eric knew if he lived to be a hundred, he could only hope he didn't feel half as old as he did now.

Even pressing the elevator button seemed an arduous task.

The doors slid open and just as he was about to step in, Dr. Clark stepped out. Freshly shaven, a red carnation pinned to his coat, his debonair appearance and upbeat, "Mornin' son, how are ya?" left no question that chronological age was a hoax on a par with snake oil.

"I'm okay," Eric out-and-out lied. "That's more than I can say for Whitney."

"Let's get out of this line of traffic so we can talk." Once in a secluded corner, Dr. Clark got straight to the point. "You look like hell. Rough night?"

"About as rough as they come."

"Was she crying, getting beside herself again?"

"No." He wished she had. Any show of emotion would have been better than her total lack of it. "She seemed to sleep pretty sound and wanted to get up this morning. The nurse said that's good."

"The only better sign is when they go for their makeup and want to fix their hair. When a person's down in the dumps, they don't care how they look. Whitney's sure to be blue for awhile, so if that's your concern—"

"It's not." Raking a hand through his hair and not giving a damn how he looked, Eric confided, "I'm down in the dumps and to tell you the truth, I'd feel a lot better if Whitney was too. She's like a zombie. When I look in her eyes, I see blank space. It's as if she's checked out and nobody's home. I've tried to reach her but she wants nothing to do with me."

"Sounds like disassociation. Know what that is?"

Eric was afraid that he did. "Isn't that when someone shuts down because the overload's more than they can handle?"

"You got it. That's how the mind protects itself from trauma until it's safe to come out again. How long that might be isn't easy to say. Think I'll have another type of doctor check her out and see if therapy's in order." Sympathetically, he added, "Of course TLC is the best therapy she could have. Unfortunately, like the other kind, the one who needs it has to first admit that they do. I'm sorry she's pushing you away. I know that has to hurt like the dickens.''

''Yeah.'' It hurt so much, Eric knew he needed to leave before he embarrassed himself in public. ''I'd better let you make your rounds. Thanks for everything. If there's anything I can ever do for you, please let me know.''

''I'll take you up on that offer right now. Do me a favor and get yourself some sleep, get cleaned up and eat a decent meal. It's important that you take care of yourself so you can take care of your wife.''

''Understood.'' The two men shook hands. As Eric turned, Dr. Clark slapped him on the back.

''Buck up, son. And just remember this—if you want the rainbow, you've gotta put up with the rain.''

''More of your dad's advice, right?''

''Nope.'' Dr. Clark chuckled and how grateful Eric was to smile even a little upon being informed, ''Dolly Parton's.''

CHAPTER FORTY-ONE

RAIN SLASHED across the windshield as Eric drove Whitney home from the hospital. She'd been there four days—four excruciatingly long days—and Dr. Clark had wanted her to stay another. Dr. Speer, the psychiatrist, had pushed for two. Whitney had refused them both, insisting she was fine, and no she would not consider some out-patient therapy or Prozac, because thank you very much she was perfectly fine.

It was a lot more than Eric could say for himself. The guilt was eating him alive. The hope he had that their marriage might be salvaged was disappearing like so much sand in an hourglass. Nothing he said, nothing he did could break through the glass wall of her eyes. And his touch was rebuffed in the most hurtful way possible.

She didn't respond, not even to push his hand away when he needed to hold hers so much it was a physical ache. When he'd brushed her hair and put on her lipstick, she could have passed for a cadaver being spruced up by a mortician.

He had been relegated to the ranks of nonexistence. What a relief it would be to be able to drive her to rage, hatred, disgust—it would provide some reassurance that she still had the capacity to feel *something* for him. Maybe if he tried to put her wedding ring back on she would throw it at him. A reaction at least, but one he didn't have the emotional stamina for. It was taking everything he had and then some to continue these one-way conversations.

"I spoke with Mr. Andrews again and he said not to worry about taking the next month off, even longer if need be. They're really missing you, especially that little Mary. She made you a card and he said he'd send it, or deliver it personally once you're up to another visit."

"Okay."

Not exactly all one-way conversation, but monosyllable answers were about as interactive as she got. With him, at least. She'd actually talked some shop with her boss when he'd brought flowers to her. Tom didn't stay long in the room, and Eric had followed him out. They'd had a private word.

"I was shocked when you called me about the accident but since she wasn't critical, I didn't expect her to look so frail. You must be terribly worried about her, Eric. Is there anything I can do?"

"Actually, there is. She's under the care of two doctors and both of them think she needs to take a leave of absence. Doing some work at home would probably be good for her, but trying to keep her usual pace at the library wouldn't, not until she's had time to recuperate."

Tom vouched his unstinting support even without knowing Dr. Speer had noted symptoms of clinical depression, and feared that the stress of a demanding job might push Whitney over the edge without the proper medication to control it.

Zoloft, Prozac, plenty of drugs around to get a really depressed person back on their feet. But nobody could force-feed chemical panaceas to anyone who refused to take so much as an over-the-counter Saint John's Wort. Eric believed in herbal remedies and certainly had consumed enough *ling-chih* to prove it. Whitney, however, had no interest in joining him again for a cup of longevity's tea.

As for joining him in any intimate activities, he could forget that, too. He cringed all over again, remembering how the nurse had come in with Whitney's release papers and gone over doctor's final orders.

"Sexual relations can be resumed in four weeks, but a six-month wait is strongly advised before you attempt another pregnancy."

"Not to worry," Whitney had blithely said while she went about packing, since his offer to do it for her had been as unwanted as the sex she dismissed as well. "Such matters are of no concern to us."

How could she be so cold? Even if she didn't want to sleep with him, how could she say as much to that nurse? And what had he done about it? What could he do?

Nothing.

Eric Townsend, the multiorgasmic man who could keep it up all night, had yet to raise a finger in protest to the humiliations Whitney had visited upon him each and every endless day he'd catered to her needs.

Where was his pride? Even now he found himself running around to open her door, juggling flowers and luggage and keys to get them inside, then apologizing for not cleaning the apartment before her return. Like he'd been here any longer than it took him to shower and shave, force down a tasteless bite to eat, and ignore the avalanche of faxes, E-mails and voice mail messages while he hurried back to where he most wanted to be—by her side—despite not being wanted.

He watched Whitney put her things up in the bedroom, moving like an automaton from luggage to drawers to bed. There, she lay down with her clothes on.

"Would you like me to get your robe?"

"No."

"How about a video? I can scoot over to Blockbuster

and be back in a flash, move the TV and DVD player in here. Something funny would be good for us both. I know we could use a few laughs.''

Whitney reached for a book beside the bed. ''I'm going to read. You can watch what you want.'' She pointed to the living room. ''In there.''

''And I suppose you want me to sleep in there, too.''

''If you don't, I will.''

He didn't argue with her about it, didn't put his foot down or draw any lines. Whitney had already done that and he wasn't going to cross her. He'd run out of steam.

Time trudged on in slow-motion seconds, hours, days that seemed like years.

He slept on the couch. Whenever Whitney emerged from her room, he walked around on eggshells while she ignored him.

He had become the invisible man. She had become...he didn't know what she'd become. She worked at home, went for walks, ate and spoke and moved. All indications she was still alive, but she had no more substance than mist. The hugs he so desperately needed had once been worth the risk of rejection. But they weren't worth it anymore, not when his arms felt even emptier with her in them.

He was living in a tomb. Cohabitating with a ghost. Lonely days, even lonelier nights, work was his only companion.

He couldn't go on like this much longer.

The morning came when Eric woke up, folded the sheets, got dressed and knew he couldn't do it again. He had to leave. A month had passed since the accident, and nothing had changed. Except for himself. He'd lost his laughter. Life had lost its lustre. And what little self-respect he had left would be gone if he wasn't on the next plane out to...

Somewhere. Anywhere but here. The people were

friendly, the scenery beautiful, and the seafood as good as it came. Not a bad place to put down some roots, as long as ample travel provided the diversity he would always need. That had been the compromise he'd hoped to work out but screw it, they had nothing left to work out beyond a divorce settlement, and he was prepared to be generous. Unless, by some mother of a miracle, Whitney woke up with her senses intact and realized Scarlett had nothing on her when it came to throwing happiness away with both hands.

Knowing he had a better chance at winning the New York State lottery, Eric picked up the phone. His, not hers. She'd made him feel as if anything he touched was defiled. Little wonder since no matter how often he washed, he never felt clean. If he put some distance between himself and the scene of the crime, maybe eventually he'd feel less tarnished.

How long would eventually be? And how far should he go? Far, far away. Yes, as far as he could get without being so out of reach Whitney couldn't find him if...

That miracle happened and she wanted him again, like she had in the beginning. When he'd searched her out and found her emerging naked from the river in Dominica.

His destination decided, Eric made his reservation. He packed up his stuff in the living room that served as the doghouse he'd been sentenced to. Severing the self-imposed chains that bound him there, he lugged all evidence of his existence out to his rented car in a spot marked Visitor.

Eric returned to Whitney's apartment. That's right, Whitney's apartment. Not his. He took a last glance around, knowing he wouldn't be back. He searched his heart and he searched his soul, seeking the best way to say goodbye.

Face-to-face? Whitney wouldn't care that he was leaving, might even send him off with a wave of her fingers and a "Ta-ta." Or maybe a woodenly spoken "Whatever."

Taking out the box which held the ring she'd had removed in the hospital, he tried to decide if it was cowardly to leave her the way she'd left him in Antigua: with a letter, her wedding ring, and a gold chain with a medallion that had belonged in the family for hundreds of years. What had possessed him to give her such a treasured piece of his history after sharing a bed for the first time?

The Way that cannot be charted, the Name that can't be described, the Truth that is unknowable. Love, so like the Tao. It had taken him over, lifted him to the heavens then beaten him down. He wasn't a coward, would fight to his death for a cause worth saving. But why knock on her door and hope she would answer when there was nothing left to fight for?

Only love, but it took two to wage a battle.

Eric penned the letter. On top of it he laid the heirloom that he'd promised his grandmother he wouldn't part with until the one true love of his life came along, and then he took one last look at the wedding ring which declared Whitney that woman.

He kissed the pearl, held in place by two reaching hands, then shut the box. Time to go. Past time, actually. So why the slow trudge of his leaden feet while he prayed Whitney would emerge from her sanctuary and ask him to stay?

He'd only taken a few steps when her bedroom door opened. Without so much as a good-morning, she breezed past him and headed for the kitchen, which didn't have the coffee already made for once.

Eric caught her arm. She looked from his grip to somewhere past his shoulder.

"Yes?"

"I'm leaving, Whitney." No response. He tapped the

hollow spot in his chest. "Not much left in here. Just a yo-yo that's run out of string. Seems you pulled it so hard, it came as detached as you. Either ask me to stay or consider me gone for good. It's your call."

She mustered a wan smile. "Have a nice trip."

That did it. He was out of here. Once he'd had his say.

"Know what? I could deal with it if you called me a cold blooded murderer because that's how I feel. But the truth is, I didn't kill our baby. I walked out and didn't turn around when I should have, and that's a cross I'll have to bear for the rest of my life. There comes a point, however, when life has to go on. I've reached that point. I love you, Whitney, love you so much it hurts. But you won't accept that love and I can't live like this. It's a living hell we're in and if that's where you choose to be, I can't save you. I have to save what's left of myself."

He waited for a response, waited for a rebuttal. But when it became clear he could wait into old age and Whitney would have nothing to say beyond, "I'm going to make some coffee," he didn't need to stick around for more.

Eric left the ring, the note he'd penned, and the treasured charm his grandmother had given him for luck in love behind—

Along with the woman he might never see again beyond a vision of the future they could have had and the bittersweet memories they'd made, which would forever remain in his heart.

CHAPTER FORTY-TWO

FOR A VERY LONG TIME, Whitney stared at the front door, which Eric had closed while she went to make coffee.

Sipping it, she tried to figure out how she felt about finally being alone, how she felt about him leaving her and not intending to come back. He wouldn't be returning with groceries, videos, Hershey's Kisses chocolates, flowers or even apologies for burning dinner because he'd been on the phone with Marcia.

Was that where Eric had gone? To see Marcia, gab it up, drink some beer, go wallow in some lava together? If so, did she care? Did she?

Whitney's emotional radar gave a slight blip then flat-lined as she continued staring at the door. She took another sip of the coffee. Tepid. Not too hot, not too cold, just sort of there like her. A very nice place to be, simply floating along without a care because nothing mattered anymore.

Oh yes, she liked it here quite a lot and since Eric had given her all the space she wanted, she'd no doubt like it even more.

Once she erased the last of his traces.

A ring, a necklace and a piece of paper with her name on it intruded on her sense of nothingness when she happened to glance at the table.

Curiosity should demand she read the letter. But she didn't want to know what else he might have to say. Maybe she should just toss it down the toilet, along with the jewelry he should have taken with him if he didn't want the damn stuff flushed.

Damn. A swearword. Now there was a start. A flicker of anger. At the man she was glad to get out of her...life.

Life? What was that? A pain in the ass, that's what it was. Life was too hard, too unfair, too ugly, too cold-hearted.

Eric, wait! Don't go! Eric...

Running after him, all she could see was his back, didn't even notice the car coming, then suddenly—

"No," she gasped out, feeling as if she were strangling on the air she was struggling to breathe in. "No, I won't go back there. Pretend it didn't happen, pretend you can't still feel it, can't see it." The coffee cup hit the floor as she covered her ears, shut her eyes, and shook her head in a frantic refusal of the nightmare beating at her brain: the image of Eric walking away. The sound of her pleading. The knifing pain and smell of skidding rubber. Her baby crushed against the grill.

"Go away, go away, go away," she moaned. Whitney willed it all to go away, tried to retreat into her safe place where she couldn't see or feel.

But she had seen. She had felt. And now there was no escaping the scene that played over and over in her mind. The unwanted past tripped into the unwanted present, the unwanted items she sneered at.

She made a clean swipe of the table and out it all flew like the tiny beads in the rattle Eric had broken. His letter winged to the floor and once it landed, she kicked it for good measure.

"Take that, Eric. And take this!" Another kick and the small velvet box containing her wedding ring bounced against the wall. "See how much I care about you and your leavings?" She snatched up the necklace, his grandmother's medallion attached, and started to hurl it at the front door he had exited.

But something stopped her. The onyx representing the male filled her eyes and seeped into the hollowed-out space that had once been her heart.

"It was a boy," she whispered, her voice cracking. "A boy, Eric! I'd wanted him to be just like you, even while you were walking out. I ran after you, just like I ran after my own father, only for him to shake me loose from his leg and walk on without a backward glance. That's exactly what you did and I hate you for it. Do you hear me? I hate you!"

She lunged forward with the medallion until she planted the fist she clutched it in against the door. *Smack, smack, smack.* She hit it until her fist throbbed and her weakening blows were spent.

But not her rage. It's all she had, just this rage, a fire in the belly she clutched. Barren, empty. All because of him.

"Good riddance," she snarled and stumbled away. With the instincts of a homing pigeon she went to her bedroom and returned to the tiny nest in a dresser drawer.

Eric had apparently put her baby treasures in there while she was in the hospital. She'd opened it once and a single glance had posed the threat of a two-ton ball poised to destroy a deserted building.

That building now had an angry tenant inside, shaking her fist at the fate she could no longer suffer in silence.

"Welcome to my living hell, Eric," she yelled, opening the drawer. "Only you couldn't take the heat so you got out of the kitchen and left the baby cereal behind."

Lifting the box of oatmeal flakes with a chubby-cheeked baby on the front, Whitney gave the picture a kiss and endured a pang of loss as she placed it on the dresser.

Avoiding the mirror above it, she dipped back into the

drawer for a skein of pastel yarn with two crochet needles and an unfinished baby blanket attached. She would never finish the blanket, clutched in her fingers. So soft, so real. More real than anything she'd felt in a very long time.

Real as the smell of talcum powder pressed to her nose. Real as knowing her baby was gone and would never be wrapped in the delicate clouds of pale yellow, blue, pink and green.

The sweet little baby things fell from her fingers and she watched them float away like the discards of a dream. That's all they were. Dreams, sweet dreams. A lullaby she would never sing. Booties that would never be filled by itsy-bitsy feet. A silver brush she would never tenderly sweep over a tiny head with downy hair.

Whitney lovingly fingered the brush, held it to her cheek. It looked so pretty against the woman's skin in the mirror. But the woman's face wasn't pretty. It was hard on the surface but chipped around the edges, hinting at something unsightly beneath.

"Who are you?" she asked the woman in the mirror.

The woman stared back at her and Whitney knew a fierce want to rip off the implacable mask hiding the stranger's true identity. She didn't know this woman who moved the baby brush from her cheek, raised her arm, and hurled it into the mirror.

Silver met silver. The mirror cracked. It spread in spiderweb veins. Transfixed, Whitney saw her image multiply into a kaleidoscope of Whitneys.

"Who *are* you?" she demanded.

The many faces of Whitney didn't answer back. They formed a jagged circle and coalesced in the middle, trapping her in the web.

She was surrounded by herself. The good Whitney. The bad Whitney. The hateful Whitney who was too blinded by her grief to seek comfort with a man she had loathed with the intensity of her love.

Whitney's eyes blurred and she couldn't see the mirror. All she could see was Eric weeping in the ambulance, his head bowed in prayer by her bed, his agony when she tried to send him away and yet he still stayed, suffering alone, his love unwavering while she spat all that he offered back into his face.

It hadn't been enough to accuse him with her silence. It hadn't been enough to make him as miserable as she. She'd wanted him to die a slow death with her so they might join their dead baby. Yet he hadn't killed their baby, she saw that now. Eric had been her scapegoat, her whipping boy. He was the fall guy she pointed her finger at so she could escape the horrible fear that it was her fault their baby was dead.

She had to face that fear. Take it out, examine it and let herself feel...

Guilt. A lot of guilt. For her misjudgment, her cruelties, her blindness. All committed against Eric, not their baby. She had loved that baby. She still did and always would. But she hadn't murdered it any more than Eric. It was an accident that could have been avoided had she been honest from the start and believed herself worthy of...love.

Eric's love. A great love, the kind that came around once in a lifetime to the lucky. Yes, he had loved her. All of her. And she hadn't been able to accept it because she hadn't been able to love all of herself.

Whitney considered the fragmented images of the woman in the mirror. Each woman demanded she look at them, acknowledge them, accept them all as a part of who she had become.

Those parts couldn't survive alone. They were interlinked facets composing the whole of who she truly was.

There was no good Whitney, no bad Whitney, but there was definitely a bitch to be reckoned with. That bitch had shot a priceless pearl out of two reaching hands as if it were some cheap marble in the dirt, not a holy globe containing the greatest riches of life.

Whitney didn't like her. She was an immature tyrant who needed to grow up and stop punishing others when life wasn't a piece of cake.

While Eric had endured the most punishment, he wasn't the only one who'd been held hostage and put on the rack.

"I know who you are now," she said to the mirror. "You're a sensual adventuress, a responsible bookworm who's as sensible as your shoes. You're a student of the world; a closet Donna Reed who can't cook, but loves the comfort zone of home. You're a lover who relishes the feel of your man inside you. You like to be dominated. You like to be on top. You're exotic. And simple. You prefer to play it safe, but you get a thrill out of taking a risk. Take it now, Whitney. Take it now, before it's too late."

Her reflection smiled. It felt odd to the muscles around her mouth; they hadn't been used for a very long time. How good it did feel, though, almost as good as using her lips to lightly kiss each frame of her face.

According to the mirror there were several more Whitneys she had yet to meet. Her smile deepened and she laughed with the rush of freedom, of self-acceptance, of love. Love of herself, of Eric, of the convoluted life that had led her to this path of self-discovery.

And where did the path go from here?

Any future children she and Eric might have didn't deserve these sorrowful castoffs. Such sad remains belonged in a box for another mother-to-be who most likely wouldn't be wearing a ring. And even if she did, what were the chances it was made of the finest gold with a perfect pearl held between two reaching hands?

Whitney went in search of the small velvet box. She found it close to the letter she had trampled.

Which to open first, the box or the letter?

Compromising, she put on the necklace and held tight to the box as she read:

Yuan-pao,

I am gone. But so are you and the child my stupid pride and a fast driver took away in the blink of an eye. I'm so sorry for breaking the rattle, so sorry for not throwing confetti and breaking out the champagne instead. That's what I really wanted to do and had I done it...well, I wouldn't be writing this letter then, would I?

If only I could rewrite the past. If only I could make you happy and you'd let me hold you again. If only the future held more promise for us than the present, then I'd hang on, even if it took another ten years to get there. If only, if only. I could fill a page with if only's and fix them all if I were God instead of a man.

I'm just a man, Whitney. A man who thought he'd never say never but finds he's given up. If there's any hope for us, it has to come from you. I leave with nothing more than gratitude for what was and a deep sorrow for what might have been. Should you feel the same way, I don't have to tell you where I've gone. Your heart will know. As for mine, it still hasn't recovered from the first moment I met you.

Eric

Whitney ran a trembling fingertip over his name. Several times before she pressed the letter to her heart.

Her heart beat fast as she called the airport and then Mr. Andrews. Faster still while she secured two pearls into her earlobes and changed into her princess bride dress.

As for packing, she had all she needed in her purse: a next-to-nothing nighty, a plastic gizmo off the toy rack at the nearest grocery, and a velvet box that matched the one she picked up from a jewelry store en route to the airport counter, where she signed away the last of her savings on a future she would fight tooth and nail to reclaim.

Her heart pounded in time with her feet as she raced down the ramp, white silk billowing behind her. The last person to board on for a flight to San Juan, with connections to Dominica, she was breathing heavily as she made it to the first-class seat on the aisle...

Where a man staring out the window with an open book in his lap unaware of her arrival, quietly mused, "A room without books is like a body without a soul."

CHAPTER FORTY-THREE

"AND WE BOTH KNOW what a body without a soul is like, don't we, Dr. Townsend?"

Eric recognized the voice. It belonged to a woman he'd once known and loved, surely more than any man had ever loved a woman. Perhaps his ears had deceived him. Perhaps his eyes were conjuring a vision. He truly couldn't believe she was standing in the aisle. Dressed in her wedding gown. And playing with a…yo-yo? In disbelief he watched the string descend, then reel back up into its casing.

Seating herself beside him, she extended the toy in her palm. "I believe this is yours. String and all."

When he didn't immediately take her offering, she leaned over and opened his sports coat, then dropped the yo-yo into his breast pocket. She gave a pat where it rested—near his heart, thumping like mad.

"Do I know you?" he asked. Hopefully. Warily. Perhaps desperation could make a man delusional. So delusional that he saw her as if for the first time. With flowing hair, a dazzling smile, a mouth that was made for kissing and a neck—

Draped with a slender gold chain. With the symbol of his heritage and its continuance attached.

Eric told himself to stay calm, not to hope too much because he'd lost her twice before and the third time was either the charm or batter out, game's over, accept your losses and go…

Home. Whitney was his home. At least she had been. When she'd made him feel like a giant amongst men.

"Do you know me?" she repeated. "Better than I know myself, it seems. But allow me to introduce myself anyway. My name's Whitney." She extended her hand. He gripped it and could feel the fine tremble in her fingertips. Or perhaps he was the one trembling from the jolt of her touch. Electric.

Her soft gasp, it was the sweetest music he'd ever heard.

"Magic," she whispered on a longing sigh, assuring him that he wasn't the only one feeling the alchemy of love and lust brewing between them again.

"Whitney…Whitney." He repeated her name like a mantra, a prayer. "Such a beautiful name. And yes, I do think I know you. If memory serves, we met on another plane a long time ago."

"A lifetime ago." She lifted her other hand in entreaty. "I've missed you, Eric."

"But I never left you. You're the one who left me and a part of me is afraid to believe you're really back. I lost you and it tore my heart out. I can't bear the thought of ever losing you again."

"You won't," she promised, her hand still raised as if to solemnly swear she told the truth, the whole truth and nothing but. "You lost me because I lost myself along The Way. It can be charted, but not without a compass and that compass resides in the heart. I followed mine and it led me here. To you and the Truth that's knowable once we have the courage to face it. I had to find that courage before I could find myself and let go of the fear that I wasn't worthy of love. Not yours and not my own."

Eric matched his hand to hers. Palm to palm, fingertips to fingertips, they held a great and painful knowledge between them.

"Love and fear, Whitney. Love and fear. It always comes down to that. Unfortunately it's hard to give either a name when we don't know how to listen with our hearts." His fingers folded in and so did hers.

"I've learned to listen to mine," she told this marvelous man who was making this much too easy for her. "Eric, I'm sorry. So sorry that I—"

"Shh." He pressed a soft kiss to her lips. "Didn't you ever read *Love Story*? If you had, you'd know that love means never having to say you're sorry."

"Malarkey. And Segal was full of it when he wrote that." Her lips tingled. All of her tingled and hummed, making her ache for a deeper kiss that ran the length of their bodies. But such a kiss would have to wait. What she had to say couldn't. "Real love, Eric, admits its mistakes and learns from them. I've learned from mine and I am so ashamed to admit that I horribly mistreated the person I love the most. I'll never hurt you like that again, Eric. Never. Say you believe me." She bowed her head in abject remorse. "Say you forgive me. Please."

"I believe you." He tilted up her chin and in his exotic almond gaze there was such tenderness she wanted to weep. "And I forgive you. Because with all my heart and soul, I love you, Whitney Townsend. Now if you're ready to move on, I'm with you every step of the way and we won't stop until we've made it home."

"As long as it's together, I'll move wherever you want. You were right, Eric. Home is a place we take with us no matter where we go. My place is with you."

"And mine, *yuan-pao,* with you." Hands interlocked, they bridged the past and connected in this priceless, present moment that would forever link them. And then they sealed their future with a hungry, endless kiss.

Well, almost endless.

"Excuse me," a flight attendant interrupted. "Would either of you care for a drink?"

Eric looked at Whitney. She looked at him. And in her eyes he saw that spark he more than ever treasured, a rare love of life, a joie de vivre that matched her lilting laughter when they said in unison, "We'll take time in a bottle."

At the attendant's perplexed expression, Whitney impishly whispered in his ear, "I don't think they have one to serve so maybe we should just ask for one of those Sex On The Beach cocktails."

"I'll give you sex on the beach," he whispered back. "And sex on the floor, against the wall, even the kitchen table once we're off this plane. Till then, I'll settle for some more naughty nothings in my ear." Eric gave a lick to hers, then nipped the pearl earring she'd never remove again.

"I'm not wearing any panties," she murmured seductively so only he could hear before placing their order. "We'll have champagne. A whole bottle, please."

"You're celebrating!" Gesturing toward the wedding dress, the flight attendant oohed and aahed.

"You bet we are," Whitney confirmed. "We're celebrating life and spending the rest of ours together. Once we land we're getting married. As you can see, I'm already dressed for the occasion since I don't want to give the groom time to change his mind."

In a flash the flight attendant was back with not one bottle but two. "I brought an extra one for the honeymoon," she explained. "Congratulations. I hope you'll both be happy."

Never had Whitney been happier, sitting in a first-class seat on a plane destined for the Caribbean, next to the most wonderful man in the world whose smile could charm the pants off a nun. Raising her glass, she toasted, "Here's to happy endings."

"And new beginnings." As glass pinged glass, Eric inquired, "What did you mean about getting married? We already are, Mrs. Townsend."

"True, Dr. Townsend, but we left something important out." Reaching into her purse, she withdrew two small velvet boxes. She laid one containing her wedding ring on Eric's lap and opened the other. "I know it's only a simple gold band but there's nothing simple about what it means to wear such a ring. Marry me, Eric. For richer or poorer, for better or worse, please marry me again?"

"On one condition." He opened the box in his lap and tapped it to the counterpart which symbolized their eternal devotion in a world where promises could be broken and so could hearts when the commitment wasn't entirely there. "Do you know what that condition is?"

"I do." Whitney knew this missing part of the commitment was even more important than the ring she slid on his finger, unable to wait for a preacher or a witness to hear the vow she would never forsake: "Till death do we part."

"No such thing." A kiss to the ring he now wore, then a kiss to her lips as they kissed the clouds, Whitney knew what he said was true.

They were immortals who would live forever because a love like theirs could never die.

HARLEQUIN®

Temptation

New York Times bestselling author

VICKI LEWIS THOMPSON

celebrates Temptation's 20th anniversary—
and her own—in:

#980

OLD ENOUGH TO KNOW BETTER

When twenty-year-old PR exec Kasey Braddock accepts her co-workers' dare to hit on the gorgeous new landscaper, she's excited. Finally, here's her chance to prove to her friends—and herself—that she's woman enough to entice a man and leave him drooling. After all, she's old enough to know what she wants—and she wants Sam Ashton. Luckily, he's not complaining....

Available in June wherever Harlequin books are sold.

www.eHarlequin.com

HTHOTKB-TR